JUDGE SAVAGE

Tim Parks studied at Cambridge and Harvard. He lives near Verona with his wife and three children. His novel *Europa* was shortlisted for the Booker Prize.

ALSO BY TIM PARKS

Fiction

Home Thoughts
Loving Roger
Family Planning
Goodness
Cara Massimina
Tongues of Flame
Shear
Mimi's Ghost
Europa
Destiny

Non-Fiction

Italian Neighbours
An Italian Education
Adultery & Other Diversions
Translating Style
Hell and Back
A Season with Verona

Tim Parks

JUDGE SAVAGE

VINTAGE

Published by Vintage 2004

2 4 6 8 10 9 7 5 3 1

Copyright © Tim Parks 2003

Tim Parks has asserted his right under the Copyright, Designs and Patents Act, 1988 to be identified as the author of this work

First published in Great Britain in 2003 by
Secker & Warburg

Vintage
Random House, 20 Vauxhall Bridge Road,
London SW1V 2SA

Random House Australia (Pty) Limited
20 Alfred Street, Milsons Point, Sydney
New South Wales 2061, Australia

Random House New Zealand Limited
18 Poland Road, Glenfield,
Auckland 10, New Zealand

Random House (Pty) Limited
Endulini, 5A Jubilee Road, Parktown 2193,
South Africa

The Random House Group Limited Reg. No. 954009
www.randomhouse.co.uk/vintage

A CIP catalogue record for this book
is available from the British Library

ISBN 0 099 44504 2

Papers used by Random House are natural, recyclable products made from wood grown in sustainable forests. The manufacturing processes conform to the environmental regulations of the country of origin

Printed and bound in Great Britain by
Bookmarque Ltd, Croydon, Surrey

This book does not pretend to offer an exact representation of English law, but where there is verisimilitude, thanks must go to Nick Syfret for his invaluable explanations and suggestions.

ONE

There is no life without a double life. And yet one grows weary. On March 22nd, 1999, having at last resolved the conflict that had dogged their marriage for many years, and with the financial confidence arising from his recent appointment to the position of crown court judge, Daniel Savage and his wife Hilary settled on the purchase of a house then under construction on the hills to the north of their town. It was, as Daniel would later recall, a clear day; there was a sharp light on a windswept, still wintry landscape; and indeed his overriding impression on taking this major decision was one of unprecedented and empowered clarity. He and his wife embraced in the shell of what promised to be a sensible four-bedroom, free-standing structure with spacious garden. I should like them to put in a fireplace, Hilary said. To be together by. Daniel agreed. They had fought each other too long. The spring will be marvellous here, he laughed, and that evening he made the unusual gesture of jotting down a few words in his diary: I feel I have at last taken, he wrote, and taken for the best, all the major decisions of my life, which is to say, all the decisions that are most difficult and self-determining. From now on, I shall be free to concentrate on the job I am so fortunate to have, to love the woman beside me to the best of my ability, to help my children as and how I can. Finally everything is clear. The time of metamorphoses is over. I have become myself.

After speaking briefly to the builder's agent, the couple enjoyed a quiet drink in the pub that seemed set to be their local and on arrival back home announced the decision to their adolescent children. Predictably, Sarah was unimpressed, while the younger Tom was delighted. Gently and earnestly, Daniel encouraged his daughter to think how much better off she would be out of town. In a bigger house she would have more privacy. The girl pulled a thin face and slammed the door. We can get a dog! Tom shouted. Hilary hugged the boy. We shall have a fireplace to sit beside, she announced. I'm seeing the builder about it tomorrow. The spring will be marvellous, Daniel repeated, up there on the hill.

Shortly after Daniel and Hilary had gone to their bedroom, the phone rang. Hilary raised then replaced the receiver. Whoever it was hung up again, she said, and when she looked over at him, Daniel knew at once what she was wondering. Lightly, he remarked: Perhaps now I'm a judge we'll get more of those. They turned out the lights. In the new house we'll make sure we're ex-directory, she said. Hilary, he whispered. They held hands in the shadowy room. This flat had been too small for them for some years now. Perhaps I could get you a better piano, he promised, for our twentieth. The date was looming. I am so thrilled, Daniel, she said. She was reassured.

The following week Daniel tried a case of indecent assault. He was still quite new to his role and savouring it. A man with many years' service in the council's child-care division was accused of having molested a sixteen-year-old. What Daniel was savouring was the freedom of not being embattled on one side or the other, whether for the prosecution or defence. The girl was retarded. The defendant had been driving her home in the council's mini-bus. In the past, Daniel thought, impassive and bewigged behind his darkly polished table, I would have had to do everything I sensibly could to find a flaw in the prosecution's case and to get this man off, while perhaps believing he was guilty. The alleged victim was not present in court. Or alternatively I would have had to do everything in my power to get a conviction and hence inevitable prison sentence, while perhaps convinced that prison was entirely inappropriate to a man in his early forties who just once had embraced and fondled a girl in the front seat of a mini-bus. If he had. There was no suggestion of violence.

Questioned on video, the girl looked physically adult and undeniably attractive, but her speech was slurred and babyish. Inappropriately, she wore a tight, low-cut blouse. Now you can just observe it all, Daniel told himself, orchestrate the whole contest, without sweating. The breasts were prominent and full. You are under no pressure, he thought, overruling some half-hearted objection from the defence, to perform or to win, only to react to the performance of others in the proper way. Propriety was the key. He had always feared the possibility of burnout as an adversarial lawyer.

At the back of the court in the public gallery, the defendant's wife made faces of scorn and disdain while evidence was given. She was seriously overweight, a bulky and bullying presence. Her husband was without charisma. His voice trembled. On the second day, the girl's mother was questioned about her claim that there had been a sperm stain on the child's clothes. Counsel for the defence wanted to know why it had been put in the wash, why it hadn't been made available to the police. But Daniel could see that the jury were entirely convinced by the girl's mother. Particularly the young Indian man. They found her reaction of disgust, her desire to be rid of that stain without delay entirely credible. It was a mistake, Daniel felt, on defence counsel's part, to keep referring to the girl as a child. She was sixteen after all. What he might have brought to the jury's attention, perhaps, was the dangerous combination of her mature sensuality and lack of those defence mechanisms that would normally scare off an insecure man long before he touched her. Consent might have been the best defence. But it isn't a judge's duty to instruct defendants and their lawyers what line to take. Freed from the fray, the judge is entirely alone. He keeps his own counsel. Both lawyers were older than himself, Daniel knew. Perhaps jealous.

On the video, ably questioned by police experts, the girl was detailed and convincing when describing what had happened. The jury were grim, the defendant's wife shifted and frowned, the mother wept. Only toward the end of forty minutes of testimony did it occur to Daniel what was so curious about it all: the girl, as she spoke to camera, was strikingly calm, even absent-minded, as though actually thinking of something else! This the defence might have drawn attention to. He might have pointed out that it was the *mother* who was upset, not the victim. As it was the mother most probably – an alert and articulate woman – who had chosen this low-cut, fashionable blouse and bought the girl her expensive cosmetics, eager perhaps – and for a moment Daniel couldn't help thinking of his own difficult daughter – to take pride in her physical charms precisely because she was a lost case in other departments. But defence counsel was not after mitigating circumstances. Possibly more afraid of his wife than of the court, the defendant had not only pleaded not guilty, but insisted he hadn't so much as touched the child. He too used the word child. Unwisely. And throughout the proceedings, bald and bowed, he examined his offending hands, unable to look the jury in the eye. There was no mention of the girl's father.

In his closing speech on the Wednesday, counsel for the prosecution used the word monster. This exaggeration – so predictable – made Daniel acutely aware, if only because he had wielded it himself and fought it himself many times in the past, of the great shift in perspective that had occurred when they made him a judge. Rather than participating, rather than seeking to colour events one way or another with colourful words, to sow doubt on the one hand, or reap conviction on the other, he was now seeing the whole thing with a clarity that was both an intellectual pleasure and an emotional strain. It was quite probable, he had thought, as he sat listening to the proceedings, and in particular to the irritating hesitations of the defendant as he admitted that he could, yes, have rearranged his rounds so as not to be alone with the girl in the mini-bus – quite probable that this man and this girl had engaged in all kinds of petting before the mother discovered that damning stain. He had been driving her home every day for months. He had had every opportunity. And perhaps it was precisely because the stain wasn't actually available as evidence that the defendant had hoped he could convince his terrifying wife that he had never touched the girl at all, while for her part the girl had been so shocked by her mother's reaction to the merest dampness on her skirt that she hadn't wanted to say that this business happened most days without her minding at all.

So your only promising line of defence was tossed away for fear of standing naked before the person closest to you, Daniel thought. Your fear of being left alone. Or at least that was one possible scenario. Convicted and sent to gaol, you can still insist on your innocence. You might even be considered a martyr. Your wife loves you all the more perhaps. She starts a campaign for your release. The important thing is not to confess. But it was merest speculation.

Summing up to the jury, Daniel invited them as ever to reflect on the words 'satisfied so that you are sure', or in the old formula satisfied 'beyond reasonable doubt'. A new judge, his appointment controversial perhaps, he was very much aware of the need to follow the conventional pattern. You must be satisfied so that you are sure, he repeated, if you are to convict. But he was in little doubt himself that very soon he would be giving the man a severe sentence. The jury would deliver a guilty verdict and at that point a judge must respond appropriately. If you are free from the tussle, he reminded himself, of prosecution and defence, you are not free from public opinion. The newspapers demand exemplary treatment for offenders of this kind, not nuanced reflection. It is a wicked thing and a terrible breach of trust to take advantage of a retarded girl in your care. So only the following morning, when the jury reached their verdict, he would stand up in court and give the defendant three years. For just a second their eyes met. He will lose his job, Daniel thought. Rightly so. He is a ruined man. Somebody led the obese wife sobbing from the court.

Lady phoned for you, Mr Savage. Twice. She wouldn't leave a name. I said you were normally in chambers late afternoonish.

It was Thursday. Daniel wasn't concerned. He knew Jane would not call again. He had grown used to that. There was even a complicity in the mutual silence that lent it a lingering sweetness. Daniel was at ease. I don't even *want* her to call, he discovered, placing his wig in its box. It would be an anti-climax, another breach of trust. Aesthetically wrong, he told himself vaguely, using an expression he knew was his wife's. There was a way in which he and Hilary were indeed two parts of the same entity. He felt safe.

Actually, I shall be out this afternoon, he told the young clerk. She too was a charming girl. Whoever it is, she'd better try tomorrow. Tomorrow's first case, he remembered, was a simple burglary. A fourth- or fifth-time offender pleading not guilty. But how is it, Daniel asked himself, slipping the relevant papers in his briefcase, how is it that you can form a single entity with a woman who is so musical, whose life has to do with music and aesthetics, with her sensitivity to the slightest falseness of pitch, when you yourself have no musical sense whatsoever, and no knowledge at all of aesthetics beyond the merest instinct for what you like and what you don't? The Bach more than the Brahms. The retarded girl more than the obese wife. Daniel smiled. Dear Jane. Yet it had made sense when Hilary said: What you are doing is ugly. Of the few expressions that remained engraved in the mind, that marked turning points, or suddenly illuminated whole landscapes of consciousness, this was the one that had cut deepest, shone brightest. What you are doing is ugly; the moral and the aesthetic met convincingly in that word.

In town he was concerned to see that the price of a Steinway grand would significantly raise the level of their mortgage payments. Not all the decisions were behind him, it seemed. But this was a detail. He smiled. He knew his mind. His wife had always wanted a serious piano. They would get a good price for their flat, which was central and not without its attractions. As the dealer played a few arpeggios to make the instrument sing, Daniel was aware of being eager – childishly eager – to show Hilary that he cared, to show her, as he had been doing more or less every day for a year now, that all was well. And it was! He would stand beside her while she played Chopin in the flickering light of the fireplace. Her small square hands were rapid and incisive on the keyboard. Life was taking on a wonderful obviousness. He was not married to a fat, bullying mastiff of a woman. He was not an insipid fellow trapped in a mundane job that constantly exposed him to the charms of his helpless charges. Leaving a pretty clerk alone is not beyond a crown court judge.

Signing the cheque for the deposit, Daniel experienced again what had become a familiar emotion ever since the terrible conflict with his wife had been – they were both agreed on this – definitively resolved: a wave of exhilaration accompanied by the thought, clearly and gratefully articulated: How lucky you've been! How lucky you are! Got away with it! An image that sometimes sprung to mind in this regard was that of his close friend Martin Shields who before Christmas had spun off the motorway at high speed, bounced off crash barriers to one side and another, rolled over and over while other vehicles braked and scattered, finally to emerge from his ruined Audi entirely unscathed. He hadn't even been prosecuted for dangerous driving! How can you be such a depressive, Daniel laughed, after an escape like that! Martin, a colleague from his old chambers, had serious problems that were all inside his head, and thus unforgivable in a way. His wife was very attractive. They had no children to obstruct their pleasures. Climbing into his own car, it occurred to Daniel that his daughter might start playing again when the new piano was installed in the new house with the fireplace and the dog. What kind of dog?

He decided to take the unusual step of picking up Sarah and Tom from their school.

It is always interesting to see your children with their friends, especially when they don't know that they are being watched. Parked just beyond their bus-stop, Daniel was poignantly struck by a certain separateness that marked out his daughter, even in this group of lively seventeen-year-olds. There was something narrow and tense about the shoulders. Her head was bowed. It would be a phase she was going through, he imagined.

What are you doing here? Sarah demanded, leaning into the side window. Where's Tom? he asked. Crowds of children were pushing by. Sarah chose to sit in the back. Daniel couldn't see her face. They waited. Can you keep a secret? he asked. What on earth have you come here for? she repeated. I thought it would be nice, he said warmly, to pick you up. I'm perfectly happy on the bus, she said.

They waited. A secret from whom? she asked. Daniel was searching in the wing mirror for his son. How correctly Sarah spoke! From whom! Young people were supposed to be slovenly. Mum, he said. You see ... No, she objected. The fact is I've just gone and ... No! she insisted. No, what? Daniel hadn't been concentrating. Tom does get out at the same time as you, doesn't he? he asked. I don't want to hear any secret I have to keep from Mum, his daughter said. People shouldn't have secrets from each other. Not in the family. But it's something nice! Daniel protested. No, I said no!

Getting out of the car, Daniel waved to Tom who came running from his friends. Dad! The boy was a charming, chubby figure, out of breath, cluttered with backpack and gym bag. Slipping back into his seat again, Judge Savage suddenly felt a soft slim arm round his neck and a mouth by his ear. Thanks for coming, Dad, she whispered warmly right against the lobe. Her breath was moist and her hair perfumed. It's so sweet of you. That's my girl! he immediately responded. Lovebirds! Tom cried. The door slammed. Where are we off to then? I thought we might drive out to the new house, Daniel suggested, to see how they're getting on, choose our rooms. No! Again his daughter's veto was brutal. I've got too much homework, she said. Then she had to go out. I have to go to Chapel. Early. It was a voice that passed from seductive intimacy to extreme authority. Daniel didn't think of opposing it. He bought his son a large ice-cream. And one for himself. I'm perfectly happy to use the bus, Sarah said, if you two want to have a drive.

Funny bloke, Daniel remarked later that evening. He put down his papers. At the kitchen table, Max Jordan was sitting over coffee after his lesson. It's lovely of Hilary how she makes the boy feel at home, Daniel was noticing. How so? Max asked politely. Oh, he denies *everything*, Daniel laughed. Police remove fragment of leather jacket from window thieves broke. Police raid defendant's council house where they find leather jacket. Tear on leather jacket *exactly* matches fragment from scene of crime. Accused is arrested and charged, but denies *everything*. Claims he never saw the jacket before. Somebody planted it in his flat.

Oh no! Max laughed. It's incredible they bother with some trials at all, Hilary remarked. She was bent down looking into the oven. My wife is a beautiful cook, a beautiful musician and a beautiful person, Daniel told himself. Max was improving his Mozart, the sonatas Gould had sighed and grunted over. Above her left ear, wisps of hair had escaped their clips. Her backside was still tight in tight jeans. She doesn't smoke, drink, or dye, Daniel marvelled. He just couldn't get over how *comfortable* life was, and he said: Not at all. The chap might perfectly well get off.

He slipped the case bundle back in his bag. It was time for his whisky, his evening whisky. I like Max, he thought. It's nice to have a handsome young guest. But that's what I meant, Hilary protested. He liked the boy's formality and politeness. It drives me mad, she said, how many people get off. Then the room was suddenly transformed by a fragrance of fresh baking. Hilary stood proudly, knife in hand. But how can he? Max enquired. His ears were rather large. There was a youthful naïveté about him – Daniel sensed – Would he care for a whisky? – that meshed exactly with Hilary's nervous, rather bossy determination to please. But Daniel actually enjoyed her bossiness these days. Max showed no resistance to her opinions on how this or that piece should be played, then rapidly lapsed back – even a layman could sense it – into a natural, sentimental generosity. He plays beautifully, Daniel thought. People lay themselves bare at the keyboard, Hilary would always say when discussing her students. And now she said: Oh you wouldn't believe, Max, you just wouldn't believe the people Dan managed to get off when he defended. The bloke who stole his own car for the insurance and still kept driving it around! Scot-free! The dealers who always say the police planted the drugs on them. As the ice crackled under the whisky and the sponge-cake steamed, Daniel felt entirely happy. It makes you sick, she laughed. Max was also laughing. We'll make love later, the judge promised himself. He was aware of savouring the moment's happiness. I'll get fat, he thought, I'll grow jolly and complacent.

But surely – Max already had crumbs on his wet young lips – surely if the police have the fragment, if the fragment, I mean the bit of jacket, matches . . . You really mustn't underestimate, Daniel interrupted his guest, then immediately was interrupted himself. In the sitting room the phone had begun to ring. There was a moment's uneasiness as husband and wife exchanged glances. You must never underestimate, Daniel repeated, the effect on twelve honest men and true of *the offended denial*. But Hilary had stiffened. It was exactly the same time as the call yesterday. Deliberately, Daniel did not move. It was Hilary who usually answered the phone. He would not have her imagine that he was eager to get there first. Those days were over. But there'll be witnesses, Max was protesting. He seemed oblivious to the sudden tension. There'll be people who'll say the jacket was his!

The phone rang on. Hilary was hovering. Daniel refused to let it bother him. He was enjoying the conversation. He made a comically expansive gesture. Picture it, he said: some steamy-faced little cockney, thirtyish, but could be fifty, whose wife and three kids have all given evidence that he was watching some soap with them at the moment of the crime, goes into the box, stares the jury right in the eye, bangs a meaty fist on the rail and shouts: I di'n't bleedin' well do it! That's all I know. I never sin this jacket nor whatever it is, not nowhere anytime in my life!

Again Max laughed, and what Daniel loved to do was to swirl his whisky twice around the glass and then down the first half in a gulp so that it rose to his head with the same rush as the smell of fresh baking from the oven. Hilary made for the door. We're going to be ex-directory in the new house, she grimaced. Too many phone-calls. Oi've got now blee-in' oidea 'ow it got there! Daniel was good at accents. He raised his voice above the ringing phone and made the gesture of banging his fist. All the man has to do, he told his wife's piano pupil, is to sow a seed, you see, of doubt. In the jury. One *tiny* seed of doubt and in no time at all it will shoot up into a towering beanstalk of innocence. Again he brought the tumbler to his lips. The ice clinked. Apparently Max's father was a mathematics professor. Parents separated, Hilary had said. A nice boy, she had insisted, as if to explain why she had accepted a private student after such a long time without. He's already played a number of small concerts. Daniel leaned over his whisky: All I can tell yer is, if it took free blokes to do the break-in, it's pretty bloody queer the cops come right off to the one poor bugger's 'ouse what's lost 'is bit of jacket. Pretty blee-in' queer is all I say.

The phone rang. If the answering machine was on, it would have kicked in by now. In the sitting room a door opened. Daniel had a glimpse of his daughter coming in from the stairwell. Immediately his wife changed direction. Oh but you're soaking, Sarah, she shouted. The girl was drenched. The phone drilled. The whisky was rising to Daniel's brain. But what about the loot? Max demanded. He seemed engrossed in the conversation. Or fingerprints? Only now did Daniel notice that the young man wore a rather extravagant earring. Get your shoes off, at once! Hilary cried. She always went over the top with Sarah. You're muddying the carpet! Computer components, Daniel said. All recovered a few hours afterwards in a stolen van. No prints.

Then it was Tom, charging in from the bedroom section of the flat, who actually took the call. The ringing must have finally penetrated his Discman. Why doesn't anyone ever answer the bloody phone, he shrilled, dashing across the room. In his freshly broken voice, he said. Hello, Savage. Then, No, it's his son. Quite unnecessarily, Hilary was tugging Sarah's wet coat off. The girl was defiant, her hair dripping. Tom raised his voice: Dad, for you! Someone called Min, Minnie?

Sorry, Dan, I thought it was you. The voice was a whisper.

Dan? And only now – though crossing the room he had sensed the memory coming – did Judge Savage connect. Minnie! Only on hearing the distinctive voice, the broken accent. He caught his breath, closed his eyes. Then I couldn't hang up, she explained. She spoke as if whispering through a blocked nose. It would have been too suspicious, wouldn't it. That's perfectly all right, he said quietly. It was not. What can I do for you? His tone was too polite. He was aware of aping the normal. His hand was shaking. Damn, damn and damn. Can't you speak? she asked. No, that's fine. But now Daniel was distracted by his wife's extravagant fussing: Oh please don't go, Hilary was turning to Max. Sarah'll just get these wet clothes off, won't you love, and come and join us. She is determined not to listen in, Daniel realised, to show she trusts me. In his other ear, Minnie's voice was irritatingly faint: Just say, I'm busy tomorrow, if you have a problem. Really no problem, Daniel insisted. But why was *she* speaking so softly? He could hardly hear her. Why was she calling? Behind him, his son Tom dropped heavily on the sofa, sprawling for the remote. There was a blip of volume before he got the mute on. Oh, hello there! Max called, coming across from the kitchen. Apparently he knew Sarah already. Daniel half turned, receiver glued to his ear. Shush! Hilary hissed. Your father's on the phone! The channels flickered one after another. A man on his scooter in the desert. It's only, I've been trying to phone for ages, Minnie said, but it's always someone else answers. That's fine, he repeated. Really, Hilary was insisting to Max, it's not late, do stay! Daniel was disorientated. I should be alarmed, he thought. He said: I'm usually in chambers late afternoon, early evening, if there's something you need to discuss. Well, I can hardly strip in the front room, Sarah was saying. She smiled sarcastically at her father as if it were ridiculous of him to be speaking on the phone while she stood at the door dripping wet with her mother tugging at her clothes. Embarrassed, Max had moved to stand behind Tom, watching the TV. But how did you get so soaked? Hilary went on. You look like Ophelia dragged from her lily-pond! No, look, Minnie was saying. Daniel tried to concentrate. This was frightening. It's a bit complicated. I've a favour to ask. Let me meet you this . . .

Leave off! Ow! There was a sudden clatter. For a split second – one ear exposed to home and the other firmly pressed to the disturbing past, to make contact, to exclude contact – Daniel supposed the sound had come from the television, so sudden was the leap in volume. But the screen was mute. A man in yellow shorts was about to take a free kick. No, it was the girl, Minnie. Leave me alone! she was shouting. Bloody hell, leave me alone! Then came something fierce in her own language and a man's voice, bantering. I'll have to change phones, she confided, dropping the whisper now. My dad, she explained. Daniel rolled his eyes for his daughter's benefit, as much as to say, these people bothering me after hours with their stupid problems! Though usually no one bothered him at all. Having protested she couldn't strip, Sarah had started peeling off her sweater, which brought her tee-shirt fleetingly up over her bra. Some kraut team, Tom was explaining to the ever polite Max. You can see from the ads round the pitch.

Waiting for the girl to change phones, Daniel noticed a sodden pile of roughly printed tracts on the low table by the door: In His Image, For Your Salvation. Fuck you, he heard a faint voice. This chapel thing was just a phase, he hoped. I'm phoning my black pimp lover, Minnie yelled, if you want to know! Daniel winced. Brilliant, Tom said. In Judge Savage's head, the whisky was making it that bit harder either to keep things apart or to put them together. How alarmed should I be, he wondered? That's wet too, his wife was saying, you'll have to pop to your room. Hilary's voice was oddly menacing. Just pop into your room and change, love, and then we can all have a nice drink together. Again there was a shout in the distance. Something fierce, in Korean. For some reason Sarah wouldn't budge. Suddenly, standing by the door, their awkward daughter was giving the unusual spectacle of appearing rather pleased with herself. Now she peeled off her yellow tee-shirt too. Sarah! Hilary was trying to speak with her eyes. To plead. Max must have seen, but had turned back quickly to the football.

Coming to his wife's aid, receiver still at his ear, Daniel began a pantomime of grimaces to get Sarah to go to her bedroom. In the background Korean voices continued to argue. It seemed there were more than two. Oh please! Sarah laughed, unbuckling her jeans. Then she started to mimic him. She rolled her eyes and mouthed remonstrations. He almost laughed himself from sheer exasperation. Hilary was suffering. It's only the same as a bikini on the beach, Mum, the girl said calmly, slipping out of her jeans. If I really have to change. But this wasn't true. The white cotton of her underclothes was damp. Her nipples and hair were dark. Max dutifully kept his eye on the ball. Minnie still hadn't come back to the receiver. Unusually, Hilary was at a complete loss, Daniel noticed. What was this call about? How many years since he'd spoken to the child? How dangerous was it? Hilary had picked up the wet clothes. Sarah's body was wiry and hard. Again Daniel heard a shout in the phone, echoed by Tom's, Bloody Borussia, can you believe it! I don't understand you, Sarah laughed. She was shaking her head.

Then all at once his other ear was shocked by sobbing. Minnie must have picked up the extension with a yell. Oh please! the voice began, Daniel! Daniel! Then, just as Hilary was forced to hurry off to the bedrooms to fetch the dry clothes herself, the line was cut. The girl's voice was gone. Daniel collected himself. More loudly and pompously than was required, he told the microphone: If it's just a question of redistributing clerical duties in the interim, I'll have no difficulty supporting you. As soon as he got off the phone, he demanded of his daughter what on earth had got into her. What in heaven's name was she playing at, stripping by the front door! But already his eyes were casting about for the whisky glass.

TWO

The clerk reported no calls or messages when he arrived at court. Daniel had slept poorly. It was foolish to drink so much. He scratched at a stain on his robe. And to force the poor boy to drink too. Poor Max. But Hilary hadn't seemed suspicious of his sudden rush of party spirit, his determined festive extravagance. If there's wine in the fridge, out with it, he had said. I have an announcement to make, he declared. He winked at Sarah. Your honour, I have a piece of information to convey, Counsel for the Prosecution announced no sooner than the court was assembled. A pompous man. Daniel was ten minutes late. The jury had barely been trooped in than they were being trooped out again. A high window showed still bare branches gleaming in rain. I've bought a grand piano for the new house, he told them. Sarah had refused the smart clothes her mother brought and gone to her room to put on her sloppiest. Why? For our 20th anniversary, he announced. A Steinway. Yes, the very same that Hilary always sat at in Blumenthal's when she chose pianos for friends. The same those friends never bought. But *he* had. He had put down a deposit. And already,

Daniel thought, as Tom and Max applauded and Hilary gasped and embraced him, already the instrument was doing its job, its music drowning out the unpleasantness of Sarah's provocations, of that strange and worrying phone-call. His wife folded her arms around him. It was money well spent. She was laughing and weeping. The English were such dilettantes, Hilary would complain on leaving Blumenthal's, the way they always went for the cheaper things, the Yamahas, the East European stuff. How was it, Daniel wondered, hugging his ever so English wife, that she always talked about the English as if she were German, they Spanish, or Greek? May I smoke? Max had enquired amid the general festivity. His politeness was touching. Hilary hated smoke and said, Of course, Max.

Your honour, the elderly prosecutor told Judge Savage, your honour, the police have just this moment informed us that the stolen goods in question, which, as you will remember were recovered soon after the crime, were, er, stolen again last night. In exactly the same manner and from the same place, defence counsel added with a hint of a smile. Despite evident differences in age, temperament and class, both advocates, Daniel observed, were performing their roles in exemplary fashion. The prosecutor coughed: Since the material in question, more than thirty thousand pounds worth of computer hardware, was essential to the operations of the company who owned it, we allowed them to take possession on the understanding that certain items would be available as exhibits as and when required. That, I'm afraid, will no longer be possible. Defence counsel's smile broadened. The bright young man seemed extremely pleased with himself. Why? Daniel wondered. The business of the jacket would surely be damning enough. Prosecution counsel had said nothing about dropping the case. Nor did the crime's repetition exclude the defendant's having taken part in the earlier theft. I wonder if you could fetch me an aspirin? he asked the usher.

Then when the defendant was brought in, it turned out he was black. Was this, perhaps, Daniel wondered, why the case had been assigned to him? So the accent was West Indian, not cockney at all. Glancing around the court, he saw that in fact he and the man in the dock were the only two non-whites present. Why had Minnie called him, of all people, almost seven years on? The only non-white judge on this circuit. A special favour, she said. What favour? Daniel invited the defendant not to interrupt the court by constantly muttering to himself. No doubt she had had other affairs since. Leaning forward from his seat the man was bull-necked and brutally handsome. Why come to him? You will have your opportunity to give evidence, Mr Conway, all in good time. Mr Cunningham? he invited the prosecution to resume. A judge ought to have everybody's names on the tip of his tongue, Daniel had long ago decided, though he was acutely aware of having had no time at all to collect his thoughts today. Sleep had been a lurid melodrama of which he remembered only the violent awakening, tossed into the morning as if from an angry sea.

It's bloody stupid, Mr Conway interrupted again. It's pathetic! He raised his voice. Once again Daniel warned that he would be removed from the court and tried in his absence if he didn't observe the most elementary of rules. It is within my power to order you downstairs, Mr Conway. As he spoke, firmly and softly, the contrast of his own measured Oxbridge accent with the defendant's rough street Jamaican could only alert the alert, Judge Savage was aware, to the cleverness of those who had made his appointment. His close friend Martin Shields had put it thus: They chose the only one of us who really *is* one of us, but with boot polish on his face. That was at the chambers party. Chromosomatism! Martin joked. They had had a lot to drink. Martin's wife Christine had tried to shut him up, but Daniel insisted that he didn't mind. They were old friends, he and Mart. On the contrary, he *agreed*. Of course, it was political correctness. He had been chosen to redress an embarrassing imbalance. I may have a little light tan on my cheeks, but at least I'm a red-blooded heterosexual, he laughed. He roared with merry laughter. It was *his* party after all. Hilary hadn't taken offence. They danced together. Martin had been overlooked *again*. There isn't room for all of us, he acknowledged. Not now the others have to be brought in too. He meant the blacks, the Indians, the women. It was the third time they had invited Martin Shields up to interview, the third time they had denied him even so much as the position of recorder. He would never make it now. But then the imbalance *was* embarrassing: not a single non-white judge on this circuit. No point in being bitter, Martin would say. He had started a collection of British fungi. He began to talk about fungi. And moths. British moths.

Presenting the case to the jury, prosecution counsel brought up the question of the theft's being repeated early on. His manner was at once tedious and entirely convincing: the theft of the same materials in the same manner had been committed the very evening before this trial. You will want to ask yourselves, of course, he remarked without looking up, whether this was pure coincidence, or whether perhaps it might have been intended to weaken the Crown's case and . . . Your honour! Young Harper was immediately on his feet. This is the merest speculation!

Daniel accepted the objection, as Cunningham no doubt

knew he would. Studying the jury, the judge was depressed to observe how often twelve people could be assembled without even one of them offering a temptation that would allow a now faithful husband to savour repression at work. The only pretty candidate had been excluded in the ballot. How can I know, Hilary had demanded, at the height of the crisis, that you're not just becoming more and more like your miserable father! Whoever he was, she added viciously. You knew my father perfectly well, Daniel objected. He referred, of course, to the recently deceased Colonel Henry Savage who had spent so much money to send both his sons to Rugby. Colonel Savage always said, *both* my sons. You were child to the people who brought you up. Certainly as much as brother Frank. The jury tittered on hearing the story of the jacket. Defence counsel, Daniel noticed, was definitely looking smugger than he ought. But this, perhaps, was theatre. Like one's wife, one's children, the jury were there to be convinced.

Aren't we spending too much?

At lunchtime the judge and his wife met briefly at the house to do some measuring. Hilary seemed both worried and delighted. These visits were already a pleasant routine. They wandered through the rooms, climbed an iron ladder upstairs. I wish we'd had three, she said. Here an old piece of furniture from the flat would fit, there another must be purchased. From her place at the piano – she had scratched out a shape on rough floor boards – she would be able to look sideways into the flames of a fire that was to sit in a modern cast iron core, but clad, distinctly Regency, in a delicate stone surround. You look – she gave him the brochure. How was it that they had stopped arguing, Daniel marvelled, turning the pages? The grey stone? he asked. Three children would have been happy here, she said. The crisis they had

had did not quite seem to explain it, he felt, this content-ment, this lack of tension. Or the marble?

The brochure showed smiling faces staring into flames. Young faces. Combustion and heat distribution (there were graphs and tables) were the most efficient technology could provide. Do you think that Sarah will start playing again, he asked, once we have the new piano? As yet their daughter still refused even to come and see the place. Hilary laughed. They poked their noses out into the rain. That was a terrible exhibition she put on for Max last night. For Max? Daniel was nonplussed. She used to play so well, he said wistfully. A bit mechanically, Hilary said. Should they terrace the front garden where it sloped down quite steeply? The religious thing is just to be provocative, I think, she said.

Then Hilary exclaimed, Oh but for heaven's sake, I forgot: Christine phoned to say they might be interested in buying the flat. In fact, she was positively gung-ho. What, Martin's Christine? The Shields? I'm sorry, I should have said at once. I don't know what I was thinking of. Suddenly, his wife turned and embraced him under their umbrella on a muddy path. As soon as they've got the doors on, let's bring up a rug and make love. All right, Daniel agreed, though sensing this was more the kind of thing one did with a mistress than a wife of twenty years. Still, he felt very happy, looking across the sloping hills in the rain. Some workers were watching from one of the other houses. Very happy, he told himself. The piano had been an excellent move. It was true Sarah's playing had been mechanical. And it would be too good to be true if they simply sold the Carlton Street flat at once to old friends. Yet at the same time − or rather this was somehow part of that happiness − he had the elusive impres-sion that his life was actually over already, burned out. It was Tom and Sarah who had the kindling in their eyes now.

Their middle aged father would just relax on the terraced lawn or on the hearthrug, listening to the ordered progressions of Bach and Mozart.

At what time was exhibit one seized? Defence counsel asked. The jury had been shown the fragment of jacket. The morning after the crime, the police officer said. I asked at what time? The policeman consulted his notes. Ten-thirty. And of course the exhibit was immediately taken back to the station? Yes. That was February 12th? Yes. And at what time was the search warrant on the defendant's house executed? The following morning. February 13th? Yes, we felt . . . At what time, Sergeant? Early. Five-thirty. And you immediately found the jacket? It was hanging in the passage by the door. With the fragment missing? Yes. And no doubt you rushed it straight back to the police station to compare it with exhibit one? We did. Taking Mr Conway back with you for safety's sake? We felt that given . . .

How wearisome this was! Daniel had his eye on the clock. Surely nothing could save the defendant. The evidence was overwhelming. Defence counsel was dragging it out. And a non-white judge, however sophisticated his accent, merely made it easier, Daniel thought, for an all-white jury to convict. He had told Minnie he would be in his room in chambers late afternoon and already it was four–fifteen. The pretty one lost in the ballot had been Asian. Would she come? Did he want her to? Yes, but only in order to have whatever it was she wanted off his back. No desire, he thought, to repeat the experience. On the contrary, he had never been so eager to get home after work, to play safe. In another couple of minutes he would invite counsel for the defence to come to the point.

At what time, then, would the arrival of exhibit two have been entered in the station's exhibit log? Daniel cleared his throat: If defence counsel could, er, come to the point, he suggested. There were wry smiles. The police sergeant was clearly telling the truth. The jury was bored. The defendant, constantly muttering under his breath, seemed sensibly to have accepted the inevitable. He had the look of a man let out of prison only in order to see how quickly he might find his way back there. We are eager, Daniel finished, to hear where your questioning is leading, Mr Harper.

Of course, your honour!

It was only then, as the young man turned rather dramatically to the judge's bench to explain himself, that Daniel appreciated that it was a set up. How stupid of him! After all these years. Defence counsel, a young and eager performer, a man with ambition glowing from his eyes, dripping from his shiny lips, had been begging to be interrupted. Begging. He had been dragging it out *in order* to be interrupted. The interruption underlines the surprise – every lawyer knows this – as a noise is louder when one is woken by it, when one is shocked out of sleep. By a phone-call perhaps. Daniel had woken the jury with his demand, put them on maximum alert for whatever it was counsel was now about to say. Your honour – the boy even indulged in a flourish of the gown – your honour, I merely wish to demonstrate that the arrival of the fragment of leather jacket, exhibit one, was not entered in the police station log until *after* the police had seized the jacket itself, exhibit two, entry for exhibit one being made at 10 o'clock on February 13th, almost twenty-four hours after alleged seizure, and entry for exhibit two after again a full twenty-four hours delay, at twelve-thirty on the fourteenth. The truth is that the police already had the jacket in their possession *before* seizure of the fragment was recorded. This discrepancy with regard to the only – ahm – evidence that the prosecution is offering fits all too well with the defendant's emphatic claim that facts have been manipulated in order to gain his conviction.

Daniel looked over to the prosecution counsel. For a moment the man had closed his eyes. He raised a hand to his brow and slowly shook his head, then asked: Your honour, given this development, I wonder if you would allow me a fifteen minute adjournment for consultation? Daniel allowed it, knowing full well that on his return the man would announce that the Crown was dropping its case. So that in the event it was only a matter of half an hour before the defendant, more bewildered than ever, would hear the judge directing the jury to acquit, and a question of minutes then before the man would be set free, though neither judge, prosecution nor defence seriously doubted that he had been involved in the crime. Sometimes it is the conclusion the jury comes to that counts and sometimes the chance to reach a conclusion is denied them. When everything seems settled, everything can still be undone. What you thought was evidence, is suddenly irrelevant. It hasn't been properly recorded, would never hold up on appeal. How could the police have made such a cock-up? It was a minor coup for young Harper to have noticed such a thing. His elderly opponent made a point of going over to compliment him while Daniel, hurrying back to his chambers, was again aware, without even needing to articulate it to himself, of the gap between reality and court theatricals. He shook his head. The CPS people would be furious. So much of life came into the court and so much escaped it, eluded it, or emerged bizarrely packaged in a quantity of money to pay, or years to serve, or years that might be served if you ever got caught doing anything again. It isn't so much arbitrary, Daniel would tell himself, as disconnected, not on the same plane. In any event, the real damage to a convicted man is not, or not necessarily, the punishment itself, but the way the conviction conditions those all around you, the jury you live your life with day by day. It would be far less damaging, for example, to Daniel, to be sent down for a month on a drunk driving charge, than for it to become generally known how he had met and seduced Minnie.

He waited for her call. Or perhaps she would actually come to the court. At six he phoned home and said he wanted to hang on an hour or so to go through the papers for tomorrow's list. Martin and Christine are here, Hilary said. She was breathless. They want to put down a deposit. Already! On the full asking price? His wife said yes. Without negotiation? That's what I said. I can't believe it. Sarah had been offensive again, his wife complained. Gone out slamming the door just because I made a comment about her appearance. Tell them, Daniel said, we'll get someone to draw up a contract absolutely as soon as possible. In the background he could hear Tom's rumbustious banging on the piano. 'Get back Joe!' We must have asked too little, he laughed. Putting down the phone he felt awed by this extraordinary run of luck. All the anxiety he had foreseen, the problem of making payments on the new house while waiting to see when and at what price their old one would sell for, was gone. Sold, done it!

Somebody's made an offer for the flat, he mentioned to the departing clerk. Oh that's wonderful, the girl said. Congratulations. Her voice was sincere. Sweetheart, he thought. Minnie too had been a sweetheart. Smiling to himself, he turned to some sentencing reports.

A social worker was recommending leniency for a man who had broken his son's wrist. The mother had walked out on the family. An older sibling, one of four, insisted that this particular act of violence was unique, the result of stress and

27

anxiety. Daniel understood the impulse to violence. There had been a number of occasions when he had hit his children too hard. Immediately prior to the incident, the victim (a six-year-old) had deliberately smashed all the kitchen crockery. Those were the details. With a hammer! But Daniel had never come close to taking Tom by the hand and snapping his wrist. He hoped they would be happy in the new house. Hilary too could be violent. She had thrown a knife at him when she had found out about Jane. How had she found out? A vegetable knife. Somebody somewhere must have whispered something. The handle caught him above an ear. How else could she have known? She wouldn't say. And she had done violence to herself too. Her fingers bled at the nails; she had gouged flesh from above her knees. He had respected this hysteria. He was impressed. He had pointed out that it was years since they had been happy together, packed his bags and left. He had gone to the Cambridge Hotel. But the convicted man had taken a child's arm and snapped it over the edge of the table. He had been drinking. Did one hear it snap? At least fifty percent of those I've defended and prosecuted had been drinking at the time of the alleged crime. It was something one often mentioned in conversation. If Daniel wasn't lenient, he would deprive the boy of his father. This was the social worker's concern. And thus of his home. That was true. In cases of this kind one's discretionary powers were considerable. What the mother had done, on the other hand, walking out on her family, wasn't even illegal. She was incapable, she had stated, of looking after children in her present situation. As it hadn't been illegal when Daniel checked in to the Cambridge Hotel. The social worker was of the same opinion. Quite incapable. But ugly, Hilary had said. Ugly. The mother was an alcoholic. The father was doing his best. He only drank occasionally. On the other hand how lenient was lenient? And could a six-year-old be expected to answer a social worker's questions in his own best interest?

It was six-thirty and still the girl hadn't phoned. It doesn't matter. The only important thing was that she stop phoning him at home. That the past remain past and buried. Pushing the seat back from his desk, Daniel remembered again his odd feeling up at the new house at lunchtime that there was something inexplicable about this new happiness of theirs. Was it really just the crisis and its resolution? The dramas of a year before seemed impossibly distant now. He knew as a fact that he must be the child of those events, but often it was as though they had happened to someone else; not to his wife and himself, music teacher and judge, but to some other person, to this man, for example, this car mechanic, who had immediately taken his son to hospital but refused to admit his responsibility to the doctors, confessing only when interviewed by the police. Even after that confession the boy had sworn blind that the fracture was a result of his falling out of the kitchen window. The alcoholic wife confirmed that her husband had hit her on three or four occasions, though never seriously. It was quite beyond her to look after children. What did never seriously mean? The father had never expected, the social worker's report insisted, that he would have to look after his children on his own. He would benefit from a period of rehabilitation. My dad, Minnie had said when she told him she was switching phones. My dad!

Daniel put down the case papers. The oddity, in the end though, he reflected, had been that the thing that ought most to have hurt him, most to have confirmed his decision to leave her, had been precisely what made him look at Hilary afresh, allowed him to rediscover a forgotten

29

tenderness. It came to him that he had seen that tenderness once in Tom's eyes when he, Daniel, in his fury over some game they were playing, had punched their bedroom door and his fist had splintered the thin ply. Tom's eyes had been full of sad love, of admiration, of reappraisal. But it wasn't the business of the knife that drew him back to Hilary. It was when she had brought up the whole story of her ex, of Robert. She had resurrected that old story in defiance, in order to destroy their marriage once and for all. They were standing in the foyer of the Cambridge Hotel. She had loved only Robert, she said. Almost sneering. *He* was the love of my life. She was *glad* their marriage was over, she shouted. The only one. Glad! It's been a farce, she said. After Robert killed himself, she no longer cared. That is the truth, if you have to know. She would never get over that, she told him. I married you entirely on the rebound, she said coldly, primly, in the foyer of the hotel. She stressed the word entirely. Hilary is capable of great feats of primness, Daniel remembered. Later, he had spent hours, days, anaesthetised before the TV, waiting for something to happen, something that was supposed to come from within himself, some decision. Martin had looked after him. They spent the evenings playing snooker together. You must look after your mum, he told his daughter Sarah one evening at the school gate. He and Hilary were agreed that the children needn't be told about Jane. I never cared, Hilary told him determinedly in the hotel foyer, about you, or anyone but Robert. I married you more to spite my parents, she said, than anything else. To spite *myself*, she said. She tried to laugh in his face. I knew you could never be the man Robert was. He was full of sensibilities you can't even imagine, she said. He was a genius. You can't even imagine. She burst into tears. The only thing you had was you weren't white. Even weeping

30

she was prim. You'll never know, she said, how much that killed my Dad.

Waiting for Minnie, reading these papers about the family circumstances of a car mechanic who had pleaded guilty to breaking his son's wrist – both radius and ulna had gone – Daniel reflected on that crucial meeting in the foyer of the Cambridge Hotel. It had taken place amid a back and forth of guests pretending, as they must, not to listen. She had meant to live an exciting life, Hilary insisted, she was spitting the words at this point, with a musician, a *rebel*, someone with real charisma, a real man. But when Robert killed himself she lost all hope. She would never understand why he'd done it. Why had they never discussed this? Love hadn't helped him. My love didn't help. We two have never talked about anything important, she shouted. Love is pointless. When she saw his body in the garage, she had known she would never love again. I knew I would never love anyone. Then she had just fallen back on him, on Daniel, and on the dull conventional life he had given her. You were a fall-back, she shouted. Understand? I'll never love anyone. The life you've given me has been dullness itself. A miserable fallback! She hissed the words. How can someone weep and still be prim? Violently prim, he thought. You fall over yourself to be conventional, she insisted, there was contempt in her voice, because you think it's the only way a black can succeed. I'm not actually black, he reminded her. Why did he always say that? Well, you're certainly not white! she yelled. In the foyer of the hotel. She almost spat, as if their marriage were something she could cough up in contempt. I never loved you, she shouted. She could vomit away her marriage. I am retching up our marriage and spitting it out. That was what she was saying.

They stood staring at each other. And all at once – he

31

could actually place the moment, the sudden surfacing of unexpected emotion – Daniel felt a great tenderness toward her for this. For having said this. He knew it wasn't true. But how sad that even the *story* of our marriage has to be destroyed like this. Hilary has to destroy our marriage, because of what I am doing to her, leaving her. What you're doing is ugly, she'd said. Yet he hadn't seen Jane for weeks now. He hadn't seen Jane at all since he'd left home. Why not? That's rubbish, he said, he took his wife in his arms. There in the foyer of the Cambridge. He reached out his arms to his wife. We had great times, he said, we had Sarah and Tom, for God's sake. For some reason he couldn't understand he really didn't want to see Jane. He kept making excuses. They held each other, standing by the revolving doors. People were pretending not to notice. She was rigid and weeping. It was the first embrace in weeks. You *know* that, he said. You can't change that, Hilary. And though the hotel stand-off was to last almost a further month, from that moment on, that embrace in the foyer by the revolving doors, his arms tight around her rigid, resisting body, their marriage was up and running again. The rest fell away. Jane fell away. As if the most damning evidence, Daniel thought, had been improperly recorded. The police had screwed up. The case must be dropped. Of course everybody *knew* about Jane, as everybody knew about Robert and his suicide, her lost first love, her musical passion, but none of this would stand up in court. There has been a mistake, your honour, an oversight. In court, before a jury of their peers, there were Sarah and Tom, and actually quite a lot of good times together, well recorded in the family albums. There was a gleam of future firelight in the children's young eyes. Then if she was never going to say what exactly she knew about Jane and who she had got that knowledge from, how could it weigh in the balance? He denied the most part – hearsay, your honour – never even hinted at the other adventures. Why should he? A jury isn't informed of the defendant's record. And he really *had* lost interest. It was strange. You can't rewrite history, he muttered in her ear, in the foyer. I thought that's what you were trying to do, she said.

So it was precisely in choosing to split up, worn down by years of warfare, that they had at last understood, without either entirely revealing him or herself to the other, that their destinies were inextricable; these were the roles they would play as surely as a judge must wear a wig in court. One might as well accept that. No, they should celebrate it! They must celebrate that famous suntan their children boasted. Oh I like my coffee well roasted, Hilary laughed, hugging Daniel when he came home – that colour that could only have come from them. Hilary loved his skin, the conventional British man, she said, in the mysterious foreign body: Daniel Savage!

Yet none of this quite explained their present happiness. There was something he couldn't quite put his finger on. Just as His Honour Judge Savage was standing to leave his room, the telephone rang. Christine said: Hilary didn't want to bother you, Dan dear, but I insisted. Her voice was charmingly breathy. Do come and have a glass of champers before we have to wander off. I mean, it's such a big day. We're buying the flat. Then under her breath, and taking advantage of what sounded like Chopin in the background, she added: you know Mart always perks up when you're there, Dan. I'm getting desperate. Evidently, Daniel thought as he put the phone down, and despite this business of their buying the flat, his friend Martin was going through one of his big depressions again. I was just on my way, he laughed.

But again the phone called him back. He had already

closed the door and now had to unlock it. Daniel? Minnie asked. Can you meet me in town? Now? With what sounded like a giggle in her voice, she named a street corner in the town centre. He was beginning to explain that it would have to wait when she said, please. Please. You'll understand why. I'm desperate. Can't speak now. She must have put the phone down.

It would take no more than ten minutes to drive home. Daniel stood at the corner of Salisbury and Drummond. There could have been no mistake. Minnie was born and bred here. But how long did one wait? He owed the girl nothing, yet felt concerned. Christine was desperate with Martin depressed. Minnie was desperate for reasons he couldn't imagine. Minnie was dangerous. Sheltering in the entrance to Hill's, he stepped out on the pavement from time to time. The town was busy in the smeared neon of a rainy evening. To cover tracks, he hurried a hundred yards to the off-license and picked up champagne. Passing Kingscote Ave, he realised he risked being seen by his daughter, whose chapel was there. She called it The Chapel. Or sometimes The Community. Sarah had hurried out slamming the door, Hilary said. Unless this was The Chapel and The Community was something different somewhere else. The business of averting his face as he crossed the road brought back all sorts of memories. The subterfuge of those many mad years. How exciting it had all been! My double life. And how stupid and dangerous. Screwing a girl on the jury! *During* the case, damn it! A big case. Daniel laughed. A Korean girl. But it was shameful too. Truly shameful. What if I had ever found out, Daniel had often asked himself, that an opponent was screwing someone on the jury when I was defending? It was such a betrayal of one's vocation. He did feel ashamed. I would never speak to them again. Not that it had actually affected the verdict though. And he had needed that excitement so badly then. An insatiable appetite for excitement and risk. For getting away with it. He had been mad. But like a hole in the head now, he told himself. Engaging in subterfuge now, you saw you needed it like a very big hole in the head. Changed, he decided. Suddenly staid. He frowned. He needed clarity now. Was it to do with this isolation one felt as a judge, this lonely detachment? He looked at his watch. The girl had definitely been a disappointment sexually. He remembered the clarity with which he had made that rare entry in his diary, the day they bought the house. I have become myself, he had written. Perhaps it was this rather than the crisis that explained their new happiness. Something physiological. The time of metamorphoses is over. That was how he had put it. I have grown up.

A taxi squealed at the crossing on Drummond. Daniel wanted to be home, with his wife and children, celebrating the new house, the new piano, the sale of the old, drinking champagne with good friends. A small man came hurrying through the rain to shelter in the entrance to Hill's. An Asian, Daniel realised. He studied the cheap jewellery behind the steel grill. She had tried to explain to him how one could tell them apart, Koreans, Malaysians, Chinese, Japanese, Vietnamese. He had never got further than excluding the Japanese. My natural parents were Brazilian, he told her. God knows what mix of races. The man turned suddenly and looked him directly in the eye. In his thirties perhaps. Awful acne. It was Minnie's stories he remembered far more than her performance in bed. Her constant chatter in the pretty accent. As if blocked by catarrh. A very pretty girl. Better dressed than un-. Perhaps the man knew her. The Korean community was so close knit. Wasn't that the burden of her stories? In which case she was risking exposure if she arrived now.

These are old patterns of thought, Daniel reflected. Risk assessment. Now he wanted to be home. Yet the very fact that you always saw it as a risk, that you never wished to be discovered, indicated an investment in the status quo, a desire for excitement, yes, but within a conventional framework where everything remained substantially the same. You go to the edge and no further. Hilary too had wanted an exciting life. I'm taking more of a risk than you are, Minnie had said. More than once. They had only made love four or five times. Impossible, he had laughed. Wrongly, he had imagined that she was worried about her boyfriend, her fiancé. But it seemed she despised the boy. My dad would kill me, she repeated. It was her father who terrified her. You're twenty, Daniel told her, just leave home and do what you want. Do it. The only thing that holds you back is what's inside your head. He wanted to help the girl. He liked her. Fuck off, she told him.

Got time please, the Asian man asked. He pointed at his wrist. Almost seven-thirty. This is ludicrous, Daniel told himself, but now it had occurred to him that the man was somehow involved. Minnie wouldn't come while he was there. How excitingly paranoid one became, running risks! How life fizzed. Career finished if even a whisper. Or perhaps she had arrived while he was getting the champagne and had thought he wasn't coming. She had gone away. Half an hour is enough, Daniel told himself, clutching a cold bottle. Perhaps she was waiting for him to make a move to his car. Then she would grab his arm. We're a tight community, she said, everybody knows I'll marry Ben. She giggled. Poor Ben, if he could see me now! She had been naked, but quite unsexy. More a child, he remembered. He didn't remember very much. She couldn't see the importance of Daniel's question, Did she really want to marry the boy? His parents were friends of the family. And in the trial, a rape trial, she hadn't seen the importance of the long debate over the defendant's mental health, the question of *mens rea*, the guilt that is in the mind. He did it, she said. He raped the old woman. Once they've admitted that, I don't see why the trial has to go on. As prosecution counsel it hardly seemed Daniel Savage's duty to argue the point.

So they've done it, Hilary sighed. They've done it! But why? Why do they want to buy our flat? Daniel and his wife were preparing for bed. I find it hard, he sighed, being with Martin these days. He's so gloomy. It's your fault, she told him. He doesn't try to make you feel guilty at all. But you get defensive. He knows it was the luck of the draw.

Turning out the light, Daniel was vaguely irritated by the sound of a computer game coming from Tom's room. How quickly elation blew over. But if he went to silence it, his wife would take the boy's side. He had done his piano practice after all. They're going to keep the big house too of course, Hilary said. Christine told me she thinks a pied-à-terre in town will be good when Mart has to work late, or when they want to see friends. A pied-à-terre, she laughed, our home! The flat was not *that* small. I just can't see all this stuff with the funguses, Daniel said. I mean, unless you're a scientist, I can't see the point of him collecting toadstools and things. He photographs them. And now moths! Hilary said. Then she said she thought actually it was rather wonderful. It was original. Who else collected funguses? Who else photographed moths? You have to have something to take your mind off Archbold. He was bored with his work. And British ones to boot! *British* funguses. *British* moths. Really, it's Christine I think, Hilary said later. They're a bit isolated out there, she wants to be closer in to town, to escape his depressions.

37

They were quietly embracing when the phone rang. Daniel knew his wife had registered his sudden rigidity. Oh it'll be silly Sarah, Hilary laughed, climbing out of bed. Another depressive! Daniel held his breath. We've sold the flat, love, Hilary announced at once. To Martin and Christine! Yes, yes, I know! And her husband relaxed. But why had the girl wanted to make a fool of him like that? No, you can't, Hilary said. Her tone suddenly altered. I don't care if it's a Christian community. I don't care if they're all vestal virgins. I'll send your father to get you at once. You've got important exams coming up. I said no! Give me the address again. No is no is no is no! You can't just phone and say you're staying out the night. A moment later Daniel was pulling on his clothes to go down to the car.

Along the ring road, girls postured at just the suggestive point where each sodium light met dark masses of hawthorn. This was one place, Daniel thought, where there had never been any need to appoint a token non-white. And there and then he decided that he could not be lenient with that poor father. He, of all people, so soon after his appointment to crown court judge, must not be seen to be soft on a man who had broken his son's wrist. One appointed different people, a new kind of person, in order that everything remain the same, indeed to demonstrate that it had always been okay. The play could go on. It was a good play, even when Lear was black. Or Hamlet Asian. The man might break a neck next time. He might break his child's neck. However rare his drinking bouts. By the road the police were bothering a potential client, examining a licence. The truck was foreign. Aware that he himself might be marginally over the limit, Daniel concentrated on his driving and, wondering now how long exactly the sentence should be, overshot the road the first time. Broughton Street. Then found it. Good.

He made the next right. A young woman immediately opened the door of a rambling Victorian house just beyond the town boundary. Daniel was astonished. It wasn't that he didn't recognise his daughter as that it took him a split second to understand how she had changed. There was singing in the background, something eager with guitars. A tubby figure appeared carrying a tray. Sarah had had all her hair cut off.

That's the Community, she said, sitting beside him. So it *was* separate from the Chapel. He reversed. They have plenty of spare beds and I didn't want to bother you to come and get me. It had been cut roughly, even savagely. Most of them are battered wives, she explained, or homeless. Girls who've left home. There are no men. When he still didn't reply, she objected: Mum's obsessed by these exams. It's crazy. She looked for a station on the radio, found something, listened, then turned it off dissatisfied. As if I had to be beddy-byes by nine every evening.

His daughter sounded belligerent. Daniel was acutely aware of being involved in some important parental test. You cut your hair, he finally said. Now they were back on the ring road again: the long line of yellow lights, the shadowy girls haunting their edges. Both father and daughter knew they were there. Why? Daniel asked. That's my business, she said. He was hesitant: There's no law against it, he agreed. M'lud should know, she said. They don't call me, M'lud. Your honour, then, she smiled. His daughter put an arm round the back of his neck and pushed her fingers into her father's hair. Thanks for coming, your honour, she said. I bet I woke you up. Her fingertips were tender. On the other hand – Daniel tried to make it a joke – if I suddenly came home in a frilly yellow skirt and suspender belt, which would be my business, you'd probably ask me why all the same, wouldn't you? She removed her arm. Should he tell her, he wondered, that she looked awful? It had just been scissored away. I mean, when you live with people, he went on, you owe them a little more than the strict letter of the law, don't you? But his daughter had burst out into a giggly laughter. Actually, it'd be pretty self-evident why, Dad, she laughed. Come to think of it, though, you might look nice in a frilly skirt. It would suit your bum.

When they had parked, he kept her in the car a moment. He said: It just occurred to me perhaps you should get it properly cropped, I mean, if you're going to have it short. Properly? You know what I mean, he said. She sat looking out of the windscreen. It's a Community thing, she explained, her eyes averted. To show that we're not sex objects. Like a Moslem veil really. A Moslem veil serves to cover what every-body agrees *is* a sex object, he said. We're all sex objects, he insisted. If we're halfway lucky. Her voice hardened to a brittleness he knew all too well. Speak for yourself, she said.

Neither made a move to get out. To anyone passing by it would have seemed that they were lovers who found it difficult to part. He tried: What if one of the universities wants to interview you? Yes, so? Well, it might be advisable to look . . . What? Suddenly she was extremely aggressive. To look what, Dad? Come on! She was scathing. Advise, Dad! Tell me what would be advisable. Daniel was furious: I'm just trying to think of your own bloody good. How are they going to react when you come in looking like . . . What? she demanded. What? Tell me what I look like? I'm think-ing of you, he repeated more calmly. You know that. You know it's a provocative statement to have your hair like that. I'm thinking of you.

There was another silence. The girl bowed her head. She was sitting with the same hunched posture he had noticed

40

a lot lately. The shoulders were drawn forward. Maybe I won't go to university, she said. I beg your pardon? I don't think I'm going to university, Dad. But for Christ's sake! The Lord doesn't want me to, she said. Then when he started to protest, she wept and turned to hug him. They were cheek to cheek. He held her tight. He wanted her to acknowledge his love. After some moments, her body relaxed. God knows what your mother will say when she sees that hair, he muttered. Don't cry now. Please don't cry. Oh Mum's already seen it, his daughter was suddenly laughing. She cheered up. She drew back. Daniel found this difficult to believe. Hilary hadn't mentioned it. How could Hilary have seen her hair like that and not mentioned it? When finally he climbed into bed, he said, That girl's driving me crazy; when you see what's she's done to her hair you'll have a fit. There was no reply. Unable to sleep, Daniel again tried to decide how long a sentence he must give the man who had broken his son's wrist. What did Minnie want from him? At last there was a soft laugh: It's just a phase, Hilary murmured. She'll soon change when she finds a boyfriend.

THREE

What Martin read, Daniel read. In the past. Aristotle, Montesquieu, Nietzsche, Sartre. Years ago now. When I choose a course of action for myself, I choose it for the whole human race. That had left its mark. At the weekend, though, and here Daniel could not follow, Martin had shown them his moth trap, a neon tube in a big muslin bag at the bottom of the lawn. This on a visit to discuss the surveyor's report. The puffy fabric, mid-morning when they saw it, was a fluttering scum of drowsy brown life. He takes photographs, then lets them go, Christine explained. Martin picked out a soft brown body. His pretty wife had put on weight. And in a phone-call on the following Monday she begged, please! Please help, Dan! The two had kissed once. After some party. Nothing had come of it. Now Daniel was playing his old friend, his old mentor, at snooker again, and the excuse he had given was that there was something he needed advice about. Why do I always feel more comfortable with Martin, Daniel wondered, when assuming a position of deference, when pretending to seek advice rather than giving it?

Driving to the pub, Daniel couldn't fathom this conundrum yet knew it was typical of the way he had always behaved with Martin. Their friendship had enjoyed its most recent flowering when Daniel had sought help during his crisis with Hilary. A stern defender of monogamy, Martin's performance on the snooker table was ruthless then, always insisting that for consistency's sake Daniel must leave home. You love another woman, so leave! Undoubtedly the best performer chambers had, everybody said of Martin. He slid his cue back and forth with great assurance and was never short of a learned quote. *Mauvaise foi*! He dispatched a colour. What I choose for myself, I choose for the whole human race. Sartre. You can't want the whole human race to be with one woman while loving another, he demanded, can you?

Daniel's hands had trembled then, fluffing every shot. If Martin was the best lawyer, Jane was certainly the youngest and prettiest. But Martin never talked about women. He wasn't the person for that kind of conversation. He never talked about children either. They had chosen not to have children, he would say. He had a sort of easy austerity. A lean, almost gaunt man. Certainly he had destroyed Daniel at snooker those difficult days at the Cambridge Hotel. Yet this brilliant lawyer and first of friends had seemed excessively disconcerted when Daniel's marriage got back together. Jane had moved south. It was as though he had lost some easy case for reasons he couldn't understand.

Had that been the first time Daniel didn't take his friend's advice? In any event, they hadn't played snooker since. Or tennis. They had barely spoken alone since that moment of unpleasantness at the chambers party given to celebrate Daniel's appointment to the judiciary. The only one of us, Martin had said, who really *is* one of us, but with . . . Oh,

43

Mart! Christine shrieked. Really! It had been a long deep kiss, years before. Chromo-somatism! Not long after the Shields had married in fact. In their garden after a party. Martin laughed. Please! she objected. Please! And she had been quite desperate on the phone Monday morning: We're lost Dan, she told him, I don't know. Martin's so strange, so changed. I've no idea what to do or what will happen. So now, instinctively, Daniel, who really hadn't minded that famous remark at the party, was presenting himself to his old friend not as the winner, the happy and successful man, but as someone in difficulty again, someone vulnerable needing an old friend's help; no sooner were they set up at their table than he pulled out the scrap of paper that had come with the post at court five days ago. Your learned counsel, Mr Shields, he asked, if you please.

Martin played listlessly. Something in the limp way he held the cue, dispatching his shots rapidly and ineffectively, without comment, suggested that it was important to him to show that the game was not important to him any longer. He wouldn't take it seriously. His shirt was soiled, the small waistcoat egg-stained. Daniel grew irritated. A year ago, at the height of the crisis, he had been desperate to immerse himself in the game, but unable to do so, overwhelmed as he was by the decision he must take, the awesome process of becoming this person or that, the man who left his wife, the husband who stayed. They were very different lives. Sometimes he'd felt the choice was between a prison cell and a bare, uninhabited planet. Now in contrast he was knocking the balls down with uncanny efficiency, but against no opposition. He couldn't get his friend either to engage with the game or to talk.

Had Martin suffered some fatal knock in that car accident, he wondered? And why is he buying our flat? A simple duplex was not the thing for the mighty Shields family. If they wanted a pied-à-terre, they could have bought a pied-à-terre, right in the centre. And surely, Daniel thought, finding once again that he had a shot perfectly lined up for him – surely an odd anonymous letter was something that could be relied upon to jumpstart an old intimacy. But Martin had made no comment, just read the thing and put it down. Still lying on the table beside their drinks, a childish scribble of capitals announced: AND THE MAN THAT COMMITTETH ADULTERY WITH HIS NEIGHBOUR'S WIFE, THE ADULTERER AND THE ADULTERESS SHALL SURELY BE PUT TO DEATH.

Nutty stuff! Daniel laughed. He was more disconcerted by his friend's silence, he decided, than by this practical joke in dubious taste. Nothing to do with Minnie, he felt sure. The old left hand for disguise, the capital letters, the torn loo paper. A schoolboy prank. Must be the Bible, I suppose. Martin only grunted, fingers in his beard. He was growing a blond beard, the usually lean face was puffy. It was part of his depression, Christine had said. Not shaving. Not looking after himself. On the phone, her generous voice, always intimate and breathy, had skated back and forth between the resigned and the frantic.

Almost at once Daniel was annoyed that he had shown his friend this stupid note. Why did I do that? At Rugby Martin had been the older boy who kindly befriends the younger, non-white and adopted to boot. Befriends and defends him. From elder brother Frank most of all. Daniel had been grateful. Frank was finally expelled, sent away. And at Oxford too, Martin had always been ready to play sage and tutor to the other's crises. He was clever, likeable, lean and athletic. He encouraged his younger friend in every way. Crucially it was Martin who had got Daniel into chambers, had pointed out to his superiors the advantages of having a non-white tenant. Half the defendants were blacks, were they not? Who better to prosecute a black than a black? And all the better if Daniel wasn't *that* black. More a sort of honourable gesture at blackness. Daniel was grateful. But there had been no way he could return the favour. Martin's Uncle Piers was a QC. One grandfather had been a lawlord. Both Christine's parents were magistrates. And twenty years later it seemed there was still no question of reversing the roles in such an old alliance, despite Martin's apparent loss of direction, the sudden scrubby beard, the inexplicable accident – over a hundred mph, going no one knew where – and now this odd collecting business: the funguses, the moths. Their relationship had a pattern that couldn't be broken. As fixed as the black and the pink, Daniel thought. I'll break left-handed, he announced. Perhaps that way he might lose.

He broke, then immediately went on to talk about the anonymous phone calls. Somebody keeps calling and hanging up, he said. Again he was irritated with himself. After all, it wasn't even true now. Minnie no longer called and Daniel no longer thought of the previous calls as anonymous. Magically, even left handed, the balls were going down.

Finally, Martin said: There was an anonymous letter on *Twins* last week, you know. His fingers were twisted into his beard. Daniel couldn't get used to that beard on his clean-shaven friend. Rachel, you know, his voice was low and toneless, gets this note saying Nikki, that's her twin, is seeing her husband. It was when he started watching soaps that I knew there was something seriously wrong, Christine had confided. Soaps! Martin! And is she? Daniel asked. For the first time it struck him that his friend might actually be mentally ill. The accident had brought on dementia. He watches *all* of them, Christine complained. There was a child-ish awe in her voice, and a sort of frustrated petulance: Dan, I'm telling you, he spends the *whole* day on the sofa.

Not exactly, Martin said. He paused to concentrate. Nikki, you know Nikki? The one with the short blonde hair. Well, she is flirting with him, Rachel's husband – Daniel had never seen the programme – but Troy, the husband, is a paragon of virtue. In fact Nikki is evil *because* Rachel and Troy are good. Get me? He spoke in a low quiet voice. And vice versa. The more one is one thing, the more the other becomes the other. Do you see what I mean? With great delibera-tion Martin cued up and missed another shot. Quite clev-erly done actually. Someone steps on someone else's territory, so they have to become someone different. You're good, but someone else's being good makes you evil. It was his first faint smile of the evening. As a result of course, neither goodness nor evil can really be said to mean anything, if you follow, though in the meantime the letter makes Rachel unhappy. That is, it gives her something to live for.

You're not trying, Daniel accused his friend. The shot had been the simplest of straight lines to an unencumbered corner pocket. Martin had appeared to take his time. Perhaps the sensation that irritated Daniel most was when he didn't know how to behave, couldn't see quite what sort of story he was involved in. This had happened frequently in the old days with Hilary, as if neither were quite sure whether they were man and wife or not, or what that might mean. Now Martin insisted on playing, but refused to take the game seriously.

What should I do? Daniel demanded. Take the blue of course. There was a wry obtusity to his friend's voice. Did he know that the evening had been set up by his wife? I mean about the *letter*, Daniel said. I want you to give me one piece of straight honest advice about this weird letter. Like old times, he added.

Old times. Martin rested his scrubby beard on his cue. His eyes were fixed on the table. Finally he said: What I don't understand, Dan, is why you went back to Hilary if you're still going to go on screwing around. With someone close to home too, if 'neighbour's wife' is anything to go by.

But I'm *not*, Daniel laughed. It hadn't occurred to him that Martin would imagine the crazy letter referred to anything recent or real. That's the wonder of it, he insisted. I'm behaving like a saint. Really. I'm even *happy* to be behaving like a saint. You don't believe me. Then I get this letter. Martin said nothing. To keep the conversation alive, Daniel went on: In fact, if anything the person acting suspiciously these days is Hilary. Keeps having this handsome young bloke round for lessons. Jewish. She hasn't given private lessons for years. He's there tonight.

This time Martin skewered the white down. Could he be on some anti-depressant? Daniel knew his friend hadn't been in court for almost a month. I'd be lying, Christine had confessed towards the end of Monday's call, if I pretended there wasn't a financial problem with his not working. It can only go on so long, she said. There was a squeak in her voice, an indignant resistance to raw emotion. The moment the receiver was down, Daniel had picked it up again to phone Hilary. They should have had children, his wife immediately said. Hilary had never approved of her husband's submission to this clever man. Now she seemed quite excited at the extent of Martin's collapse. Isn't he working at all? she asked. No.

But you must have done something, Martin was saying, otherwise why would they write? People don't write unpleasant letters completely out of the blue, do they?

Nothing, Daniel insisted. I don't know what on earth it's about. Well then, consider it a blessing, Martin told him. He suddenly put the cue aside, mid game, as if snooker were not a thing that required a beginning and an end. He stood the stick in its rack and sat at their table. Yes, a blessing, he said, rubbing his hands. His gesturing was odd, Daniel thought, oddly troubled, oddly condescending, and at the same time, animal like. He has the nervous gesture of the alert animal.

The letter gives you the impression, Martin began to speak, that you're in danger, you know, and so the illusion of having something to live for. You call old friends, as one does in such circumstances, and start talking it over. It keeps the mind busy. A good old threatening letter. What more can one ask? Everybody should get one.

Pulling out a chair opposite, with no protest about the abandoned game, Daniel said he didn't need such stimulation. His mind was kept busy enough trying to decide how long a bloke should go to gaol for for a third car theft, or what to do about his daughter who was now telling him God didn't want her to go to university. It's not the same, Martin objected. Those things don't put you personally in jeopardy, so your mind never engages with them entirely. They don't threaten to rearrange the landscape. We're sending her to Italy, Daniel said. For the summer. Give her a different perspective. Then he protested: But the person who wrote the letter wasn't thinking of the need to get my mind engaged, was he? Martin chuckled. That's the beauty of it. It's for real. Only a real nut would write something like that.

For the first time that evening, the two men made eye contact. The old relationship has been re-established, Daniel thought. He felt relieved. His friend was playing mentor again; the familiar, school-masterly tone was creeping into his voice. But Daniel's brief from Christine had been to tackle Martin on the problem of his depression, his not accepting briefs from solicitors; and his instructions from Hilary were to get some definitive reassurance about payment for the flat. The last thing they needed was to find their buyer had money troubles. I'm to consider myself lucky then, Daniel asked, if someone chooses to worry me to death? Of course, Martin smiled. Under threat, the status quo becomes more precious. Your life seems more worth living because it has to be struggled for. Daniel leaned forward: In that case, would it be wrong of me to submit, Mr Shields, he raised a comic eyebrow, that six months ago you drove off the motorway at terrifying speed in order to make your life more intense, thus reminding yourself the status quo was worth defending?

Martin shifted his eyes elsewhere. The pub's carpeted spaces and sham decor were so familiar, yet the two friends were completely estranged. Daniel drew back. Only fielding an idea, he remarked. Two other men had taken up the snooker balls, in complete ease, laughing, concentrating. After an uneasy silence, Martin asked: Do you still care about what happens in court? I beg your pardon? For a moment his friend said nothing, then remarked: I hear you sent down a Colombian woman for eight years last week. Daniel nodded. Crack courier, he said. So actually your sentencing is the same as everybody else's. Why shouldn't it be?

Martin shook his head. With peremptory earnestness he leaned across the table: About six months ago, I defended a bloke on dangerous driving – he'd killed a cyclist, a little boy. Anyway, at a certain point, perhaps because of the way this man looked in the dock, I don't know, I was just watching him sitting there, he was completely bored, unable to follow the court rigmarole – at a certain point, as I said, I had this, I don't know, I can only call it a revelation. The word carbon came to my mind. You know? Carbon. Do you ever get words like that? It suddenly sang in my mind. We are all just a certain proportion of carbon material and water. It doesn't matter. Or rather, it's only matter, it soon dissolves. Whether I won the case or lost was quite irrelevant. If I died this minute, it wouldn't matter.

Martin sat back. Daniel was puzzled. I'm not talking about an *intellectual* argument, Dan. You follow? It's not a book I read. I long ceased to be convinced by *books*. It was a *revelation*. A relief really. Suddenly I *knew* it. I just heard that one word blocking out everything: Carbon. The man's just carbon, I thought. No, I knew. The boy he killed too. I kept thinking it for weeks. His body composition. You know that coffin they have in the British Museum with the various substances of the human body. A few little bottles lined up on the bottom. Carbon. Chemicals. And then on top there's this farce, this veneer – no I don't mean veneer – this sort of sticky surface, if you like, this cocooning film, wrapping round and round. Of parody. Our lives. What else can you call it. Parody. Irony. Soap. Cloaking the basic matter. It's hard to take seriously, isn't it? The way the stuff manifests itself. You must have noticed, Dan. You must have seen how nothing can really take itself seriously any more. Nobody does. Do they? Not *really*. Though the more you can't, the more everybody insists on pretending. Do you follow? The harder everyone *tries*. That's why everybody's so loud these days. Everybody's so shrill. It's so hard to convince *yourself*. Wasn't that the case with you and Hilary after all? You try to take life seriously and do the proper thing, split up. Then you suddenly realise there is no need. Why make the effort? It's just carbon.

Martin put his beer-mat on the edge of the table, flicked

it into the air with the back of his hand, missed the catch, shook his head. I won the case of course. He laughed. But then the funny thing is – suddenly he was excited again – they make *you* a judge, Daniel Savage, fast-track promotion, their high-visibility policy of showing sensitivity to the victims of discrimination, the ethnic minorities, and sure enough along comes a Colombian woman who's been doing nothing worse than supplying the British middle classes with the thrill of an illegal substance, a game they're playing with their vacuous minds, and you, the new judge, the solemn black judge, steam on regardless, and send her down for eight years, though you know of course that she would have been operating under her men-folk's orders, and you know that people who want cocaine will always find someone silly enough to risk getting it for them. For all I know you take it yourself from time to time. In short, your sentence was perfectly in line with the norm, the great charade. You're an instrument of the charade, Dan. No, listen. Don't be upset. I'm not *criticising*. Because the hilarious thing is – try to see it from my point of view – that now you make a big show of wanting advice from me about some silly anonymous letter because you're screwing around again, pretending to fall in love here and there, no doubt, to cheer life up, while at the same time pretending to be married, and somebody else is pretending to bother you about it, but not doing a very good job of it. You're ludicrous, Martin was suddenly exclaiming. Ludicrous! But we *all* are. I'm not criticising. The mad thing is not that we wear wigs, Dan, you know, but that anyone wants us to take them off when we leave the courts!

Daniel was astonished. For a moment he stared at his old and very English friend. He had always thought of Martin as older and very English. Instinctively he objected: Mart, you wouldn't be talking like this, if they'd made you a judge.

At once Martin nodded: That is absolutely true! I've often thought that that's exactly what responsibility is for. You're right. We need more and more power and respect if we're to stay in harness. That's why older people are given more responsibility, not because they're more expert, please, but because if you don't give it to them they'll start treating life as the farce they're always in danger of discovering it is. They get bored, they start playing. Okay then, give them the thrill of power. That way the pretence can go on a little longer. It's really the only explanation why the young would let their lives be run by the old.

He sat back. Suddenly the energy seemed to leave him. Still, he said vaguely, I'm enjoying my moths at the moment. You know? He trailed a finger in some spilt beer. I love the way they're such a blatant example of mindlessly animated material, bits of fluff and silicon fizzing and flitting about. He laughed nervously. Then the farce of those extravagant patterns on their wings. It's fantastic.

Unasked, Daniel stood up to get in another round. On the television behind the bar they were showing a Hollywood shootout in the customary abandoned warehouse. Hispanic policemen, Chinese traffickers. Or was it vice versa? To date Daniel had never had to try a case involving actual use of firearms. On returning to his seat he could see no other way of proceeding than with complete frankness. Pint in hand, he said: Two things, Mart: to be brief: first, Christine is frantic, I mean about you. I've had her weeping on the phone. Second, Hilary and I are concerned that if you're not working, it may change your plans for purchasing our flat. We're pledged to a schedule of payments that depend on you honouring yours. We don't have a lot of cash in reserve.

Martin had rested his chin on his hands. The beard has overgrown his personality, Daniel thought, obscured it. There was dirt in his nails. Have you told Hilary about the anonymous letter? his friend asked. Judge Savage said he hadn't. Why not? It's obvious, isn't it: because she might imagine there was something behind it. And you maintain there isn't? No! So actually, you're just protecting your wife from a dangerous idea. You're patronising her really, the only reason for not telling her is if there's something behind it. Oh for Christ's sake, Martin, I just don't want her to get the wrong end of the stick.

There was a pause, then Daniel asked, So do you tell Christine everything? Actually, yes, Martin said. He stared straight across the table. Yes. You have no secrets at all? None. He was oddly belligerent. Really? None; it always seemed to me that that was the only way to give marriage any sense at all, no secrets. Well, I don't see, Daniel objected, how that's actually possible; I don't know how you can tell another person *everything*. I mean everything that's in your head as well. Martin smiled. He is horribly smug, Daniel thought. And she has no secrets from you? Daniel insisted. No, why should she have? So you know that she phoned me on Monday, desperate to get me to talk to you because she feels you're going crazy? Of course I know, Martin said evenly. I thought it was rather funny when you called and said you had a problem you wanted to discuss.

And the kiss? Daniel wondered.

Martin said: I know Christine is worried, but I've told her not to be. You know she's a bit of a drama queen. As for cash, you know our family's not poor. I've never not met a commitment. I can work or not work as I choose. Suddenly he stood up. And now I think I'll be off. Daniel was taken aback. Without another word, Martin Shields walked briskly to the door. On the table a pint of shandy was left untouched, as the snooker table too had been abandoned mid game, and likewise in a sense, Daniel thought, his friend's career.

Daniel Savage sat on for a few minutes alone, a handsome man of obscurely mixed origin wearing a sober suit and tie in this mostly white and very English suburban pub. He drank up his beer, then sat alone in the front seat of his car. What did Martin mean, So your sentencing is just like all the others'? Why shouldn't it be? The Colombian woman had been found guilty. Martin is ill, Daniel thought. The Savages, he remembered, had been bled dry paying for Frank's various addictions. One way or another, his brother had drained the Savage family resources with his endless requests for money. Trafficking is a serious matter. Matter in general, Daniel thought, whether carbon or whatever, is serious. But all at once he was aware that what was troubling him lay elsewhere: What if Minnie were brought before my court? Minnie had always said, Dad is the boss, Dad would kill me. What if the girl were forced to commit some crime, to carry drugs? Minnie stands in the dock and says, my father made me do this. I phoned my old boyfriend His Honour Judge Savage to ask for help, but . . .

The fireplace for their new house was being prepared on the trading estate to the south of the town. Daniel and Hilary had driven out there on the Friday to decide on some final details: lacquered or natural finish, the kind of scrolling beneath the mantelpiece. And so you drove right past Minnie's factory, Daniel remembered, without even thinking of her! You parked within a hundred yards of Minnie's factory, Minnie's father's factory rather. You walked along the ugly, amorphous trade-estate street, hand in hand with your wife of twenty years, discussing the sort of shapes and colours your new sitting room will have – Shiny surfaces clean easier,

Hilary had said – all within sight of Kwan's Asian Fabrics, and you never thought of Minnie at all!

Daniel started the car and pulled out into the road. I didn't even think – he took the ring road with its fast stretches and busy lay-bys – didn't recall, that is, any visual image of the three or four times we made love at Kwan's Fabrics, lying on heaps of oriental rugs. But why should I have? That part of his life was over now. Twenty minutes later he stopped the car beside one of a series of low prefabs behind railings and barbed wire. An amorphous gritty street. There had been five or six keys as he recalled, a rather nasty dog who used to recognise her at once. Dad'd kill me, she giggled. He remembered her turning the keys, speaking Korean to the dog. After a few weeks of the water torture, she added.

The place was dark now as it had been then. No, she hadn't been good in bed, perhaps not even really interested sexually. What she wanted was contact with an older and, as she presumably saw it, intelligent man. She wanted knowledge from outside her closed community. The Korean community's so tight, she told him. He'd beat me to death, she said. Her accent was comical. You have no idea. And what Daniel had enjoyed, as with other younger women for that matter, was the opportunity to reverse the sort of role he seemed obliged to play with Martin, the endless deference he had learned to deploy as a non-white performing on sufferance among powerful whites. Unless that was just part of his character *anyway*, something he would have done, whatever his race. How could you know such things? Or to do with being adopted, with being invited into a family, rather than bred there. He had learned deference, he had learned to be a good boy, to hide his misdemeanours. Perhaps adoption was far more important than race. Other blacks showed no deference at all. Quite the contrary. Many were assertive, even belligerent. It was Daniel's adoption his brother Frank had resented, not his colour. Daniel had always sensed that. Frank was not racist. With Minnie on the other hand Daniel Savage could play mentor. Now *he* gave the wise advice. He became authoritative. In that sense his affairs had been a rehearsal for promotion. There was an odd thought! For finally having the whip hand.

Minnie's body was pretty rather than seductive, he remembered, better fantasised beforehand than when actually lying naked on the high platform of rugs in the gloom of smeared windows. They couldn't risk the light. And she never stopped talking, never stopped pouring out her problems, her future, her father's plans for her future, the claustrophobic life laid out for her. With Ben. Ben! She laughed. She despaired. Ben! He's so thick! She giggled. So hopeless! The only thing holding you back, Minnie, Daniel said, is what's inside your head. Fuck off, she told him. And then she said: Maybe, could be. People say they'll kill you, Daniel told her, but they never would, would they? A father is not going to kill his daughter. Still sitting in his car, out in the street, the crown court judge at last formulated the question in its most appropriate form: What if I were the only person in the world who knew that Minnie had been killed?

FOUR

Before we go any further, your honour, a matter of Public Interest Immunity needs to be considered. Judge Savage had not been expecting this application. Can I address your honour in chambers? In his pocket was a scrap of paper that said, The eye of the adulterer waits for the twilight, saying, No eye shall see me, and disguises his face. Judge Carter, who ought to have been sitting, was ill. To avoid emptying a surprisingly packed court, Daniel decided to hear the matter in his own chambers, his office. Judge Carter is always ill, he thought. Counsel for the prosecution and his CPS solicitor, a woman Daniel had never seen before, followed him along the corridor together with a police officer. Inspector Mattheson, your honour. Of course. They took seats. Then as counsel began to put the prosecution's application in tediously circumlocutory fashion, Daniel was suddenly struck by a photograph of Hilary on the filing cabinet to the left of his desk. Taken a dozen years ago it showed her in a pretty dress leaning back against a farmyard gate in the golden light of early evening. The eye of the adulterer waits for twilight! Mr Nicholson, he interrupted. The young man was obsequious and complacent. Mr Nicholson, despite the short notice I have read through the papers in question and I'm not sure that I am entirely convinced. Actually I'm not convinced at all. Soberly dressed, a determined set to her lips, the solicitor immediately leaned over to whisper to the police inspector. He nodded and half stood: Your honour, if I might be allowed . . . But now there came a knock on the door. The court usher appeared and hurried across the room to pass the judge a note. Your wife asks you to call home as soon as possible. Daniel was perplexed. Hilary never contacted him at work. It was a rule. Superintendent, ladies and gentlemen, he apologised, if you would bear with me for just five minutes. The three of them filed out.

Sarah won't come out of the bathroom, Hilary told him. Her tone was grim and somehow demanding. Daniel's attention began to fragment. He didn't like PII's, particularly when it was a question of protecting informers. Then what purpose does it serve, he had been asking himself, to send a man vaguely threatening notes obliquely accusing him of something he had done ages ago but did no longer? She's been there since you left, Hilary said. It's driving me crazy. But why? Don't ask me. She won't speak. She's just sitting in there crying. The only thing she said was that we were incredibly cruel to go out like that last night. Daniel couldn't understand. To the concert? Yes. But why shouldn't we go out? We haven't been out together in ages. Don't ask me, Hilary repeated. Ask your daughter. Tom certainly didn't mind.

Then Daniel remembered that Sarah was to start her A levels this afternoon. I don't understand what she wants from us, Hilary was saying, or why she's doing this. I was supposed to be up at the house this morning showing them what we want done with the bathroom. I've a lesson at eleven. Then I have to see Charles about the organ recital. Why is it,

Daniel wondered, that Hilary is so generous with Tom, so hard on Sarah? As last night she had been so hard on the Russian's performance of Froberger. Froberger is bad enough on a piano at all, Hilary had said in the interval in a voice that turned heads all along the bar. But to add the *pedal*, as if we were at the height of Romanticism, as if the whole philological movement had never been! For heaven's sake! Just tell her, Judge Savage said, that you've got me on the phone, and that I'd like to have a word with her. Right away.

Waiting, he stood by his desk, playing with a paper knife. A light flashed beside the number pad, indicating that someone else was trying to get through. He ignored it. He had had the impression, speaking to his daughter at the school gate a year ago, telling her, I want you to look after your Mum, that the girl had suddenly matured; she had flowered in that brief month he was away. There had been something composed and adult about the way she'd said: Don't worry Dad. I can handle it. Mum'll be fine. One Saturday he had spied on them when they went to do the morning shop as he knew they would. They had been chatting, very cheerfully he thought, pushing their trolley through the car park. He had felt a pang of jealousy.

Now he heard the clatter of the receiver. She says she won't speak to you, Hilary announced, unless you come home. But I'm in court, for Christ's sake! Basil's ill again and I've got to do his list. There was a silence. She says she's not going to do her exam. What? She's not going to go to school. She bloody well is! Daniel said. She says that since she doesn't want to go to university it doesn't matter. God doesn't want her to go. But I thought, Judge Savage said, that we'd agreed to postpone the university decision till after Italy. Apparently not. Hilary's voice was dry to the point of sarcasm. God has decided, she said.

Oddly, Daniel now had the impression that he and his wife were arguing. Though presumably they were united over Sarah. Christ knows, he protested, we let her choose the subjects she wanted, didn't we? Now she can bloody-well go and do the exam. Some parents don't even let their kids choose their own subjects. I don't understand, Hilary said coolly. I mean, he explained, that some parents wouldn't let their kids study Theology and Classics, would they? They make them do what'll get them a job and that's that. Do they? His wife didn't seem to have grasped what he was talking about. Who? she asked. Then Daniel realised that he could only have been referring to Minnie's father. He was thinking of Minnie again. The girl's studies had been entirely geared to her father's miserable business. She'll damn well go if I have to drag her there, Daniel was saying, when Adrian, the court usher, put his head round the door. Court Three also waiting, your honour, he whispered; he raised his eyebrows in a smile of shared sufferance. Adrian was comically gay. We minorities, his smile said, holding the fort! Look, Daniel told his wife, I'll try to get back before one and take her to school myself for two. It's at two, right? Two-thirty? Tell her I'll come back and have lunch with her. I promise.

No sooner were they back in the room than it was clear that the threesome had decided to change tactics. The point is, Inspector Mattheson was saying – and doubtless he was right to go over the head of the dithering prosecution counsel – that young Harville is being most helpful to us in all sorts of ways. He has all sorts of contacts in all sorts of fields. The epithet young is palliative, Daniel told himself, resuming his thoughtful judicial face over the relevant papers. That may be so, Superintendent, but in this particular case I can't help noticing that he is also the defendant's brother-in-law. That's right, your honour. In fact it's significant, that the young fellow's wife, the defendant's sister, is Irish, they are very much involved in the Irish community in all sorts of ways. Mattheson likes the expression all sorts of, Daniel noted. To reveal his name in court, your honour, as the source of our information would be to lose a – er – potential national security advantage, the policeman was insisting. From all sorts of points of view, Daniel suggested. Exactly, Mattheson agreed. Quite apart, I imagine Superintendent, from putting the man's life at risk, perhaps. I'm afraid so, your honour.

Daniel caught the eyes of the CPS woman for a moment. She was staring at him most intently, as if this might somehow convince him of their case. Clearly she would have liked to speak, but that would be a breach of the normal procedures. He turned back to the thickly built Mattheson. Where had they crossed paths before? The man had aged. Superintendent, let us go over the story, can we, just to make quite sure that I have got the facts right. Of course, your honour. Mr Colin Rigby, Daniel glanced down at the papers before him, or young Rigby as I might say if I felt so inclined, is stopped in his car and searched in response to information supplied by Mr Harville, who is Rigby's brother-in-law. A kilo and more of cocaine is found in the glove compartment of the car. Rigby swears he knows nothing about it, never saw it, doesn't know how it got there. To complicate matters, Harville himself was tried some nine months ago for ABH. He was accused of beating up another young man who had a record of drug related offences. In that case the victim stated that the attack was in response to his inability to pay for the drugs that he had been using and that, so he claimed, Harville was supplying to him. Am I right so far? Your honour, Mattheson saw at once where this was leading, Harville always denied that the fight had anything to do with drugs. He claimed both men were drunk and arguing over a woman.

But his victim was a cocaine addict.

He was, your honour.

Daniel paused. Superintendent, Mr Nicholson, and er – Mrs Connolly, the woman said quickly. Thank you, Mrs Connolly. Superintendent, naturally when I consider an application for Public Interest Immunity I must bear in mind the importance of the information in question to the defence position, were it to be disclosed. Of course, your honour, prosecution counsel said too eagerly. Now, correct me if I am wrong but I believe that as far as regards the previous trial, in which Mr Harville was the defendant, an initial charge of GBH, section 18, a most serious crime, was altered to ABH, upon which he, Harville altered his plea to guilty and was given a non-custodial sentence. Two weeks after that he was entered in the registry of police informers.

Daniel waited a moment. Nobody corrected him. Being a judge, he was aware, meant not being party to the un-declared agendas of those who petition you. He must only consider the fairness of the trial. There are inferences, he said at last, that the defence counsel might draw from this state of affairs, are there not? He might question the informer's motives. The man has been accused of involve-ment in the drugs world. Could he perhaps be setting up a rival? Does he have a score to settle with Rigby? Is there some quarrel in this family which might prompt Harville, now he has access to the police, to have his brother-in-law sent down for a few years? These are all areas that the defence might wish to explore with Harville in the witness box. In fact, this is a situation where the moment the defendant knows the name of the person who has informed against him, he might supply an entirely convincing explanation of how the cocaine came to be in the car.

Counsel for the prosecution began to make some bland remarks about there being plenty of other evidence to suggest that Rigby had been dealing in drugs for years. Nevertheless, Daniel interrupted him, a seizure and arrest was only possible after information received from an informer who seems to me, Mr Nicholson – this man is inept, he thought – to be in a most problematic relationship both to the defendant and the crime.

Mattheson stood up from his chair, went round the solicitor's chair and stooped a moment beside the barrister. He said a few words in a low voice. Of course, Nicholson protested. He still seemed absurdly confident. The policeman returned to his seat. Your honour, the prosecution counsel said hurriedly, as you are no doubt aware, most convictions in the area of drugs, and terrorism, come thanks to the services of an informer. He paused and glanced across at Mattheson, apparently looking for approval, then added: We are all here to fight crime after all. Frankly, if the prosecution is obliged to disclose the names of informers, then . . .

Mr Nicholson! Daniel was furious, as far as I am aware I am not here to fight anybody or anything, but to help decide disputes, that is, to administer justice. He stopped. I will not be patronised! he thought. The policeman was looking at his feet, shaking his head. I repeat, this relationship between informer and defendant is suspect and would render a trial in which it remains undisclosed to the defence unsafe. But then it suddenly occurred to Judge Savage that what he was really reacting to, perhaps, was Martin's wounding criticism of the evening before. It's not true that I toe the line, he told himself. Concession of immunity is a most serious matter, he said.

Your honour, Mrs Connolly stood up, if I may have a word with my learned friend. Of course. He watched as they whispered. Nicholson had assumed an air of offended dignity. The solicitor was in her early forties, Daniel thought, the mother returning to work after the kids perhaps. Your honour, Nicholson began again. Your honour, after consultation, I'm afraid I must say that if immunity is not granted we will almost certainly be obliged to drop this case and forgo possible conviction for a most serious crime. Again while the prosecution counsel repeated his inadequate formulas, Daniel noticed that Mrs Connolly's eyes were alert and determined. She cared. Daniel Savage shook his head. I cannot grant immunity in these circumstances. Not unless I can be convinced that the informer could have no personal interest in the defendant's arrest beyond his remuneration as informer.

Your honour?

Inspector Mattheson?

The policeman hesitated. No doubt he knew more than the case papers said. But whatever might or might not be at stake for the police, he decided not to say it.

Your honour will not grant PII?

No. The identity of the informer must be disclosed to the defence

Your honour?

Yes, Mr Nicholson.

Your honour, this really is most . . .

The policeman shut his eyes. Judge Savage sympathised.

Mr Nicholson, do you have any further argument which might cause me to change my mind?

The young man floundered. He looked at the others.

I am here to be persuaded, Daniel went on.

No, your honour, the prosecution counsel eventually said.

Well in that case, ladies and gentlemen, we have a very

busy morning ahead of us. Daniel stood up and smiled. Mattheson was already at the door.

Your honour? Having gathered his papers, Judge Savage found that the CPS woman was waiting for him. Your honour, I just wanted to introduce myself properly. I'm Kathleen Connolly. Despite the setback she had suffered, the woman was smiling. Charmed, Savage said. He gave her his hand. I believe you're trying the Mishra case, Mrs Connolly went on. Again she seemed eager to find his eyes. He nodded. There was to be a pre-trial review that afternoon. I shall be there, she told him. A most unusual case, she said. She seemed excited. I've been following it closely. It's an area I'm particularly interested in. For a moment, standing together by the judge's door, Daniel feared the woman might be about to do the unthinkable and try to engage him in some kind of discussion about the case. It is indeed most unusual, he added gently, We'll leave it at that, shall we? Kathleen Connolly insisted on shaking hands again.

Anybody phone? he asked Laura, hurrying back to his chambers after adjourning a trial for lunch. There was a man who refused to leave his name, the clerk said. Oh, and your wife. Left a message. Shaking her curls, the secretary, Laura, read from her note pad: They've put the doors on, exclamation mark. She insisted on the exclamation mark, Mr Savage. She said you would understand. The girl smiled generously, her nails were long and shiny, as if she too understood. Excellent, Daniel said. He smiled at her. Excellent. But then driving home too fast, he was aware of an unpleasant mental clouding. Six weeks ago, when they had settled on the house, everything had appeared so clear. Now the landscape was shrouded under the humid skies of early summer. I must save Sarah from making a decision she will regret, he told himself. He took the corner with Primrose too fast. What was the point of these anonymous messages? The only person inviting me to venture forth at twilight these days, Daniel smiled, is my wife. They've put the doors on indeed! Hilary was prickly one minute, passionate the next. Mattheson, he remembered, as he let himself in the front door, had given evidence in some theft case he had defended. Way back. Daniel paused, key in lock. Had he called the policeman a liar? There had definitely been a certain hostility.

Sarah?

Food's ready! came the voice. It sounded cheerful. Daniel was relieved. Walking to the kitchen, he found the table carefully laid, red napkins mitred in Hilary's best crystal. Her back towards him, his daughter was bent forward over the oven so that the apron tie – she was wearing an apron! – crossed her slim bare waist between charming green pyjama shorts and a white tank top, bright against her dark skin. Sarah's skin was much darker than her brother's. Hi, Dad! she sang. It was a strange thing, Daniel sometimes told himself, that he had never had sex with a woman of his own colour. There are so few of my class, he once joked.

Fantastic, he told his daughter. He took his jacket off and sat down. But what's this story about your not going to the exam? Christine Shields phoned, Sarah said. She came from the oven with a steak steaming on the family's best china. Why had she got that out? Only the cropped hair reminded him of her recent insistence on not being a sex object. But that too was glossy, freshly washed. The long neck was even more in evidence. The girl smiled slyly. Something about a problem moving money around. Another month before they can pay. Please, Sarah, listen, Mum told me . . . Eat up, she said. Wine? She had opened a bottle of wine, a good bottle. His glass was full before he could move to block it. It would be a busy afternoon. What's the story? he demanded. Your mother said you wouldn't come out of the bathroom. Sarah laughed. I gave her quite a shock, didn't I? You gave *me* quite a shock. But then she went off, Sarah remarked, to do her various errands anyway, n'est-ce-pas?

The girl seemed both angry and pleased with herself. Daniel ate quickly. I'll run you in as soon as I've finished. It's always best to be there half an hour early for an exam. If you take the bus you'll be worrying about time. Sarah pouted: Mum said your honour would drag me there kicking and screaming. I'd been rather looking forward to it.

There was a note of flirtation in her voice. It was odd. She was wearing make-up. He glanced at his watch. You'd better change, hadn't you? How was your concert? she asked. It was a concert you went to, wasn't it? She wasn't eating, but watching him. She'd made the meal for him, but only to watch. Her eyes sparkled. The concert? He tried to smile: Mum said Froberger should never be played with a pedal. Inappropriate and anachronistic sentiment, she said. You know how she passes judgement.

Sarah laughed heartily, head cocked to one side. Then she got up, flouncing, to bring him salt and salad. She has pretty ankles, he thought. He would not bring up the business of her having complained that it was cruel of them to go out.

But did *you* like it? she suddenly demanded.

Me, the music? He was swallowing steak. His daughter reached across the table and wiped a spot from his chin. I don't really listen to music you know. Just shut my eyes and let my mind wander. Again his daughter stood smiling too brightly: And where did Froberger pedal you to, may I ask? Daniel didn't think: To you, he said. You still have to change, he reminded her.

Picking up the bottle, his daughter very quickly poured

herself a glass of wine. Not before your exam! But already she'd drunk it down. And what did you think about me? Her voice sharpened: That it was stupid of me to get involved in a Christian community and sit around singing to guitar music?

What I thought, he said, then stopped. It was all such a far cry from presiding at court. No, I'll only tell you what I thought if you get changed first. Come on, love. He tried to make his voice light as if talking to someone much younger. Sarah looked at her watch and without protest went out of the room. She seemed to be away a long time. The minutes ticked by. Daniel felt his alarm growing. I can't physically force her to go, he told himself. She was taking a ridiculously long time. Would he force her? It was pure provocation.

Then Sarah reappeared in tight skirt and blouse. She had shoes with heels. By the way – she did a little pirouette – you know I'm only doing this for you. There's really no point in my taking the exams if God doesn't want me to go to university. I haven't revised at all.

Daniel chose to let this pass, he was so eager to have her out of the house and into the sensible harness of school and exam papers. But then despite himself he was telling the truth: It makes me so mad, Sarah. What the hell's God got to do with it? You're too intelligent to believe you know what God thinks. All we're asking is for you to sit the exams you've been studying for.

She burst into laughter. They were on the stairs now. Temper temper, Daniel, she said quietly. She had used his name, his Christian name. Daniel was rigid. Have you got your pens and things? he demanded. What things? she sweetly enquired. Do I need anything?

They went down to the car. Weren't you going to tell me what you were thinking about me, she asked again, buckling herself in. While Froberger pedalled along, I mean.

Actually, it was the pianist who pedalled, Daniel corrected her, not Froberger. Froberger never saw a pedal in his life. Fill the space with banter, he told himself. The Russian pianist, he insisted. You know what your mother thinks of the Russian school. Sarah smiled. Okay, so what were you thinking while the pianist pedalled and mum squirmed? He didn't reply. The girl was so sharp and so wayward. When had she ever called him by his first name before? It's Ancient History isn't it? he asked. I don't believe you haven't revised. Everybody says that before an exam. Dad, please, I asked you what you thought about me. Now come on.

Well, first – he was driving quite fast, but relieved to be back with Dad rather than Daniel – yes, at first I was just thinking it would have been nice if you could have been there with us. You didn't invite me, she objected. Well, as I recall, he said, it was the first time we've been out together just us two for ages. Quite, she said. But that doesn't stop me wishing you could have heard the concert, does it? I suppose not. She seemed bored now. Perhaps she was at last beginning to think of her exam. They drove on. The silence was promising. And then, Daniel picked up the conversation, well then, to be honest, I was thinking that a year ago, you know, when I was away for a bit, how cheerful and sensible you seemed to have grown and how . . .

Stupid! She howled. Suddenly she was banging her fists on his arm. Stupid man, she yelled. I'm not doing your stupid exam. I'm not going to your stupid university. And I'm never, never, never going to live in your stupid house. Don't bother setting up a room for me in your stupid house with your stupid dog and your fireplace and stupid bathroom and terraced gardens.

She was pummelling him. Daniel had to pull the car over. She howled. Idiot! Idiot! Idiot! He slapped her face. She fell back and stared. It was a hard slap. Sarah, please, calm down! Please! There was a short silence. Her eyes were wide, the nose worked like an animal's. Forget whatever it was made you mad, Daniel ordered her. Forget it. Okay? He softened. Listen, we'll talk about it when the exams are over. But please, please, don't miss your moment, Sarah. You'll regret it. You really will, love. For me. No, for yourself. Please, just go there and do it.

There was a phone-box just outside the school gate. The children used it to call home when for some reason they were allowed to leave early. As soon as he had watched his daughter join her friends at the front door, Judge Savage stepped into the box and phoned directory enquiries, then the number they gave. Minnie Kwan, please, he asked. There was a short silence. I'd like to speak to Minnie Kwan. One moment, sir. The accent was Korean. She's there, he thought with relief. He waited. A different male voice said, Who is this? Could I speak to Minnie Kwan please? Daniel was aware of disguising his voice, eliminating Oxbridge for something more local. I asked who is it? The voice was aggressive. Who is that? Daniel put the phone down. Perhaps he should just have said, Accounts, please. Her future was to work in Accounts. Wasn't that what she hated? That she hadn't been able to choose. As he pushed open the heavy door, the phone started to ring. Judge Savage hesitated. All around, glossy visiting cards offered sexual services, some with photographs of girls not unlike Minnie, or his daughter for that matter. New Girl on the Block. Thai. Norwegian. He picked up the receiver. Who is this? the foreign voice demanded. Who is it?

FIVE

It is not one decision that makes or unmakes a man — Daniel had read this somewhere, at Martin's bidding no doubt — but the consistent concatenation of all his decisions over a lifetime of action and reflection. Quite probably this was true. Yet inevitably some choices will be more important than others. Daniel had been aware of that on his narrow bed in the Cambridge Hotel, and again on the bright slope to the north of the town when he and Hilary first stood before the shell of a house that corresponded to a dream they shared. Certainly as a judge some rulings, some sentences, would be better remembered than others, more highly praised, more vehemently contested. Trying the Mishra case, Daniel Savage rather unexpectedly found himself at the burning focal point of public attention.

The facts were as follows: the Mishras, man and wife, who ran a small deliveries business, had lost the guardianship of their thirteen-year-old son because they repeatedly refused to permit a leg amputation that the NHS insisted was essential to save his life from a highly malignant form of bone cancer. The boy was made a ward and his doctor became his legal guardian. Forty-eight hours after this ruling, the parents took the child from the cancer ward of the local hospital, drove to Paris and boarded a flight to India. There the boy eventually died after apparently undergoing alternative treatments. On return to the UK the Mishras were arrested and charged with abduction of a minor and manslaughter.

Even after a first cursory reading of the case papers, Daniel had been acutely aware of the extraordinary problems the trial posed. First and foremost there was the question of jurisdiction. All those involved, parents and child, were British nationals, yet the death itself had occurred outside the United Kingdom. Then although it seemed indisputable that the parents had abducted a child to whom they were no longer *in loco parentis*, thus becoming the indirect cause of his death, nevertheless to apply any of the normal sentences for the charges involved would surely be both obscene and unpopular. It was curious, Daniel thought, that CPS should pursue the matter so vigorously, when thugs were allowed to go free to inform on their brothers-in-law. Even more curious, though flattering, was the fact that he, who was hardly one of the senior judges, had been assigned the case. Could it be put down to the acute shortage of qualified judges on the circuit at this particular moment? Was it paranoid of him, he wondered, to imagine some kind of racial matching? In any event, the question of intent will be crucial Daniel guessed, and likewise the admission of evidence. It was in the latter area that a judge might greatly influence the outcome. What he did not expect, however, was to spend that whole afternoon in pre-trial review discussing an area of Archbold with which he was entirely unfamiliar.

If I may refer your honour to chapter eleven, paragraph 24 Dying Declarations. Thank you, Mr Stacey. Defence counsel, it seemed, had a video of young Lackbir's fourteenth birthday party, only days before his death, a party at which he had declared he would rather die with his family than have stayed in an English hospital. Dying declarations, prosecution objected, quoting Archbold, are admissible only where the death of the deceased is the subject of the charge and the cause of the death the subject of the declaration. May I submit to your honour. . .

Daniel watched the video. Tediously static, the camera showed a garishly furnished flat, apparently in Chandigarh. The parents, older son and younger children fussed around the drawn face of the dying boy. Sound and language were both a problem with the bearded and turbaned father reading out a passage from what was apparently a holy text in Punjabi, while the boy's voice was so weak that his comments, fortunately in English, but scattered in broken sentences through twenty minutes of muddled festivities, could only be understood with the help of the accompanying transcript. Nevertheless, Daniel ruled the evidence admissible, not as a 'dying declaration', but rather as part of the court's need to understand the child's, or rather, after his fourteenth birthday, 'young person's' ability to decide matters, even questions of life and death, for himself, and again to clarify the extent to which the various family members had been conscious of the gravity of their decisions. Mrs Connolly, who, as promised, was attending, was visibly annoyed with the decision. Had she been instructed, Daniel wondered, or decided on her own account to undertake a campaign of prosecutions against parents who took the law into their hands? Would there soon be a law that would imprison a father for slapping his hysterical daughter in the car?

What would you have done, though, the judge asked Hilary as they lay on the quilt she'd brought in lingering light the following Sunday evening. Would you have taken the boy away? His wife did not immediately reply. These hours snatched between Tom's afternoon football tournament and the organ recital later on in the evening were proving more of a success than Daniel had expected. As a rule, he distrusted moments of organised intimacy, but a series of obstacles had unexpectedly come to their aid. Not only had the builders got on the doors to the house, but, in far less time than seemed possible, all the windows, too. The Savages had no key. We'll have to break in, Hilary decided.

They had parked beside the fence. STRICTLY AUTHO-RISED PERSONNEL ONLY, it said. Daniel was for leaving be. What do we want to damage our own property for? I want you, she whispered. I do. She leaned her forehead on his chin standing by the car. There were threads of grey in the once gold hair. When he put his arms round her, she shivered. She wants what she imagines I stole from her with my affair, he thought. They must break into their own house.

She led him through long grass to a place where the perimeter fence was easily passed. He hadn't known this. But she came here more often than he. She was thinking of this home in a quite different way from in the past. A new building needs air, she was saying. They can't lay the parquet till everything's dry. This is mad, he protested. But sure enough, at the back, an upstairs window had been left open. Mad, he shook his head. It was quite a climb.

The day was still bright at that point, still very bright and breezy. The town sprawled beneath them, a sharply focused muddle of which this development, the builder had insisted, would be the last outpost. The final frontier, the man had laughed. They had laughed at that too. We'll call it Laramie, Hilary had chuckled. No, the Enterprise, Daniel said. Then he had asked could she remember the name of the token black member of Kirk's original crew. Hilary's primness was shattered by a sudden giggle. She put her hand in her mouth. Seeing them happy, the builder knew he had a sale. Behind the house fields rose quite steeply. A rabbit! Hilary pointed. Now, two months later, she was laughing again as her husband propped various planks against the wall.

You're getting fat, Judge Savage, she called. He was exaggerating the trickiness of the climb, but honestly a little nervous too. I'm proud of you, she said more softly. Knees shaky, he balanced on an upended plank. There won't be any water! he called now, looking down. What'll we do for a pee? We can't flush. He was balanced on the top of a protruding sill over the kitchen window. You look so funny! He clutched at the guttering. Pee out of the window, she laughed. My reputation, he protested, a crown court judge pissing out of the window! Oh don't be so *boring*, she pleaded.

It was strange dropping down onto boards in the bare room. There was a dry clatter. Once we've moved in, he knew, Hilary will become terribly fussy, protecting all her clean new surfaces. This was a moment of grace. He went downstairs, but they had put on security locks. The front door wouldn't open even from the inside. He had to let her in through a downstairs window. Before climbing up, she passed him the bin-bag with quilt and champagne and glasses. He shook his head. We'll be arrested. But it's our own home! We haven't paid yet. Oh come on! The bank manager had seemed surprisingly easy about their money problem. Christine had insisted it was the merest logistical glitch. Just a question of bridging a month or two. We consider a judge about the safest security a bank could ever have, the Lloyds man laughed.

The pop of the cork ricocheted round the bare walls. They drank the first glass with elbows awkwardly entwined.

How awkward it is to make those celebrated gestures! But when they wrapped themselves in the quilt, more or less where the Steinway would be, it was suddenly as if they had never been so naked together before. Certain situations can generate this tenderness, Daniel thought, this shedding of the most tenacious clothes. They kissed more slowly and deeply than was usual. It was not that the light was particularly forgiving of their no longer youthful bodies. But somehow the generous emptiness of the house lent itself to the idea that this moment was special, or even symbolic. He whispered obscenities in her ear. Horny Savage, she praised. In the past he had vaguely thought of his wife as a sort of providential policeman who kept him from excess, while she perhaps yearned for an excess he couldn't give. And now – how strange! – in the aftermath of a crisis that had been entirely unplanned, destructive at first, they finally seemed to be the right two people for each other. I can hear Chopin, she whispered. She pressed an elaborate seventh into his back. Two fingers trilled. Oh, I can just hear how perfect it will be. They hugged, laughing with relief. I can't believe you bought that piano, Dan. You lavish, lavish, reckless man! I love you for buying that piano.

When they broke apart, she told him: Light a fire! What? Let's light a fire! The cast iron core of the fireplace had been installed, though not the fancy stone surround. There was a grate, a chimney. We can do it, she said. But what if people see the smoke? Oh don't be boring! she cried. Do anything, please, but don't be boring. Come on, there are plenty of scraps of wood around. Light a fire.

You skip your organ recital then, Daniel said. Incongruously he was on his feet, padding naked round the boards, picking up odds and ends of wood. But I can't. I set the whole thing up, the whole series. You're not actually involved tonight, he objected. You don't have to do anything. But Dan . . . Skip it! he told her. I'm supposed to be picking up Max, she said. What will people think if I don't turn up? They'll think you're off making love to your husband. Of twenty years! Her peel of giggles was so unrestrained that Daniel himself burst out laughing. We are happy, he noticed with some amazement.

Hiccuping, Hilary stayed wrapped in the quilt while he forayed to other rooms for wood. There were off-cuts of skirting board, a chunk from a beam. You know we're social deviants, she called. To be married for *twenty years*. You do realise that at Gordon's party we were the only couple still on first marriage. The only ones. Suddenly it seemed she couldn't get over this. Fucking after twenty years! She had to raise her voice when he went upstairs. It's obscene! She hiccuped. People don't *do* that! We'll be ostracised. It's far worse than inter-marrying you know. There's Mart and Christine, he reminded her. Twelve years, Hilary said scornfully, and no children! Wasn't Tom a darling, she added. Poor boy! In the closing minutes of his tournament, their son had missed a penalty. He had wept.

Daniel came back with a bundle of rough cuttings, scratching an arm. There were nails and splinters. Don't know how we're going to light it. She held out her arms. Come here and kiss me. We should do this more often, she sighed, as he stooped over her. It's not every day, he pointed out, that you have a new house to break into. For a moment they looked into each other's eyes. We'll grow old here, she whispered. Hard to avoid, he agreed. Probably it'll be here one day we'll realise we're never going to make love again. At least there'll be a big garden, he said. But you hate gardening! She raised herself on an elbow. You never know, the global warming thing might stir a dormant gene or two. He felt happily facetious. We'll plant a coconut tree. Speaking of which, I'm freezing. She shivered theatrically. Her breasts were still attractive. Are you going to light that fire, or aren't you? Are you going to skip that recital? he asked.

Then she said yes. Yes, I'll skip it. Daniel was astonished. I don't believe it. You'll skip it? Yes, why not? A vague anxiety stole across his nerves. I was beginning to think you were in love with Max. Oh shut up! she threw a sock at him. I only want Max around in the hope the great clod'll take a fancy to Sarah. He threw the sock back. She threw her bra. He made to put it in the fireplace. She leapt to her feet, grabbed it, embraced him, naked, only slightly over-weight, and whispered in his ear: The girl's seventeen and still hasn't had a boyfriend. She's a Jesus freak. What can a mother do but assemble a few gallants?

Daniel eventually found a lighter in one of the workers' overalls hanging in the kitchen. What would you have done, he asked, if we'd had that problem? They were lying on their stomachs, wrapped in the quilt. Hilary watched the first flames catch at the little pyramid he'd built. Isn't this wonder-ful, she said. I do love it when you talk about your work. You always used to complain, he reminded her. Especially in company. Well, now I love it. See the spurts of green flame! I love looking at fires.

Dimly, Daniel was aware that life really could be made to change. This moment proved that. Even the past can always be changed, he thought, or just understood differently. He leaned over and placed his cheek against her neck. See the creamier smoke, she whispered. The wood spat. It draws pretty well, doesn't it? What would you have done though, he asked again, in the Mishras' shoes?

The house had darkened round them as the flames shone out. The still unplastered brickwork was all rough potential, trembling with shadows. Three or four moths milled where the mantelpiece would be. It's such an awful story, she said. She leaned into him. What would I do if it had been Tom, you mean? Or Sarah, he said.

The crackle of the wood seemed extravagantly loud. For some reason they were whispering. I don't know, she said at length. I really don't know how you can decide such things. If they honestly believed the doctors were wrong – you say they got advice elsewhere – I suppose I'd do what they did. They thought they could save him and his leg. They believed in their traditional medicine. So that he could play and run and miss penalties. Then the boy wanted to go with them, she asked, didn't he? What's his name?

Lackbir. Actually, the prosecution claim that the parents lied to him about the treatment in India. Naturally, he was terrified by the idea of having his leg cut off. Hilary was silent. One of the things she liked to do was massage his hands. Daniel has long elegant hands. My playmates, she called them. There's some evidence, he began, that after they . . .

Let's not talk about it. She gripped his hand tight. It's too much. Other people's lives are really too much. I don't want to be mixed up in them. She shook her head, as if to chase dust or moths from her hair. I want it to be just you and me.

He watched her. She knew he was watching. Her face was sombre but youthful too; he could see the flames burning in her eyes, her contact lenses. In firelight, the hair lost its grey. And then he remembered what Martin had said, that he and Christine told each other *everything*. Could that really be true? Suddenly, he found himself yearning for that complete communion with his own wife, a complete knowing between themselves that would seal their closeness forever. He hesitated.

I loved – he reached out to pour the last champagne –

how you slagged off that Russian the other day. The Froberger? She smiled. Why's that? I thought you hated me being critical. Aren't I always too critical? Isn't that what everybody says. Mum you're so critical! He stroked her shoulder. It's just that when we used to go to concerts, ages back, you'd always fall in love with the pianist and I'd feel like shit. I could never compete. Not actually *in love*, she said. Anyhow, the thing with Froberger is it's not sentimental, is it, it's pointless making him sigh and swoon like a young Romeo. It's false. You lose all the – she was looking for her words quite carefully – all the austerity, and somehow the fun of it too. He listened to her. A certain coolness and gaiety, she explained, go together in music like that. You know?

Daniel didn't reply. He hadn't understood. But eventually, after they had finished the champagne and were still lying there staring somewhat dazed into the fire, he began: Oh by the way, there's something I thought I should tell you, only then I thought it would just be an extra worry. Can't be worse than borrowing fifty thousand pounds, she laughed. She said: Anyway, you'll have to tell me now, won't you? I've been getting these strangely threatening notes, he announced. Oh yes? She pulled herself up on both elbows. Anonymously. The dying fire was only a red glow on the curve of her shoulders. It had turned chill. I can't understand them, or why anybody would send them. I mean now, rather than, well, a year ago, if you get me. But what do they say? Where have you been getting them? At court. From memory he quoted the two notes. Shall surely be put to death. Hilary seemed puzzled rather than hurt. Strange! Suddenly she laughed. Oh, silly, it must be *Sarah*, don't you think?

What?

It's Sarah!

Daniel Savage was astonished, both at the idea, and the lightheartedness with which Hilary jumped at it. His daughter was sending the letters. But why . . . Committeth adultery with his neighbour's wife! Hilary laughed. It's nutty religious stuff, isn't it? They're quotes from the Bible. Don't they read a chapter a day, at the Chapel, every afternoon, Obadiah, Hezekiah? But why? Daniel floundered. Anyway, I didn't think she knew. I mean about me and, and . . . They stared at each other. Of course she bloody-well knew, Hilary said quietly. The girl's not stupid, is she? After a moment she said vaguely: Quite probably *I* told her.

Daniel was appalled. But didn't we agree we wouldn't, that the children . . . I don't remember, she said. I was out of my mind. We definitely said we wouldn't tell them, he repeated. She was impatient: What did you expect me to do, for Christ's sake? While you were away all that time doing God knows what. I thought I was going to die, to lie down and die! Daniel backed off. How stupid to have brought this up, to have disclosed something that there was no need to disclose. Carefully, he asked, But why now? Why a year on? Why start sending me such rubbish *now*. Hilary had turned back to the embers. A moth was dying in circles on the grate. God knows, she muttered. It's so pretty isn't it, when the last sparks come and go? She shook her head. God knows what's got into her.

Then they both sensed it was time to gather their things and get out before any more damage was done. Forty minutes later, on arrival back at the flat they found Max and Tom on the sofa watching football and Sarah again locked in the bathroom. She was furious, Tom said, when you were late. The boy, on the contrary, seemed extremely pleased with himself.

SIX

Professor Mukerjee, would it be true to say that relationships in traditional Sikh families are no different from relationships in the average English family? Counsel for the prosecution was examining Peter Mukerjee, Professor of Oriental Studies at Birmingham University. On three occasions Daniel had over-ruled objections as to the relevance of the questions. With Mrs Connolly watching carefully and the press gallery packed, he did not want to seem biased against the prosecution. One is vaguely intimidated, he was aware, even when someone has no official power over you. Even a pair of eyes, he thought, exerts a certain pressure. Having eyes full of adultery they cannot cease from sin, the latest note said. Should he confront his daughter, or wait to see whether the notes stopped when she went to Italy?

No, it would not be true, the Professor said solemnly. On the contrary, I think it would be hard to exaggerate how profound those differences are in many many areas.

Is the area of parental authority one such area, Professor Mukerjee?

It is indeed.

Could you explain the nature of that difference.

The professor coughed into his fist. Like so many expert witnesses, he had a vested interest in indicating that special knowledge was required in his field. In the English family, he said, obedience is rarely unconditional. A child is not expected to obey any and every command. He, as it were, chooses to obey, and by doing that shows his love and respect. But in many of the cultures of India, and other hierarchical communities too of course, there is a longstanding tradition of total, unquestioning and immediate obedience of children towards their parents, in particular their fathers. If I might be permitted a metaphor: the children stand in relation to their father as the fingers to the hand. They are not, as in the English family, independent agents.

Professor, would you consider the Sikh culture, which you have spent much of your life studying, a culture where such unconditional obedience is the rule. Stacey loves to prosecute, Daniel observed. He was not unlike Martin in that way.

I would, Mukerjee said.

In the case in question, Professor, it has been said that Lackbir Mishra, a thirteen-year-old boy, acquiesced when his parents told him they were arranging for him to leave the hospital. As an expert in these matters Professor Mukerjee, do you think we can infer from that that the boy wished to leave the hospital?

Not at all. Professor Mukerjee was giving Stacey what he wanted on every count. On the contrary, it is unthinkable that he would disobey.

Can we infer that he agreed with his parents' assessment of how he should be treated?

Not at all.

Can we infer that he had decided that the so-called

alternative treatments were a viable alternative to the treatment offered by the National Health Service and the doctor who had become his guardian?

Again, no. You see, really this is a conceptual problem. It probably would not occur to a boy to decide for himself. He hasn't developed that habit. Of course, much depends on his education, but in the strictest families, a child simply would not think of weighing up the pros and cons. He would just obey. This is his destiny.

Professor Mukerjee you have seen a video in which the young Lackbir declares that he would rather die in India with his parents than have stayed in an English hospital. From your knowledge of Sikh family culture, what weight would you give to this statement.

This is a very difficult question, said the professor. He shook his head, bit a lip. Watching the video, it's clear the boy is sincere. But in this culture this is the kind of thing you do think. It does not indicate a personal choice in the way it might with someone from a western cultural background.

Stacey smiled. Stacey, Daniel noted, shares Martin's gift, the gift of those educated according to a certain tradition, for participating in a case with measured professional passion. The jury was paying serious attention. True there was one Indian, or perhaps Pakistani, in the twelve, but he wore no turban, so even in the unlikely event that he was a Sikh, it was hard to say how much he might be in sympathy. Why then, Daniel wondered, had Martin gone to pieces and this man not? It was a conundrum.

Professor Mukerjee I am now going to ask some general questions about Sikh culture. Stacey paused, appeared to steel himself to say something unpleasant. Is it true, Professor, that there have quite recently been cases where female foetuses have been aborted because only a male child is desired? Around the court there were sharp intakes of breath. The Indian, sitting with fists tightly clasped under his chin, nodded vigorously, as if to answer the question himself. This is true, Mukerjee said, of many oriental cultures. He paused. And indeed many traditional and hierarchical cultures the world over. There is nothing specifically Sikh about it.

Can you explain to the jury why that is so?

Well, in such cultures, the family is very often also a business enterprise and the boundaries between the two are not clearly defined. The business is the family and the family the business. But this is true of older cultures in the west of course. Anyway, a male child may well be seen as more valuable to the business.

Given this context, Professor Mukerjee, I mean the family and its business, its livelihood, how would a male member of the family unable to take his place in the business, due to illness or handicap, be considered?

I'm sorry.

Would a handicapped male child be considered a liability, an intolerable economic burden? Much as the unborn female foetus.

Packed with relatives of the defendants, the public gallery had begun to complain. A man raised his voice. Judge Savage interrupted: Members of the public must be silent or leave the court. But now counsel for the defence had risen.

Your honour, I object. When the admissibility of this, er, expert evidence was discussed, we did lay down precise boundaries of relevance. May I submit that my learned friend has now overstepped these boundaries.

Mr Stacey – Daniel was determined not to be seduced by the man – could you perhaps reassure us very briefly as to the relevance of these questions.

Stacey seemed pleased to have been interrupted. Perhaps in the end Mukerjee would have given a negative answer to what was the most insidious question of them all. Perhaps he would have said that a handicapped son would not be seen as an intolerable economic burden at all. Now the insinuation lingered in the air.

Your honour, so much has been said and as this case proceeds no doubt will be said about the positive values of traditional family solidarity as opposed to the bureaucratic procedures of our state hospital system. I am just trying to establish the nature of that, er, traditional solidarity.

Savage accepted defence counsel's objection. Mr Stacey, you must keep your questions to the point.

Of course, your honour. Prosecution counsel turned again to the witness. When the Mishras travelled to the Punjab, they took their elder son with them. When they returned two months later, he was accompanied by a young bride he had not met before that trip. In your expert opinion, is that normal procedure in this culture?

It is not unusual.

Would the son have met and fallen in love with his bride to be by chance.

Mukerjee explained that families tended to be in touch with each other for some time before such marriages.

Very astutely, Stacey hesitated. For a long silent moment the court waited for some awful question that would seek to suggest that the real motive for the Mishras trip to India was not Lackbir and his alternative treatment at all, but the marriage of the elder son now solely responsible for the future of the family dynasty. Swaying slightly back and forward, rubbing the tips of his fingers up and down his chin, Stacey appeared to reflect. That will be enough, thank you very much, Professor Mukerjee, he eventually said and sat down.

In the dock, turbaned and full-bearded, sitting closely beside his wife, Mr Mishra remained impassive. The decision of both defendants not to give evidence would keep proceedings disturbingly brief.

Yep, the Crown's really going for the whole hog, Daniel remarked one evening later that week. Fashions in Fire had now finished the stone surround. Abduction *and* manslaughter. No doubt hoping for an exemplary sentence. Having picked up Sarah from her last exam, Daniel, Hilary and Tom drove to the industrial estate to view the artefact and pay before installation. Then there would be a celebratory dinner in the centre of town. It was the end of Sarah's school career, the beginning of another summer holiday. They always dined out at the end of the school year, a tradition carried over from Colonel Savage's family. What traditions could I keep but the traditions of the Savage family, Daniel thought? Having adjourned the Mishra trial before the next day's summing up, he noticed at a scheduling meeting that the case against Rigby had been dropped. The police had chosen to protect their informer. On various occasions during the afternoon he had found Mrs Connolly looking at him most intently.

But do they honestly want the poor people sent to prison, Hilary asked? Everybody was relieved that Sarah had gone to her exam and hadn't objected to an outing related to the new house. It seemed important not to draw attention to the fact. There've been four or five cases recently, Daniel remarked, tabled against parents for cruelty to children, 'excessive correction' usually. In the back of the car his own children were listening hard. And funnily enough the accused are almost all from immigrant communities. If you can make 'em judges, Hilary laughed, you can send 'em to gaol. Daniel mentioned a Japanese man arrested for having locked his son in his room for the weekend. On the Monday morning the boy had skipped school and gone straight to the police. Young Tom was scathing: What'd be the point of sticking these Mishra people in gaol, Dad? Then we have to pay to bring up their kids with our taxes. Tom liked to join in adult conversation, endearingly taking, Daniel knew, in his craving for approval, an extreme form of what he perceived to be his parents' position. It's not that simple, love, Hilary remarked. Sarah wouldn't be drawn. Oh fine, she muttered when Daniel again asked how the exam had gone. So, tell us what you wrote about! Marriage in the early church, she said. She was looking out of the window. Apostolic succession. Zoroastrianism for the Comparative. Zorro-what? Tom demanded. Do people worship Zorro? Nodding to his left, as if seeing it for the first time, Daniel exclaimed, Oh talking of comparative this and that, perhaps we should pop in there afterwards. There might be something special for curtains or carpets. Hai ching, mi phong, Tom giggled. Foi shi bo yung! Oh shut up, idiot! Sarah elbowed him. Daniel had contrived to park outside Kwan's Asian Fabrics.

The Savages were now in considerable debt. A schedule of payments had been agreed with the builder in order to guarantee a fixed total price on completion late July. A small concession had then been made to the Shields in return for two lump sum advance payments on their purchase of the Carlton Street flat. This money would allow the Savages to meet the builder's requests. Everybody trusted each other. But when the Shields didn't pay on time, Daniel and Hilary had taken out a bridging loan which, combined with their old mortgage, sent them six figures into the red. The plus side had been the banker's confidence in Daniel's ability to meet almost any commitment. Least sacked category in the land, he laughed, judges. So now, writing out the cheque for Fashions in Fire, Daniel felt quite confident. Stupid red tape, Christine had said. Question of days. Martin had now apologised about their evening at the pub. When I get depressed, he explained, there are these moments when I'll say anything. He was suffering from a constant low level fever, it seemed, but refused to leave the house to see a doctor.

Although it may appear delicate, an assistant reassured them as he pulled a cloth from the dove grey stone, it can actually take more or less any heat or bashing. The fireplace was laid on its back on a pallet, the fine fluting across the top lacquered to a glassy finish. State of the art resins, he explained. Traditional design, modern toughness. Looks straight out of Jane Austen to me, Sarah complained. Tom asked if he could see the machines that cut the stone. I can't remember – Hilary stood on tiptoe to whisper in her husband's ear – anybody having sex on the hearthrug in *Pride and Prejudice*. Daniel smiled and took his daughter by the arm. We can sit and play cards by the fire, he told her, while the flames toast our toes. Happy Families? the girl asked caustically. Strip poker? Tom giggled. Then Sarah giggled too. Their silly laughter echoed in the cavernous prefab. Daniel was encouraged. I can already see my whisky on the mantelpiece, he announced with a loud chuckle. Dad, please! The girl was embarrassed now. He sniffed clownishly. Double malt, smells like. He's terrible, Tom informed the assistant. A fish! The stone surround alone had cost two grand. The Steinway grand was now under wraps, waiting to be delivered. They were all set.

But I've always hated oriental designs! Hilary didn't want to visit Kwan's. They were late. They're hardly likely to have anything that'll go with our fireplace, are they? Max had been told seven at The Duck. And they still had to pick up Crosby, a friend of Tom's, the organist's son. The traffic would be hell. Hilary was already climbing into the car when Sarah said: Well, I'd really like to see what they've got. I'm interested in oriental stuff. Oh, Sarah! Come on! The fireplace isn't going to be in *my* room, the girl was saying, is it? We don't all have to have the same look, do we, like some crusty old English manor? We can have one room Regency and one Ming Dynasty.

Daniel pulled faces at his wife. Let's just take a peek, he said. Couple of minutes. But listen, Hilary began, if we wanted . . . Who's always telling people not to be boring, Sarah demanded? Her mother hesitated a moment. Father and daughter were arm in arm. Again Daniel winked. Perhaps with exam pressure off, the girl would get over whatever it was that had been making her so impossible. She would take an interest in the house. They might be happy. His wife gave way and apparently in good spirits took Tom by the elbow, so that they crossed the road together, laughing.

Inside, the smell was immediately familiar, as Minnie's voice had immediately been familiar on the phone that evening. I should have reacted at once, Daniel thought. They waited, chatter muted in a gloomy space, half-showroom, half-warehouse. The young Asian man now appearing in attendance seemed taken aback and addressed himself exclusively to the white woman in the group. Daniel had seen this behaviour so many times he wasn't even offended.

We're wholesaler, the Korean said. We don't sell to public. Just a peek at some of your designs, Hilary asked. Typically, having got into the place, she wasn't to be put off. She walked directly to the great heaps of fabrics under neon by the far wall. This was where her husband had first undressed Minnie. If you think the English are racist, the girl had laughed, you should hear the Koreans! Her skin smelt faintly different. The young man was well dressed in grey suit and bright red tie. For wholesale only, he repeated.

They stood over a garish play of gold and blue, the Korean peeling off layer after layer, looking only at Hilary, though it was the dark and suddenly beautiful Sarah who was fingering each material and murmuring oohs and ahs. Do the characters mean something, the girl asked? The acnied young man appeared not to have heard. Ninety-five percent, he was telling Hilary. Daniel was suddenly irritated. My daughter asked whether the characters meant something, he said. But the design had been covered by another. The Korean stared blankly. Oh, it doesn't matter, Sarah smiled. This is wholesale store, the salesman repeated. Then Daniel asked: And are you Mr Kwan? Immediately, he sensed his voice had taken on a false ring. But if he didn't pursue the matter there would have been no point in coming in here. Mr Kwan's son, the Korean answered. And is it a big family, are you all involved? Hilary raised her eyes in surprise. We are two brothers, the young man said, walking them through the gloomy warehouse. We are not a big family. Only wholesale.

In the dining room behind The Duck, Sarah became extremely voluble. She needled Max mercilessly, but seemed in good spirits. Doesn't it drive you crazy when Mum keeps telling you you're too sentimental. Doesn't it make you mad when she says, Oh, but that's such a boring way to play. Don't be boring, Max! You've had too much to drink, Hilary laughed. Having finished her exams, the girl had been allowed a full glass of wine. She had taken two, but refused to eat anything more than a salad. Usually heart and soul of any party, Daniel explained his quietness by remarking that he would be summing up tomorrow in the Mishra case. My first time in front of the national papers, he said. Interrupting, Tom asked Max if he did any sport. They were both eating steak. The piano was enough, Max said. The piano is all the voices all on its own, you see, so you don't need any accompaniment. He was clearly a delightful young man. Whereas when I'm in company, you know, I almost always feel awkward. He blushed. And no of course I don't mind, he told Sarah, when I'm told I'm doing something badly. Hilary had made sure the young people were sitting side by side. That's why one has a teacher, isn't it? But what *is* badly, Sarah demanded? Who's Mum to decide what's badly? When did she ever tell anyone they were playing well?

Max had put his fork in his mouth. Tom and Crosby were shovelling chips. I must stop thinking about Minnie, Daniel ordered himself. Hilary was smiling over her fish and across at Max with a look of general complacency. Judge Savage suddenly said to his daughter, Why don't you start playing the piano again, Sarah love? Now the exams are over. He spoke sincerely. The girl was sitting opposite. That would be such a treat. Oh no! Tom cried with his mouth full. Spare us that! He put his hands over his ears. Not the piano! Shut-up, Tom! Daniel told him. Oh you should worry, Crosby grimaced, my sister plays the *violin*! Both boys burst out laughing. Then beneath the table Daniel felt his daughter's leg brush against his own. I'll start playing again when *you* do, Dad, she said. There was an odd mix of challenge and composure in her voice. Oh, did you used to play too, Mr Savage, Max asked? Sometimes the young man's politeness seemed to verge on mockery. For God's sake, call me Daniel! the judge responded. It's bad enough being called Your honour all day. I'd love it if you did start again, Dan, Hilary told him in her softest voice. She had her velvety black concert dress pulled tight at the waist underneath a pale green cardigan. You mean so you can tell him how badly he plays, Sarah announced. Too much pedal! she mimicked. Make it sing!

Oh for heaven's sake! Hilary turned to Tom on her left. Tell me, Tommy, am I really such a bully? The boy's lips were smeared with ketchup. Asked the question in the presence of Crosby, he hesitated. The youngsters exchanged glances. Well, a little bit, the boy hazarded. Everybody burst out laughing. Tom! You traitor! Hilary shook her head but managed to smile. Oh poor Riliree! Daniel laughed. At last forgetting his other worries – he owed the girl nothing, he thought, and anyway she had no intention of destroying his life – the judge turned to his left and embraced his wife. Unexpectedly, she raised her lips to kiss him more fervently than she ever would in public. She too had been drinking. They were both so relieved Sarah had done her exams! School was over. The girl sat opposite watching. Max clapped heartily. So when's the twentieth anniversary, he asked? When's the great day? October! Tom shouted. With any luck they'll go away for a second honeymoon and we'll have the whole new house all to ourselves. Cool! shouted Crosby. Hilary detached herself. She appeared to be laughing and crying together. Sarah said sharply: And to think, this time last year Dad was living in a hotel and everybody thought they'd broken up.

The dining room at The Duck was a favourite with families. No sooner had Sarah spoken than the noise from the other tables seemed to invade their own, in particular a fat man laughing raucously. No that's too funny, he was shouting. That's too funny, the fat man roared. Hilary had closed her eyes. She put her forehead on her fingertips. Max seemed tremendously embarrassed. Tom glanced furtively from mother to father, head down by the tablecloth. Only Crosby was cheerfully unaware of any unease: My folks say they're going to break up every day, he grumbled, but in the end they never do. Do I call the girl to order in front of Max, Daniel was asking himself? The last thing they needed was for the child to walk out. She had put her fork down. Her palms were pressed down on the table as though about to rise. Dad's always moaning, Crosby went on, that he'd rather live on his own in the garden shed with Camomile, that's our cat. He says. . .

Recovering abruptly, Hilary patted the organist's boy on the head. Would anyone like some dessert? She beckoned to the waitress. By the way, she addressed herself to Max, Sarah's off to Italy tomorrow. Aren't you, love? Having filled his mouth to cover his embarrassment, the handsome young man took a moment to reply. How wonderful! He turned to face the girl beside him. Sarah seemed locked into an unapproachable resentment. The dark skin thrilled with angry tension. Where exactly? Max asked. We should have said something, Daniel told himself. We can't let her get away with this. Perugia, Hilary was explaining. There's a sort of all round course on Italian culture and language. Or was it wisest just to wait for the girl to leave home? Minnie, perhaps, had finally been allowed to leave home. Could it be that Koreans only mentioned the male members of the family? They were as chauvinist as Sikhs perhaps.

Do you have a lift to the airport? Max unexpectedly enquired. Having decided to stay in her seat, Sarah reached across and drank off the wine in her father's glass. The flight's in the afternoon, she said. I'm going to go and hear Dad's summing up in the morning, then I'll take the bus from the station. Again her parents were caught by surprise. You've never been interested in court before, Hilary objected. Since it's Dad's big moment, Sarah explained, and I've finally finished school, why shouldn't I go? She half giggled and tossed out: If I get good results, I might even study law. For Daniel this was such excellent news that he at once forgave his daughter everything. She would come right. She would leave home for university at the end of summer. A completely normal kid. Perhaps I could come along too, Max suggested, I'd love to see how a trial works. Then I could drive you on to the airport. Daniel picked up Tom's pantomime wink at Crosby. The boys had started to giggle. Well, I can't stop you, Sarah told him. Sarah, her mother demanded, what kind of reaction is that! When somebody makes such a generous offer! She finally seemed to have found something she wanted to be openly sharp about. But won't it be difficult for you to get off work, she turned to Max? He was on flexitime. The young man shook his head. And of course I'd be delighted to be of help. Daniel watched, trying to understand. How long will you be away? Max enquired. Only a couple of weeks, Sarah said. Wasn't it a month? Daniel asked quickly. Again his daughter's knee nudged against his own. Oh yes, a month, she said. Lucky bastard, Tom announced. Please! Tom, dear! his mother said. Just because you've a friend here, doesn't mean you can start speaking as if you were in the playground. You'll miss my concert then, Max told her. At the church. Before the summer holidays Hilary encouraged all her students to give a concert. Smiling shyly, he added, Perhaps it's just as well, with all the mistakes I make. Sarah hesitated, half smiled, Ask for extra lessons, she said. I'm sure Mum will oblige.

Towards two a.m. that night Daniel replaced his old Opel Estate with a golden Aston Martin. The garage he parked it in was a long way from home. Acceleration was awesome, but for some reason the bonnet kept popping open. Hilary would not be pleased about the lack of luggage space. Then he was just settling down on his side of the bed when it occurred to him that his Aston Martin wasn't insured. He had driven it dangerously, parked it miles away in the flimsiest of prefab garages – there had been a smell of urine – and it wasn't even insured! It could be stolen and he would have no compensation. Daniel woke in a panic.

Later he went to the medicine cabinet in the bathroom. The events of a year ago had taught him to recognise that particular chemical tension in the head that tranquillisers will resolve. For a while he sat in the dark in the sitting room, waiting for the drug to work. Hilary had already begun the process of dismantling the flat and packing up. Prematurely, he felt. The books had gone from the shelves. She was in such a hurry to be out. She phoned every day to hear if the new house might be ready earlier. There were dusty boxes, a roll of carpet, a stack of Tom's games. In our minds this period of our life is already over, he thought. The period of difficulty and crisis. When Tom and Crosby had left the dinner table that evening to go to the Children's Room and play computer, Sarah had stood up and gone with them, leaving himself and Hilary to talk to Max. There's something I never penetrate, Daniel was aware.

Standing up, Judge Savage began to wander round the flat. It was at least a decade since they'd redecorated. Where Hilary had taken down the pictures, the wallpaper almost glowed. He looked in on Tom. It was the room they called the cubby. Then he pushed open Sarah's door. Her face was solemn in the shadow, her thin body covered only by a sheet. How many people had he sent to gaol since he became a judge? The Colombian woman would not look in on her children. I should cherish this responsibility, Daniel told himself. The curve of his daughter's neck was so right, so perfectly geared to all a man would ever want to gaze at and adore. But am I responsible for Minnie? *Recover everything you remember about Minnie*, a voice suddenly ordered. *Everything*.

Then Daniel knew he was in panic. My life is changing. He hurried to the kitchen, found pen and paper. MINNIE, he scrawled. Named after the Korean Queen Min. Age? 20 then. What, 25 now? Studies? All their talk, her talk, had revolved around her studies. Accountancy. They had only met, what, five or six times? But she had wanted to go to art college. Was that right? Her father made the children do different subjects that would be useful for the business. The business was essential to their survival. They were immigrants. The community is everything, she said. She had definitely spoken of two brothers. We are one person, she said. And a grandfather too. But why did they save the accounting for me? He heard her voice in those words, that wail. Accounting! She was laughing and crying. It was her voice, her accent to be precise, that had most attracted him.

As the only daughter, she had had to play nurse to a decrepit grandfather. That was it. Accountant and nurse. The old man woke her at night. He was incontinent. Lying beside Daniel on the pile of cotton in the warehouse, the girl wept with frustration. As soon as she left him, she would have to go and clean her grandfather. She might spend all night with him. After only their second or third meeting, Daniel knew he wanted out. She sensed it. You only pretend to listen, she laughed. She woke up exhausted to a day of accounts. Her father wouldn't get a professional nurse. Not for a member of the family. Koreans don't put their fathers in homes. Mother was dead. He'd kill me if he knew, she laughed, naked on the cotton pile.

Daniel put down his pen. That's all I remember, he

thought. No, there was a boyfriend too, a boyfriend she was supposed to marry. Ben. Daniel had told her she didn't have to. Nobody *had to* marry. It was all inside her head. Fuck off, she wept. Just fuck off. That was the last time. At least five years ago. And Daniel wondered, Did Ben work in the business? Had she told him that?

Anything the matter? Hilary's voice called softly down the passage. Just worrying about money, he called back. Returning to bed, he said, This is ridiculous, I'm going to go and see Martin as soon as I've got a couple of hours free time and demand to know exactly when they're paying. Sleep now, she whispered. She began to stroke his back. Big day tomorrow, Dan. Lying awake as she dozed off, Daniel knew that other men would not have allowed themselves to be seduced by this dilemma.

SEVEN

Judge Savage proceeded with quiet authority, addressing himself solely to the jury. He had made no sign of acknowledgement to Mrs Connolly. He explained the function of judge and jury. Or to his daughter for that matter. Max was not beside her. He considered the question of the burden of proof and the standard of proof. People were standing in the press gallery. He defined abduction. Outside the court there had been a demonstration, a television camera. He defined manslaughter, by unlawful act, by gross negligence. He analysed the elements of each crime that had to be proved. Could a family seeking alternative treatments for a life-threatening disease be accused of gross negligence? Stacey held his pen poised. No doubt he was ticking off the routine items a judge must include in any summing up. If so, could the essence of the crime be said to have taken place in the UK, even though the victim died in Chandigarh?

Daniel looked up. He spoke without flourish, working from notes. The packed court was attentive. He would not be tempted by the theatrical gesture. The cases for the prosecution and defence, *The Times* would say the following morning, were succinctly put. Someone sneezed. Had the family taken the child to India at the first hint of illness, Daniel reminded the jury, there would be no question of their standing trial today. Such a decision would have been perfectly legal. Then he tackled the question of the *mens rea,* the guilty mind. It was here that the jury must interpret all that they had heard and reach their decision. Nobody disputed that the child had been suffering from bone cancer. Nobody disputed that an amputation of the right leg would, at the very least, have prolonged the boy's life. Nobody disputed that the parents had taken the child to India when they were no longer *in loco parentis,* though equally no one was suggesting that they had used force.

Over the last two centuries, there has been a considerable shift, Daniel announced, raising his eyes, in the way we try, judge and sentence crime. He paused. He was departing now from standard practice, yet the case seemed to demand it. From a black/white, yes/no decision as to whether a certain incident considered to be a crime actually happened, and if so who did it — his eyes went down to his papers again — we have struggled more and more to establish the level of guilt of the perpetrator. His colleagues would be on the alert. We ask ourselves whether they were in their right mind when the incident occurred. We ask ourselves whether they are mentally ill, whether they acted under the influence of a passion, or a drug. We ask whether they were under duress. The decision of a jury, Daniel spoke very slowly but without emphasis, may be and indeed has been, influenced by the fact that the defendant was suffering from some kind of stress at the time of a certain crime, or experiencing menstruation perhaps, or by the fact that the defendant has recently been abandoned by his wife, or has experienced a bereavement. Stacey whispered something to Mrs Connolly. To a certain extent – Judge Savage slipped one piece of paper behind another – this willingness to consider mental states may seem to complicate the principle that the law is equal to all, in that one person may be condemned and another acquitted for what was to all outward appearances the same action. To that we can reply that the law is equal to all, *given the mens rea*, the guilty mind, in so far as we have been able to establish it.

Are they following me, he wondered, am I making myself clear? Certainly nobody could accuse him of being a conformist after a summing up like this. He focused his eyes on the jury, looking at each in turn. In certain cases, however, establishing that mental guilt may be a very difficult thing to do. Five men, seven women. Above all it is something that is more open to debate than the simpler questions, did this person shoot this gun, did this person take that money. It is here, then, over the issue of the guilty mind, the defendant's perception of the nature of his intent, that your judgement, the pondered judgement of a jury on the basis of the evidence heard in open court, is crucial.

We say that the defendant is tried by a jury of his peers. What does that mean? It means his equals, people in the same position in life, people who can be expected to understand what they themselves would do and indeed what it would be right and *not* be right to do in similar circumstances. At the centre of the line of jurors, a pallid man in his sixties, diligent, self-important, was taking copious notes. The Indian sat with his chin in his hands. He was gazing intently. There were two blacks. Another way of putting it has been to suggest that the jury assesses what the *ordinary reasonable man or woman* would have done in the same circumstances and compares this hypothetical behaviour with that of the defendant.

Judge Savage hesitated. For a moment he caught his daughter's eye, but looked quickly away. Here our problem, he told the jury gently, is that such behaviour is indeed hypothetical. It is clear that over many issues the ordinary reasonable man or woman behaved very differently a hundred years ago than he does today. It is also clear that people in other countries act in different ways. You have heard an expert witness who has told us that in this case the kind of family under scrutiny would have very different customs and attitudes than a traditional English family.

For a moment he broke off. He lost his thread. What was he thinking? But the pause only served to give his delivery greater authority, as if, despite the copious notes, he were pondering these weighty ideas even as he spoke. Fortunately – he half smiled to acknowledge his stumble – fortunately ladies and gentlemen we are not obliged to try the people of a hundred years ago. On the other hand, and with greater and greater frequency, as I am sure you are aware, we do find ourselves trying the people of other cultures, and this may make your work as a jury doubly difficult.

Again he paused. It was stupidly melodramatic to imagine Minnie might be dead. Why had he allowed his mind to be invaded like this? He cleared his throat: I think that this is true of the case you have been called upon to try here, ladies and gentleman of the jury. I am not suggesting to you, of course, that the law can be different for different sections of the community. Nevertheless, it is my duty to remind you that where the *mens rea,* or the guilt that is in the mind, is important, then personal factors, and those must include cultural factors, can hardly be discounted. Again, I am not suggesting to you that we should allow ourselves to drown in a sea of relativity. Mr and Mrs Mishra chose to live in the United Kingdom and in so choosing they bind themselves to live by the laws of the United Kingdom. Their son is a native born citizen of the United Kingdom. But where the law itself considers the guilty mind important in determining whether a crime has been committed – in this case the very serious crime of manslaughter – then we cannot shy away from considering the individual circumstances, cultural and psychological, of the defendant. With these thoughts in mind, let us now consider the evidence offered against each of the two defendants for each of the two crimes.

Some hours later Judge Savage paced nervously up and down the narrow hallway of the Shields' beautiful house. Bent over an antique sideboard, Christine was writing out a cheque. There, she said. This is bizarre, Daniel thought. Twenty thousand. Somewhere upstairs the television struck up a brash tune. Pounds. I love him so much, she sighed, laying the pen down. If only he'd, oh I don't know, even go out and have an affair!

She was half-laughing, but in tears. Anything! Just to get him out of the house. Out of the house! To be himself, you know. She had leaned back against the door, hugging her breasts, very aware, Daniel sensed, of the melodrama of this intimate conversation in the passageway. He had spoken to no one after the jury retired, left the court almost at once. There had been shouts and angry voices out on the pavement, some kind of demonstration. But he had turned neither to left nor right. These things mustn't concern a judge. The call to Ben he had made from a phone box. Both the house sale, he told himself, and the Minnie business must be put behind him at once. His work was suffering.

The moths, Christine was shaking her head, the soaps! You can't imagine how much they give me the willies. It's just not Martin at all, you know, the way we knew him. No, Daniel said, slipping the cheque into his wallet. He couldn't understand how the woman had signed away in the porch, with no problem or explanation, as if to the milk-man, what had been due to him by contractual agreement three weeks ago. She seemed distracted. And you really have no idea at all, he asked, what brought it on? She shook her head. Her hair was thick and perfumed. The good thing though, he tried to be encouraging, is that Mart was saying, only the other night, how close you two are, that you're a world unto yourselves. She smiled warily. Yes, it's true. And yet there's nothing that would explain . . . Nothing, she insisted. But why did you decide to buy our flat? Daniel asked. Buying a property's a major move, after all. Again Christine told him they had simply decided it would be nice to have a place in town. But why? What are you plan-ning to do in town? She shrugged her shoulders. Use it to stay over. If there are concerts or dinners. Avoid the drive back and forth. I know it's only half an hour but after all these years you go crazy in the car.

It's not, Daniel suggested carefully, that one of you doesn't have the courage to say that you want to separate? Or at least be apart more? The cheque, he'd noticed, was in her name alone. Oh for heaven's sake, she laughed. She had given her whole life to being his companion, Daniel knew. No regular work, no children. The wealth was on his side of the family. She liked to play hostess, to throw dinner parties. She played tennis, attended church functions. Now she stood hugging herself tight in the panelled hallway of a very expen-sive house with lawn to the riverbank and swimming pool, a little overweight perhaps, hair dyed obviously, yet younger and prettier than he usually thought her, that prettiness that comes from a constant feminine care for femininity. I just don't know, she said. She looked softly in his eyes. Daniel knew she wanted to be kissed. He looked at his watch, announced, Right around now Sarah should be landing in Rome. You know we packed her off to Italy, he explained. How wonderful! Christine sighed. Standing up, she gave her bra a little downward tug through cardigan and blouse. It must be such a relief, I suppose, when they finally leave the nest. Her breasts were generous. Got it in one, Daniel laughed.

Upstairs, Martin didn't want to be disturbed while his soap was on. He barely greeted his friend. With twenty minutes to kill before driving back to town to meet Ben, Daniel sat in the armchair across the room from the bed. I would be glad to meet any friend of Minnie's, sir, the voice had said. The accent reminded him of her. Martin was lying in bed, tissues and aspirins by his side. But do you know where I can get in touch with Minnie herself? Daniel had pressed. I'm eager to be in touch with her about a job she might be interested in. Let's meet, sir, the Korean insisted. What's your name, sir? The room smelt stale. Clearly the windows hadn't been opened all day. The phone box had smelt of urine. Steve, Daniel had said, and please don't call me sir, Steve Johnson.

On the screen a man and woman were kissing when apparently they shouldn't. Martin was absorbed, infantile, munching biscuits as he watched. Daniel felt uneasy. There was something unfriendly about it. Yet he owed the man more than he did Minnie. Why hadn't he insisted that Ben say whether he knew where she was or not? Help me, the girl had said. Martin didn't want to be helped. She'd said it twice. I did nothing, Daniel thought. I should have acted at once. Now the problem invaded his mind, even during his work in court.

That's Rachel, Martin said, nodding at the screen. Christine had explained that he had a fever. That was why he was in bed. More than a week now. Above the thickening scrub of beard, his cheeks were pink. One of the twins. Oh right, Daniel remembered. So has she finally bedded her sister's husband? No, Rachel was the faithful wife, Martin told him without taking his eyes off the screen. Nikki's the flirt. Except that now Rachel's going with this computer rep because the letters she's been getting – we still don't know who they're from – have convinced her that the husband's sleeping with Nikki, while in reality he's resisting valiantly. It's quite a story.

Understanding nothing, Daniel watched Martin watching. His eyes were intensely engaged. Bit tame after the real thing in court, the judge ventured. Don't you think? He would have liked to discuss the Mishras, to have talked it over with somebody truly competent. Martin didn't reply. The man's hands were busy with each other, picking at the quick around the nails. Oh by the way, Daniel tried again – suddenly there were adverts – by the way I found out who my own threatening little letters were from. He waited. My daughter. At last Martin turned: Sarah? At last they made eye contact. Yes, it seems Hilary told her, about me and Jane, that is, and these letters are the belated result. Oh of course, Martin said brightly. There was a smile on his face. Of course *nothing*! Daniel retorted. We'd agreed we. . .

Then *Twins* started again. Martin raised a hand. Rachel's husband, who was West Indian, was arguing with a doctor in an old people's home. His father was not being properly treated. The man's a saint, Martin chuckled. Have a biscuit. Turns down the sexy sister, looks after his dad. Positive role model for black men in world of fickle whites. Slick reversal of the old take. But when the actor climbed into his car and for a moment the camera panned across some futuristic cityscape, Martin said musingly, I can't see though, Dan, why you always blame others rather than yourself. Perhaps it's a sort of judging bug. Obviously Sarah's upset to think that the dad who's sticking people in gaol is also cheating on her beloved mum, no? It's obvious. She reads it as hypocrisy.

As had happened in the pub, Daniel noticed, the opportunity to criticise seemed to return Martin to himself. For a moment he pulled himself away from the TV. Their relationship meshed again. Now she's determined to punish you, his friend was explaining, on behalf of her mother. She hates her mother, Daniel said. Rubbish, Martin laughed. No really, Mart, she gets on far better with me. She's going through her Oedipal phase, or whatever it is with girls. She even plays footsie with me, despite being terribly Christian. It's embarrassing. Came to watch me in court today, the Mishra summing up, don't know if you've heard of the case.

Martin shook his head. Last time I saw Sarah and Hilary they were the best of friends, he said. They came over two or three times when you were playing bachelor in the hotel there. Last year. They were perfectly happy then, laughing and joking. They played tennis, then took a dip in the pool. I distinctly remember. The girl no doubt hates you for what you did to her Mum. Daniel was confused. He shut his eyes. What would he say to Ben? At least I have the twenty thousand, he told himself. Maybe you're right, he said vaguely. I don't know. Anyway, Sarah went off to Rome today, so that's one thing out of the way. He tried to laugh. Her boyfriend took her to the airport. Martin's eye was drifting back to the screen. Any chance of seeing you in court? Daniel threw in quickly. Be fun to be sitting when you lose a case or two. Martin wouldn't reply. Daniel waited, then in a sudden frustration he demanded: For Christ's sake, Mart, what's up? You offer me pretty sharp criticism about my life while you go on behaving like an idiot, stewing in bed over soaps. What in God's name's going on? You've got Christine downstairs going completely crazy. Her whole life's hung on you. And even the dumbest hearings are twice as interesting as any television show. For some reason Daniel felt furious. He stood up, grabbed the remote from the bed cover and switched the set off.

Martin scratched at his beard. He swung his legs out of bed, walked a little stiffly across the room and turned the TV on directly from the set. He selected the channel. As the screen popped into its mimicked life, a woman in church was trying to decide whether to enter the confessional. You don't understand, he said flatly when he was back in the bed. And because you don't understand you get angry. He smiled at the corners of his mouth, with a condescending, falsified expression. Actually everybody's getting angry with me. He turned back to the screen. Even Jane came and gave me a good talking to yesterday. Yes, your beloved Jane. Perhaps I shouldn't have mentioned it. Back for a week or two.

Then nodding to the set, Martin remarked, Rachel tried to confess a couple of programmes back, about this computer rep, but ended up just saying she'd smacked their daughter too hard. Come back to court, Daniel told him, before it's too late. In a toneless voice, Martin said: Anything I can do, others can do just as well. Then his face lit up. Speaking of which, you know they even managed to substitute one of the actors on this show instead of having them die or leave like they usually do. Just introduced a different actor one day playing the same guy. But really different. Tall instead of small sort of thing. They made a sort of joke out of it, everybody saying how much he'd changed. Wonderful touch.

Daniel was silent. Anybody can do what I do, Martin repeated. There is no need for my presence. When the man talked about himself, the life went out of his voice. The eagerness was replaced by a dull solemnity. Standing up, Daniel demanded: But what if that wasn't the case, Mart? You know? What if there were some huge moral issue, that only Martin Shields could solve? What then? Dream on, his friend said quietly. He wouldn't take his eyes from the screen.

Take me into town, Christine begged at the bottom of the stairs. She had changed into a dress, put on some make-up. Please! Her voice was squeaky. Daniel explained that he had an appointment. He had to meet a bloke in town. In fact it was already beginning to look rather tight. Cancel, she told him. He noticed the perfume now. Had the mention of Jane affected him? Take me into town before I kill that man. She gestured upstairs, then giggled. I need a drink, preferably in male company. For some reason Daniel remembered then that Christine was Sarah's godmother. She had even taught the girl in Sunday school at some point. He hesitated. Is it an important appointment? his friend's wife insisted. You look worried, Dan. Her tone was maternal. He asked, can I make a call?

The sitting room was a default setting of old English elegance. Green upholstery, floral curtains, antique furniture. What did the Shields do of an evening, Daniel wondered? The place looked unlived in. He sat at a polished desk littered with dusty photos. Warehouse, please, he asked. He couldn't imagine a childless marriage. We're closed, sir, said the voice. Again a catarrh case. Can you try it, please. I'm a friend. Who's speaking, sir? Steve, he said. I'm sorry, sir? Steve, he repeated more loudly. Concentrating, he saw the photos were all of moths. He was tense. Blurred creatures right up against the lens. There seemed no point. Soaps and moths. Ben, he asked? He doesn't kill them, Christine had explained, so they're never still when he clicks the shutter. Ben, look, yes, I'm sorry but something's come up, I can't make it this evening. The pictures were unfocused, as if the things had just flown into your face. Let's meet tomorrow. Okay? You almost felt the eyelids flicker shut in self-defence. Daniel stared at them. Good.

Immediately afterwards he called Hilary. Christine was hovering at the door. It was a light, summery dress she'd found, pleasantly airy about the knees, charmingly girlish. They've given us the dough. Yes! In his lowest voice he said he'd have to stay the evening to understand what on earth was happening with these two, their old friends, and whether they were going to pay the rest on time or not. Tom's clamouring for you to go and watch his six-a-side, Hilary said. It's too bad, he agreed. Tell him it's a crisis. And everybody's been phoning about the summing up. Oh really? Judge Savage wished he was home, but he could hardly back down now. I'll be back around nine-thirty, ten. Has Sarah phoned? She hadn't.

Her whole life had been a mistake! Rrruhh! Christine clenched her fist till it shook. She pushed the hand into her hair, then held her head in taut fingers, looking down at the table. She had been explaining that she and Martin hadn't had sex in years, three years. She looked up. I think it's three. She sat like a girl knees wide apart in her skirt jerking nervously. Cigarette? Daniel declined. There was a fracas at the porch; a large party had changed its mind and chosen to leave before all its members were properly inside. There was a confused back and forth at the door. And just, Christine was telling him indignantly, just when I thought I might slip in a baby at the last minute, you know? people do, at that very moment, can you believe it, he stops wanting it altogether. Libido, gone. We don't have sex at all.

There were tears in her eyes. Daniel half smiled. Having been through them himself, he was weary of these intense emotions. I'm sorry Christine, he said, I'm not being a good listener. Let's eat.

She came back with menus from the bar, a second pint he hadn't asked for, a second gin for herself. Why didn't I go and see Ben? Daniel looked at his watch. The chicken, he said. She went back to order. There are so many worries when you have children, he told her as she pulled her chair up, played with the ice in her gin. Sarah's quite impossible. You know the day of her history A level she decided she wouldn't go. Didn't want to do the exam. I almost had to drag her there. Then she made me stop on the way for this most awful tête-à-tête, I'd said something wrong, I don't know. It's incredible with kids how you can say something wrong without having any idea what it was. I still don't know. They live in a different world. Anyway, she was howling and screaming. I had to slap her round the face – I'd've been arrested in Sweden, here too before too long – then we hugged of course, and all the time I'm worried stiff she's going to be late for her exam. He shook his head. So perhaps, you know, you might actually be better off without in a way. No, I don't mean that. He drank some beer. I was just thinking, right now the thing to do surely is to concentrate your mind on Martin, on getting him out of this state. Has he seen a specialist?

Christine leaned forward across the table. She kept picking out a pendant that hung in her cleavage. A little silver cross. She fished it out, then let it drop down there again between the full breasts. Now, as she pushed her face toward him across the drinks, it swung forward. Is that why you started cheating on Hilary, she asked with soft intensity? What? He was surprised. This frustration, Dan, the other person being unhappy *on purpose* and not telling you why. So far not a single word, not a single bloody word to say *why* he's doing all this. Endless silences, days in bed. He's doing it *on purpose*. It's infantile. It's cruel! Her voice too, Daniel thought, was oddly infantile; she had the squeaky indignation of the little girl. And there's something of that in Hilary, isn't there? Christine said, sitting back. I remember you telling me. You remember that night? She's always been famous for her depressions. She was giving you hell, wasn't she, sitting in corners refusing to speak to people. They punish us with their depressions, Dan!

Oh, Hilary's fine, Daniel said. He didn't want this. People have their moments. No, the affair thing was just that I got infatuated, you know. He tried to be offhand. Pretty banal choice, Christine was objecting: strawberry blonde in the same chambers, fifteen years younger, all legs, tits and bottom. She seemed almost peeved. No, she insisted, I'm sure it was more to do with how things were at home, Dan. Otherwise – she sat back brightly – it would be unforgivable, wouldn't it! To have an affair when you were happy at home.

Daniel wouldn't reply. He tried to keep some sort of smile on his face. Marriage is how you describe it, he had decided. He wouldn't speak ill of Hilary. She dropped by yesterday, you know, Christine went on. Jane, I mean. I suppose Mart told you. Looking fabulously coltish of course. And of course I sent her straight upstairs in the hope the sight of all that prettiness might wake up Rip Van Winkle. I've been calling him Rip Van Winkle. You don't believe me, she urged, suddenly assuming a voice of grim desperation, but really, I wouldn't mind at all if he ripped off all her expensive clothes and had her right there in our bed. She downed her gin abruptly. I'm sure you would if it happened, Daniel assured her. Maybe, she said. Fingers playing constantly with her face or round the corners of her lips, or dipping the little silver cross in and out of her cleavage, she told him, You've had loads of women, haven't you, Dan? Lorry loads. He opened his mouth. It wasn't just Jane, was it? Oh, don't deny it, you rogue! You've had millions! No, don't be *silly*, Martin tells me everything, he says you're still seeing. . .

No!

Now Judge Savage was upset. His voice was firm and sober. No, that really isn't true, Christine. She looked at him carefully. She is carefully made up, he thought. There was an evident element of premeditation about all this. She had decided how she was going to behave while he had been upstairs with Martin. Or even before, perhaps. She had been determined to take him out. If I remember rightly, she said, you'd have gobbled me right up that evening we kissed. He shook his head. Christine, that was really so . . . You had your hand up my dress! she squeaked; she bounced up suddenly on her seat as if he had only just that moment touched her bottom. That was ages and ages ago, Christine, Daniel said firmly, after a very long and very drunken . . . Well now I'm in the same position as you were then, she said brutally.

Rummaging for cigarettes, she forced a pause in the conversation. Her bag was beside her on the floor. He knew she wasn't listening to his quiet remark about being very happy with his life. He repeated it anyway. When she began to speak again, interrupting him, it was in an entirely different tone, low and straightforward, but as if communicating something of great importance: Dan, listen, please, don't misunderstand me, I don't want to leave Mart, I couldn't, I mean, I don't want to start some kind of grand passion, then when I think what he's probably going through, you know, clinical depression and so on, but at the same time I do feel this huge . . . She stopped. This . . . she shook her head. Oh I don't know, she wailed. Perhaps to punish him. Being unhappy makes me silly somehow. Do you understand?

Daniel prayed the food would arrive. If only one could call people to order as one might a wayward witness. Suddenly afraid his body language was all wrong, he sat back in a deliberate gesture of disengagement. He tried to seem easy where he had been tense, sprawled where he had been upright. Confront him with it directly, he told her. You'll save yourself a lot of time and effort, believe me. He might have been telling her how to fix a computer. Or perhaps it was Martin's guru voice he'd assumed. He was playing Martin to Martin's wife. Tell him you're at your wits end and thinking of going to bed with someone else. No, I couldn't, she said quickly. I couldn't do that. She too sat back, glazed, thwarted. She shook her head. Try, he insisted. Talk to him. Once you've started it'll be easier than you thought. If there was one thing that he knew wasn't true, it was this. He tried to laugh. Aren't you famous for telling each other everything? I won't even phone Jane while she's back, he decided. There must be no contact at all.

Christine shook her head. I might be able to betray him, she said. But I couldn't *tell* him I was, or even that I was thinking about it. Do you see what I mean? I couldn't hurt him directly. I've never been able to do that. The same way he's never hurt me. Did you know, Dan, that he's never, never hurt me? I don't believe I've ever hurt him. I take him his Lucozade poor dear. He *has* got a temperature actually. I've checked it. It's been going on about ten days now. Low, but always there. And he has this odd rash on the back of his leg. I can hardly put his hot water bottle down and say, Listen Martin, lovey, since we're not having sex, I'm off to screw someone else. I'm not that kind of person. Daniel observed: Things didn't improve with Hilary, you know, until we had a head on collision. Right, she nodded. Only it was she found *you* out, wasn't it, not you deciding to tell her. She told us everything, poor thing, while you were holed away in your silly hotel. Actually, if you want to know, I told her that as I saw it you'd only done it because she was always so bloody moody and depressed. Christine laughed, I thought Martin might get the hint.

Then just as the girl appeared carrying their plates, Martin Shields' wife actually began to giggle: Oh if you knew how many times Mart and I were lying in bed – she didn't seem to have any qualms about letting the waitress hear this – criticising you for all the women you were having and saying how lucky you were Hilary had only found out about the one, and not the other twenty, when really of course we were jealous! Because we weren't having sex at all! The truth is, she drained the second gin to make room for her plate – the waitress smiled – the truth is, maybe we never had children because I had to look after Martin, who after all is the biggest baby the world has known, you know? Always needing to hear he is better than everyone else. Always! You really are the best, Martin, she mimicked herself, shook her head, picked up a knife in her fist. Ruhhrr!

Daniel asked, By the way do you know how Hilary found out? Thank you, he told the waitress. Christine frowned into the bottom of her glass. How did she find out? I've no idea. Tell me. No, I was asking you, Daniel smiled. Christine looked puzzled. Oh, I see. Why? Does it matter? You had lipstick on your collar, I suppose. She overheard a phone-call. Actually, she did say there was a period when you were constantly on the phone.

Then it occurred to Daniel that all of this must have been discussed *in Sarah's presence* on those visits Martin had mentioned. Hilary had taken Sarah to eat with Martin and Christine and the whole thing, his affair, Jane, the possible break-up, had been lengthily discussed, in his daughter's presence! Perhaps Tom was there too. This was alarming. Oh, before I forget, he said abruptly, he put his napkin down, I was hoping you would tell me if we're likely to get a repeat of the problem with the payment – we had to take out a loan you know.

Mouth full, Christine looked up in surprised amusement. Are you upset, she asked? Have I upset His Honour Judge Savage? She looked hard at him, then down at her plate. Business-like, she said: There'll be no more problem now, Dan, okay, because from now I'm going to pay it directly myself from my own account. So let's say no more about it. Apparently the hints about not having enough had been the merest melodrama.

On the way back, fifty yards from the gate of the Shields' house, she put her hand over his on the gear stick. Stop, Dan. Look! He pulled in. To the left, beyond the fence, there was a pool of neon in the middle of the lawn. They were looking down a slope with the river beyond. His moth trap. Lives of exemplary brevity, he says. He's in bed all day, but then goes down at dawn to see what he's caught. He pulls them out by handfuls and tries to snap them with the flash. They damage their wings in the muslin. So even if he doesn't kill them, they die anyway.

As she spoke, she put her left hand on his. Daniel was expecting the request for a kiss when it came. I know you don't want to, she said easily, turning her face to him. But please. Just a kiss. It's been such a lovely evening. She laughed, snuggling to him. At least I got a few things off my chest.

Kiss me. No, he said. Otherwise I'll tell Hilary! Daniel laughed: So if I don't, you'll tell, and if I do, you won't. Right! She was smiling. There were tears in her eyes. And remember, I'm signing the cheques! It was a joke of course. They kissed for four or five minutes. He enjoyed it, enjoyed those breasts in particular, and driving back to town felt furious. Abruptly he turned off the ring road and headed for the centre.

The Capricorn Café was on the corner of Soames and Cruft. He went upstairs and squeezed through three or four small rooms. How often in life this gesture of poking into bars, wandering between the tables had been accompanied by an intense awareness of the colour of his skin. Was he welcome? When he finally found a group of Asians in an upstairs alcove, he felt quite sure he wasn't. I'm looking for a Korean guy called Ben, he said. I know he often drinks here. He's the boyfriend of a girl called Minnie, Minnie Kwan. Her father has a fabric import business. There were four men and two women eating an assortment of ice-creams. Immediately they began to speak in their own language. You are Korean, Daniel asked? One of the women said, yes, yes. The man beside her cut in. We don't know Ben. But you do know who he is? Again they spoke among themselves. You know Minnie Kwan? We don't know, the man repeated. We can't help.

Various calls, Hilary yawned. She was in the bathroom. Gordon Crawford said someone was saying your summing up was 'daring'. Daniel hurried to Tom's room, but the boy was asleep. Did he win? Yes, I think he did. Or at least scored. Oh, and Martin phoned: someone had been phoning them, wanting to speak to someone who'd made a call from their house. I don't know. I think that's what it was. He thought it might have been you. You'd used the phone or something and their phone had registered the number. Then Christine called to say the same thing. She thought you'd be home already. Daniel went back to the sitting room and filled a glass with ice and whisky. In the bedroom again he undressed quickly. They're splitting up, he said. Christine's going to buy the flat on her own. No doubt she plans to move here herself. Lying down, the two of them began to criticise their friends. They should have had children, Martin's being a baby himself was just her excuse. A man isn't a baby. Did Sarah phone? Daniel asked at length. No, Hilary said. Why should she? And did Max take her to the airport? Hilary laughed: It seems she told him she wouldn't get in his car until he stopped making mistakes at the piano. He told me when he came for his lesson.

EIGHT

It was in the nineteenth century, he remembered Hilary pontificating, that composers began to allow chaos into music. Waiting for the jury to return, Daniel read how nine youths were accused of having thrown, from a bridge over the town's fast ring road, the rock that had destroyed Elizabeth Whitaker's life. His wife had been trying, as he recalled – but she had stopped bothering years ago – to get him to appreciate Wagner, a strange passage where the harmony disintegrates into a noisy crowd scene, then is regenerated from within the confused voices to swell out even stronger. Her teacherly tone had irritated him. The harmony swells out stronger, she said, *because* of the chaos. A crowd of people, Jonathan Whitaker had testified. At least a dozen. He had glimpsed them racing across the bridge as he dragged his wife from the shattered car. Unusual willingness to tackle the deeper issues, *The Times* said. Two passages were actually quoted. Deeply troubling in its implications, claimed a *Guardian* leader. Daniel put the case reports down beside the newspapers and reached for the phone.

Hello? It was her voice. Nothing unpleasant in the papers,

he announced. I'm glad, she said. Jury still out? She seemed relaxed this morning. You know I was just remembering, he told her, something you once said about Wagner. Oh God, Dan! They've given me that stone-throwing case, he explained. The ring road thing? Yes. The story had been in the news some months before. How awful! Hilary said. And please don't remind me of my Wagner days. Why not? She said she had read in a magazine somewhere that the embryo was going to survive. That's why they were keeping the woman alive. What's her name? Whitaker. Apparently an embryo can survive even when the mother is brain dead. These things turn my stomach, she said. And she said: By the way, your brother phoned. It seemed the notorious Frank Savage wanted a loan. Talk about out of the blue! Tell him no. *You* tell him! He's your brother. News from Sarah? he asked. What a relief not to have her around, Hilary told him. No, she hadn't phoned. But that was healthy, wasn't it? Why should an eighteen-year-old call the moment she was away from home? I'll be back a bit late this evening, he told her. Something he needed to discuss with Crawford, he said: The way the people from the CPS were behaving. You do know Tom's demanding a game of chess, she reminded him. You know how he gets in holidays with nothing to do. I love you, Daniel told her.

He found he was on edge now waiting for the jury to return. Unless it was the business of seeing Ben in the evening. This evening he really must. Guilty of abduction, he thought, not of manslaughter. That would be the right result. He hadn't expected this much attention. Then everybody could claim a victory. Mrs Connolly would have her conviction, the Mishras could soon return to their life, their business.

Collectively, he read, struggling to concentrate on this new case, the accused, all under 25, had named more than twenty other youths as being frequent visitors to the bridge. Five spoke of a white-haired man with a foreign accent who offered tenners to the first person to smash a windscreen. Others denied all knowledge. Someone had heard of a points system for hits and near misses. Forensic experts stated that the boot of a Ford Mondeo had been filled with whitish stones of a variety found in the Hartingdon quarry to the south of the town. A similar stone had been found smothered in blood on the floor of the Whitaker's car. Once again there would be questions as to the *mens rea*, Daniel thought.

On impulse he picked up the phone again, this time to call the number his wife had just given him. You set off round the ring road, he imagined, to do a perfectly ordinary spot of shopping, the wife is pregnant, and suddenly a rock crashes into your life. Chaos. Photographs showed that the woman had lost the entire left side of her face. What harmony could swell out from that?

Saw your name in the paper, Frank said, my dear little bruv. Thought I'd call. Frank! You never told me they'd made you a judge. I told Mother, Daniel said. I imagined she'd tell you. The two brothers hadn't spoken since the colonel's funeral. You'll have no problem giving me a couple of grand then, Frank decided. As always he had a pleasant, persuasive voice. Daniel had frequently argued with Mother about her willingness to finance Frank's various schemes and addictions. What are you up to these days? he asked. Minding my own business, thank you, squire. The careless humour was carefully provoking. Are you working? Daniel asked. Working on getting these two grand, Frank laughed. Fuck off, Dan, will you lend it or not? Lend or give? Daniel asked. Where's your sense of humour? Frank objected. Is euphemism the pinnacle of civilisation, or is it not? No, Daniel told him. No what? No, Judge Savage said. It was the same automatic voice he had used to reject Christine's request for a kiss. Immediately he felt apologetic. Look Frank, right now we're not in the best position . . . At the same moment Adrian put his head round the door. Verdict, he sang. The fact is, Daniel resumed, we have this . . . The line was dead.

Mr Foreman, asked the clerk of the court, have you reached verdicts on either of the two counts against either defendant on which you are all agreed?

The public, still squeezing in, were immediately hushed. The defendants stood expressionless in the dock. Even as the clerk spoke, Daniel noticed two wilfully ugly youths in the public gallery, one with a Union Jack tattooed on his neck. The usher demanded silence.

We have reached a verdict on one count, for both defendants, but not on the other. It was the pallid, elderly man, they had chosen as their foreman. No doubt retired, he was clearly enjoying the attention and spoke with exemplary gravity.

Have you reached a verdict on count one on which you are all agreed.

Yes. Manslaughter. The court held its breath.

On count one, do you find the defendant, Sunni Mishra, guilty or not guilty of manslaughter?

Not guilty.

Judge Savage didn't move a muscle while the usher hushed two or three voices in the public gallery. The formula was repeated for the man's wife.

At the second not-guilty, somebody rushed out, banging the door. The clerk continued: Have you reached a verdict on count two on which you are all agreed? They hadn't, despite eight hours' deliberation. Daniel sent them out for a further two hours, while he got on with the more routine work on his list, then had them recalled. Again no verdict had been reached. Ladies and gentleman of the jury, he told them, we have now come to the point where a majority verdict would be acceptable. The public sighed. Stacey, Daniel noticed, had seemed resigned after the summing up to losing the manslaughter count. Fair enough. Abduction, after all, could hardly go any way but his. It was a mystery why Mrs Connolly cared so much.

Ladies and gentlemen, we call it a majority verdict, if ten, I repeat ten of you, are agreed, one way or another. I cannot of course, he told the foreman, ask you how you are divided over the count of abduction, in what numbers or in what way, but I must now ask you, to retire once more to see if you can return a verdict on which at least ten of you are agreed.

The foreman wore a small thin moustache, white polo neck, tweed jacket. Your honour – wisps of hair were trained across a bald head – one or two members of the jury would like to know what kind of sentence the defendants would get for abduction of a minor. Daniel responded on automatic pilot: While it is understandable that members of a jury should show an interest in the fate of the defendants, I cannot comment on the nature of any eventual sentencing. It is the jury's duty to reach a verdict on the basis of the evidence they have heard, not to reflect on the consequences of that verdict. As he finished speaking the court usher leaned over and handed the judge a note. Your wife asks you to call home urgently. Daniel stared. From the poise of an impeccable judicial performance in a packed court, Daniel Savage suddenly felt himself sinking under a wave of nausea. He felt dizzy. Why? Why do I feel so fragile? Just because my wife says she needs to speak to me. For a moment it was almost panic. Oh this has to be settled, he told himself. This stupid business. Under the thick wig his scalp thrilled with heat. He took a sip of water, shook his head. Your honour, the foreman now turned to him. His manner was unctuous. I am not sure whether any more discussion will help. Don't agree! one of the women behind him objected. Daniel recovered himself. Ladies and gentlemen of the jury, I will now ask you to retire and to seek to arrive at a majority verdict. Please do not feel under any pressure. If there is any matter on which you would like further instruction, you need only ask.

Back at his desk in chambers, Daniel listened to the ringing tone home in the flat. Urgently, she had said. Laura was off photocopying. It had been a day of phone-calls. But Hilary wasn't answering. Then the clerk was back. She knocked on his door. Judge? He met the girl's clear eyes. Your wife said she had to go out, but to tell you there had been a call from Italy about your daughter. Yes? She didn't say what it was? Only to call back later. I think she said she had a lesson. Well, it couldn't be that urgent, Daniel thought, if Hilary had gone to her lesson. For a moment he had seen himself postponing the meeting with Ben again. Having an excuse to postpone it.

In the meantime, Judge Savage started to leaf through the Whitaker papers. There were accusations made in initial interviews, then retracted. An elderly cyclist had seen a group of youths clustered at the parapet of the bridge at the exact time of the crime. A retarded boy had been arrested and had confessed to a quite unrelated, indeed unreported rape. The police were not investigating. None of the defendants denied having visited the bridge on various occasions, or even having seen stones thrown. But nobody had been directly involved. In a series of identification parades, the cyclist had picked out only two of those charged. These people are guilty in general, Daniel thought. While the person who destroyed Elizabeth Whitaker in particular was merely unlucky. Sometimes it is the merest bad luck that turns a guilty action into a major crime.

An usher came and asked if Daniel could hear an application to vacate a plea. Crawford's case had gone on longer than expected. Judge Savage reached for his wig again. So it would be an hour and more before he spoke, not to Hilary – still out – but to Tom. And almost five-fifteen before the jury finally returned their verdict in the Mishra case.

Can you play Super Star tonight? Tom asked. He had worked out how to do the 'incredible control' thing, that chip shot over the keeper. Mum told me you wanted a game of chess. Oh Dad! I played Max yesterday. He must be good, Daniel said. No, I killed him. Well done! At Super Star, Dad, not chess. I kill everyone at Super Star. So what's the point of playing me? We can play together against the computer. Japan against Nigeria's good. What's the story with Sarah? Daniel interrupted. Sarah? I don't know. But Mum phoned me about her. I don't know, Tom said. Putting the phone down, Daniel remembered Sarah's exam results were due soon. What would that jury decide?

Have you reached a verdict – the court clerk repeated his formula – on count two on which at least ten or more of you are agreed. People were still crowding in from the corridors. The whole Indian community had mobilised. There were people from the National Front. Laura said she had seen three TV vans out on the street, a line of demonstrators. Blown up out of all proportion, Daniel thought. It was raining heavily and the summer afternoon was dark. Entering court, Judge Savage felt confident again. It always had that effect, the three knocks, the court rising to his entry. He felt strong. And he could see at once that the jury had managed to agree. There was that familiar expression of tired relief on their faces. Yes, we have. On count two do you find the defendant, Sunni Mishra, guilty or not guilty of abduction. Not guilty. The verdict was repeated for Mrs

Mishra. Not guilty. There were shouts from the gallery. How could they? Daniel asked himself. How could they not find at least one parent guilty? Of abduction. At least the father. And how are you divided? the clerk asked. Your honour! The defence counsel was immediately on her feet to protest. For a moment Judge Savage was so surprised he failed to grasp the error. No breakdown question was required with a not-guilty verdict. But the foreman had already replied. Eleven to one, your honour.

He tried to call Hilary. Outside the court he was shocked by what was going on on the pavement. Do you want to speak to Max? Tom had asked. Max? Paki Child Killers read a placard. The Mishras were Indian. Hilary was still out. Max was there playing the piano. The police were temporising, keeping two groups apart. We're All White Trash, said a banner. Somebody threw something that thudded against the wall. There was a bright light, a TV camera. Daniel had had no idea. Racist shits! Obviously these people were sufficiently well informed to know that a judge left the court from his own special side entrance. Two constables appeared and escorted Daniel under an umbrella to a car and thence round the block to where he kept his own vehicle. You never know when everyone's going to go nuts, the driver shook his head. He seemed pleased with himself. Just two lots of crazies waiting to have a go at each other, your honour.

Twenty minutes later, Daniel climbed the stairs to the upper room of the Capricorn. It was strange that they didn't have their own ethnic place, he thought. A Korean place. It was a good sign, perhaps. Upstairs was empty. He was calling Hilary again, from the payphone by the bathrooms, when the men came in. It seems she isn't eating, his wife explained, and she's been skipping all her lessons. They wanted me to phone her this evening and talk to her about it. Daniel asked why had she asked him to call urgently, then gone out like that? They were three Asian men, all in sober suits. I thought it would be better if you called her, Hilary said. You're better with Sarah, you know. Am I? Ignoring Daniel, the men sat down at a corner table. Presumably they had nothing to do with Ben. Then he recognised the young salesman at Kwan's warehouse. The son. Where are you now? Hilary wanted to know. Could you pick up some milk coming back? At the Polar Bear, waiting for Crawford, he said. The Paki shop should be open, she told him. They said we should call her around nine o'clock our time. Why was Kwan's son here? he wondered. Minnie's brother. Their point of view is, either she mucks in with the others or she should leave. Oh, and the good news, Daniel could hear the sudden lift in his wife's voice, the good news is the builder said we can store anything we want in the house now. Furniture, anything. To all intents and purposes it's finished. Just the utilities to hook up. Great, Daniel said.

He walked across the room. A dark carpet under violet light created an unreal field of colour. Oddly green. There were no windows. He had reached their table now. Fifteen minutes after the appointed time. Excuse me, he asked, is one of you Ben? As always he tried to strip the education from his voice. The result was unconvincing, brittle. Who are you? the older man asked. He was shorter than the two beside him, but had the weight and solidity of middle age. He wore glasses. Steve Johnson, Daniel said. Now, if you don't mind, I'm late for an appointment with a guy called Ben. I'm looking for. . .

Sit down, Mr Johnson. The accent was so strong it was comic. Daniel hesitated. A group of teenagers appeared at the top of the stairs. Abruptly some music struck up, some urgent rhythm. Nothing can happen here, he told himself, in a café off the town's high road, beside the main shopping centre. The garish furnishings were innocuous. Sit down, the man repeated.

Determinedly, he took a seat, planted his feet on the carpet and his hands on his knees, keeping a little back from the table. Mr Kwan, he said, I presume you are Mr Kwan, I'm trying to get in touch with your daughter, Minnie. The young man who served in their warehouse said something rapidly in Korean. There was a back and forth, apparently irritated. The father looked sharply at Daniel. Only four or five years between them perhaps. Why? Why do you want her? There was an ugly broadness to his face. Almost broader than it was long. A job has come up, Daniel said. Minnie asked me for help a while back, to find her a job.

The older man didn't appear to have understood. The music was loud. Or perhaps his English was even poorer than his accent suggested. Daniel began to repeat, but again the son he had met in the warehouse spoke in Korean. The others stared across the table. How oddly the light transformed the Asian man's skin. And mine? Daniel wondered. Their white shirts took on a cathode glow.

What job? It was the son addressed the question, but clearly it came from the father. A tradition, Professor Mukerjee had said, of unquestioning and immediate obedience of sons toward their fathers. That was what Minnie had fought against. It's a good position, in an office. I'd like to discuss it with her personally. Perhaps, if you. . .

He was interrupted by the waitress. The café was filling rapidly. Cokes, the father decided, holding up three fingers. Gin and tonic please, Daniel smiled. The girl was tiny, Indian. Yesterday it had been Christine drinking gin. So, if you could just let me know how I can contact. . .

He stopped. Only now, as he spoke, did Judge Savage become aware that his approach had been based on the

129

assumption that nothing was wrong, that he would check that all was okay with his ex-girlfriend, if that was the word, and then, duty done, go back to concentrating on wife and family and career. This is a formal gesture you are making, he realised. You're not prepared for a calamity. But why, when he had made an appointment with the boyfriend, did father and two sons come to meet him? There was a pause. Perhaps he had never spoken to Ben at all. The silent son took a packet of cigarettes from his top pocket. Lighting up, he never once took his eyes off Judge Savage.

Minnie Kwan, the warehouse son announced, has no need for work. She would never speak to a black man. She would never ask for a job. The older man leaned forward, gazing intensely: We don't speak to blacks. Even as he said this, the tiny Indian waitress began to set the drinks on the table. The cokes gleamed black. In the gin the ice winked with violet light. Only an hour ago, I was a figure of authority, Daniel was aware, in the sane, aseptic lighting of court number three. I'll get the tab, he said. He found his wallet. The girl smiled, a jewel sparkling in her nose. You are a pimp, Mr Johnson, the father said directly. You leave Minnie Kwan alone. Daniel had to take the glass from his lips and set it down. A pimp! His bewildered indignation was the kind a jury immediately recognises as sincere. I would hardly come to your ware-house with my wife and children if I was a pimp.

At once he knew he shouldn't have said this. He remem-bered Minnie's shout of derision on the phone, My black pimp lover! Presumably it was the worst scenario her father could imagine, the worst possible provocation. The man was speaking grimly, in Korean, but staring straight at Daniel. There is no other reason, came the son's translation, why a Korean girl would speak to a black man. I'm Brazilian, Daniel said. Actually, he was English. And no other job, the boy

parroted, that a black man could offer than to be a prostitute. Looking from one to the other, Daniel realised they
might be in good faith. They honestly couldn't imagine that
a black could offer work. They wouldn't believe it if he
explained why he was dressed in black suit and tie.

Look, he said smilingly, let's all go and see Minnie together.
I offer her the job, in your presence, it's a secretarial thing,
not a bad position, and we can see what she thinks. This
time a command from the father had the smoking son pull
a mobile from his pocket. He began to speak, the others
waited. Daniel sat back and drank. Was this the catarrhy voice
that had passed for Ben? You mustn't be home too late for
Tom again, he told himself. The rush of alcohol was always
a pleasure. And there was the phone call to Sarah of course.
Then the old man cut through the monotone of his son on
the mobile. In English he asked: When is the last time you
see Minnie Kwan? We spoke on the phone, Daniel said
cautiously. When? Look, Mr Kwan, I have to be getting on
home, so why don't we go and see her now and . . . I asked,
when did you see her last? The sullen boy snapped his phone
shut. He seemed to be the older. Daniel was silent. We don't
understand why you must see Minnie Kwan. We don't understand how Minnie Kwan can know a black man.

The three waited. Unable to tell the truth, not even sure
himself now why he was here, Daniel said lightly: What if
I am a policeman? What if Minnie Kwan phoned us to say
she needed help. The father turned to his son for clarifica-
tion. All three spoke urgently. You show some identity, the
articulate one said. Where is Ben, Daniel demanded. It was
Ben I had the appointment with. Show your card! The boy
had remembered the right formula. That was just a joke,
silly, Daniel shook his head. Of course I'm not a policeman.
Let's go and see Minnie now. Then I promise I'll leave you

all alone. The three conferred furiously. The music had grown louder. The waitress was hovering again. Daniel smiled at her, chewing his lime. I'm going to use the bathroom, he said.

Walking between the now busy tables, Judge Savage felt he had done the right thing. The father seemed an unpleasant piece of work, but hardly the kind to have done violence to his daughter. They are just immigrants, he told himself. Imagining themselves in a hostile environment, they have paranoid ways. Minnie had perhaps been in some trouble and they were protecting her. They hadn't had the good luck of his upbringing. On the other hand, at least they kept their children in line. All I have to do now, he decided, standing over the urinal, is get some assurance that she's okay. But when he came out of the bathroom, the Korean men were gone. The table had already been taken by a group of young white girls.

Daniel stood in the strange light, at once theatrical and commonplace. He felt relief more than frustration. I tried, he told himself. He shook his head. Good. He looked at his watch. It had been a strange experience. Ten past eight. Down in the street, he hurried through heavy rain to the mall, waited for the lift to the car park. No doubt the weather had broken up the demonstration, he thought. He strode between cement columns three floors up. The first blow struck him as he bent down to open the car door. Even before he fell, some sort of bag came down over his face. He was struck violently in the back. A string bit into his neck. There was no sound but his own suffocated cries. Blind on the cement between his own car and the next, he was being kicked left and right. Bright colour rushed from his spine, filling his mind with pain.

NINE

A judge, the *Telegraph*'s Saturday supplement remarked, may easily become notorious, but rarely popular. The investigator and the criminal, the editorialist went on, the prosecution and the defence were two pairs of archetypal antagonists. Their back and forth would always command centre stage, while the judge, for most of us, was no more than the astute referee who allows the story to unfold. This is not a role likely to arouse widespread excitement. All the same, as the paper was then bound to admit, when the story broke, after a night of vicious race riots, that Daniel Savage lay in coma in the local hospital, all the same, this first non-white judge on his particular court circuit, had immediately become a hero nationwide. Occupying considerably more space than these few brief reflections, a photograph of the country's newest celebrity showed an almond-coloured man with faintly negroid features and a reassuring hint of grey in woolly hair. Not a child of empire, read an enigmatic caption.

Meanwhile, as newspapers pontificated, the police were under some pressure to identify the judge's assailants, the doctors to save his life. Hilary, the sick man finally whispered on the third day. Groping upward through an oppressive mental dark, he had become aware of her fingers in his. Hilary! But simultaneous with this first flicker of consciousness that would be such a relief to millions – Savage Survives, a headline would declare – came an enormous anxiety. His hand clutched hers. Take me home, he whispered, I want to go home. Hilary was thrilled. Yes, yes, she said. Yes! Her lips brushed his bandaged face – Don't move, keep calm – she stood up to call a nurse. Nurse! The shrillness rang in his skull.

Apparently Tom was staying with Crosby. That much he gathered. You are beside me though, he kept muttering. Yes, she said. Yes, dear. She had chosen not to tell Sarah, she explained. She had begged the organisers of their daughter's trip not to let the girl know, to keep her there in Italy till the end of the month. The last thing she needed was Sarah now. You're awfully famous, Dan, she told him. They're all waiting to interview you. I was afraid people would bother the poor girl.

He barely registered the words. Or the hours and days. Bandages were removed and replaced, painfully. New tests were run. The silly child – Hilary had taken to embroidering, she sat beside his bed – claims she swallowed the top of one of my perfume bottles, six months ago. Can you imagine? Since then she's never felt well. It's blocked somewhere, she says.

Daniel was lost. I like you doing embroidery, he whispered. His mind was in constant alarm with sudden pains that flashed and would fade. He shivered. Can you see, she asked? She was leaning over him. A blur. Flowers, she said. Two roses against a lattice. He couldn't see, couldn't think. Where did it happen? she asked. There was another operation, another morning's unconsciousness. I don't remember, he told her. You didn't meet Crawford, she said. Crawford? Should I have?

The hours passed in a slow swell of pain. He remembered, he said, leaving court, somebody had thrown something. A red point of light tortured the dark. There were riots, she told him. He winced. She told him of cars burned, hails of stones. All weekend. The TV called you the emblem of order and sanity. What happened to the stone-throwing case? he asked one early morning. She didn't know. She'd done nothing but sit in here by his bed. It's a mercy Sarah's away. A relief that she doesn't know. Nobody blames you, she said. Every day I leave the hospital there are people asking me questions, waiting to interview you. Don't let them in, Daniel muttered.

She sat in silence working on her embroidery. This was so unlike her. The stems go in and out of the lattice, she explained. She described it to him. I was so afraid you were going to die. Then twine together. It's like a meditation, she said. He sensed her calmness. You're a hero, she whispered.

They had bandaged his eyes now. She told him: CPS have been taking some ferocious criticism, you know, in the press, for bringing the case in the first place, in such a race sensitive town. I love you, he whispered. I don't want to talk about what happened. Crawford, she said, has no recollection of your arranging to meet in The Polar Bear. I can't remember, he repeated. Again he made the mistake of trying to shake his head. Perhaps in a day or two, he promised a police inspector, taking the man's hand in the darkness. His mind was racing. There were trays of medication. My teeth, he protested. Christ!

He asked Hilary to explain about Sarah again. The bandages had been removed now. One eye could see. There was an operation to repair a kidney. Another twenty-four hours blank. Tubes in and out of his body. But he was definitely getting better. He could sit up in bed and swallow some soup. My neck! She says she swallowed the top of one of my perfume bottles by accident, his wife repeated. He could almost savour the pain now. When a wave came he knew it would ebb. Dental work next week, the doctor had said. About six months ago, Hilary went on. And that's why she's been acting so strangely.

Daniel was troubled. He tried to focus. At least, Hilary said, she's admitted that she has been acting strangely. From one eye he could see the concentrated, stern expression of his wife's lips as she pricked her needle back and forth.

She began to tell him about the house. The fireplace was in, the piano was in. Christine had been so sweet. No more problems with money. As soon as the water is turned on, the blokes can come to organise the garden. I don't understand, he said. Did you actually notice a bottle with its top missing? She claims she didn't tell me when it happened because she was afraid I would be angry about her stealing my perfume. She says she threw away the bottle so I wouldn't notice. And that since then she's been feeling weird – actually it *was* about six months ago she started getting strange, wasn't it? Wasn't it then she went evangelical – due to this thing blocked in her stomach. Anyway, I told the people running the school there to have her see a doctor, which she did, and of course he said it was all rubbish. A plastic bottle top would have gone straight out in the faeces. I didn't mention your being in hospital, Hilary said, because I knew that then she would come straight home. You know how she is about you. How, Daniel asked? Protective, Hilary said. She laughed. Haven't you ever noticed? She needs this time away, his wife insisted. It'll do her good.

A television camera was allowed in, briefly. Sitting up, something of the pirate with a patch over one eye, Daniel said he hoped to be back in court as soon as possible. Couple of weeks at most. Judges were overworked enough as it was without people like himself shirking. He smiled painfully. The nurse was furious about the bright lights. Although he declined to comment on the Mishra case, or the riots, or even the assault, nevertheless it seemed he had found exactly the words to gratify the public's interest and reward their unrequested sympathy. His scarred features made all the front pages, arm half lifted in salute. England Needs You, was a tabloid view. Not allowed to watch television as yet, he heard of a possible MBE on the radio. You deserve it, Hilary said.

Got our memory back now, have we? Inspector Mattheson asked. Daniel was profuse in his apologies. He honestly hadn't recognised the man before. Was it you Inspector? I was completely out of it. We felt in the circumstances, the policeman said, that you might like to see someone you knew. He seems friendly, Daniel thought. The officer pulled a seat from against the wall and sat for a few seconds, breathing heavily. I want to go through everything you remember, he announced, for at least three days before the assault, okay. Everything.

Hilary was plumping out the pillows to help her husband sit up properly. You might as well take a break, Daniel told her. She said no. She wanted to listen. Perhaps I can help, she said. They must catch these monsters. A friction of unease passed over Daniel's nerves. I was in court most of the time, he began. He remembered some unsavoury characters in the public gallery. There was one with a Union Jack on his neck. A bull neck. Two young men covered in tattoos. They had descriptions of everyone in court, Mattheson said, and video of the people on the pavement outside. With your mug all over the telly, the policemen went on, all sorts of people came forward. In a way it's been marvellous, Hilary agreed. Daniel shut his good eye and lay back.

Matteson smiled. Relax. He pulled out a handkerchief and clamped his nose. Don't want to sneeze in here, do we? No, what I was saying was that we shouldn't restrict ourselves to the Mishra case and the situation immediately outside court. You give me everything you can remember about those three days, or even anything strange you may have noticed in the weeks before. It was a pretty ordinary month really, Hilary said very quickly, wasn't it Dan? Daniel knew she wouldn't mention the embarrassing letters. Her husband was a hero attacked by racist thugs. Nor the phone-calls. There was no need to mention them. Nobody would start investigating a judge's phone-calls, surely.

We made a few trips out to the house, he said, to see how it was progressing. You know we're buying a new house. We drove over to look at the fireplace, Hilary reminded him. We've had a period fireplace fitted. There's a small factory in the industrial area. East India Street. Dinner afterwards at The Duck, Daniel got in quickly. You know The Duck? Then he confessed, I'm afraid I'm finding this terribly exhausting. I think they must have me on sedatives or something. We've plenty of time, Matteson reassured him. Is there anywhere I can get myself a coffee? He disappeared into the corridor.

Hilary fussed over her husband. Just tell him to go if you've had enough. He grimaced. She put a hand on his forehead. They seem stupid questions to me. It's obvious who did it. I'll manage, Daniel said, but if you want to take time out, do. If there's some shopping or something, he offered again. She wouldn't go. You know, thinking about Sarah, he said. Yes? It just occurred to me she must be wondering why I haven't called her in all this time, especially with her not feeling well. I said you were hellishly busy, Hilary laughed, with one of the judges being ill.

Mattheson came back holding a plastic cup. Daniel smiled wanly. How is it? he asked. They won't let me have coffee yet. The policeman frowned. Could be worse. Or maybe not, he laughed. Well, Hilary said in a louder voice, the evening before it happened, Dan, you went to Martin and Christine's, didn't you? Oh right. Daniel began to explain about the money problem. The inspector nodded. You were there from when till when, he asked? You went out to dinner afterwards with Christine, Hilary said, didn't you? She must show she was privy to her husband's life. At The Raven, Daniel agreed. You know the place? Poor Martin's got some odd nervous illness, Hilary explained. Mattheson said he wondered why he hadn't seen Mr Shields in court for a long time. Such a good lawyer. We left the restaurant about ten-thirty, I suppose, Daniel said. And I imagine, the policeman began, that you drove straight home? Look, Daniel interrupted, you don't think it could be something to do with some defendant I sent down or something. Someone with a grudge?

The policeman sat squarely on his chair. He drained his coffee. I'm ready to consider all sorts of suggestions, he said, but seemed perplexed. Do you have anyone in mind? Hilary remarked: I've already told the inspector about your brother calling the very day of the attack, demanding money. Oh, but that's silly, Daniel protested. He felt relieved. Well, he *did* phone, she said, he was demanding money and he certainly hasn't called since to express his sympathy. Hilary had always been afraid of Frank, the bad apple in her husband's family. He was up on an assault charge once wasn't he? she justified herself. Daniel managed to laugh now: If poor Frank had the cash to pay three people to beat me up, he wouldn't have been asking for money in the first place.

There were three attackers then, the inspector asked, you got a glimpse of them? I was walking across the car park, Daniel said cautiously. Where from? Where had you been in the meantime? Daniel shook his head a fraction, stiffened with pain. Sorry, but I have no recollection. He mustn't move his head. Is there a lot of time to account for? About an hour. It would be so useful for us to know, Mattheson said, for all sorts of reasons. Of course. You said you were going to the Polar Bear with Crawford, Hilary reminded him. She didn't say he'd actually phoned her.

But anyway, there were three attackers, Mattheson repeated. Daniel asked: Wasn't I sighted anywhere? That would help. All I know is, I was crossing the car park. On one of the upper floors. I seem to remember being in the lift. Anyway I have the impression then – I've been over it a hundred times – this impression of being bashed in the back, gripped in a vice and feeling this bag pulled hard over my head, all at the same time. That sounds like at least three people to me. Hilary shook her head. And why do you think they put a bag over you? the policeman wanted to know. Daniel closed his eyes. I have no idea. I feel guilty for being assaulted, he realised. After another ten minutes, the policeman left.

The left eye, the consultant told him, will regain some sight in due time. He could walk up and down the corridor now. Anyway, the right had always been the strong one. Discharge in a week, he was promised. Back to work as soon as strength returns. Meantime, he spoke to other patients. Wonderful girls, someone said of the nurses. They were all black or Asian. He had a television now, and a phone by the bed. His head ached. Justice is not primarily to serve society, but to guarantee dignity to the individual. Across the corridor Father Shilling was dying of lung cancer. There were five beds there. Voice bubbling with catarrh, he quoted St Augustine: When a man doesn't serve God, how much justice can there be in him? Daniel played the elderly priest at chess. A non-believer couldn't be denied a concept of justice, he objected. My mind's beginning to work again, he told himself. It was a relief that Hilary had gone back to her lessons.

Christine came. They've taken about a thousand photos of the inside of my brain, he laughed. I was hoping they might be able to tell me something useful. She glanced round the small room. See what happens, she said coyly, when you kiss a married woman! She has dressed up for the occasion, he saw. Please, he said, I've been talking to a priest all morning. Apparently I can't be a judge if I don't go to confession.

Christine enquired and sympathised. The breasts were very much on show again. But she wasn't happy. Martin, she told him, hadn't moved an inch in all this time. It's as if he were willing himself into a fever. He's always taking his temperature. He has the thermometer in his mouth all day. She laughed nervously. She was wearing high heels in red lacquer. One day he says he's a modern day renouncer, you know those Brahmin blokes who gave up on everything and crept off into the forest to meditate, leaving their womenfolk in the lurch. The next he says he must have some virus or something. Her shoes clicked. It's silly! She began to look around to see where she might put down some flowers. I brought flowers, she said. Men always get fruit, so I bought you flowers. When Daniel enquired, she said that Martin was refusing to see a psychiatrist or have any tests or anything done. Not even their GP. How will he live, she asked rather brightly, if I leave him? She smoothed down her blouse. You won't, Daniel smiled. He'll get over it soon, whatever it is. Going out, she asked: did Hilary tell you that Jane's marrying? A black girl came in with the tea trolley. Daniel watched her impossibly slim wrist as it tensed under the weight of the pot. Yes, he lied.

He watched television. The talk was all of some reservoir that had been polluted. The riots had been forgotten. Three weeks would be a long time to remember an evening of summer madness, a riot, or a kiss. His eye ached. He should have asked Christine about the last house payment, now due. Things go back to normal, he told himself. Knowing Christine couldn't be home yet, he called Martin.

You've survived then, Martin said quietly. If it's really me, Daniel laughed. Then he told his friend he needed help. There was silence at the other end of the line. No, it's not about the house or money, he reassured him. No problem there, Martin said slowly, I've handed over everything to Christine. She's making the payments. But it's not about that. Listen, I need to find someone. Ah, Martin said. He seemed to be fiddling with something, the remote perhaps. Not Jane, I hope? No, of course not. Daniel himself had to keep his eye on the door. Hilary would arrive before too long. Perhaps with Tom. Then Martin said: You do know, Dan, that she's marrying Crawford? Gordon Crawford, Judge Savage's colleague, had been Jane's long-term boyfriend before the affair with Daniel. I don't suppose she ever quite broke off with him, Martin said. Then clearing his throat, his voice oddly matter of fact and mechanical, he began to say that there was a similar situation in *Enemies and Relations*, a South American soap: The lead actress, you see, is having two rather steamy affairs while still proceeding with arrangements to marry her dull doctor fiancé of five years standing. Of course she broke off with him! Daniel interrupted. I should know.

Still holding the receiver, he stood up sharply beside the bed. At once he felt dizzy. He put a hand on the window-frame. You should have heard the kind of things she used to say about him! Again Martin left a short pause before speaking very quietly and calmly: I can't remember you actually covering Hilary with compliments. But you never really broke with her. Did you?

What was it? Daniel knew he had taken another blow, in a part of himself that he hadn't visited for a while. Every time he spoke to Martin he took a blow. Jane was marrying Crawford. What on earth had his colleague and ex-rival thought then, when Hilary asked him if he'd met Daniel in The Polar Bear? Collecting himself, he said: Hilary's been so wonderful these weeks. I can imagine, Martin agreed. There was definitely the sound of the television in the background. No, listen, Mart, the person I need to find isn't someone you know. Again there was a silence. Can I trust you? Daniel asked. His old friend said, Of course. No, I mean, can I trust you not to mention it to anyone, not even Christine. Silent as the grave, Dan, Martin promised. A tomb. The fact is I need, don't ask me why, to find a young Asian girl whose father may have done something awful to her. Police, Martin said abruptly. But, listen . . . Dan, you know that if there's any chance of a crime having been committed, you must go to the police and that's that.

This was good advice. All the same, Daniel felt confused. Seeing the world through one eye is a big strain at first, the consultant had told him. Frustrated, he changed tack. Anyway, how are you, Mart? Fine, his friend said. You're not going back to work? No, I'm not. I'm in bed, I've got the TV on, you know, bit of a temperature still. Always between ninety-nine and a hundred. But I'm perfectly happy.

This whole thing should have happened to him, Daniel

suddenly realised: Minnie, the beating up. It should have happened to Martin. For some reason this appeared to be a useful thought. It clarified things. This insoluble little dilemma – it *was* little – should have happened to someone who had lost interest in life. It would have woken Martin up, obliged him to act, to live, to see he was important in other lives. But not to a man newly in love with hearth and home. Sarah will think I've abandoned her, he realised. I must get Hilary to give me her number.

Lying down again, Judge Savage phoned his brother. I'll give you the two grand if you earn it, he told him. Perhaps the essence of those years of excitement, he reflected, when the call was over, his head on the pillow, was the feeling you always had of putting your life in another's hands. You hadn't wanted to lose anything, your wife, your job, but you needed, for some reason to place your safety and everything precious in another's hands, in the hands of someone you barely knew. That was the essence of the kind of risk-taking he had indulged in. It created a sort of society, a secret below-the-surface intimacy more intense than any afforded by conventional relationships: this person, whom I scarcely know, could ruin my life – that was exciting – but they won't. Do I really know anything about Frank? he wondered vaguely.

Judge Savage? In his sleep he had been searching for a clean lavatory, all blocked and laughter coming from behind every door. Your honour. Judge Savage. He woke to see the CPS woman. What was she called? He couldn't remember. How kind of you to come, he said. He struggled onto his elbows. She had brought peaches and grapes. We were all so upset about what happened, she smiled. I hope you don't mind my visiting.

The woman sat down on the edge of the chair beside the television. I can remember everything it would be more convenient to forget, Daniel thought, but I can't remember her name. Cunningham? Catherine? It all seemed, she was saying, so totally out of proportion to anything at stake in the trial. You know. Why has she come to visit me, he wondered? What do we have to say to each other?

He asked: I gather you returned to the profession quite recently. In particular, it struck him as extraordinary that she had woken him up when he was sleeping. Something like that, she said. Surely the rule is that you let sick people sleep. There was an awkward silence. Sounds mysterious, he tried. He'd got into a sitting position now, in his dressing gown, the pirate patch on his eye. His head came level with hers. Casually dressed in trousers and light sweater, she had shed a certain brittleness that he had sensed in court. The creasing round the eyes, communicated eagerness. Absolutely without make-up, he noticed.

It's not a secret, she laughed. My son had a problem at birth, there was a lack of oxygen to the brain. He's retarded, I suppose you'd have to say. My husband left as a result. Anyway, for a long time I couldn't work because of all the care he needed. Left her *as a result*, Daniel was wondering. For a moment he lost the thread. *As a result?* My mind still isn't quite right. Then she was saying that she felt that as the institution of the family broke up, the law would inevitably be forced to become more active in this area.

How old is the boy, Daniel managed. Steven? Fifteen. She smiled. She was Irish, he remembered. He goes to a special school now, so I was able to start work again. Connaught? Was that it? But we should be talking about you, she suddenly announced. Everybody's eager to have you back. When is it going to be? So then they spoke of work. Court three had been closed for renovation. I think this awful business has given everybody a new sense of how much responsibility we all bear, she said. Crawford was busy with an excruciatingly complicated and quite interminable fraud case. Perhaps she will be a friend, Daniel thought. An ally.

Now that you remind me, he said, I was wondering, just this morning in fact, about the stone throwing business. Is it . . . She hadn't heard anything, she said. Since it wasn't scheduled for some time she couldn't imagine that it would have been allotted to anyone else. Not yet. This news cheered him. Very soon, he would resume his old position. He would be in court again, even better respected than before. Life's other problems would recede into the background.

To go back to the Mishra business, he said generously. To be honest, I can't understand how they arrived at their verdict on abduction. I felt the prosecution had an overwhelming case. They looked at each other. Sometimes I think they just decide on character, you know, she said, not the crime at all. They weigh the accused up and decide, especially where it's the kind of crime they know won't be repeated. He objected: But the Mishras never spoke, never gave the jury a chance to weigh them up. I thought it would work against them. She shook her head. Speaking is more often than not a way of betraying yourself; silent, people seemed dignified, don't you think? They seem focused, above the fray. It was so kind of you to visit, Mrs Connolly, he said. That was her name. Please call me Kathleen, she laughed getting to her feet. Oh, and I'll remember, he found himself saying as she turned a moment from the door, not to give evidence when finally they put me in the dock. Oh, but you could charm the hind leg off a donkey, judge, she smiled. You really could. Daniel felt he was getting better.

TEN

The jury's decision, one of the weeklies had said, seemed less a pondered response to the evidence than a gut reaction against dominant trends. Daniel discussed the press cuttings with Father Shilling. Hilary had brought a pile. It can be interpreted as a last ditch defence, he read aloud from one eye, of what is now the only traditionally hierarchical institution to have survived the pressure of individualism and egalitarianism: the family. Emaciated as he was, Father Shilling insisted on playing chess while they talked. His fits of coughing made it hard to concentrate. And this for the simple reason, Daniel read the conclusion, that the helplessness of the young child obliges society to recognise a state of *natural* subordination that it would not countenance between adult individuals.

Easy to write articles, Daniel put the paper down. Not stupid, though, the priest said. Head sideways on the pillow, the dying man considered the board. When he opened the game in an unusual way, Daniel felt disorientated at first, but always managed to turn things back to something recognisable. The priest had an oddly oblique approach –

pawn-to-queen's-rook-three sort of thing – but the middle game always forced the general engagement. Daniel had done well at school. He counted on winning those complex exchanges where the mind boggles at what might happen when the swapping starts. I can never get my son to play, he remarked regretfully. Kids don't appreciate that to get into a position where you can win, you have to go through a period of losing. In fact, he said, the thing the article doesn't take into account is that children themselves don't accept this state of subordination past about age eight. They want to decide for themselves.

Father Shilling moved very rapidly. The priest lives outside the family, he said, because the Catholic Church knows that it is impossible for one man to embrace every aspect of experience. His voice was bubbling with catarrh. That's what hierarchy means if you follow me. Accepting your own specific area. The right hand or the left. The little finger or the thumb. The Protestant aberration, he claimed, he cleared his throat, was to suppose that men are all equal, not only before God but also here on earth, in every department.

Flat on his back, head twisted to one side to study the board, Father Shilling suddenly became earnest. They imagine that every man, and now every *woman* for heaven's sake, can be sex partner, parent *and* priest. That is an extremely dangerous mistake, don't you think? I wouldn't know, Daniel said. He was vaguely aware that Professor Mukerjee had also spoken about fingers on the hand. It is evident to everyone – the priest cleared his throat again, he had been a heavy smoker – that social order – this according to Aquinas – consists mainly in inequality. But who would ever dare say that today?

Daniel chose not to exploit Father Shilling's own more obvious mistakes. Finding it awkward to reach out an arm

148

while his drip was running, the priest dictated his moves. Are you sure? Daniel asked. His opponent had a tendency to assume that two pieces were both safe when only defended by a single other. His faculties were fading. His skin was grey. But he never seemed unhappy with his game. He accepted defeat graciously.

Were you always quite sure, though – Daniel was dressed today and ready for discharge – that you wanted to be a priest, the celibate life, I mean? He smiled. It was the kind of personal question one felt one could ask a dying man before parting. Actually Daniel was thinking of Martin. The priest had that same mentor's air to him. Wherever I go I seem to find myself a mentor. Father Shilling said nothing, engrossed in working out what he might still do to win their last game. He chuckled: If they cannot contain themselves let them marry, for it is better to marry than to burn. St Paul, he explained. Then coughing fiercely, making yet another unwise move, he said he felt the *New Statesman* piece had been on to something when it claimed that the family was now under house arrest – a nice pun. The more people don't know how to behave, the more the State extends its power. Knight to king's knight five, he said.

Oh I often have no idea at all how to behave, Daniel admitted, making the man's move for him. He could see the end now. Again the priest looked up from the game. Are you sure there isn't something you want to tell me, Daniel, the dying man asked, before you leave? His rheumy eyes were neither inviting nor discouraging. After all, we'll probably never see each other again. It's just I feel there's something you're eager to tell me. I sense it.

No, no, Daniel said. I meant, I don't know how to behave with the children. My daughter, for example, has got herself attached to some sort of evangelical group and is talking about giving her life to Jesus. I don't know whether to try to force her to go to university or let her do what she wants. I suppose it's better than her running off with a married man.

Father Shilling smiled. I preach, or preached, almost every day, he said. A habit, a duty. But if there's one thing I've learned, it's never to give advice. Why so? Shifting the rook, Daniel thought, Got him! You can never know, the priest explained, what sort of equilibrium you might be upsetting, you know? Once, in the confession box, I told a man that he must give up his mistress. He was having an affair with a schoolgirl, for heaven's sake, one of his students. I told him it had to stop. Shortly afterwards, he killed himself. Hardly your fault, Daniel said. The priest looked at the game, looked away. Good-humouredly he said: I think it was because I knew I'd be a terrible father that I became a Father, if you see what I mean. Check, Judge Savage told him.

Uncovering the bishop's attack, a second queen was suddenly assured. Father Shilling resigned. He lay back. Soon all the pieces will be queens, he chuckled. I think that's what your man in the paper is trying to say. There will be no bishops, no rooks, no knights. Above all no pawns to sacrifice. Everybody will be able to move any distance in any direction. A massacre! When Daniel turned, Hilary had appeared at the door. It's been a great pleasure to talk with you, the priest said. He held out his hand.

They went down a service elevator, accompanied by a policeman in plain clothes. You'll get better faster now, Hilary whispered. She's thrilled, Daniel realised. The consultant had insisted on dark glasses. In the gloom of the lift he kissed her cheek. It was the change he had always yearned for in his wife. Dan, she put her arms round him. Then even with the glasses, the light and space of the street was overwhelming. A bus roared. His head spun. An unmarked car was waiting. They told me to leave mine very visible round the front, Hilary laughed.

The car sped through bright streets. Max had done his concert Sunday, she said. He was wonderful. Not a single fudge. In three weeks, Daniel hadn't once thought of the young man. I'm pleased, he said. Hopefully they're going to let him play at the town-hall, next month. He felt frail and inadequate. It's the sudden change of air, he thought. One feels so vulnerable sitting in a moving car. Funny way to go home, he whispered at last. The young policeman was driving rapidly along the ring road. In the mirror Daniel managed to focus on a regular patrol car in close attendance. He had a sudden reaction, a frightening sense of entrapment. Jerking his neck round brought a jab of pain. Where were they taking him? Just wait and see, Hilary said. He turned back and found her prim, petite features lit up in delight. Her eyes shone beneath a fresh perm. The perfume was strong and sweet. My wife! She had his hand in hers, triumphant. We're going home, she said.

The car turned up the steep hill. Another police car was parked outside a fresh brick wall. Tom, Max and Christine came towards them as Daniel rose carefully to his feet and looked along a paved garden path with sieved and seeded soil either side. Dad! Dad! How wonderful, he said, embracing the boy. What a wonderful surprise! It's great, Tom was saying. It's a fantastic place, Dad. Our home, Hilary announced. At last!

Although it was July, a fire was burning. Just for effect, Christine said. A couple of logs. You can burn wood here. The woman was pouring champagne. One glass to welcome you and I'm off. Same here, Max agreed. How are you feeling, Mr Savage? Already Daniel was in an armchair, its blue upholstery new to him. There were flowers everywhere. The room was quivering with colour. If you knew what a help Max has been! Hilary hurried to and fro. I thought blue would be right, don't you think? Then the walls exploded with sound. Tom was playing Get Back. The beautifully reso-nant piano, hugely present in the centre of the room, hadn't changed his gung-ho style. He hammered it out, held the pedal down hard. The new brick strained to contain the noise. Please, Daniel protested. The house would burst. He got to his feet. Tom! One sip of champagne had made him dizzy. A bunch of roses was too pink. Then the sudden silence was equally stunning. I'm still not well, he muttered.

Come in the kitchen, Dad! Come on! The adults laughed at the boy's excitement. Daniel followed him across the ample sitting room, already carpeted, fully furnished, there were even paintings he didn't recognise. You open it, Tom said. Daniel pushed the kitchen door, and at once some wild black thing tore past his legs and chased its tail round and round, yapping furiously. *Out* of my sitting room, Hilary shouted. She was laughing, but serious. Out! Max grabbed the creature and tugged it back. I'm overwhelmed, Daniel said smiling. I can't believe it. He stood at the door to say goodbye to Max and Christine. How elegant she looked! She had a girlish red ribbon in her hair. It's only sad that Sarah couldn't be here. The police car was still at the gate. House arrest, Daniel remembered. Forbidden to drive, he was entirely dependent now.

You've done everything! he told his wife. It's been fantas-tic, she agreed. With what happened to you everyone was so generous. Everything was speeded up so you wouldn't have to come back to a packed-up flat. Look at the flow-ers people have sent. And frankly I had to have something to be busy with when I wasn't in the hospital. I couldn't bear just sitting alone. I've been working like crazy. Look! She had framed her embroidery in a gilt oval behind the piano, a simple lattice and two roses intertwined. How clever. That's us, she smiled. It will always remind me of the hospital. My first embroidery for thirty years. He shook his head. What about the money, he asked. All sorted, she said. Not to worry.

When Tom had been packed off to bed, she played very softly for him. With the windows open to the fields, the air in the house was fragrant. Don't turn the light on, she warned. Only trouble with the country is it's full of flies. She played something soft and slow, music that moved as delicately as the dying light. He came to stand beside her, and as she played, so gently and softly, but not solemn, some slow sonata from memory, they grew intensely conscious of each other, conscious that happiness was within their grasp now, the life they had planned of solid affection surrounded by sensible beauty, the house, the flowers, the paintings, the rich music rolling out into a peaceful countryside. I can't believe it, he whispered, he leaned down and kissed her hair. She broke off. I did it all for you, she said. They were silent, both watching her small square hands on the keyboard as if waiting to see what they might do next. If you have problems, at first, she murmured, getting back into things, I can help. I don't need to teach till September now. I don't need to teach at all, if you don't want. I can drive you around, read your papers for you in the evening. I'm going to do some more embroidery. She looked up. I'm going to relax for you.

Daniel sighed. She struck up something from Chopin. He had always begged his wife to relax. He kept his hand on her neck as she played. How straight and somehow expressive of her whole character, the shoulders were, the back, the erect, controlled posture. Riliry, he whispered. She was lavishing attention on the piece, determined that it seduce both her husband and herself, it must generate an enchantment worthy of their dreams. He had survived. They had survived. The notes lingered in the air. Shadows darkened the new furniture. How far away he was now from that awful moment in the high-rise car park, from the medicated anxieties of the hospital! Only three weeks had been lost. I am neither desperate to drag it out, Father Shilling had said, nor eager to go soon. Did he mean that?

Little trills subsided over the last gentle breathing of the bass, the piece expired on a broken chord. Mmm, Daniel applauded, perfect, he said. Suddenly, he felt completely well. Lightly, he kissed her neck, smelt its lovely perfume. Hilary has such excellent taste in perfume. I should phone Sarah, he announced. Not now, she murmured. Let me play something else. I've thought out a whole concert for you. All your favourites. He looked at his watch. It's an hour later there, isn't it? If I don't phone now, it'll be too late. Oh don't be boring, she told him, why do you always think of Sarah when we're enjoying ourselves?

She began playing again. But the sentiment was coercive now. Daniel felt it. I am being constrained. Yet this was his daughter he wanted to phone. He hadn't called Sarah at all while she was away and soon she would be back. I must call her. He went to sit on the small sofa beneath the window beyond the fire. Then not having thought about it at all till now, he said: Shouldn't her exam results have come through, have you got them?

Abruptly, Hilary stopped. As the sound quickly died, the distant buzz of the television became audible. From upstairs it seemed. She has allowed Tom to have a TV in his room! Hilary walked round the huge piano and came to sit on the edge of the sofa, turned toward him, bowed forward, a little tense. Her hair was neat, her face prettily made up. She took his hands, sought his eyes. Ready for it? she asked.

What?

Three fails, she said.

Daniel stared into the pleasant space around him. A tall vase crammed with flowers stood on the table. Through the open window, presumably from the estate at the bottom of the hill, came the very distant jangle of a late ice-cream van. He sighed.

The examination board got in touch with me before the results were announced, Hilary said. It seems she covered all three papers with obscenities and Biblical verses. But Hilary, why didn't you . . . I could hardly tell you the moment you came out of a coma, she said, could I? Or between one operation and another? You should have, Daniel said. He pushed her hands away, got to his feet, looked about the room. This was awful. In extreme agitation, Hilary wailed: I thought you were going to die, Dan! I was terrified. When the school called, I hardly registered what they were telling me. I was thinking of you!

I must call my daughter, he thought. Have you spoken to her? What did she say? Why did she do it? Get me the phone number. He couldn't see the phone in the room. Where's the phone?

Dan, for God's sake, sit down. Let me . . . He had started to sit, he felt suddenly dizzy, then found himself on his feet shouting, But how could you? How could you arrange all this, this – he gestured to the flowers, the piano – and imagine I was going to have a happy evening, with such miserable news waiting for me? He was beside himself. His patched eye throbbed. It's grotesque. Grotesque. After a year's peace they were shouting again. He heard her voice raised over his: I don't see why we should ruin our lives just because she wants to ruin hers. She's your bloody daughter, he was protesting. He was exhausted. Three fails! Alarms pulsed round his gums and teeth. Where's the phone? he demanded. Tight-lipped, she said they hadn't connected any of the houses yet. She had a mobile. She kept forgetting to charge it.

Can I call Italy from a mobile? Give it to me. Dan, Dan, she said, Dan, listen, Sarah's not in Italy. He stared at her. Where is she? Hilary didn't reply. She was shaking her head quite theatrically. He kicked out at her sofa. He could see at once that she cared for the thing. And immediately it was like old times. His body stiffened with the shock of the blow. Where is she? Why wasn't I told? Somehow Hilary was standing by the French window looking out across the raw slope of the garden. It hardly makes sense, she said, to have the poor policeman hear us yelling at each other, does it. The policeman? I don't give a toss about the policeman! It's my daughter I'm . . . Well, what about Tom, she spun round. Tom? He was confused. What *about* Tom? You come back and the first thing the boy has to hear is that you're shouting at me. Tell me where Sarah is, he demanded.

Calm down and I'll tell you. She tried smiling now. I just hoped it might wait for tomorrow. I wanted to give you a nice homecoming, time to get your strength up. Tell me, damn it! Then he spied the drinks cabinet. It was an elaborate thing in some dark satiny wood with a frosted glass door. Hilary has been spending money. You're not supposed to drink, she said. For Christ's sake, tell me! He poured from a bottle, barely registering how unsteady his hand was. The stuff splashed onto the carpet. *Her* carpet, he thought. Dan! Tell me! He was ready to kick again. I've lost control, he realised. But the thought was a relief too. This argument is a relief. Already he felt better, even exhilarated.

Last Tuesday, she said. She was very tense. Yes? Making a huge attempt to calm himself he sat down abruptly sending another splash of whisky onto the upholstery. He poured the whole glass down his throat. Please Dan! The effect was an instant flooding and blurring. His hand came up rapidly to his head. He covered his eyes. Just tell me everything. Quickly.

On Tuesday, she repeated. She also sat down. Daniel waited. She just suddenly appeared. Let me think. Everything had already been moved in here, or almost, I had . . . Where is she? No, listen, please Dan, you won't understand if you don't know what the situation was. I had some people shifting the last stuff from Carlton Street in time to be ready for today. Also it seems Christine is eager to get some of their stuff in there as soon as possible, but that's another story, I don't know what's going on with them. Daniel was suddenly struck by the cautious tone in his wife's voice, her roundabout way of telling. She is looking for mitigating circumstances, he thought. At once he was doubly hostile, but at the same time more attentive.

I was about to close up Carlton Street, she was saying, I was planning on sleeping here for the first time – and there was a phone call. From the transport police. She'd arrived at Dover, on the train. She'd travelled all the way without paying. All the way from Italy? From Perugia. They said they'd put her on the train up here but only on the understanding that we picked her up at the station and paid the whole fare, from Italy, when we got her. She'd told them she was sick and the whole story about the bottle-top again. She needed to see a doctor. She hadn't eaten for forty-eight hours, because of this obstruction, all kinds of things.

But that was three days ago. Where is she now? Wait,

Hilary said, more firmly. So I went . . . Why don't you give a damn about Sarah? he demanded. Daniel, please. How could you sit at the piano and tell me not to be boring when we have a major crisis on our hands? Dan, if you hear me out perhaps you'll understand. Again they were staring at each other with intense hostility. So I picked her up at the station, Hilary said, and paid her fare, plus a considerable fine. Obviously they'd made trouble for her at passport control, with her not being white as well, not having paid and not saying she was a judge's daughter.

Where is she?

Hilary drew a short breath. Since Carlton Street was empty I brought her here, obviously. Well, she threw the most amazing scene. Hilary is making a show of speaking very evenly and sensibly, he saw, as if to emphasise that my anger is childish. And of course Max was practising here, he said.

Hilary looked up. As a matter of fact, he was. She frowned. He was having some trouble with his mother's piano, no, I think she had guests or something, and of course it was the day of the concert. That evening. I told him he could use the Steinway since it had just been tuned. Anyway, Sarah threw this quite incredible fit, said she would never never live here in this house and ran off. What do you mean, ran off? She walked out. But walked out where? Where did she go? I followed her in the car. With Max too. He was so kind, poor boy. He didn't know what to say. She said she was going to her Community. I gave her the keys to Carlton Street just in case and fifty pounds.

But she was ill, this thing she's swallowed.

When I asked her about that, she just looked sheepish, like they used to when you caught them fibbing. You know? She wouldn't talk about it. She's never mentioned it to me herself, I only get the story from others. She knows I'm not so gullible. Of course, I offered to take her to the hospital, to a doctor. She wouldn't answer, and she wouldn't get in the car. She said she would never get in a car with me again, and so on. Poor Max did his best too. She spat at him.

Daniel smiled. Spat?

Yes, in his face.

And then?

I waited a couple of hours, then phoned the Community. I thought it wouldn't be the end of the world if she stayed there a while. I know the vicar at St Mark's has dealings with them. Christine says she knows someone whose daughter's there. You know Christine goes to church. It took ages to find the number. Then she wasn't there. I finally got her at Carlton Street. She said she was going to stay there on her own and hung up.

And you didn't go and get her? he asked. Dan, she's 18, she's an adult! She's not an adult, he shouted. She's a mess! Why did she come back from Italy, why didn't she wait for the flight? It was only a few days off. Hilary repeated: As I said, she wouldn't tell me. She went completely hysterical when I brought her here instead of Carlton Street. Hilary sighed. She found her husband's one seeing eye. Dan, I don't think you can begin to imagine what she was like.

I'm going to get her, Daniel said. He got to his feet. The blood rushed to his head.

That's what she wants, Hilary said.

Well then let's do it! Let's do what she wants. Why shouldn't we? We can't leave her in an empty flat.

The old fridge is still there. And there are chairs and things.

That's not the point.

I told her she'd have to be out of there by Monday because we're supposed to exchange contracts at which point

159

Christine is eager to have possession. And then we've *got* to exchange contracts because if not we can hardly expect the rest of the cash.

You'll have to drive me there. Daniel was swaying on his feet. Hilary sat still. She was curved forward on the armchair, her hands pressed tight together, eyes half closed. Her body swayed slightly back and forward. I told her you were away till next week, she said. You're not well, Dan.

You didn't even say I was in hospital?

No.

But why on earth not? Somebody else will tell her. Hilary! Hilary! he sat down again. He must try to be understanding. I don't know who's crazier, you or her.

She's hostile, Hilary said abruptly. She looked up now from joined hands. Can't you see that? She's determined to be a spoke in our wheels.

I can't believe I'm hearing this, Daniel said. So you didn't tell her I was in hospital? Hilary started to speak, but he wouldn't listen. This is too much, he announced. Uncertainly, he started for the door. There was still a curious novelty about every move he made, his one eye guiding him across the now dark room. Embers from the fire made the space cavernous. She wants to break us up, Hilary said. Daniel was furious. How ridiculous, he said. He rounded on her. It gave him strength. You're mad. You should see a psychiatrist. Something must have happened to her that we don't know about. Like what? Hilary demanded. Come on, tell me what! She stopped. Dan, this whole thing's changed you. You're not thinking straight. Let's talk about it for a bit, ten minutes won't make much difference, will it, then I'll take you over there if you want.

He had steadied himself against the door. Our daughter is having some kind of major crisis, he told her, this is the age when teenagers have crises, and you planned to sit there playing the piano. My husband, she retorted, has just come out of hospital after a violent assault, coma and all kinds of surgery. I was eager to protect him from a spoilt kid who's always played her father's generosity and general guilt in her regard for all it's worth. I'll get the policeman to take me, Daniel announced. He went through the porch. It stinks of fresh paint, he thought. Now he was out on the garden path.

Daniel! He had reached the gate. He didn't turn. Obscurely, he sensed that this anger towards his wife would be useful somehow. Dan, she cried, this is stupid! You're not well. He would go straight to Mattheson perhaps, as Martin had advised. Who cares if Hilary finds out?

Dan! She called in a low shout across the seeded earth, fresh and damp in warm July. Dan, come here. When he stopped her voice dropped further. Dan, how do you think I found out about you? I mean you and Jane? Why do you think I wouldn't tell you? He turned and stared at her. Now he climbed back to the doorway. What was that? He stepped inside. What did you say? She looked pale and brittle. The petite, permed radiance was gone. His wife was shaking. What do you mean?

But Hilary had caught a glimpse of Tom there on the stairs, behind the piano. Go to your room, Tom, she called. She pulled herself together, false and jovial. We've seen you there, Tommie. Go to bed! Dad, he said, are you all right? Go to your room! No, the boy said. The quick brown face was peeping over the banister at his father. The boy has never seen me like this, Daniel realised: dark glasses, stumbling gait. Despite his confusion, Judge Savage managed a reassuring smile. Go to your room, Tom. Or do I have to kill you? The boy laughed and scampered off. Oh, and you'd better enjoy that TV while it lasts, Daniel shouted. Rascal. Tomorrow it'll be coming out of there.

The couple looked at each other. He knew his wife appreciated his authority with the children. It was Sarah told me, Hilary said. Again Daniel was sitting down. Sarah told me, not me her. And she made me promise not to tell you. Why else do you think I wouldn't have? Why would I have hidden it? Actually, I thought you'd guessed. How else could I have known it was her writing those silly letters to you? She was very upset. She said, as soon as Dad leaves chambers he always goes to see that woman he works with at her flat. Everybody knows, she said. An edge crept into Hilary's voice. And she was right. Everybody knew except me. Christine said she'd known for ages.

Shit. Daniel had his head in his hands. Then Tuesday, Hilary, went on, when she threw that fit – she was banging her head on the wall, in front of Max – she began to say all kinds of wild things. That I was stupid to stay with you because you had lots of women, not just one. She said she'd only told me about just the one because she thought it would be enough to wake me up, but apparently it wasn't. She said you were having women all the time. She said – Daniel kept his face in his hands – where did I think you were when you always got back late from everywhere you went and people always phoned imagining you'd be back already. To whores, she said. Hilary's voice had become dull and flat. She said that's why you'd gone away for the week no doubt – because I'd told her you were away on a different circuit – to see prostitutes. Like I said, Max was here. She said it was a farce our staying together, our buying a new house as if we were in love, and she would never live in it, she would never live with two such sick people again. She kept banging her fists on the wall saying we were sick.

She would never sleep even a night in this house, it was a false house, unless you left for good and stopped pretending to be different from what you were. She said that watching you in court she'd felt ashamed and that I should divorce you at once and marry again. There was a pause at last. Daniel looked up. A moth fluttered at the porch door where a naked bulb had been switched on. He met his wife's eyes. She said – can you believe it – she said – there was almost a moment of hysteria in Hilary's voice, that she was glad I had Max. That I should marry Max because he was nice.

We'd better go and get her, Daniel said.

ELEVEN

If I had always had Hilary to drive me around, it passed through his mind, perhaps I would never have become adulterous. There would have been no opportunity. I'll call Mattheson tomorrow, he decided. I'll explain exactly what happened. Perhaps a whole life could hang on something as simple as a driving licence. At a traffic light, he glimpsed a tear shining on Hilary's cheek. Hilary, he said. You didn't believe any of that rubbish she came out with, I hope. His wife shook her head. She drove. Daniel felt enormously agitated. And ashamed. No, I'm calm really, he thought. And I don't feel guilty. Or I'm beyond knowing. Then he changed his mind. I must sit tight and save everything. My marriage. My daughter, my job. An enormous effort of will. There is nothing incompatible about having all these things.

On the ring road his one strained eye caught a dark glimpse of two girls giggling by the bushes. Three fails, he thought. Why had the child blown her chances so stupidly? If she wanted to protest, why not to his face? I'll go back to court Monday, he suddenly said. Just to see how it feels, sitting at my desk, looking through a few papers. Perhaps there would be a note from Minnie. The girl was fine after all. What do you think?

There's no hurry, Hilary replied. Her voice was a whisper. But if you want to. She was holding back sobs. First I hurt her, he thought, then I'm overwhelmed with tenderness. No, but it was Sarah had hurt her. Not me. It's complete rubbish, what Sarah told you, he said. I don't know why she would make up such stuff. Hilary shook her head and this time kept shaking it from side to side. That was a lovely evening you planned, Daniel told her. If I believed the half of it, his wife finally whispered, I'd have told you to fuck off and leave me alone forever. Daniel sat still, watching the familiar streets slide by from this unfamiliar seat. I hate being driven, he thought. His headache was fierce.

Go on, she told him. The car had stopped in Carlton Street. She put the keys in his hand. We should go together, he said. No, she wants you not me. But didn't she say she wouldn't live in the new house unless I left? She wants you, Hilary repeated. I know her. He said: Listen, even if she does want just me, shouldn't we go up together to show we're united. Hilary stared through the windscreen down the street. In the end it was an attractive street in a nice part of town. Carlton Mansions was a pleasant building. What delicate equilibrium had been upset by moving away from here? If we were united, Hilary muttered, we wouldn't be here at all. Daniel bunched the keys in his fist and swung a stiff leg out onto the pavement.

Oh, Mr Savage! The lift door opened on their erstwhile upstairs neighbours, the Fords. How wonderful to have you back! His dark glasses and impaired vision in the dim hall light only just allowed him to see how flustered the two elderly ladies were. So brave of you, how awful, are you well now, we prayed for you, Mr Savage, we're so proud of you, have they caught them? Daniel tried to smile. Pushed for time, he apologised. The ancient sisters were used to being dismissed. Of course, of course. At every meeting, he realised, I will be inappropriately praised. The lift doors closed. Alone in the small humming space he was assailed by a shiver of vulnerability. Take a deep breath. Crossing the corridor, he slipped a key into the familiar lock.

Sarah! How strange to see the place so empty! He walked across the sitting room. His voice echoed. Then Daniel was shocked. She was sitting on their old mattress in their old bedroom. Why hadn't Hilary told him? Hilary misses out the most obvious details, he thought. There was no bed. It was the room they had slept in for years. Back to the wall, cross-legged on the mattress, Sarah was frighteningly gaunt. Her cheeks are hollow. Dad! The young woman jumped to her feet, Dad, what's with the shades? Oh Dad! She threw her arms round him. I had an accident, he said. Nothing to worry about.

They hugged. Her body is all bones, he thought. But immediately she asked, Have you brought any food? I'm starving. He released her. Let's drive over to the new house, he said, and cook something up. Promptly she sat down on the mattress. I'm staying here. This is my home. I want to eat my food here. So why haven't you? There isn't anything, she said. Your mother gave you fifty pounds, didn't she? Sarah said nothing, a sudden vagueness seemed to come over her. Don't ask her about the exams, Daniel told himself.

We could go to a restaurant, he suggested. Okay! She jumped to her feet with that lightness that had always delighted him about her, about young women in general. Certainly she seemed to have plenty of energy. Okay! On the landing he said: Mum's waiting in the car. Great, she smiled. He was relieved. Had it not been for the bags under the eyes, he would have called it a seductive smile. Mum told me, by the way, about what happened when she picked you up from the station, he said. Again the girl looked sheepish. And everything you said to her. They were in the lift, but she contrived to look at the door; she was watching the landings pass by through the tiny grill. Daniel didn't know how to go on. I must put my fate in Mattheson's hands, he thought. Or perhaps Frank would find the girl with no trouble.

In the street, he was careful to open the back door for Sarah, then took the front seat beside his wife. They must stress their unity. To the Kossuth, he announced brightly. The girl must eat. What if you're recognised, Hilary asked. Does it matter? We don't want to be mobbed, Dan. He said nothing. You don't know what it's been like, she insisted, outside the hospital, with the press and everything. Now she's inviting the girl, Daniel realised, to find out what she wouldn't tell her before. If Sarah had known he was in hospital she would never have imagined he might be with another woman.

Why aren't you driving, Dad? his daughter asked. Your father's become a hero in your absence, Hilary tossed over her shoulder. Perhaps I should have told you. I was rather badly beaten up, Daniel said. After the Mishra trial. Right after you left. I've got a problem with an eye. Who did it? Sarah asked. I've no idea. I didn't see them. But where were you? In the high-rise car park, he said. Queen Street. They think it must have been some racist group after those Indians were acquitted, Hilary explained. They were cleared? Yes. Apparently some people blamed my summing up. Of abduction too? How marvellous! Why? he wondered. Why was his daughter pleased that the Mishras had been allowed to abduct their sick child? Now dead. Just temporarily, I'm blind in one eye, he told her. Your father should really be in bed, Hilary remarked. I'm so pleased they got off, Sarah said. She leaned over to the front seat and pressed her cheek against her father's. Poor Dad! You were so clever when you spoke to the jury like that. So convincing!

In the restaurant the young woman ate voraciously while her parents watched. She didn't seem unhappy with the situation. She spoke enthusiastically about Italy. Thanks for letting me go! She had enjoyed herself immensely. It was amazing what the Etruscans had done under the city. There was something slightly dazzled and false about her, Daniel noticed. Something hurried. And almost no reaction to his having been hurt. There are these huge caverns, Mum, they tunnelled down to, an incredibly complicated system of water distribution. Latin turned out to be quite a help.

Eventually, while her head was down over her dessert, Daniel began, Sarah love, Sarah, I'm not going to be angry, really I'm not, but you must realise that we've got to talk about a few things. She ate on. You've failed your exams, he said. He stopped. Talk away, she said without looking up. You didn't even try to pass them, it seems, Sarah, love. Hilary is watching, it suddenly occurred to Daniel. He remembered Kathleen Connolly's eyes at the Mishra trial. To check that everything was being done properly. Then you came back, he told the girl, completely unexpectedly from Italy. And however much you say you enjoyed it, you weren't eating much, were you? And you baled out early. Now your mother tells me you don't want to live with us in the new house. Naturally we wondered – when he paused, she just kept on eating – if anything particular had happened that might explain all this, and also, he went on quickly – also, we need to know what you plan to do next and above all, I suppose, where you're intending to live.

The girl glanced up from ice-cream. No need to be so bloody solemn, Dad. She ducked down again. Are you going to answer? Hilary demanded. Her mouth full, the girl said: I would have done the exams properly if he hadn't slapped me in the face. Rubbish, Hilary snapped. I'm sure your father did no such thing. Ask him, Sarah said, still without lifting her eyes. Let's talk about things one by one, Daniel tried. Leaving your education aside, what we . . . Yes, your honour? Suddenly she looked up so perkily, with such an air of mischief and fun that Daniel couldn't help but smile. It was like when they all played cards together in the evenings on holiday. He was disarmed. Hilary was furious. Treat your father with some bloody respect and answer his questions! *Jawohl*, Sarah replied. Leaving your education aside, he began again – the fact that he had previously lost his temper with his wife somehow saved him from the need to lose it now with his daughter. But what had he meant to say? Leaving aside the question of my education . . . Sarah was on the edge of giggles, Hilary livid. Where do you plan to live? he finished.

At home, she replied.

Excellent.

In Carlton Street.

But I told you, Hilary jumped in, that you had to be out of there by Monday. And there's no furniture. You see what I mean, she turned to Daniel. She's completely unreasonable. The flat has been sold, Daniel told his daughter firmly. Okay? Monday you have to be out. You have no legal right to stay. They were late with their part of the bargain earlier on, Sarah said evenly, so why shouldn't we be late now with ours. They haven't paid all the money yet, he explained patiently. We need the money to reduce our loans, and they won't pay till we give them possession. Aren't they old friends? Nobody is friends when it comes to a hundred thousand pounds, Hilary cut in. But her daughter's eyes seemed to be concentrated on a group at another table. She said quietly: That is my home, that's where I've been brought up and have always lived. I'm staying there. You're not moving me, and if you try I'll walk out and you'll never see me again.

She turned her attention to her dessert. The sound of the spoon scraping the bowl seemed unnaturally loud. Daniel stared at her. The waiter came, hovered, departed. Hilary looked ferocious. It was getting late. As the seconds passed the contrast between the apparent cosiness of this small Hungarian restaurant and the impasse in which they found themselves could not have been more complete.

Then Hilary was on her feet. I'm putting up with no more of this! She stood and walked to the till to pay. The waiter moved promptly across the small room to meet her. Sarah smiled indulgently at her father. Can I see what it's like under your glasses, she asked. Just a patch, he said, removing them. You poor thing. She raised a finger and gently touched his brow.

Getting out of the car at Carlton Street, Sarah turned and knocked on the window: Oh sorry, I forgot to say, there was a phone call from Uncle Frank. At the flat. Thanks, Daniel said quickly. But she insisted on saying more: He said to be in touch at once because he has earned his money. Fine, good. He was already buzzing up the window. How are you feeling, Hilary asked, a few moments later. She was driving quickly through deserted streets. Shattered, he told her. Why doesn't she enquire about that message? Daniel wondered. She must have heard. Home and bed, his wife smiled. She said, I can't wait for a real cuddle. Up on the hill, the young policeman was playing Tomb Raider with Tom.

TWELVE

That Colonel and Mrs Savage had made a calamitous mistake adopting him, Daniel had appreciated – fully appreciated – only in his mid teens. Their radical side-taking over Frank's expulsion suddenly made him aware, in an adult way, of what he had always known intuitively: I am my dear father's revenge for the love Mother lavishes on Frank.

But why should he remember this now, Sunday morning very early pottering around his new house? This is not at all analogous, Daniel told himself – there were so many chores to be done – to our relationship with our own children, or their relationship with each other. Light fittings to be bought, wall cupboards to put in. It's quite different, he thought. A new house, a new family, is a completely different world. He felt decidedly better this morning. A little safer. It's a miracle, he decided. He touched the fresh wallpaper. He had slept well, woken early. Don't worry, he had promised his wife as they embraced before sleeping, she'll come round. Now he stood in the kitchen sizing up the new fridge, the new oven, new sink, all perfectly fitting in a domestic dazzle of polish and lacquer. The little dog snapped at his feet. Pushing back the curtain – she had even managed to get curtains made – he saw there was a TV van outside.

Rather talk to you in person, squire, than on the phone, Frank told him in a low voice. Daniel spent the morning getting to know the house and playing with Tom. With the help of the police a bargain was struck whereby three cameramen were allowed into the front room for exactly ten minutes. The sunglasses are no good, they complained. We need the patch. Hilary was angry. Blacks in sunglasses make them think of pimps, Daniel whispered. He smiled. He was good-natured. Best-Bred Bloke in Britain, the *Mail* would say. For two minutes he let them film him sitting over a fake game of chess with Tom, patting the dog – what's he called again? – then standing at the French windows with Hilary. Wolf, she whispered. It was a warm day. We don't want the general public to identify the house, the policeman insisted. Wolfie! Hilary called. Everybody loves a dog, the cameramen agreed. Afterwards Tom wanted to play something together on the computer, but Daniel said his eye ached. The TV comes out of your room, he insisted. Your father's right, Hilary said. She was breaking up cardboard boxes. Then when she drove the boy off to his football, Daniel at last had the privacy to make his phone calls. A mobile of his own would be essential.

Frank said he had earned his keep, as it were, but they must talk face to face. Fucked if I tell you over the phone then don't see the cash for weeks. How had his brother come to speak like this? It wasn't so much a working class accent he'd adopted as that of the society card, the racecourse tipster. I'll see what I can do. Good on you, squire. Agitated, Daniel remembered he must wipe the number off the gadget's memory. He wrote down Frank's address. More and more police reports spoke of mobile phone memories.

He called the Shields. Christine answered. She wanted to move into Carlton Street *immediately*. Despite the sophisticated voice, her anxiety was unmistakable. The exchange of contracts was at five tomorrow. He's doing it *in order* to push me out, she said. I can feel it. He refuses to talk at all now. So if that's what he wants, I'll go. I can't fight it any more. I can't bear it. He lies in his room, doesn't eat, doesn't talk. It's been going on for months. For months! I don't know what to say, Daniel told her. Her voice was so present to him he felt he was seeing her there in her panelled hallway, trembling, hugging her breasts tight. Then for some reason, the cab company wouldn't answer. He could get to Frank's and back, he thought, having looked up the address, before Hilary reappeared with Tom. It shouldn't be difficult. If only he could call a cab. But now they put him on hold for an age. The line broke up.

Daniel found a light jacket and stumbled out of the house. If it's okay with you, I'm going to take a stroll, he told the policeman. Doesn't look like there's anyone to bother you, the young man said. He was listening to the test match. In fact if no one else bothers you today, I think they'll be telling us to leave you to it, sir, as of Monday. They've overestimated the problem, I suspect. Fine by me, Daniel told him. How's the match going? How do you expect it to go, the policeman grinned. It was Pakistan. You teach people a game and they beat you at it. With respect, he suddenly said. Daniel laughed.

The mobile in his pocket, he set off along a track that cut directly down to the estate and the main road. There might be cabs on the move, or he could call again from the roundabout. The track was rutted. Or from the pub that they had drunk in the day they decided to buy the place. A cat brushed his legs. He looked down in pleasure, but

173

already the creature was gone. This is a lovely place to live, he thought.

For about three hundred yards he walked steeply down beside a field. The air was soft and full of scents. Something moved rapidly in the hedgerow. He turned. A twinge in his right side only reminded him how fit he was after all. These were just muscle pains. He was stiff. A month in bed was a month in bed. He had got better. I feel okay, he realised. Rested. Bar the eye. It was strange his attackers hadn't actually broken a bone. The attack was to keep him away from Minnie. Just a warning. Perhaps they'd hurt him more than they meant to. I've earned my keep, Frank had said. Frank had found Minnie's whereabouts. He was going to see Frank again.

Judge Savage quickened his step. Did I actually do anything wrong, he wondered, in the business of Frank's disgrace? He kicked a stone. He had never told on his brother. But Martin had seen what was happening. Mother's accusation was that had he told her first, she could have nipped the situation in the bud. She could have saved Frank. He doesn't need saving, Father shouted, he needs whipping! How different would it be, Daniel felt, to know that a father really was your father when you called him that? Perhaps not at all. He had definitely felt more attached to Colonel Savage afterwards. Whereas Mother had been less and less his mother, more and more the woman who had made a mistake adopting him. That was really the moment when a bud might have been nipped. Six thousand miles away, in 1955, or perhaps '54, a woman's womb had expelled him into the world. No certain birthday. No star sign, he would joke with earnest women at parties. With me anything can happen. It was a good line. The women liked to guess. The preponderance was for Aquarius. And fifteen years later, he reflected, Frank

Savage had been expelled from Rugby. The most unexpected things connect.

They look like claw scars, Hilary said in wonderment the first time she saw. She kissed them. Did she love him partly because of those? Some sort of stigmata. Daniel swore to the headmaster it was just a dare. I agreed to it. But it wasn't true. The pain was excruciating. You were always looking for some way of pleasing Frank, he told himself. Pleasing and appeasing Frank. At least we'll be blood brothers, he gasped. Frank was grim. On the adoption certificate, they had fixed his birthday on the same day as Frank's, So that you can celebrate together, Mother said. It was a mistake. And suddenly Frank was blown away, expelled, gone. The Savages were irrevocably split. Martin Shields had lifted the back of his younger friend's jacket – why? – to find his shirt soaked in blood. You're my real son, the colonel told Daniel. And years later, after Frank's dishonourable discharge, the colonel said, You are my *only* son.

At the bottom of the hill, the older housing estate was mainly Indian with a few white winos where the round-about met the dual carriageway into town. A big black girl was cleaning dog-shit from her rollerblades. The afternoon was warm. Wondering if a taxi might materialise, it occurred to Daniel that he might even walk it. It was only a mile or so to the address he'd been given. He need spend no more than five minutes with the man. They had nothing to talk about. Perhaps I can walk it, I seem to be okay, then call a cab from there and be home more or less at the same time as Hilary. She would never know he'd been out.

He called the Shields again. It was the first time he had spoken on a mobile while walking along the street. He had always resisted the things. There was the gypsy camp to his left, kids burning rubbish, to the right some industrial buildings in disuse. Edwardian. His mother perhaps, his natural mother, was herself the product of some weird cosmopolitan mix, some nameless place where country and city met in a clutter of wasteland and fast roads. Thank God we managed to buy, he congratulated himself, just that stone's throw beyond the urban mess. This is where the town stops, the estate agent had promised. That side chaos, this side peace.

Hello? It was Christine's voice again. Doesn't Martin ever answer? he asked. A black plastic bag caught at his foot. Sorry I exist, she laughed. He kicked it off. No, I told you, he won't speak at all now. He has to think apparently. He says he has to think. A heavy truck passed. Greek plates, Daniel noticed. Listen, he said, about the flat. He told her about Sarah. Hadn't Martin been defending a foreign truck driver when he had his terrible revelation? The signal faltered. We are all carbon. It's embarrassing, I know, he said. But look, don't worry, she will get out I'm sure, I just wondered if maybe you would talk to her. It might make it easier if she realises she's bothering someone outside the family, her godmother no less. Probably she's quite reasonable with everyone but us. Christine said yes. She didn't seem perturbed by this new problem. Rather the opposite. Pleased to be distracted, perhaps. I'll do that right now, she said brightly. What did Christine do all day, on her own with Martin? You didn't get the police contacting you at all, he enquired, after what happened to me? No. Should we have? she asked.

Then Daniel panicked. He had just entered a street of sixties maisonettes; FREE HONDURAS someone had sprayed over a road sign. It wasn't that he was lost. The cooling tower was his landmark. I've always had an excellent sense of direction. But suddenly he felt a violent urge to run, and at the same time the impossibility of doing so. His breath wouldn't come. I'm sinking. He had to press his back to a wall. If the half of it was true I would tell you to fuck off at once. Hilary had never spoken like that. She didn't use the word 'fuck'. He looked at the phone. That's my word. I'm ill, he thought. Could he call the police? His hand was shaking. He called the cab company again. Two girls were in a tiny garden with tennis rackets. Not ten feet away. What's the name of this street, please? His voice wavered. Balaclava, they spoke with Scottish accents. Everybody has sports equipment, he thought. Balaclava? They're all battles, she explained. The one on the right's Ypres. Don't know how you pronounce it, the other giggled. Amazingly a polished voice came on the line. Someone called him sir. Corner of Balaclava and Ypres, Daniel said.

Waiting, he was afraid the girls would think he was ogling them. He forced himself to walk back and forth. They weren't attractive. The sudden thought that the situation was comic increased his anxiety. You all right? the taller girl called. Fine. He had his back against the wall again, eye closed. Are you sure? The panic welled when he heard her laughter.

As soon as he was in the cab, he felt better. He breathed. This is to be expected after all, he realised, when a man's been beaten within an inch of his life. A life event of this nature, the consultant had said, can have traumatising consequences. He had read out such reports in court. A life event. Apparently things sprung up on you when you least expected. The loss of peripheral vision consequent on using an eye patch – he had listened to doctors giving evidence – can generate a sense of insecurity. How reassuring everything was when explained in court. I can't make it, Frank, he said on the phone. I'm not up to it. Not well. Chambers Hall Sports Centre, he told the driver. Feeling awful actually. I'm not supposed to drive for at least a week or two and Hilary's busy with Tom. Why don't you come to court tomorrow morning? I'm going to get her to take me to the court to look through a few papers. Frank snorted. You can bloody well come here, Danny boy, if you want to find out about your little Korean wench. Daniel closed his eyes.

Summer meant six-aside. They played on a special pitch of synthetic turf. Max was there! Daniel stopped. But then so too was Crosby's mother, Rosalind, and a tall older man he recognised, parent of some school friend. They were all together on the low stand that rose to one side of the pitch. In the open field beyond, a cricket game was in full swing. How desirable it all is! How good to see such a mixed group of kids. A thin cloud moved across the sun. There must have been half a dozen teams shouting among themselves. The scores were chalked on a blackboard. The light was beautifully diffuse. But how was it that his wife had this companion, this young man who sat in an office all day and played the piano so wonderfully and may or may not have been interested in their daughter. Dad! Tom ran across to him. What are *you* doing here? He pushed through a knot of boys and parents. Dad, we're playing next, come on! He was dragging his father past a tea stall.

But it's Daniel Savage! My good man! A group of people were around him. Marvellous to see you. Feared the worst. I took a cab, he told Hilary, felt better, wanted to be with you. She gripped his arm, delighted. Have they caught the bastards? someone was asking. Oh watch the game, Daniel told them. Don't remind me. But people needed to congratulate him, to shake hands. It made them part of a larger world. He'd met them before at parents' evenings, church concerts, other sports events, or perhaps he hadn't met them at all. An honour sir, one younger man said. A real honour. For heaven's sake, Daniel protested, watch the game. Are you all right? Hilary whispered. You should have stayed in. Fine, he smiled, what a lovely afternoon!

I am granting myself a reprieve, he observed, smiling, shaking hands. He'd earned it, he thought. Panic earns reprieve, he noted. Perhaps he should see a shrink, not Frank at all, never mind Mattheson. Tom's team went back on. Semi-final. The synthetic surface was marked in white for tennis, in yellow for football, in blue for volleyball. It didn't appear to be a problem. Hilary had urged him to see a shrink when he went to the Cambridge Hotel. You may not realise it, she said, but you actually force me to be bossy, do you know that? You force me to be unpleasant, then say you have to leave me to be free. Where's the sense in that? The whistle blew. The boys rushed and yelled. Tom was the team's Brazilian, their genius playmaker. Being black can confer that status. The boy ran rings round the others on the fake turf. Sarah had never been good at sport. Pass! Hilary screamed, pass! He never passes! she complained. I hope you don't mind my coming along, Max asked politely. Tom's been begging me. He begs everybody, Daniel laughed, the little beggar. Then hogs the ball.

They stood together at the rail. When Judge Savage cheered, his sightless eye throbbed. If he closed the good eye he found himself in a bright light, but as it were beset by darkness. A bright darkness. They all cheered. From time to time someone leaving or arriving would offer a hand or tip an imaginary hat. Great to have you here, your honour. There was a roar from the cricket field, suddenly a breeze. They were pleased, Daniel knew, to be generous to a man from an ethnic minority. A little girl bounced up and down screaming, Go on, Matthew, go on, go on! Hilary pointed out the propeller spinning on her cap. They laughed. Daniel imagined Minnie walking by. She would have a short skirt, pink sneakers and a tennis racket. Squeezing his wife's hand, he leaned the other way and said: Max, why don't you go and see Sarah, find out what she's up to. If you think that will help, the young man said, I'll go willingly. Someone scored. Oh dear, Hilary groaned.

Actually, it's getting a bit embarrassing, she acknowledged in the car going back, but he's so well behaved and obviously lonely. I rather took advantage of him with the move and everything, so I suppose now I'll have to put up with it. Ref. was biased, Tom grumbled. Rubbish, Daniel said firmly. You wouldn't believe how much he arranged for me, how much to-ing and fro-ing he did. In a low voice Daniel asked, If the idiot's lonely, why doesn't he go and see Sarah, not us? He was only the father of one of the guys in their team! Tom objected. Didn't you see when . . . A bad loser loses twice over, Daniel told him abruptly. That was Colonel Savage's voice. Oh but he's tried to see her, Hilary moaned, poor chap he has, but the stupid girl chases him away.

Towards eight they drove into town again for the organ recital at the church. No I really don't want to stay at home, Daniel insisted. Again people flocked around him. I feel fine, he repeated. Hilary had invited a professor of music from a nearby university, an expert on William Byrd. Max should have been here, she said, looking round. The boy hadn't come. We are so relieved you are well, a reassuring voice said. It was the vicar padding down the aisle. A good crowd, Hilary said, neck craning. Not just churchgoers either. It was important for her, he knew, that it be a distinct community that came to these recitals. She didn't want it to be considered a Christian function. Let's hope the man's good. The problem was that only churches had organs. But Daniel didn't so much as look at the typed programme on their seats. He sat holding his wife's hand and let his mind wander.

Organ music, he knew, was good for that, complicated and rambling. Various possible tunes seemed to be sizing each other up. Presumably there were rules governing the different themes. I won't try to understand, he thought.

When there was a concert they brought the organ console down to the chancel steps so that you could get a better view of the organist. There were three keyboards, four if you counted the one beneath the feet, then an umbilical bundle of cables snaking back behind the Lord's table to the bellows and pipes above. On his polished bench just yards away from them, bald scalp and broad back to the public, the visiting professor displayed a frenetic, elderly man's agility, left hand racing on one keyboard, right springing up and down between the other two, flicking switches, setting stops, feet all the while clomping at the pedals with the mad vigour of a marionette.

You look glum, Daniel whispered to Tom. The boy was biting the skin round his nails; it was one of Hilary's habits. I'm missing the Test highlights, he said. Organ stuff is always the same. It was a rule Hilary had invented that if she took Tom to his football games he must come to her concerts. He mustn't grow up musically illiterate. Daniel whispered: Not that test matches are all that different. The boy smiled. His father almost burst out laughing. How wonderful Hilary was with her endless rules. I broke them all, he thought.

At home, the dog had to be walked. Here was a new routine. They sidled to the end of the close and back. Two of the other houses looked inhabited now. You don't know how lovely this air tastes, he said. After the hospital. Later, very carefully, they made love. I thought it was the end of my love-making days, she whispered. You would have married Max, he teased. Holding her husband tightly, Hilary didn't reply.

THIRTEEN

There were forty photographs. A good dozen of them of Koreans. Could you look at these? Mattheson had scribbled. Already I'm in a state, Daniel thought, but calmly. On the floor were three boxes of letters, presumably from well-wishers. Leave them there, he told the clerk. I'll go through them myself. One might be from her. Get well, love, Minnie. It might. Get well, love, Jane. From married bliss. Or perhaps Sarah had started her comminations again. Oh the clutter, he laughed, he rubbed his hands, before one can get down to anything! Telling me! It was Laura's voice. They'll have to burn me out, his daughter had told Christine. So it seemed. She had phoned first thing. Adrian popped his head in. All well are we? Perhaps a little smoke will be enough, Daniel had joked. One jokes. Fit as a fiddle, he lied. But he had sensed that Christine was concerned now. The woman is at a turning point, he thought. She is moving out on her husband. Anything could happen. She needed a place to stay, a place of her own. Could he simply drag his daughter out of the flat? Should he physically force the girl to come and live with them? What power does one have? As far as scheduling was concerned, he agreed that he would start next Monday. Another week. Meantime, I'll test my one eye on the stone-heaving papers. Am I going to be able to work, he wondered? He was worried. But when he sat at the bench again these other problems would dissolve. There are various other small matters, judge. Bail applications. Sentencing recommendations. Of course, Judge Savage said. As soon as I'm ready.

Putting the phone down, he went back to the photos. None were of the Kwans. My hands are remarkably steady, he thought. Every minute or two he had to close his good eye for a few seconds. He opened it again. Mattheson seems to think I was assaulted by a Korean, he said to Laura. The young clerk held a mug of tea. She stood over him. I thought you must have been to a Chinese restaurant, she remarked. She bent over him. How can you tell they're Korean? Good point, Daniel said. He looked more closely. She set down the cup on his desk. For a moment he was vaguely jealous of the Shields and their imminent separation. How civilised! The man simply lies in bed until his wife finally goes for the door. Call me a cab, he told the girl.

Having asked Hilary to drive him in early, Judge Savage now had from ten-thirty till after four in the afternoon on his own. Before four-thirty I resolve everything, he decided. Then the exchange of contracts. Life right back on the rails. It can be done. In the bathroom mirror he found a tall handsome man with close cut grey hair, tinted glasses. Tall, dark *but* handsome somebody had once said. The patch is fairly discreet, he thought. It was reassuring. I look good. Danny boy! Crawford came to knock on his door as he came out. He was holding a copy of Archbold. You're back! Are you okay? That's just what I was trying to decide, Daniel laughed. Why this automatic laugh when I speak to people?

Look, Crawford asked, he was a prematurely portly, affable man, apart from saying hello of course, I wondered if you could you jog my awful memory a moment. I've got a rather curious application to have a charge dropped because the police failed to carry out an identification parade. Forbes, Daniel said at once. Yes, yes, I know, but the circumstances are rather odd. I've . . . From the corridor they heard Laura calling, Your taxi, Mr Savage. Tell me, Daniel said. Well, the problem in this one, Crawford began, is that the defendants are on record as having asked for a parade, and now the delay's been six months. What's the charge? Daniel interrupted. Rape. Your honour! Laura called. No but rather unusually, you see, there's an independent witness and since the victim is supposed to have some long-standing grudge against the suspects – two brothers – they claim it's a set up and that witness should have been called to identify. Tangled web, Daniel pursed his lips. Let'em put it to a jury, is what I say. Crawford is mediocre, he thought, hurrying down the passage. Having to ask him a question like that. Defence counsel was trying it on. Bear brain, Jane had called him. Yet it was Martin they had passed over. Why do I keep thinking of Martin?

Because Martin substituted for my brother. Twenty minutes later Daniel was climbing to the third floor of a once grand terraced house now split into small flats. He and his elder brother Frank had last met, but hardly spoken, at the colonel's funeral. But then they had hardly spoken at all since that afternoon thirty years ago when Martin Shields had taken it upon himself to tell the house-master about the blood on his younger friend's back. Was it entirely coincidental – Daniel stopped on a patch of old carpet – that the crisis with Hilary had come simultaneous with Colonel Savage's death? On the landing, as if in some Masonic trial, there were two identical doors, left and right, with nothing to distinguish between them. Certainly he had frequently felt, during the old man's interminable illness, that he had to sleep with every woman he met. *Had* to. He would visit his father, then use the excuse to rush off to a girlfriend. Stink of death. The stairs smelt of cat. Tanned as ever! a voice called. Daniel looked up. I thought you said the third floor. Did I? Sorry squire. Daniel climbed the last flight. His brother greeted him with a mocking bow. My name is V-Vrank. Velcome to my ha-umble ha-ome!

Frank had always been a fat boy. Now he was a flabby, shambling, bespectacled man in his late forties. They had seen each other so little. Generous trousers, clean white tee-shirt. No neck. Daniel watched his brother as he walked ahead along squeaking boards to an ample sitting room, thickly carpeted, cluttered with the sort of moderately priced antiques, plaster busts and brass bric-a-brac that Hilary was always so scornful of. English muddle, she called it. As if Hilary didn't belong in England. Take a pew, Frank said, but Daniel went to a window that opened over the patternless scribble of the southern side of town. It was quite a view. To his surprise his brother came to stand beside him. Three hundred thousand souls, Frank commented. There was heavy traffic. Or none, of course, he laughed, depending on how you look at it. Was it bad? he enquired when Daniel sat down. He seemed genuinely sympathetic. Coma, briefly, Daniel said. So the world was told, and the eye? Another couple of weeks, then we see what it can see. Frank scratched at the corner of his mouth. He has, Daniel was aware, a slovenly, sensual mouth, yet it was the colonel's mouth too. The colonel had never been slovenly. But the fat face was the same. The man was his son.

Frank seemed pleased to have got his brother into his flat.

Pain? he asked. He was immediately more accommodating than at any time on the phone. No time for it at the time, if you see what I mean, Daniel explained. There was a short silence. Daniel said: Actually, it wasn't as painful as when you used to cut strips out of my back, Frank. They looked at each other. Still thinking about that? Frank raised an eyebrow; his broad face assumed the wry expression that had always awed his younger brother. The fat man laughed. Course the person who should have been expelled, he remarked lightly, was yourself, squire, for letting me do it. He's at ease with himself, Daniel realised. My wayward, sponging failure of a brother is at ease with himself! Arthur, Frank was shouting. Arthur! A door opened along the passageway. Want to make some tea, can you?

Still, you probably did me a favour in the end, Frank went on easily. *I* didn't do anything, Daniel said quickly. No, Frank agreed. He sat down in a second dusty armchair. No, you never *did* anything, did you? He put his feet up on a low table. None of the furniture in the room seemed to be from the same set. On the other hand, the place had a wayward cluttered cosiness to it. Brightly painted and carved as if flapping, a wooden Union Jack hung askew on the grey wall. The man called Arthur appeared with mugs and teapot. Stick'em on the table, kid, Frank said. And he said: Only now, three decades later, that same impeccably-behaved brother finally gets in touch again because he wants bruv to find a tart for him. Nice, eh?

How's Mother? Daniel asked, I see some newspaper managed to get a few quotes out of her. Enjoying her dotage, Frank said. I presume, Daniel said, that she's run out of money. Frank sighed, that's right, squire, more or less, if she doesn't sell up, that is. So my badly behaved brother waits thirty years, then calls me to ask for money when his mum runs out? Touché! Frank smiled. Depressing isn't it? He seemed in excellent spirits. The man called Arthur wore blue shorts and a tank top. Perched on a bar-stool by the window, his body was wiry, his thin, clean-shaven face alert and solemn. Daniel had expected something very different. No one had ever said that Frank was gay. But then the only news he ever got of his brother was through Mrs Savage, when she deigned to speak to him. Mrs Savage spoke to Frank, and Colonel Savage spoke to Daniel. They were sponsors of competing teams. Your mother always loved a loser, the colonel had confided.

Presumably you know that mum always tells me not to get in touch with you, Daniel said. Claims it would only upset you. Is that so? Frank asked. And you very wisely obey her? I don't imagine you were waiting by the phone, Daniel said. To tell the truth, I thought you were in London. Frank sniffed, shook his head, exchanged a glance with Arthur. Let's get to the point, he said, have you brought the cash? Daniel took an envelope from his jacket pocket, he had his court clothes on, and laid it on the card table beside the teapot. This, after all, was exactly how the police went about finding information. They paid informers. People like Harville. People who often enough had had a part in the crime they informed about. So the stuff about the mortgage and bridging loans was all bull, Frank smiled affably. Not at all, Daniel said. I'm in rather a difficult situation actually as far as cash is concerned. Yet willing to spend generously when it comes to skirt. Just tell me where she is, Daniel said.

Arthur? Frank made a gesture. Unsmiling, the younger man went to the table between the windows and picked up a small notebook. Flat 72, Arthur read, Sandringham House, Dalton Estate, Sperringway. His accent was American, but of the kind that suggests the best New England education. In his late thirties perhaps. That's all? Daniel asked. He found a scrap of paper in his wallet and fiddled for a pen. I don't recall the master asking us anything else. Frank again hammed an extravagantly ironic expression. It was the sort of thing that used to drive Colonel Savage mad. Daniel ignored it. But you're quite sure? he insisted. Arthur said: A young Korean woman called Minnie Kwan – that's K-W-A-N right? – definitely lives at that address on Sperringway. How did you find out? Any fool can find out this sort of thing, Frank interrupted. Then he said: Arthur and I have a stall in Doherty Street. Actually we need the cash, you might be reassured to know, to buy some better stock. There are plenty of people at the market you can ask for help when it comes to finding someone.

Doherty Street market? Daniel could hardly take it in. Running a market stall hadn't seemed one of the possibilities available to Colonel Savage's children. Antiques, Frank smiled. And in case you were wondering, yes, we have already sold most of Mother's stuff. The vanished inheritance. I have to be off, Daniel stood up. He felt dazed. As a child it always seemed that the only options in life were professional English success or nameless, third-world poverty. Now his brother was running a market stall.

He got to his feet, offered Arthur his hand. Behind him Frank hadn't risen. Why don't you stop a bit? he asked. His air of avuncular superiority was annoying. But perhaps he means to be friendly, Daniel thought. I'm in a rush, he said. Quietly Frank announced: Someone's screwing you for cash, aren't they, squire? Daniel turned and smiled. Nothing so dramatic, he laughed. That nervous laugh again. Comas and eye-patches sound pretty dramatic to me, Frank remarked. Someone's blackmailing you.

Having climbed onto his feet, Daniel now found they wouldn't move. Standing still in the middle of the room, he was again struck by what a different world this was, these dusty rugs and armchairs, this quiet view of the drabber suburbs. But complete in its way. I could live here, he thought. It was this domestic solidity he hadn't expected. News of Frank had always had to do with addictions and bookmakers and unpaid rent in threadbare boarding houses.

Having shaken hands, Arthur had gone to a cabinet in the corner and was shuffling through a stack of CDs. Frank, Daniel said firmly, I am not being blackmailed. Frank looked at him, lips pursed. But you are going right away to see this girl whose no doubt numerous friends and relations beat you up, right? Not at all, Daniel lied. Danny, Frank said, for a moment his voice shed its customary self-parody, can't you see? I'm actually worried for you, fuck it. I'm even beginning to like you. You're a judge, a public figure, you've been all over the papers and TV, you've always been Mr Clean, then all of a sudden you're spending two grand just for an address, for a child anyone could have found if they'd thought about it, and then rushing off to the Dalton Estate of all places, Shanghai, Bombay and Khartoum banged together in British prefab. I love it. He smiled: What I'm saying is. Perhaps I can help. Your old useless brother can do a bit more for his cash, squire, he finished. The bantering tone was unmistakably affectionate now.

I don't need help, Daniel said. But he seemed unable to move. Someone had clearly told the police that a dark man, well dressed, had been sitting at table with a bunch of Koreans. In the Capricorn. Why else the photos? They were digging out their criminal Koreans. Judge Savage was struck by a sense of unreality, the frightening counterpart to that exhilaration he once used to feel making love to a young

Asian girl on a heap of rugs, or to a colleague's fiancée in a seaside hotel. Jane's yellow hair! That too had been quite unreal. Carnival, the word came to mind. He should have been wearing a mask. Is Judge Savage amongst us mortals, Frank enquired. Or is he communing with powers above? Daniel looked at his brother. It *was* this girl's people beat you up, Frank insisted. Some abuse of nuptial rights, I presume. Dan, brother, I'm on your side. I'm pleased you had it in you! Daniel shook his head.

Only now did he notice that soft jazz had begun to play. He had always loathed jazz. In particular soft jazz. Very practically, perched on his bar stool, the man called Arthur suggested: Perhaps we could come along with you at least and offer our, er, moral support. Right, Frank said. Bit difficult to start hitting three of us. I'm *fine*, Daniel insisted, he even managed to smile. The situation isn't at all what you imagine.

Sperringway, he told the cabbie. He had never been in these estates before but knew that they tended to be divided up into different ethnic groups. A black in an Asian block might be even more obvious than a white. So many of his clients had come from Sperringway, in the days when he defended. The truth was that without his wig on, he wasn't entirely sure how people saw him. Sandringham House, he said. He was against the movement to scrap wigs. Then it occurred to him that perhaps it was Father's death that had allowed Frank to do something other than succeed or fail, as in a way it allowed me to imagine leaving Hilary, he thought. Somebody dies and quite unexpectedly you can be someone else.

The driver pulled off the main road into a group of council high-rises. It was when the flats were sold off, Daniel had heard, that people started to sort themselves into their ethnic groups. Then it occurred to him that if he had a mobile phone – he must get one at once – he would be able to call Hilary at a moment like this, from the back of a cab. Not to discuss this business with her, of course. But to touch base, to run a hand along the solid wall of that side of his personality. Man in carnival mask phones wife! No doubt that sort of thing does happen.

He paid the driver. There is nothing frightening about the place at all, he told himself, standing by a bin. The few kids hanging out didn't seem surprised to see a taxi. They were kicking a tennis ball. My defence is surprise, Daniel thought. They can't be expecting me to arrive at the door. This place has been harshly judged, he decided, walking across the hard mud of what designers must have planned as a lawn. Where was it he had seen the Dalton estate mentioned recently? He looked around. You have to move your head more with only the one eye working. He looked up and was dazzled. As yesterday at Tom's Sports Centre, the weather was halcyon, the July sun brightly blurred behind a haze of high cloud. Never judge a place in sunshine, Hilary always said.

Yes, it was the man who broke his son's wrist. Daniel stopped by the first block. Not the stone-throwers, they came from the other side of town. A better area. Is this Sandringham? he asked. A freckled little girl ran away chased by her dog. There's too much dog shit here. Trying to work out where the name of the block would be written, he remembered that the social worker in the case had made much of the cramped circumstances in which the man's family found themselves. It's ridiculous that it doesn't say which block is which! The boy claimed he had fallen out of the first floor window, but in his confession to the police the father had pointed out that the windows didn't open enough for anyone to fall out of them. How long did I send him down for? Then he saw a sort of swimming pool mosaic on the column beside the door. Balmoral. Good.

He walked on. Sandringham was the third. Odd, it occurred to him, given how well-off the Kwan family must presumably be, that Minnie would be living in one of these small, erstwhile council flats. Perhaps she has escaped from home. She is well and happy. A five-year-old was going round and round the lobby on a bike too big for him, a woman with chin in hands watched from the stairs. It was hard to say what the smell was. Does the lift work? Daniel asked. I should bloody well hope so, she said. It wasn't urine. She was cheerful and uninterested. How can I know which floor to go to for which flat? You what? Is 72 on the seventh floor? The bicycle went round and round him, the boy scraping his toe on the cement. Where else would it be? she asked. As the winch whined and the box lurched upward, Daniel felt the same rush of fear he had experienced two days ago in the lift at Carlton Mansions. Is this courage or folly? he wondered.

A narrow balcony ran right across the front of the block. It wouldn't do to suffer from a fear of heights. I'm going to see Minnie at last. The doors were orange. Daniel knocked. There was a chrome knocker. The window was curtained. The men will all be at work, he told himself. A muffled voice said something incomprehensible. Then again. Was it a woman's voice? It's incomprehensible my being here. He almost panicked. Still the door didn't open. I'm looking for Minnie Kwan, he said. Who is it? came the question. Yes, a woman's voice, he realised, an old woman. His fingers unclenched. Daniel Savage, he said. He felt a certain satisfaction. Daniel Savage, he repeated, very slowly and clearly. I'm looking for Minnie Kwan. The door opened on a chain, showing a wrinkled cheek. Who are you? They all speak English the same way, he told himself. They're all the same. But now a younger, shriller voice intervened. There was the sound of rapid movement, a voluble exchange, the door tensed, then swung inwards. Behind a small, flustered elderly lady stood Minnie Kwan.

They were still arguing. Beyond the narrow entrance, Daniel glimpsed a sitting room choked with colour and ornament. There was a strong foreign smell, the den of a species he didn't know. He felt so relieved to see her. Finally, Minnie reached across the older woman, grabbed his sleeve and tugged him inside. It was incense, he realised. Alarmed, the tiny lady, whom Daniel now saw had sharp wooden skewers in her hair, retreated, almost scuttled, from the door to stand defensively at a point where three other doors were closed. She was still speaking rapidly. Don't worry, she won't understand a word of what we say, Minnie told him, then turned to continue their argument. Daniel watched this girl he had once made love to, jabbering away high-pitched, brushing hair from her lips. She wore blue jeans and a simple white smock. More attractive dressed than un-, he remembered. What pleasure there had been was quite insignificant now. The danger, on the other hand, had multiplied. Minnie turned. She's agreed you can stay for ten minutes, but she has to watch us. That's fine, Daniel said.

Quickly then, she asked, why on earth have you come? She sat on a green cushion, facing His Honour Judge Savage where he was now perched forward on a low wicker chair. In the opposite corner, he noticed a thin line of smoke rising vertically before a niche of photographs. Think clearly, he decided. He was so relieved to find her. Really, he could get up and go now. They were extravagantly framed. I've done my duty just seeing her.

Well? She was looking up at him, her eyes expectant and charming, forcing him to assume the role of the able older man. He clasped his hands together, as he tended to do on the judge's table: You called me and said you were desperate. I was worried for you. I thought perhaps something had happened to you. As he spoke, he remembered the charmingly cocked inquisitive gaze she had had as she sat in the front row of the jury. You'd said your father was violent. So finally I got in touch with your boyfriend, Ben. You remember you'd told me about him. I was supposed to be going to meet him, to find out if you were okay, and instead your father and brothers came and, I presume, though I can't be sure because I didn't actually see them, they beat me up.

Beat you up? She was alarmed.

Daniel realised he had his sunglasses on. He took them off to show the patch. The room was brightly yellow and red. You didn't know that?

They beat you up? She was on her feet, shocked. You are hurt? She came to stare at him. She doesn't follow the news, Daniel realised. These people have a different community. They don't bother about the English news. They have satellite TV. Briefly, he explained what had happened. I can't be absolutely sure it was them, he said. She sat down again, staring, shaking her head. I'm so sorry, she was saying. She shook her head from side to side. That's terrible. Obviously it isn't unimaginable to her, he noticed, that her father and brothers would beat someone up. You poor thing, she kept repeating. I shouldn't have mentioned this at all, he realised then. I could have seen her, said hello and left. No, I could have waited outside the block, till I caught a glimpse of her – she is thriving – and left. There was no need to speak to her. So that made me even more concerned, he explained, that something might have happened to you.

You still worried for me! she sang out. Even after being beaten up! Her bright voice conveyed a charming exoticism. Daniel, how nice! She frowned. You never loved me, though. Why did you do this? Why did you try to find me? From the door, the elderly woman interrupted with a dry word. Minnie turned and spoke extremely harshly. As she swung round, Daniel caught the flutter of breasts beneath the smock. The old woman muttered her disapproval. For me? Minnie turned back to him. She was shaking her head. I'm so sorry you were hurt. Daniel repeated: I didn't want to feel that you had appealed to me and that I hadn't helped, that maybe you'd got into some kind of trouble. As she watched him, she began to smile. The English gentleman! she laughed. She was shaking her head again, then brushing back her hair. You're the English gentleman! I did all this for nothing, Daniel realised. I risked my life, my livelihood, for nothing.

Abruptly he asked: So why *did* you call me? She sighed. He noticed a green neck-band. It was elegant. She looked at him, but didn't reply. It was as if she couldn't even remember. She said she was desperate then, but now she can barely remember calling you. By the way, he said, I should warn you, the police know that the people who attacked me were Korean. The police? When a judge is beaten up – I'm a judge now – the police inevitably work a bit harder to find out who did it. They know it was a Korean. Her eyes widened. I doubt if I can stop them finding out.

You mean you didn't tell them? To tell them, Daniel explained, would mean telling about you. Yes, she said, yes. She hasn't thought about this at all, Judge Savage realised. Her right knee had started to rock with tension. She is taking it in now, he saw. Did the Kwans themselves know? he suddenly asked himself. It seemed impossible that the three men wouldn't once have watched the news, seen his face. My face has been all over the papers, he told her. She brushed her hair from her cheek. Sooner or later the police will find out. That's their job. They will arrest your father.

Then she was very practical. Everyone will deny it, she said. You will deny it, because you must never admit about me. It would be bad for your family and your job. I will deny it. My father will deny it. My brothers will deny it. Maybe so, Daniel said, but what if the police find concrete evidence? They will still deny it, she said, always, even if they were in prison they will deny it, because they would never want people to think that I had a relationship with a black man. They nearly killed me . . .

The expression irritated Daniel. The girl was healthy. Her breasts are bigger, he noticed, than when I knew her. Yet she talked lightly about being nearly killed. And how many times had she said, he'd kill me if . . . he'd murder me if . . . ? Wasn't it that, in the end, that had tricked him into worrying about her? Her stories about her violent father. But here she was positively blooming. So why didn't they kill you? he demanded. You seem fine to me. I'm going to have a baby, she said.

Again she waved away the old woman. Ben's mother, she explained. Ben had been going back and forth from Korea for years. I doubt if you spoke to him at all. Ben doesn't know a word of English. I'm sure he doesn't know anything about this. He would have left me. They smuggle people in, she said. That's what these flats are for. We have five of them. Then I got pregnant. It was stupid. I was putting everything off, but when I was pregnant then I knew we must marry. She drew a deep breath. I couldn't dream of escaping any more. I had been living two lives in two worlds. That's when I called you.

Daniel watched the girl. Every time you went to bed with a different woman, he had once told someone, perhaps Martin, you came into contact with a completely different world. You established a secret chain of contact between different lives. That was the excitement of it. You never knew who else was attached to the link you had made. It was a secret chain stretching out across the world, through all the communities you would never know or understand. It's a stupid risk, Martin had said. And a shameful breach of trust.

And what did you imagine I would do for you? Daniel asked her. She looked down so that the hair fell over her face. You used to say: the only thing holding you back is what's inside your head. Remember? She looked up. How presumptuous of me, Judge Savage said. I don't know, she sighed, I wanted advice, I wanted to get an abortion and disappear. I don't really know. Sometimes I think of myself as a normal English girl. I'm not Korean at all. I just wanted to hear what you would say. So why didn't you come, that evening, he asked. Because Mark, she said, my brother, that's his English name, I don't know, he'd heard something I said on the phone. We had a fight. He is always worried about the honour of the family. He is very Korean. You wouldn't understand. There is this whole honour of the family thing. By the time I got there you had gone. She sighed and smiled. And when I got back I told them I'd been to see my black pimp lover. It was a joke. I always said it. You know? Anyway, Mark started hitting me. Then I told them Ben had made me pregnant. Now I'm married, she finished. It was bound to happen. This is me.

Daniel was aware he should be quick. The old lady was fretting, making signs. Look, he was suddenly earnest in spite of himself, some voice was speaking that wasn't quite his own, look, if you're not happy, Minnie, wouldn't it be better for you if these people were arrested so that you could be free. You can always divorce. You see, he paused, at some point I may be obliged to tell the truth.

These people? The Korean girl's eyes widened. My father! But she smiled. No, I don't think like that now, she said. This is my life. She smiled again. You said yourself I was flourishing. Look at my tits! That's just hormones, Daniel said. She shook her head: You were quite right about it all being in my mind. But the fact is that it actually is there. That *is* my mind. Anyway, they'll never be arrested, she smiled. Dad's never had problems with the police. You needn't worry.

Standing up, Daniel again noticed the candle and photographs. The family shrine? She had explained once how her father would kneel before the photos of his grandmother but not his grandfather, whom he'd hated. It had fascinated her that Daniel didn't even know who his real mother was. She looked at the photo. Ben's Dad, she said. He died before I was born. There was a flower too, he now saw. Don't kiss me or even shake hands, she warned. Her eyes flickered to the older woman. I'm so sorry you were hurt.

The door closed behind him. Walking along the balcony, Daniel glimpsed, beyond the corner of the block through a hazy distance, the hills that rose to the north of town. If I looked hard enough, if my one eye was sharp enough, I could pick out our house. But the girl had told him to leave quickly and discreetly. Glancing at his watch in the lift, he realised it was only twelve. Two grand well spent, he thought. Deny everything.

FOURTEEN

It would be unrealistic to expect a cab in these parts.
Walking along Sperringway, Daniel Savage was struck by
the thought that resolving his problems seemed to involve
going from one young woman to another. He grinned. In
the end Minnie is in much better shape than my daughter.
Why did I ever allow myself to be so distracted?

He came to a bus stop. Three Hispanic boys on a low
wall were laughing at him. Needless to say the glass over
the timetable and route map was gone. They laugh at the
impeccably dressed black, he thought. Does it go to the
station? he asked. Yeah, yeah, one boy said. The others burst
into giggles.

The road was a slow dual carriageway through housing
estates both sides. He had done the fashionable reading in
his time on the social causes of crime. Yet he was aware of
having fallen back over the years on the rather simplistic
notion of the bad penny. That was one of the colonel's obses-
sions. Frank was a bad penny. Most of the people in the
dock were not evil at all. The Mishras, the man who had
broken his son's wrist, the fool who had fondled the retarded

girl. It was painful to sentence such people. But others were decidedly and inexplicably bad pennies. The stone-throwers surely. It would be a pleasure to send them down. Minnie's father. It is a character thing, he thought. He had no real take on it. Perhaps there were trials where the jury was right just to base a verdict on intuition of character. Kwan is evil, Daniel told himself. They had that bag ready, he thought. They came knowing they would attack me.

But then someone dies and a character changes. On the bus a middle-aged white woman stared. She had recognised him. I've certainly changed, Daniel thought. And at the station the cabbie too. If you don't mind my saying so, sir, we should have the bloody death sentence for the bastards who did that! Bet you'd love to try'em yourself, sir. Daniel didn't reply. Nice looking missus you've got, if I may say so, to judge by the photo, sir. I'll tell her, he said. He was thinking that in the end the colonel had been wrong about Frank. Frank had been kind this morning. Perhaps then, by some miracle, Sarah might change too.

From the phone box at the bottom of Carlton Street he called Hilary. I'm here he explained, Carlton Street. She asked where he'd been. That police inspector was eager to speak to you. She couldn't remember his name. I felt claustrophobic at chambers, I thought I needed a walk. I've got someone in, she explained, to sort out the plumbing for the washing machine. Listen, he said, I'm going to tell Sarah that if she wants to live away from home, I'm happy to rent her a small place for a while. Are you agreed? There was a moment's hesitation. Indignantly, his wife declared, Well, fairer than that you cannot get. Did the inspector say what it was he wanted? No. The solicitor's at four-thirty then.

So what do you want to do? he asked his daughter. He had noticed there was a plastic bag on the kitchen floor.

I'm glad to see you're eating. Max brought it, his daughter said. He had found her on her mattress in shorts and tee-shirt listening to her Walkman. That was kind of him. Oh it was Mum actually bought the stuff, she added. For a moment Daniel didn't understand. Come on, only Mum would get me things like plain low fat yoghurt. *And* Mon Cheri. She knows they're my favourites. Daniel sighed. Do you like Max? he asked. Taking a moment to think about it, she answered: He's okay. I have time, Daniel thought. It was something he used to tell himself when cross-examining. You have time. Don't hurry. He was aware of being anxious about Mattheson. It was one thing to be satisfied that Minnie was okay, quite another to feel sure that the case was closed.

Sarah, we've got to sell this place. The new house was expensive, love. We don't have unlimited funds. She didn't look at him. I have a good salary now, but it will take a few years to mount up. He paused. Quite apart from the fact that we've signed a contract to sell. We're honour bound. She was sitting on the mattress with her back to the wall, knees open wide, chin to the window. He had turned a chair round and was gripping its back between his hands. She has my chin, he thought. There's nothing left here, he told her. There's no table, no sofa. We don't live here any more.

The girl shrugged her shoulders. Her father tried to joke: You can't even go back to nature in a place like this. She groaned. That's such a stupid expression, Dad. Nature doesn't go back so why go back to nature. They exchanged glances. To go back is unnatural, she said. He waited. She is very much my daughter, he thought. He felt reassured, but intensely aware of the mistake he had made that day he persuaded her to go to her exams.

What would you like to do? he asked again. Now you've finished school. Tell me. Her lips were set and she shook her head as if in disbelief that he couldn't understand. Minnie too had sat on the floor, while he was on a chair. Minnie is infinitely more disadvantaged than Sarah, he thought. Yet conversation with the Korean girl had been remarkably easy. He needn't worry for her. At last Sarah asked, Want a Mon Cheri? He took one. She giggled: Chosen for me by Mum, delivered by Max, eaten by Dad. He smiled. I've got three full hours, he thought.

Listen, Daniel said. However softly one spoke, the voice took a sharp ring in the bare room. This morning I looked through the case of a Chinese man accused of assaulting his daughter, your age more or less. Bloke has a small business and trained up his children so that each would have a particular role in the company. Also, they had to marry inside the community. You know. The two older children were brothers. Anyway, when the third child, the daughter, rebels and starts seeing a white guy instead of the bloke she's supposed to marry, her father goes and beats her up. Pretty badly actually. Her wrist was broken in two places.

And? Sarah enquired. You're telling me I'm well off, I suppose. Not exactly. I'm just asking you: is there anything we are forcing you to do, or even to *be*, if you see what I mean, that you don't want to do or be, or anything we're preventing you from doing that you are dying to do?

Sarah appeared to be thinking, but as he watched her Daniel was struck by the realisation that this was a sham. She wasn't thinking at all. Why did he have this impression? Smirking, she asked: Do I have the right to silence? Everybody has the right to silence. He smiled: But these days the jury has the right to draw such inferences as may seem appropriate. She cried: I knew it was a cross examination! In the end, you'll drag me out kicking and screaming. Won't you!

Sarah! Judge Savage stood up. For God's sake. Let's have a cup of tea. There's no kettle, she remarked. So let's go out to a café. I'm not leaving here, she said. In case I don't let you back in? She was silent. Daniel was struggling to contain himself. Why, he should have asked Minnie earlier, had she insisted on provoking her father with that line about the black pimp lover? No wonder they had hit her!

By the way, Sarah said, when I'm silent, do feel free to draw inferences. I want you to. There was a superciliousness in that smile. It was as if she'd inherited it from Frank. Which was a ridiculous notion. If ever there was a father, he'd often joked, who can be a hundred percent sure he *is* the father, it's me. He said: Sarah, let me tell you an odd thing I heard this morning. You know your Uncle Frank. Not really, she interrupted. Not at all in fact. Okay, you know *about* your Uncle Frank. The only time I spoke to him was at Granddad's funeral. You know the *story*, he insisted, of your Uncle Frank. Yes, your honour, she smiled. I know Mother never wanted to see him. This surprised Daniel, that she should have looked at it this way. But it was true of course. Well, this morning, I found out that he's got a stand at Doherty Street market, selling antiques. Cool! the girl said. For a moment she was enthusiastic. And so? Judge Savage groped for a moment. The point is, it's something nobody ever thought he'd do, or anybody in the Savage family and I just thought . . . Don't, she told him. She smiled. She had already seen the whole discussion. She is smart, he thought. Abruptly he decided: Look, Sarah, you've got to leave the house immediately. We've got to get this exchange of contracts. If I can't pay the builder tomorrow, theoretically he can repossess the house. If we take out a further loan to pay him, the interest will exceed even a judge's income.

This is the only house I've ever lived in, she said. Again she had turned her face away. So what's that supposed to mean? he demanded. People don't go from birth to death in the same house. You don't get buried in your first nappies. You have to move and change. She turned her face away and when she spoke her voice had become flat and dull. You can drag me out kicking and screaming, she said.

All at once Daniel was exhausted. As on Saturday, he felt the irrational urge to go straight to Police Inspector Mattheson and tell him everything. I fucked a girl, yes, on the jury. I got mixed up in her personal problems. It was her father had me beaten up. Arrest him. Daniel could see the scene as the interview finished. He could see Mattheson reaching for the phone to give the order. Why was it so seductive? The ensuing humiliation, the showdown with Hilary, perhaps they would be a relief. A sudden weakness came over him and he rested his face on his forearm across the back of the chair. Unthinking, he asked: How did all this happen?

I don't know, she said. Sensing she was looking at him now, he looked up. Their eyes met. There was a sympathy, he knew. And hostility too. I can see, he began. He stopped. It is always me exposing myself, he thought. She had told him nothing. Go on, she said. He sighed. I can see why you would feel upset about what happened with your mother and myself. I even think I can see how that might encourage you to get attached to an evangelical group. She was looking resolutely at the floor. In the sense maybe that when you're young you find it difficult to accept any distance between ideals and reality. A thing has to be perfect or it's nothing. I can even see why that might have started you sending me those unpleasant letters. Those quotations from the Bible. He waited. It was you wasn't it? She was silent.

But even accepting all that, I mean, that you find the lives of your parents, I don't know, difficult to deal with, or even sick, you know, what I really can't see is why you have to take it out on yourself, why you go and throw away your exams.

Again he paused. Having begun blindly, he now felt he should choose the words very carefully. Perhaps I've found the right thing to say, he thought. Don't spoil it. Her young body was vibrating with tension. Her dark face, still averted, would be a beautiful prize for someone. She had such fine lines. Daniel had often looked forward to having a son-in-law, he had imagined the look of fulfilment on his daughter's face. There would be complicity, about happiness, and about how difficult relationships are. Max was an attractive man.

For example, if you want to live on your own, I don't see why you have to do it 'in spite of us' as it were. I mean, we'd be quite happy to pay your rent somewhere. He stopped. At least for a while. If you . . .

She looked up. Her eyes were streaming tears. But she was laughing too, almost giggling, a knuckle in her mouth. She was shaking. He was swept by the impulse to embrace her, to take his dear child in his arms. My daughter. The first child. You are my first real kin in this world. That was something he used to say. The first person he had known to be in a blood relation to himself. He was getting to his feet. He too was laughing and crying, shaking his head. Sarah, I don't understand, he was saying, you really must explain to me why you have all these problems and dear Tom is so bloody normal! And why did you go crazy on me that day in the car on the way to school. What did I *say*, for Christ's sake? As he moved towards the reconciling embrace, the girl stiffened. I have to go to the bathroom, she said. She bounced to her feet and walked out of the room.

Judge Savage was left alone. He waited. Outside the curtainless windows, the sun lay brightly along the pleasant street; it never penetrated the flat in the afternoon. What has Mattheson found out? he wondered. My life is on the brink. On the wall were the cleaner rectangles where the furniture had been. I didn't want everything to get so complicated. A patch of mould followed the outline of the big wall cupboard. Beneath it lay a small heap of moths and spiders' webs. We lived here fifteen years. Almost all my career really. Tom was conceived and born here, he thought. How much of it had been spent fighting! They had bought a wall cupboard that was too big for the room and then been stuck with it for fifteen years. The girl is being a long time, he thought.

He took off the tinted spectacles and touched the patch. The eye had stopped hurting. Minnie is fine, he repeated to himself. That's a relief. They will take it off and I will see. Everything will be as it was. He looked at his watch. Melodrama nearly over, he thought. The girl's coming round. He had begun to feel hungry. As after a tough exam. She'll see reason. In the end I was the only victim of all this. Even if Minnie had managed to see you that night, it wouldn't have made any difference. You couldn't have advised her. The false premise of all advice, it occurred to him, is the proposition, if I were you. How can a man of my age advise a young woman from a different community? The interrelationships between the members of these families are quite different from those an average English person would grow up with, Mukerjee had said. If Minnie had wanted an abortion, he told himself, she would have gone and got herself one. She wouldn't have asked for advice. People already know what they have to do, even as they pretend to be desperate and ask you for advice. I'm pleased Jane has married Crawford, he decided. How could I ever be jealous of Gordon Crawford? It was always unreal.

Close your eyes! his daughter sang out. She must have been in the passage just outside the door. Why? Close your eyes, she repeated. Eye, he said. Okay, close your eye. He heard her come in then sensed her presence close to him. Hug me. He folded his arms round her and immediately jumped back. His head struck the bare wall. Standing beside the mattress, his daughter was naked.

FIFTEEN

The solicitor was discussing his hay fever. Judge Savage arrived breathless. His mother had had it and his daughter had it and now his grandson had it too, poor little chap. The place stinks of menthol, Daniel noticed. The windows were shut and the venetian blinds lowered against the sun. There was a neon glow. So it's obviously congenital, the man was apologising over piles of papers, an uncle of Martin's apparently. Sins of the fathers, he joked. To the left, his screensaver was a constant tangling of coloured tubes. What happened? Hilary whispered. It was almost quarter to five. I'll tell you later. Daniel sat down. But she did agree to leave? I'll tell you later. Hilary was alarmed. Sensitivity to timothy grass, the man was still explaining. That's what they make hay from. We'll have to come to some kind of arrangement with Christine, he muttered. It would have been easier if he had sat next to her instead of leaving the central seat empty. There were three seats and then the sneezing solicitor behind his desk beneath his certificates beside his smoothly complicating screen. Just when it seemed there was no more space imaginable, a tiny green tube, bright as neon, began to penetrate rapidly and confidently into the mesh.

So she won't go? Hilary closed her eyes rather dramatically, as if to avoid looking at the end of the world. Some sort of difficulty? the solicitor now enquired. This was typical Hilary. She whispers, but loud enough to be heard. No last minute hitches, I hope? He spoke through a slurry of congestion. The room is suffocating, Daniel thought. Just a detail or two we have to go over with Mrs Shields, Daniel told him. And by the way, the elderly solicitor now rubbed his hands together, my warmest congratulations, Mr Savage. Thank you. But Daniel hadn't understood. It's official, Hilary explained, you're getting the MBE.

As he tried to smile, Judge Savage was aware that he really hadn't wanted this. Hilary would be telling everybody. There's no merit in being assaulted. Where's Christine? he asked. He had done nothing courageous. Late, Hilary said. Daniel recognised her official-situation primness. She is nervous. It's only because I'm not white, he thought. They would never have given Martin such an honour. If Martin had been assaulted. Probably the traffic, the solicitor smiled from his Kleenex. Not to mention the parking problem since they opened this Saver Centre. When it seemed it must go on filling forever, the screensaver suddenly dissolved to a blank. Did Mattheson phone again? Daniel asked. A single red tube appeared in a corner and started to snake this way and that.

The solicitor launched into a spiel about what a pleasure it was when people managed to sell a property on a friendly basis, a basis of mutual trust, without all the usual gazumping and price haggling and people not vacating the premises when they should. There's no consensus about how things should be done. He had a client – he is one of those men who are perennially pleased with themselves, Daniel thought – who had sold his house and vacated it on schedule, you see, but the owners of the house he was buying didn't vacate despite the exchange of contracts with full payment. The solicitor sighed, held out his hands palms upward. Now he's stuck in a hotel with wife and three kids! Terrible, Hilary agreed. On the edge of bankruptcy, the solicitor pointed out. Absurdly, Daniel was reminded of The Cambridge. In the end he had enjoyed his time there. You should never have come home, Sarah shrieked. Never never never. She banged her face into the mattress. I was so happy when you left! Perhaps we'd better phone her, Hilary suggested.

There was no response from the Shields' phone. No one knew if Christine had a mobile or not. They sat waiting. Their buyer was now forty-five minutes late in a town that could be crossed in half an hour at the worst of times. Odd that Martin doesn't answer, Hilary said, since he never seems to leave home these days. You heard that he's stopped working? she asked the solicitor. The elderly man, at once gaunt and merry, hamming his hay-fever, declined the opportunity to talk about his nephew. Suddenly concerned, but perhaps about something that had nothing to do with them, he could only remark on how fortunate it was that this was the last appointment of the day. We can wait without keeping people waiting, if you see what I mean. Could I borrow a hundred grand privately, Daniel wondered? Fame and honours should serve at least for that.

I'm going to be late for Max's lesson, Hilary announced. The solicitor's secretary put her head round the door to ask if she could leave. I gather, Daniel found himself saying to his wife in a low voice, that Sarah actually knew Max before you did. The image of his daughter's body still filled his mind. Hilary narrowed her eyes over her watch. Yes. It seems she button-holed him, would you believe, on one of her silly evangelical outings. She tried to convert him. But you know what's happened, don't you, she went on; they're making up, aren't they, Christine and Martin, and so they've changed their minds. They were buying the place to split up, pretending nothing was happening, probably so as not to upset the parents, his parents are still alive, aren't they, but now that push has come to shove they've gone and had it out between them and changed their minds and we're going to be left holding the baby. This was a crazy idea. They've already paid fifty grand, Daniel said acidly. They're not the kind of people not to honour a commitment.

Again the screen's impossible tangle magically dissolved and shortly after six, driving home, both in a state of some anxiety now, or at least aware that all kinds of practical problems would have to be looked into, Judge Savage told his wife how Sarah had stripped all her clothes off. I thought she'd finally agreed to leave, he explained. She said she had to go to the bathroom for a moment. Then when she came back she had no clothes on. I shouldn't have told her, he immediately thought.

Hilary kept her eyes fixed on the traffic. I didn't know what to do, he insisted. He felt he had betrayed the girl. And she asked you to hug her, I suppose, Hilary said quietly. Yes. Is that the first time? Of course it's the first bloody time, he shouted, or I'd have told you! Hilary snapped: How am I supposed to know what you tell me and what you don't? She turned and glared. It was a fine round English face of grey-blue eyes and greying blonde hair. She drove straight-backed. She told me, Daniel said, that I had ruined her life when I came back home. She said if I was going, I should have gone. She did, did she? Hilary remarked. And she needed to be naked to tell you that, I suppose.

Judge Savage didn't reply. Hilary drove. She always kept both hands at the top of the wheel, the forearms stiff. Her mouth was determined. Streets appeared and twisted this way and that and dissolved. My wife gives the impression, these days, he was aware, that life is an exhausting task, an oppressive burden. Even when she's exhilarated, he thought, and shouts not to be boring, she does it to spur you on to some exhausting task, to have you take up your heavy burden. Bringing up children, making music, making love. We're both exhausted, he said.

Then Hilary told him: She's done it twice with me. What? Taken her clothes off like that, like you said, asking to be hugged. But why didn't you tell me? You had enough on your plate. You'd just started as a judge. I thought it was the last thing you needed. Daniel experienced a strange leadenness. His eye ached. So how did *you* handle it, he asked. I told her that if she wanted to do something silly like that, she should do it to Max, not me. To Max? A bell rang in Daniel's mind. Get dressed, he had told the girl. He was aware of having spoken too sharply. He had shouted. Perhaps some different kind of response had been in order, something more tender. But he couldn't imagine what. Hilary braked hard for a dog. Don't imagine – he had spoken very sharply – that you can make a fool of me! Why had he said that? The dog didn't cross after all. His eye had rested for just a moment on her sex. It was the first time he had seen her naked for many years. Where were you, Hilary asked evenly, that evening immediately before they beat you up?

They were out of the centre on dual carriageway now. He had been expecting this challenge at some point, but was unprepared. I don't prepare my lies any more, he realised. You do know, she said, that you actually phoned me to say you were in the Polar Bear waiting for Crawford. You said you were there in the pub. It must have been just before it happened, she insisted.

In the silence that followed, as she tried to make a difficult right through fast oncoming traffic, he was aware of the danger – they should put a light here, she was muttering – of simply telling the truth in spite himself. Out of exhaustion. Careful! he cried involuntarily. Hilary released the clutch with a jerk. The car rushed a few yards, then was stopped again. She gripped the wheel and waited. I mustn't, he decided. Oh, but he hated the way his wife knew to leave long silences at crucial moments. Things would fall apart, he thought. She stared at the traffic ahead. They were moving again. Finally, he said: Well then I must really have been in the Polar Bear. What can I say? I don't remember. Why didn't you tell me this before? It was for her sake he was lying. This time she spoke immediately: But Crawford says he didn't know anything about being supposed to see you. Daniel shook his head. I don't know. Perhaps a message went astray somewhere.

Five minutes later, with a little premonitory cry Hilary announced: Jane Simmons came back that week, didn't she? Abruptly, she pulled the car over at the bottom of their hill and turned away from him to the side window. Above rising cornfields clouds were piled in soft layers on the horizon. I was *not* with Jane, Daniel said at once. He put his hand on her shoulder. She was rigid. I've told you a million times . . . So you *do* know what you *didn't* do, Hilary came back. Hilary, Hilary . . . I don't want to know! I could have checked up on the call, she said. I could have phoned BT, or told the police. But I didn't? I don't want to know.

He tried to embrace her, but she grew more rigid. She was like Sarah, he thought. Then she turned abruptly to the wheel and put the car in gear. We've got to get this money problem sorted out, she said grimly, before we're kicked out of house and home. Daniel was furious. It was exactly the kind of remark that drove him insane. You know it's not that dramatic, he shouted, they'd never kick us out. I've just been given the bloody MBE, for Christ's sake. It's a miserable little money problem! Hilary was accelerating. With the salary I have, he went on, he wanted to force her to admit it now – she pushed the accelerator to the floor – even if we had to pay it all and keep both flats forever, which we don't, I could borrow . . . He knew she was not listening. We would be so happy together without her, Sarah had said. She never listens. You ruined my life when you came back, his daughter had wept. She had kept shaking her head back and forth. I understand nothing, Daniel thought.

Hilary turned into the gate and pulled the handbrake hard a second too soon. A Mr Mattheson called, Tom announced cheerfully, coming to the door. He wants you to call him back. I took the number. Oh well done, Tommy, Hilary told him in her most ordinarily jolly voice. You've started writing down the numbers at last, have you? Max, she cried. I *am* sorry! Poor Tom never used to write down numbers, she explained. We'd come home and he'd say, some bloke called and he could never remember the name or the number. She laughed. Max was polite as ever. So, Debussy, she cried! Let me hear where you're up to. Daniel took the piece of paper with Mattheson's number on, a mobile. He slipped it into his pocket.

That strange and elusive music! Bloody Debussy, Tom groaned. In the gleaming new kitchen, Daniel and his son heated up a tin of soup. Looking out through French windows, the boy made a bowling action. There's nowhere level enough to practise, he complained. Football was suddenly behind him. The back garden rose to a stone wall and the thickly piled cloud beyond. It seemed solid. Daniel went back into the sitting room where Hilary was pacing up and down beside the piano, beating time on her thigh as Max sat handsomely at the keyboard absolutely intent on his music. Accountant by day, musician in his spare time. Perhaps it had been a mistake to buy the thing so soon, Daniel thought. The mockingly solemn notes filled the room. It was thirty grand more to borrow in the end. He noticed the flowers she'd chosen. No one could deny Hilary's taste, the sober but sunny ease of the room that she'd put together.

Shall we keep some soup for you, he mouthed. Hilary shook her head. She began to tell Max he was doing it all wrong. Don't be so boringly sentimental! I must get Max's phone number, Daniel decided. I must talk to him privately. Forgetting why he had come into the room, he went back to the kitchen. You haven't phoned that Mattheson bloke, Tom said. He said it was urgent. The boy dipped a chunk of bread in his bowl, turning his head sideways to fit it into his mouth. His hair is too long, Daniel thought. The room was silent between them and at the same time filled with the sound of the piano, stopping and starting round the same soft phrase. Debussy is all about not being sentimental, came Hilary's voice. Tom grinned at his father. When most he seems romantic is when you can be most sure he isn't! So there you are! Tom giggled. Trying to laugh, Daniel remembered what it was he had wanted, got up and went back into the sitting room to retrieve the phone from her handbag. Again he set it to call the Shields number.

Is there something wrong, Dad? Tom asked. Judge Savage looked at his son. *Of course Tom knew*, Sarah had said. He isn't stupid, is he? Weren't they the very same words Hilary had used when she told him Sarah knew? She isn't stupid, you know. Tom knew. Yet his parents' problems didn't seem to have bothered the boy. He reads his war books, has his computer games, his sports, and now the dog. He's a completely normal kid. Where's Wolf? Daniel asked. Mouth full, Tom shrugged his shoulders. Daniel watched his son. What do you think of Max? he asked. Tom was looking under the table for the dog. He's all right. The animal came wagging from behind a chair. The house rests on Tom, his father suddenly decided. We have to protect Tom.

Vaguely Judge Savage hazarded: I never worked it out, Tom; is there actually anything between him and Sarah? Oh I think she fancies him, Tom said offhand. But you know what she's like. No, I don't really, what *is* she like? Tom looked up: Great when she's not here, the boy laughed. Dad? he asked. Now he was on his feet, rooting in the freezer. You know that tree they cut down – he found an ice-cream – beside the back wall. You know? He wanted to start burning the wood. But what's the point when it's already so warm? Don't you miss your sister at all? he asked. Please Dad. Can I chop it up? It has to be cleared. We can stick a couple of logs in the fireplace. All right, Daniel said. When those two have finished their lesson.

Max was in good spirits and helped them carry in the chunks of wood. He held the trunk while Tom chopped and sawed. The evening was suddenly blowy as the light dimmed. All the better, Hilary clapped her hands. We can pretend it's cold! There was something unsettling about the way she would move from alarm to lightheartedness. She'll start to bake a cake, he knew. She did. Let's have a crumble, she announced. I can bake a crumble. Fussing in cupboards, clucking back and forth, saying not to worry about the crumbs of bark falling on the new carpet, no problem, I'll hoover, she said, it was suddenly, Judge Savage thought, as if they were *both* her children, Tom *and* Max.

She was happy with this family. While Sarah sits alone in the old empty flat with a radio and a box of Mon Cheri.

Crouching, he started to tear up *The Times* and place it in the grate. Don't you want to save your picture, Mr Savage? Max was the perfect addition to the family. Hilary said abruptly: Dan, I think you should go out to Martin and Christine's and see what's going on. But they're not even answering the phone, he pointed out. So it seems unlikely I'd find them. I think you should go anyway, she told him. Leave a message. It's so strange she didn't come. Oh, not just now Mum! Tom protested. We're just about to light the fire! Can I use your lighter, Max? It's the best moment. I think you should go and see, Hilary insisted. Suddenly she was anxious again. After all, we need to know, don't we? We'll have to have something to tell the bank people tomorrow. We can't just arrive at the deadline not knowing what's going on.

Judge Savage had got his jacket back on and was at the door before he remembered the obvious. I'm not supposed to drive. Hilary looked up sharply. I'm sure you could, she said. You said yourself you were seeing perfectly. If I had an accident, he said, I'd be responsible. I haven't got a sense of distance yet, he explained to Max. Hilary said nothing. She doesn't want to be alone in the car with me, he realised. We're exhausted. She's convinced I was seeing Jane. His head ached with the stupidity of it. And they had given him the MBE. A member of the British Empire! I can take you, Mr Savage. Max wiped his hands. Hilary opened her mouth, then shut it again. Oh Dad! Tom protested.

Surprisingly okay thanks, Daniel told Max, just a bit tired, you know. The tall young man was larger still in his small car. He drove efficiently. When he shifted gear a cuff-link gleamed. He is the polite son-in-law from American films,

Daniel thought. Of the fifties. There is no harm in him. I heard today, he tried, that you actually got to know us through Sarah. Max was good-natured. She took me to one of Mrs Savage's church performances, he laughed. It was kind of you, he said, to take her some food at Carlton Street. Oh I just delivered a few things Mrs Savage gave me.

It came to Daniel then that Tom had been even more put out by Max's leaving than his own. It's a family Max wants, not a woman. And apparently the family wanted him. Sarah is going through a tough time, he said. Max drew a deep breath, nodded and sighed: She certainly is. Daniel insisted, Between you and me, Max, I mean, not a word to Hilary, but do you think she needs to see a psychiatrist? The young man didn't immediately reply. Deliberately messing up her exams like that, Daniel added, you know the story don't you, then the strange on-off tale of the bottle top, and coming back from Italy early when there were only a couple of days left anyway.

Actually, I did suggest to Mrs Savage, Max cautiously said, that she might contact a psychologist, an analyst or something. Frankly, I thought it was more a behavioural problem, you know, whereas psychiatrists always want to give you medicine. Daniel was surprised by this elaboration. You're right, he told him. And what did Hilary say to that? She said she felt the moment we conceded that Sarah was ill, the girl might feel she had carte blanche to behave as weirdly as she chose. Daniel recognised his wife in these words. And I do think she's got something there, Max went on. But do you have any idea, Judge Savage asked, what her problem is? An unwanted intensity was creeping into his voice. Max pulled out the lighter element to touch it to his cigarette. Daniel watched the purposeful pursing of his lips. Why am I so impressed, he suddenly asked himself, by the beauty and good manners of this young man? His generous red lips. Smoking is a stupid habit! He thought of Father Shilling and his racking cough. At least Sarah doesn't smoke. Well, Max said, in his even, pondered way, I really don't know, Mr Savage, it's hard to guess. He blew out a stream of smoke. Then he said: It's pretty obvious she has some kind of problem that prevents her from having a boyfriend.

It was quite a surprise when, on pressing the bell at the end of the small drive, the gate clicked immediately. Daniel had taken it for granted that the trip would be fruitless. Through the bushes a light came on over the front door. I'll wait in the car, Max called. And Daniel's mind now made a sudden shift. At the click of the gate, he was entirely engrossed by the question of Christine and Martin.

Dan! The breeze of an hour before had already died. It was Christine. The rain hadn't come. Dan, I just spoke to Hilary! Daniel found himself embracing a woman soft from the shower in a towelling robe on her doorstep where the outside light in the summer evening was quickly gathering a storm of moths. Mmm, she said, it's nice to see you. I'm not alone, he told her. I know, she said. There's that boy with you, isn't there? But despite Max, Christine decided to shut the door behind him. That's better. And she explained then that she had called Hilary's mobile around four-thirty, found it engaged, wasn't able to get hold of, in the heat of the moment, the solicitor's number and so had called Carlton Street and spoken to Sarah who had promised to phone her mother and father at once. Only it now turned out she didn't of course. I'm so, so sorry, Christine said. She pushed damp hair back from her face. It seems you have real problems with the girl. Then she told him that Martin had had to be rushed to hospital. He couldn't breathe. He kept vomiting.

They stood as they had a month before in the panelled hallway. Perhaps she liked to see him here. There was a box by the door, full of bottles to be recycled and another of newspapers and on the wall a portrait someone had painted of Martin as a child. But why? he asked. She sighed. He could just see the freckles on the swell above the cleavage. Something he caught, she said vaguely – her eyes were pale green – from all that fussing with funguses and moths. Then she asked, Kiss, Dan? There had been a colleague's wife, he remembered, who would only make love to him in the basement. So lovely, she breathed.

They drove back to the ring road, then round to the south and the hospital. Max wouldn't accept thanks. The sodium lights raced by. The weather had disappeared. Max began to say how amazed he was that whatever time he drove round the ring road, no matter when, it was always busy. It's one of those things like thinking your heart is always beating, he said. This thing always always always going on. Let's hope it does, Daniel commented.

Then while Judge Savage was noticing, as ever, the girls and their bored posturing in the wind that the cars made as they rushed by, Max said: That's the bridge they threw the rocks from, isn't it? Daniel glanced up but already it was gone. Already one would be dead. You know, he told Max, they loaded up stones in a quarry miles away and actually drove them to the bridge on purpose. Can you believe that?

Martin had been given a private room. Can't hold down anything, he whispered. Do they know what's wrong? They've run some preliminary tests. The two men exchanged glances. Martin's face was white, his beard grey. Well, I was up on the fifth floor, Daniel finally said. Intensive care. And if I got out of here, you're bound to. But that sounded wrong. This man had climbed out of a high-speed accident without a scratch. Now he looked seriously ill, above all gaunt and beaten. Christine said something about having got infected from your toadstools and whatnot. It's just an idea, Martin said weakly.

There was a silence. Was his old friend happy to be visited? It occurred to Daniel to tell him about the meeting with Frank. He's living just off North Side, he explained. Really? There was a flicker of interest in dull eyes. Daniel sat on the chair beside the bed. Can you believe he's opened a stall at the market, Doherty Street. Having a whale of a time, it seems. But he was always the eccentric. A nutcase, Martin said. There was a time in their lives when they'd spoken endlessly of Frank. Of the colonel's family. Antiques, Judge Savage explained. It had been Frank had brought them together after all. Frank was in Martin's class. Did you ever think he was gay? Daniel asked. Because he's living with this young American man. They run the stall together. I suddenly thought it might explain everything.

Martin seemed to be in trouble. For a moment Daniel thought he had burst out laughing; in fact he had begun to choke. Now he was retching so violently that Daniel reached for the switch hanging by his bed. No one came. Daniel moved to put his arm round his friend and pull him up. Martin! Come on mate. For Christ's sake! Martin struggled, coughing furiously. His face was livid. The main light snapped on and an Indian girl was shooing the judge out of the room. He needs to rest! Another nurse appeared. A fat, white, middle-aged woman. There aren't supposed to be visits, she said, after eight-thirty.

Driving home, Max agreed that it was the most normal thing in the world for someone to make themselves ill when a relationship was breaking up. After what I went through with my parents, he laughed, I doubt I'll ever tie the knot!

Apparently his mother and father were separated. Mother had got breast cancer immediately afterwards.

Thank God, Hilary said, that whatever else is going on, at least we've got our health! By the time they arrived back she was in quite an emotional state. She'd been on the phone to Christine again. Thank God! She must have said it four or five times. Later, watching the dog pee in the mothy dark of the garden, Hilary leaned against her husband and put an arm round his shoulder. Martin's crisis has given us an excuse to make up, he realised. He was relieved. The grass is just sprouting, she whispered. It has that green shadow. Let's not argue, she said. Please Dan. Let's be happy. He kissed her.

Shortly after 2 a.m. the phone rang. Daniel had been sound asleep. Mattheson! He sat up. It's Sarah, Hilary said. She shook her head. She wants to speak to you. Sarah! He sank back on an elbow. Is that you, Dad? Sure it's me, love. The girl seemed very cautious. He caught a glimmer of his wife's eye watching. I just got a weird phone-call, Dad. Oh yes? Then Judge Savage heard his daughter explain that she had spoken to a distraught person called Minnie. She said she didn't have your new number, I think her name was Minnie. He kept the receiver firmly to his ear. She says she really needs somewhere to sleep. She said she was in trouble. And? Well, I didn't want to give her your number. Uh huh. So I told her she could come here, Dad. I thought that was the best thing.

SIXTEEN

If society is held together by the respect people somehow nourish in each other's regard, together with the belief that it really is better to live a decent rather than a criminal life, then the function of a trial and the task of a judge becomes clear enough. Or so Judge Savage had always thought. Sitting down at his desk, he opened a drawer and pulled out a pad of plain paper. Wherever such respect and belief have been shattered by some awful crime, then the trial must publicly assert the significance of what has happened. The community, even if it can't quite believe Man was made in God's image, nevertheless gives notice that such matters are very serious. They won't be tolerated.

Daniel had often reflected in this way. He leaned across the desk and chose a pen. Woe betide the person who decides all this is farce. We will punish him.

Yet if a breach of the general trust hasn't actually been noticed, he once put it to Martin, what then? Daniel stared at the blank paper. He had once defended two Irish menials, man and wife, who had defrauded the elderly lady they were looking after to the tune of half a million pounds. The lady had long since succumbed to Alzheimer's and hadn't even noticed. She had no heirs who stood to lose from the theft. The Irish couple looked after her well and even affectionately. Half a million was less than half her fortune. In this case, to make the crime public knowledge actually damages public faith, finding evil where before people had only seen good. After the couple were gaoled, the old lady made her exit in very short order.

Or what about this, Daniel had suggested (he always enjoyed playing devil's advocate with Martin): what if some sportsman, long dead, some soldier, politician, national hero, admired in biographies and lauded in school – there were monuments to him no doubt – were found to have cheated in some way, or to have fondled a pretty retarded girl in the back seat of a car? Does such knowledge help? Daniel gripped the pen tightly. Does it help the young first-time taxpayer to know that almost all his elders and betters have evaded something sometime somewhere?

Yes, many crimes perpetrated remain undiscovered, Daniel reminded himself this morning, sitting at his desk, waiting for the moment when he would begin to write. He ploughed a hand into a grey fuzz of hair. Still waiting, he turned to his diary and discovered he was supposed to attend a meeting. Trial scheduling for young offenders. It was annoying.

But what had Martin said on that occasion? He couldn't remember. Something about having confessed to his mother, as an adolescent, that he had stolen money from her purse. Was that possible? Daniel was perplexed. Perhaps he didn't remember rightly. It was too stupid. Begin, he told himself. Begin with the date. For God's sake! The biro wouldn't write. For a moment he dragged it angrily back and forth across the paper.

August 25th.

Then of course many crimes that are discovered remain unsolved. He had come into chambers early. The police solve only one in ten reported. Or some such statistic. Despite doctor's orders, he had driven here himself. But how much the worse off are we for that? Could we imagine the police solving everything? The courts would be packed. Yes, Martin had spoken about confessing a theft to his mother, about his personal experience of the cleansing powers of exposure and shame, the way these feelings reintegrated one in a larger society, released you from the isolation of guilt. He's a Christian, Daniel remembered. Suddenly it was astonishing to him that his old friend and reader of Sartre was a Christian. Or had been. Martin had been irretrievably solemn. That was why you respected him. Even pompous. But what would the world be like if every everybody confessed to everything? Nothing had been said of Christianity in these months of Martin's strange despondency, and now very real illness. He is mortally ill, Daniel muttered. Though Christine too was a churchgoer. How did that business in the King's Head about us all being carbon, fit in with Christianity, with the cleansing power of confessing thefts to your mother? I should have put that to him. Unless it was the very rigidity of Martin's earlier vision that had made him vulnerable to being swept away like that.

And, finally, how many crimes that are solved remain unpunished all the same? Many of those Daniel himself had defended, for example. This was another thing they had talked about. Many whom the CPS didn't even bring to court. How much does that matter? How much would we gain if absolutely every misdemeanour were brought to court? How much had been gained by bringing the Mishra case to court? People adapt their point of view to suit their situation, Daniel thought. Albeit unconsciously. Your daughter becomes intensely Christian, fundamentalist even, she talks about it endlessly, for six months she goes out every evening proselytising. It's disturbing. Then quite suddenly she stops talking about it. She stops mentioning God. She stops visiting the Community. He put the pen down. She becomes Christian, to solve a problem, to overcome some discrepancy between the way she sees the world and the way it is. She cuts her hair short and shaggy. She's ill at ease. She talks about divine intervention in her school curriculum. Daniel reflected. It was forgivable, surely, to postpone your confession for a few moments to think about your daughter. Then a few months later she writes obscenities on her exams. The anonymous letters, Daniel remembered, were a mixture of fundamentalism and obscenities, a radical discrepancy.

The August morning was clammy. In a moment he was going to start writing. Daniel wiped his hands. He wasn't worried that he might change his mind. He had understood what must happen the moment he put the phone down last night. How could he go on living with such vulnerability? He had explained to Hilary that Sarah had wanted to apologise for her scene earlier on. That's why she asked for me. But already he had seen what he would have to do. How could he function under the constant threat of scandal? Minnie had left home. Belatedly, she had taken his advice of seven years ago. She has decided on a Western life, rather than an oriental. She is rejecting rules of total obedience and coming out into the open. Now you too will be obliged to adapt, he thought, now the shit will hit the fan.

And it had been such a meaningless misdemeanour, such a casual tangling of utterly different lives!

Judge Savage looked at his watch. These philosophical issues might be interesting, but they were hardly appropriate just at the moment. Mattheson, after all, was working on something that had been most visible: the assault and battery of a crown court judge after a controversial verdict in a matter fraught with repercussions for local race relations. Far from being hidden, the crime had been broadcast nationwide as an outright attack on the community and the due process of law. Its perpetrators must be punished. Even if the truth was that it hadn't been what it publicly appeared to be at all. On the contrary it had been a defence of a different kind of community, a defence based on a misunderstanding. But this is irrelevant, Daniel told himself. This is the kind of crime that, once solved, will be brought to trial with great rapidity and punished with exemplary severity. Again his pen hovered. I have a suspect Mattheson had said. Who?

Only after I had confessed, Martin had explained on that occasion, did I feel that the thing was truly behind me and that I would never do it again, precisely because of the shame I'd felt confessing it. Was it possible that an intellectual like Martin had offered such a feeble and personal response to such a complex question, the exposure of evil in the public domain? Was it possible that he had spoken about the need for total candour in marriage? Perhaps Martin had *always* been ill, Judge Savage thought. What was the value, for example, of putting something behind you, if you destroyed your whole life in the process? And perhaps the lives of others too. This was Sunday School talk. Again Daniel wiped his hands. My womanising was just a phase, he told himself. Frank's life had been entirely determined by one single exposure of what was probably a brief aberration, his rancour against his parents cruelly taken out on an adopted younger brother. It would have stopped the day Daniel had stopped trying to please him.

But such reflections were pointless. For quite apart from

what might or might not be a policeman's particular take on the administration of justice, there was Mattheson's career to consider. Mattheson is a career policeman, he thought. Abstract argument dissolves in the acid of personal interest. This was something Judge Savage had often thought. To catch the men whose crime had filled the newspapers and made their town the centre of national attention for some long time would be a major coup for Inspector Mattheson. He has a suspect now. A Korean? And it would be even more of a coup, would it not, if the eventual solution was not the one that everyone expected? It hardly seems likely, Daniel thought, that Mattheson will put my family and my privacy before his career. Or me before Minnie if it comes to that. Why should he? The girl might well be in danger. I've left, she had said on the phone. Who could know how her family would react? Daniel had called her this morning immediately after leaving home. She knows about their immigration racket, Daniel thought. To be part of her family is to be an accomplice in a crime. They can't let her walk out on them. It was seven-thirty in the morning from a call box. I changed my mind, she said. I'm not going back. I don't even really like Ben. I want a different life. You were right, she said, to tell me to leave. I should have done it ages ago. Have you told Sarah? he asked. About us? I think she knows, Minnie said. In any event, Daniel insisted, I *want* you to tell her. And I want you to tell her that I *told* you to tell her. I don't want her to think I'm trying to hide anything. The time had come to be clear. Prevarication has exhausted me. My double life has tired me out. I'm proud of you, he told the Korean girl. I'm proud you had the courage to do it. The girl said nothing. Daniel had phoned Mattheson at nine. I'm preparing a written statement for you, Inspector. Let's meet at twelve. The policeman was thrown. I have a suspect, he said lamely. I'll come to you at twelve, Daniel repeated. And now found he was supposed to be in a meeting.

Suspect in the singular, he had said, not suspects plural. Who? Judge Savage was curious. But I can't allow him to charge the wrong person. STATEMENT, he started to write: In 1992, during a rape trial at which I was counsel for the prosecution. . .

Hilary phoned. All the morning's thinking had been a not thinking of Hilary, a blotting her out. Now here she was, eager and friendly. With Martin in hospital, she was saying, Christine says she isn't so eager to move in absolutely at once. But she says she'll definitely pay the money into our account today. We can exchange contracts as soon as the solicitor has a free moment, then decide on a rent to pay her pro tem for as long as Sarah's there. That's a wonderful idea, Judge Savage said. Sarah's bound to see reason in a week or so, don't you think? Probably as soon as she knows she's not causing trouble, Hilary said. You could be right. Or if Christine still isn't in a hurry to move, she could find a couple of flat mates to help with the expense. Right. That might be a solution, he agreed. He hung up and wrote:

. . . I made the acquaintance, as a result of coincidences which needn't concern us, of a member of the jury, a young Korean woman called Minnie Kwan, though I believe her actual baptismal first name may be different.

Writing, Judge Savage felt a flow of power. Something you'd like me to type? Laura asked. The clerk was coming toward his desk. He made no attempt to hide the paper. She brought a reassuring aura of expensive perfume and youthful cheerfulness. So different from Sarah. Another brick to add to the stone-throwing bundle, she said. She dropped a thick file with a thud. No need for the moment, he told her. Just making notes for today's meeting. Oh, right. Judge Carter's ill, she added and they laughed. It was a court joke. I'm still laughing, he noted. I'll still be myself whatever comes of it all.

Should he admit that the affair had begun during a trial? Because of course that would be grounds for a re-trial. Daniel stopped. There was a web of consequences here. A rapist and thief might find his sentence quashed. It would be a ridiculously inflated effect of an otherwise insignificant cause. Again the pen waited. The power you feel, he wavered, is only the power to pull down the temple on everybody's head. Should he hang on, perhaps, until he knew who Mattheson's suspect was? Could you erect a barrier between Sarah and Hilary so that it never comes out? How could I do that? Minnie would have to be spirited off to some other town, a job found for her, a place to live. People do do such things.

Judge Savage opened the file newly arrived on his desk. There were psychiatric reports on the various accused. There had definitely been an inflation in psychiatric reports of late, Daniel felt. Ms. Singleton, he read, describes her relationship with Mr Sayle as follows (verbatim from tape): *We met at St Mark's youth club a few years ago. I think I must have been fourteen or fifteen. Like, he's four years older than me. He's twenty-three now. Anyway we both went to church then. I stopped, he still goes. Not always. David's very straight and very respectful. I mean, he does volunteer work and stuff. Paraplegics and old people. You can check with his mum. I know because it pisses me off. I mean like, I'll be wanting to go out and he's like helping somebody in a wheelchair at Saver Centre. Sometimes he goes with Jamie (Mr James Grier, another of the accused). Or he used to. Jamie's changed now. He doesn't go to church no more. I suppose you could say David's hung up. I think so. At the beginning, it was funny, I liked*

*him especially because he didn't just want to have sex with me,
you know how most boys are, it's like the only thing they want.
Then it got weird. I mean he didn't do it at all. We never have.
He says he doesn't want to harm me. We go to a party or even a
rave and he gets going up to a point and then stops. Or it's just
like he disappears. In his head. It gets on my nerves. I'm nineteen
now. I've. . .*

Daniel turned the pages. It really was hard to see how
the inclusion of this verbatim material could have any relevance at all. Where was the statement's conclusion? He went
straight to the end: My assessment is that this is a group of
people in their late teens and early twenties who are all
extremely infantile. Rather than couples, or just a loose
group, it is as if the accused were in a brothers-and-sisters
relationship to each other (7 of the 9 accused are the only
child in their families, none of the supposed boyfriend/girl-
friends spoke of a normal sexual exchange) with the result
that they (and in particular the older male members) seemed
to have no idea how to free themselves from their innocence. In this light, the stone-throwing, if we assume that
the defendants are indeed the perpetrators, which always and
exclusively (according to witness reports) took place on
Saturday nights and always immediately after closing time,
can be seen as an attempt to establish an initiatory ritual
which might allow those involved a sense of having become
adult.

Free themselves from their innocence! Daniel slapped the
paper down on the table. He felt angry. What was this all
about? Immediately he picked it up again. It should be noted,
the paragraph continued, that in many societies the performance of an indiscriminate act of violence, even a killing, has
been seen as a necessary introduction to adulthood and in
particular sexual maturity. Such initiation rituals. . .

Again Daniel slapped the paper down. You get killed because someone else needs to become an adult and have sex! Fantastic! The psychologists forgive everybody, he remembered a colleague saying after one trial, because the most important gesture in the modern world is to show understanding. I prompted that acquittal of the Mishras by pretending I'd understood them, Judge Savage thought. No, by fielding the idea that it was impossible to understand them. Even better. Even more understanding.

Very determinedly now, he wrote: I had a brief sexual relationship with the above-mentioned Miss Kwan after which I heard nothing from her until a few months ago – March, I believe – when she phoned me asking for an urgent favour. She didn't say what she wanted, but during the phone-call she became involved in a violent altercation with her father. I was unable to grasp the reason for the argument because it was in Korean. Apparently as a result of the argument the call was interrupted. Some time later Miss Kwan telephoned me in chambers and begged me to meet her. I agreed. She did not then come to the meeting. Since she had always spoken of her father as being dictatorial and extremely violent in her regard, I became concerned for her safety and attempted to contact her without success. Eventually I spoke to a man whom I believed to be her fiancé. He refused to answer my questions on the phone and said he wanted to meet me. I went, on the evening after the Mishra trial, to the Capricorn Café on Market High Street. Instead of her boyfriend, her father and brothers were there to meet me. I recognised them because I had once visited their fabrics warehouse as a potential customer. They refused to answer any questions about Miss Kwan's well-being. They appeared convinced that I was a pimp attempting to lure the girl into a life of prostitution. While I was using the bathroom, they left the café and it was immediately afterwards, on returning to the car park, that I was attacked. Although I did not see the faces of those who attacked me, I have every reason to believe that it was these men. In any event I finally contacted and saw Miss Kwan yesterday at a flat on the Dalton Estate, Sperringway (flat 72 Sandringham House). She was well. However, and as of last night, the girl has now decided to leave the flat and her family and is staying temporarily at our old family flat in Carlton Street (she is presently there with my daughter). It seems she is pregnant and quite possibly, given her family's attitude to personal freedom, in need of police protection. I did not explain these facts earlier in order to protect my reputation and, obviously, my family situation. I wish to say how much I regret the considerable amount of police time that could have been saved had I made these facts available earlier. The Kwans can be found on East India Road in the South Side Trading Estate where they have a company called Kwan's Asian Fabrics. I am willing to give evidence in accordance with this brief statement and will furnish all further details that you may require in a full and properly recorded statement whenever and wherever you may see fit.

Daniel signed the three sheets of notepaper, put them in an envelope and asked Laura to call a courier. Oh, I've only just been told, Judge, she cried over the phone, congratulations on the MBE!

SEVENTEEN

It had often occurred to Judge Savage that on a different day, or even in different weather, or a different room, a jury might decide things differently. Everything happens now. The thing is decided round this table at this minute with this group of people on the basis of this evidence. He had sent the letter. Twenty years of double life, he told himself, end in that statement. Looking around, he thought: I must speak to Hilary, I must tell Minnie what I have done. Expect months of confusion. Then a voice was asking if he felt well enough to sit. Just very briefly, if you could, Adrian asked. There was no other court available.

A few moments later Judge Savage heard a man proclaim himself not guilty of causing actual bodily harm to a drunk who habitually shouted on the street outside his flat. Judge Savage granted bail. The accused had no record. The court usher had a cold. Sooner or later I was bound to send that letter, he told himself again. Just one more, your honour, if you wouldn't mind. A frail, belligerent boy pleaded not guilty to burglary. My client does not want bail, your honour. He believes his life is under threat if he leaves the prison. His defence will be duress. I have done nothing which could lead to my being imprisoned, Judge Savage reassured himself. He would not grant bail, if it wasn't asked for, he agreed. A heroin addict, the boy claimed he had been forced to burgle by a dealer to whom he owed a substantial sum. Duress, Daniel Savage knew, was a very difficult defence. At knife-point, the boy claimed. Could the libido constitute a source of duress? Your honour, there is one other small matter for consideration. The defendant is a registered addict. I have a statement from his doctor indicating that he may have to absent himself from the trial for about half an hour at some point to receive his dose of methadone. Disrobing, Daniel experienced a moment of vertigo, a rapid clouding of the mind. He gripped a table: it was all bound to happen, he thought. Everything is bound together.

Back in his office, he phoned Jane. Jane? Sorry, this is her sister. I seem to be moving through a fog. Daniel shook his head. Would you like her mobile number? Before he could dial, Hilary phoned again. The solicitor can see us at six. She was excited, delighted. I'll be there, he promised. No problem. A man in the fog, he thought, with a telephone, a list of numbers. No sense of direction but everyone present.

Hello? Jane! It's Daniel. She was thrown. Sorry, Dan, I'm in the car, let me pull over. I'm in trouble, Judge Savage told her. What is it? There, I've parked. She hesitated: You do know I'm marrying Gordon? Of course I know. It's not about that. Their two voices were strange. You didn't love me, were the last words he'd heard from her. Eighteen months ago. I never really believed you'd leave your family. She hadn't cried. You never loved me, Minnie said. Women make these discriminations. What is it? Jane repeated. He said: It's going to come out I had sex with someone on a jury. But Dan! Listen . . . No, Dan don't talk on the phone. Don't! Jane, keep calm. It's only . . . But you mustn't! Don't say a word more. When can I come and see you? How can I help. Perhaps a visit in the cells, he laughed.

Pathetic! He hung up. No one was going to put him in cells! I'm behaving pathetically. A few moments later Judge Savage was in the car, though it wasn't clear where he was going. It is harder to know where I am going than if I were driving through a fog. Or phoning at random. The eye doesn't help either, he thought. It is more of an offence for me to be in charge of a motor vehicle, he told himself, than to have had an affair. My sight is impaired. Even if it was with a member of the jury. It is more prejudicial to public welfare – he spoke out loud in the car – for me to sit at the wheel of a motor vehicle than to have sex with a member of a jury in one of the most open and shut cases I was ever involved in. Though it was a shameful breach of trust. Could Martin advise him? Martin had defended in that trial. It was one of three or four cases in which they had been pitted against each other. I might kill someone, he thought. But hadn't Martin himself been lucky not to kill anyone when he spun off the road like that, headed no one knew where? How attractive that was. Or Christine? Now he was on the ring road. Or even Frank. He could go and see Frank. There were other names too, but none promised release. No one is interested in a traffic offence, Judge Savage thought, however serious. Martin hadn't even been charged. Prince of Wales caught speeding, who cares? Why had he called Jane? We will never call each other, they had agreed. Daniel Savage had never felt so completely alone. A man who enters and leaves his place of work at a separate entrance, he thought, who has his own separate bathroom, who eats separately from others at a separate dining room. The judge. As if the only way not to be compromised was to avoid all contact with the world around.

It was eleven o'clock. People often speak of the ring road as if it were a clock. At nine o'clock there is the court, at 12 the exit home. Driving to six o'clock, or half past, he could go to the industrial estate to confront the Kwans. I could do that. I could discuss the state of play with them. Or Carlton St at ten. My old home, my daughter, Minnie. I have nothing to say to Minnie. Or Frank at two. And prostitutes at various half hours. There were two girls in short pants standing by a traffic light. Prostitutes are available twenty-four hours a day. A city encircled by prostitutes. The local newspaper loved to comment on the fact. Sacrifices on the altar of monogamy. He had read that somewhere. Whenever I'm out on the ring road there's always traffic, Max had said. Did Max go to prostitutes? Somebody has to. There is a geography of prostitution, Daniel chattered to himself. There's a particular place people go where they can be someone else for a while. As when a woman will only have a lover in the basement, or kiss a friend in the corridor. She feels excited in the corridor. It feels less inappropriate in the basement. He was at eight now, heading anti-clockwise. Ladies and gentlemen of the jury, the defendant may be one thing on the ring road but he is quite another in the city centre. Not to mention the mask he wears in the office and the different voices he assumes on home phone, work phone and mobile. Daniel remembered sentencing a respectable stockbroker for repeated violent affray at the away games of his childhood football team. If I drive, Daniel thought, straight to the police station, take the next exit, fast, I might still be there before Mattheson reads the statement.

But I didn't get into the car to drive to Mattheson. He pulled up in a lay-by. That appointment came later. He sat quietly for some minutes, waiting to see what he would do. I need to breathe. This crisis will pass, he thought. He waited. Could it be, he suddenly thought, that Martin had been lying in bed quietly waiting for some crisis to pass? The same crisis he had tried to exorcise in a high-speed accident. He hadn't even invented a story to explain where he had been going that day. I must not drive in this state, Daniel Savage told himself, sitting in the lay-by. It is a shameful risk of other lives. Cars flew past. Until, with lying in bed, a moment's disorientation had become a month, three months. The crisis hadn't passed. It doesn't matter if I get this man off or not, Martin had said. It was a denial of his whole life to date. All human experience is essentially the same, he said. The condemned and the acquitted. All matter and no matter. The outcome of any trial is irrelevant.

Judge Savage was startled by a tapping on the window. You want? the girl asked. She opened the door. I get in? She sat beside him. A girl of indeterminate colour. She wore a short pink dress. What you like? The accent was foreign. She was chewing gum. He still hadn't replied. The question he had always asked himself when he drove by these women was, will I ever end up there? With a prostitute. He hated gum chewing. Her hair was short, but not curly. 'End up' were the words he always used. Her lips were generous. I was bound to, he thought now. One day. I was bound to write that letter.

The girl gestured to the road. We go to nice place? She was brash and anxious. She was working. Daniel was locked in himself. He was churning tension. As he drove, she took out a phone, pressed buttons, spoke rapidly. What language was it? What if the police stopped him? To the right, she interrupted herself. Portuguese? Could it be? Her left hand made an elegant gesture. I'm attracted to slim elegant forearms, Daniel thought. Oriental dancers and young black nurses pouring tea. Now they were driving through streets of council housing not far from the Dalton Estate. Here. You pay now, she said.

There was a Hispanic man at the bottom of the stairs. Forty pounds, sir. Ancient terraced housing. Judge Savage was struck by the sir. A sir-vice industry. End up. She led him by the hand. The room was a bare mattress on the floor, a small boarded fireplace, and on the mantelpiece, boxes of condoms. Already she was naked. The light was pale through curtains patterned with cartoon figures. A slim narrow body stepped out of its clothes. His eye rested on her sex. There was a small white dresser, the kind you carry home in a box and put together yourself. The kind Hilary despises. You like? She asked. She was almost too slim. But she made no attempt to embrace him. She took a sheet from a pile and already she was lying on it, adjusting the thing under her buttocks. She raised one knee. The Disney curtains must have been for a child's room. Naked, she was clothed in indifference. The knee swayed provocatively open and closed. There were Tom and Jerry. And the rooster. Still chewing, she said, Come. She knows, he sensed, how to be here and not be here. This girl is more balanced than my daughter, Daniel thought. She held out a condom.

Judge Savage lay on her violently. He was rough and quite violent, his face averted. She had her strong young fingers in his hair, but he knew she was still chewing. Stop chewing, he shouted. He had always forbidden the children gum. He always ordered witnesses to remove chewing gum from their mouths. Stop fucking chewing! It seemed to galvanise the girl. She began to move. His eye throbbed beneath its patch. She'd spat the gum out. Then he was staring at her dark skin as the room tumbled into place. Her collar bone, her shoulder. It was a fine body. Gently, he touched her neck. We have the same coloured skin, he said. He was aware of speaking softly. She shook her head. Her hand was reaching for her dress. Where are you from? he asked. When their eyes met, hers were blank. She was perfectly protected. You take me back now. Back to the road? His own movements were sluggish. She looked at her watch. Yes.

When she climbed out of the car, he noticed the bridge. He turned off the engine and sat still. The girl walked away. The Whitakers' car had been heading clockwise, as he recalled. He too was now pointing clockwise, towards the bridge. He drove forward a few yards to where the girl had already taken up her stance again. Did you ever see people throw stones from the bridge? He pointed. She was puzzled, made a face. It turned into a smile. All at once, she seemed carefree. The professional sullenness was gone. She was smiling. She seemed pleased. She has no need to hide now. Then at last he desired her. If only she could speak, he would have spoken to her. Could she be Brazilian? He would have expressed affection. He loved women, women of all kinds. Perhaps he would have asked her advice. You come again, she said. He couldn't tell if it was a question or an invitation. She waved quite cheerfully.

So the prostitutes stood in the lay-by right beside the bridge. Judge Savage pulled out into the road. The killers stood on the bridge beside their girlfriends and threw the rocks they'd brought in full view of the prostitutes. The bridge is a stage, Judge Savage realised, for a public of prostitutes. Had the police thought of this? For an audience of destitute immigrants. Illegal no doubt. The white boys show off to the black girls. Had they interviewed them? These young people – what were the words of the report? – had no idea how to rid themselves of their innocence. All those arrested were white he remembered. Young white men with their young white women.

Towards midday, more or less at the same time as he should have been sitting down to discuss sentencing schedules at the courtroom, or alternatively sitting down with Mattheson to discuss his own life sentence, Judge Savage turned his car into the drive of his new home. His eye was aching. He hadn't had an accident. In the end he felt okay. Sarah is seeking to rid herself of her innocence, he thought. Does that make sense? A gardener was raking wood chips around the freshly planted bushes. Daniel stopped a moment to watch him, then hurried to the door.

Mum's out, Tom sang. The boy didn't look up from his Playstation. Daniel stood at the door to his room, watching his young, intent face in the glow of the screen. Game of Super Star? Judge Savage proposed. Dad! Tom was thrilled. Great! Let's play. It was almost three o'clock before Mattheson arrived. By then England had beaten every major football team in the world. Dream on, Judge Savage told his son, and informed the policeman that he had an important appointment at the solicitors at six. I don't expect I shall keep you more than an hour or so, Inspector Mattheson said.

That evening, after the papers were signed, the contracts exchanged, Hilary announced: Now that's done, I think we should go straight to the flat and talk it over with Sarah, all together! An estate agent had suggested that an average rent would be in the region of eight hundred pounds a month. Quite a sum. Christine stood on the pavement confused. I don't know where I've left my car, she said. It's so silly! She was shaking her head. She is as lost as I am, Daniel realised. He had realised it a half an hour before across the solicitor's desk when their buyer couldn't understand where she was supposed to sign. Where the cross is, the solicitor kept saying through his hay-fever. That's where you sign. Sorry, I'm being silly, what cross? Euphoric, Hilary hadn't noticed. We all have our crosses, she giggled. She had her husband back, her financial problems were settled. Her daughter had been outflanked. When we explain it's eight hundred, perhaps the child will see reason, she repeated. Christine repeated that she really ought to be getting on to the hospital. She had to see poor Martin. But she didn't move. She doesn't want to go to the hospital, Daniel realised. She's had enough of Martin.

I still don't understand why they bought the place, Hilary chattered once they were alone in the car. Christine would follow them. They would see Sarah all together. His wife was squinting in the rear-view mirror. Does it matter, he asked, now they've paid? I was so sure they were going to let us down somehow. That we'd be ruined, you know. I had visions of us losing house and home. Just paranoid, I suppose, Hilary laughed. You always said I was paranoid. The more secure you want to be, the more vulnerable you feel. I've bought champagne, she chattered on. Hilary is determined to be happy, Daniel saw. She hasn't noticed I'm a million miles away. For years she is frustrated and now she is happy. Christine too had been a million miles away. Hilary has abandoned any serious professional ambition, Daniel realised. Soon they would be in Carlton Street. This had allowed her to be happy. With my attentions, my success. With a pleasant student or two. She is determined to disbelieve the things she has heard about me. She is an excellent wife. I read in a magazine, Mattheson had said as they shook hands at the end of their conversation, about this film director bloke, does thrillers with shootouts and assassinations, can't remember his name, anyway, it seems he was so scared of telling his wife that he wanted to leave her, one day he says he'll be back at such and such a time for lunch, right? and when she goes to open the door there's a lawyer and a removal van to take away all his stuff. Mattheson laughed. Bloke said he found it easier to imagine an assassination, or even a torture scene, all sorts of awful things, than a confrontation with the missus. Funny, no? I don't want to leave my wife, Daniel reminded him. The inspector had divorced twice. When exactly did this relationship with the girl begin? he had asked. Daniel told him the truth. During a trial. And now, as she turned into Carlton Street, Hilary was talking about Brahms. Can I drag you along to hear Brahms? Oh Dan, why don't we go on holiday together, she cried. Just us two. Her hand left the shift to rub along his leg. Someone was doing the *Liebeslieder* waltzes. We can leave Tom with Crosby. I must say something, he thought. Just us two, she repeated. It had been such a pleasure to play all afternoon with Tom. Minnie will be in the flat. He knew that. How will Hilary react? What will be said? We could have a week in a hotel together. Venice, Vienna. Do what we want all day. He imagined a life where he played cricket and computer games with his son. They were about to confront Minnie. The truth about Martin and Christine, he was suddenly speaking very earnestly, is that there's some key fact they're not telling us, isn't there? There must be. Do you think so? Hilary asked. But now they had arrived. We would understand why they bought the place, why they paid the first instalment late, he said, if we knew whatever it is there is to know and that they're never going to tell us. Christine's car appeared immediately after them. Christine looks rather prettier distracted, he thought. Who cares now they've paid, his wife chuckled.

They climbed in the lift. Hilary put her arm round his waist. What I have to know, Judge Savage had asked the police inspector, is whether I must tell my wife. She was squeezing him. You're overweight Savage, she laughed. I mean, what will come out and what won't? Martin was all skin and bones, Christine told Hilary. He wasn't getting better at all. He can't keep anything down. Even water he vomits. Again she said it seemed he had caught some weird thing from his moths. They had him on a battery of drips: nutrients, drugs. Hilary tried to listen. Or it could have been the funguses. He has this romantic thing, Christine was trying to smile, about the most humble life forms. It was in line with his spending his whole life defending riff-raff, I think. She is lying, Daniel thought. Given the course of action you've chosen, Mattheson said, I don't see how you can avoid its coming out. A courageous course of action, he repeated, in all sorts of ways. He had insisted on knowing exactly when the relationship with the girl had begun. They said it might be why he's been so odd this last year and more, Christine was saying. Again Judge Savage had told him the truth. The fourth or fifth day of the trial. Can I see you? he whispered to Christine as Hilary rang the bell and called Sarah. Alone.

The door swung open. Sarah was beaming. She was radiant. She announced: Oh, Dad, Mum, this is Minnie Kwan, she's a friend of mine. She just came over for a bit. Keep me company. And the girl directed a huge wink at her father. It was a wink, he immediately understood, of ugly complicity. This from the girl who a few months ago hadn't even wanted to share the secret of a present he had bought, a grand piano for a twentieth wedding anniversary now only weeks away. Minnie did not seek his eyes as she shook hands. The Korean girl seemed confused and uncertain. How do you do Mrs Shields? Sarah meanwhile was embracing her mother with an exuberance that was unsettling. Again she winked broadly at her father, actually over her mother's shoulder. Mumsie! she cried. It's ugly, Daniel thought. She pressed her dark young cheek against her mother's grey-blonde hair. Minnie stood back, then took one formal step forward to smile and shake hands when Hilary had freed herself. We were thinking maybe she could stay and share the rent, Mum, Sarah was saying. She put an arm round her mother's shoulder. She'd like to leave home, you see. How rare it was for Sarah to call Hilary Mum! If Auntie Christine will let us stay, that is. Since when had she called anyone auntie? At least until we find somewhere else. We can start looking right away. Again she winked at her father. Daniel realised that she might equally well start shouting out the truth. She might leap in one bound from exuberance to hysteria. He would not accept the alliance offered. One day she would betray him. He would be forever vulnerable, always on edge. The police know who did it, he told Hilary that evening after Tom had finally gone to bed. What, Dan? The police know, he said. They know who did it.

Exactly how the ensuing conversation with his wife had gone, Daniel Savage wouldn't properly remember. Why would one try to remember such things? But it was clear that it ended forever a great phase of his life. They had taken the dog out, this creature who in just a few days had become the symbol of their middle-aged domestic happiness. She let it off the lead at the beginning of the path that led up across the field to the top of the hill. Of all animals, the dog is the most easily domesticated. The evening was pleasant. There was a harvest moon in the sky. Hilary wanted to walk, to enjoy the feeling of the last problem resolved, of relief at last. This happy, sensible, middle-aged couple, Judge Savage thought, who've been through it all, are taking a walk in the country near the handsome, but not extravagant new house they have bought. The police know who did it, he began.

A half hour later she was sitting with her back to a tree, hugging her knees. He tried to touch her. Leave me alone! She started shouting. Leave me! You've killed me. What do you want to do, kiss a corpse? Leave me here, I don't want to talk to you. Where's Woolfie? he asked. I don't care where the stupid dog is. How can you think of a stupid dog? Go!

He obeyed. In the sitting room at home, he poured out a whisky. Quite a few, I suppose, he had told her. It doesn't matter. Yes it does. How many? I don't know, a dozen. Or more? I can't see the point in counting. I bet you did though. He grew angry. Twenty-one, he said brutally. Okay? Obscurely, he felt she deserved it. Who? She demanded. He was furious. They were girls, he said, who do you think? There were friends' wives. They were clerks. Who else would they be? Oh, let's name them, shall we? she shouted, let's name the sluts! You asked for the truth, he said. You asked for it. It had been an ugly scene. Now Judge Savage sat on the sofa his wife had chosen. He knew how carefully she would have chosen the fabrics. To make the house beautiful. Or can't you remember them? she shouted. Hilary liked to put together an environment carefully, he thought, the same way she liked to study a piece of music, meticulously, to build it up line by line, to colour it, to feel the weight of the right hand, the left, the pedal. To make it beautiful. There are so many you can't even remember their names! she was shouting. Is that it? Actually, it was. He poured another drink. He had sensed from the way she had reacted that she wasn't so much disbelieving of *what* he was telling her, as of the simple fact that he *was* telling her, he had made her life impossible. She could no longer go on believing that rumours were just rumours. For how many years has she been hearing rumours, he wondered. She depended on me to lie.

Sitting on the sofa, Judge Savage thought: she likes to eliminate clutter and mistakes. He looked round the tidy room, draining his glass. The embroidery hung over the piano. She wants a man who is a man, but she wants tidiness too. The whisky rose rapidly to his head. There's a discrepancy there. Though he very much appreciated how she kept the house. I don't usually drink two whiskies. Now he was pouring a third. The shock is *that* I did say it, he thought, gazing at the embroidery. Probably she believed what Sarah had told her. She half believed. But it was clutter out of sight. On one side of the cloth you have a strong and carefully woven picture – Daniel Savage MBE no less – and on the other, unseen, the knots and the messy snippings. What a lot of clutter I've brought into this house, he thought. He actually laughed. What a lot of mess!

Standing at the piano Judge Savage played a scale and a chord. For years he had taken lessons. The fingers wouldn't move. Major and minor chords. It's a question of understanding progressions, Hilary had explained. Judge Savage tried to remember how to switch a major chord to a minor. There was a trick. Every major calls to its minor, Hilary said. She had been explaining this to Tom only recently. They don't exist apart. One grew weary of her explaining things. The whole business with Wagner was another. You grew weary of her talking about it. As she had grown weary of his reflections on the courtroom. Marriage. What a bore, Daniel Savage repeated. He banged down the lid over the keys. At the same instant the dog came barking across the room. He turned. The door was open. You're a fool, Hilary announced. She was brittle and icy.

She had tidied her hair, he saw. She was trying to control her breathing. Hilary! Why on earth did you tell the police, she hissed. You're a fool! A great fool! She still loves me, he saw. The whisky had taken away his normal anxiety. Now they're going to fire you, she said. They'll have to, won't they? You're finished.

She stood by the fireplace hissing at him across the top of the piano. Quite apart from anything else, how are we going to pay for all this? Tell me that, Daniel Savage. When they've fired you? Not to mention eight hundred a month for your pampered daughter and pregnant ex-slut. Why in God's name did you tell the police? Why did you go and see the little whore? Daniel was silent. She left home, obviously, because kind stupid uncle-lover Savage went to see her and gave her a lesson on human rights, the superiority of Western culture. Daniel said: Quite probably. Idiot! If you'd told me first, if you'd discussed the whole thing with me the moment you started getting those phone-calls, then we could have helped the girl together, couldn't we, we could have got her a job in a different town. Without going to the police.

Daniel was silent. Another tone had crept into his wife's voice. Why are you so afraid of me? she demanded. It was a mocking tone. She faced him across the piano. That's what's caused it all. Don't be afraid of the notes, she used to tell him when he sat at the piano. You're in a funk, she said. Not at all, he replied. You're terrified of the black notes, she laughed once. Look at you, she repeated. You're terrified. If I was afraid, Hilary, he said quietly, I'd never have told you, would I? You want me to be afraid. How stupid, she repeated,

If you'd told me when this idiot girl started bothering you – we could have sorted the problem out together. *Together*, she repeated. Together we could have sorted it out.

He had to admit that this had never occurred to him, this idea of himself and his respectable, conservative wife coming to the aid of a luckless ex-mistress. She was just a little fool in a scrape, Hilary insisted. For God's sake, Dan, what do you think people do when they're in a scrape? Especially little girls. They phone everyone they know, don't they? Especially the older ones. They see if anyone will help. If anyone has an idea. And she's not even pretty, for Christ's sake! For the first time it occurred to Daniel that the Kwans wouldn't have beaten him up if he wasn't black. If he hadn't been black they might have accepted that he was actually concerned, that he had had some sort of relationship with the girl and was worried for her. But a black! Probably all she wanted was help with an abortion, Hilary was saying. That would have been easy enough to arrange. Only now you'll end up fired. We'll have to sell up. What a fool! Tom will have his friends at school laughing at him. He'll have to change school.

Suddenly Hilary was quite beside herself. Did you ever once think of the children? Did you? You'd better go, she told him. Get out! Oddly, she picked up the whisky bottle and splashed some into his glass. He'd parked it on her score of Debussy, on the piano, spilling a few drops over the precious wood. You'd better just get out of here, she repeated. I don't want to go, he said. It's stupid to act on the spur of the moment. Aren't you worried about your daughter, she mocked him? Aren't you concerned about your little Asian slut. Aren't you afraid her nasty folks'll come and get her back. They must be out there scouring the town for her. Go on, you've already given up everything for the girl. You've

249

let yourself be beaten within an inch of your life for a slut. You've allowed your marriage to go to pieces because of your morbid relationship with your spoilt daughter. Because you had to let your daughter know that you had other women, that you weren't just a henpecked husband. Well now, thank God, the two objects of your concern and affection are in the same place. Go. Go on. Go. You can live with them.

But he told her no. I don't want to leave you, and I'm certainly not leaving Tom. Hilary, he said flatly, I'm not going. Actually I love you. She stared. Don't you dare say that. Don't you dare! I'll stand firm, he thought. He drained the glass. Go! she shouted. No, I've told you, I'm staying here, where I belong. We all belong here. He looked up and saw her arrested in her icy rage. It's an anger greater than she can express, he saw. I caused it. Her body was rigid. She was wild with perplexity. If I'd wanted to go, there'd have been no need to tell you anything, would there? I'd have just gone. But I don't want us to split up. That was in the past Hilary, I'm sorry about it and I'm sorry it had to come out.

She walked rapidly to the door. Hilary always walks with remarkable straightness, shoulders straight, walking straight from A to B. Don't leave, he told her. Come on. She crossed to the door. It's midnight, don't be silly. Let a day pass. The door slammed. Daniel stood still. From outside she opened it again. He heard her forcing in the key. He waited. The door stood ajar. She hesitated, then she slammed it again. Expect chaos, he thought. He waited. At the top of the stairs, he found Tom sitting in his pyjamas with his chin in his hands. Go to sleep, kid, he told him. Go to bed, Tom.

EIGHTEEN

Notoriously, one of the greatest impediments to rapid justice is the difficulty of gathering the parties involved and keeping them together at the same time in the same place from start to finish, or for as long as each one is required. A member of the jury is injured in a motorcycle accident. The key prosecution witness has flown to New York where his father is dying of cancer. Or the constable who responded to the initial emergency call has gone on holiday despite his summons. Your honour, my client is in prison while PC Mulligan is sunning himself on the Costa Brava.

Every pertinent witness must be heard, every pertinent fact set forth. On the second day of R. v. Sayle, Grier Davidson, Simmons, Crawley J., Crawley G., Riley, Bateson and Singleton, Crawley J., one of the two sisters accused in the case, jumped bail. The logistics are inevitably more complex in a group trial: nine men and women in the dock, nine defence lawyers, almost a thousand pages of evidence. The charge was Section 18, Grievous Bodily Harm. What is the point of my beginning this trial, Judge Savage wondered, when I am bound to be an object of scandal before it is over? On August 25th Mrs Whitaker, in coma, gave birth to a baby boy. Daniel had gone into and come out of coma in less than forty-eight hours, while this woman had been marooned there for months before and weeks after. At the outset five defence lawyers submitted that if her life support were removed during the trial her eventual death would unduly influence the jury. Judge Savage remarked that the court had no jurisdiction over the possible decisions of competent doctors and that the defendants might consider themselves fortunate they were not being tried for manslaughter or even murder. We will proceed without Miss Jennifer Crawley, he ruled after an adjournment of twenty-four hours to see if the girl could be rearrested. It was unusual but not unthinkable. The defendant would be back, he was sure. The Crawley sisters were the two who had accused their friend David Sayle of throwing the stone in an initial interview, then retracted.

Equally notoriously, once told, all the evidence must be weighed together as it were simultaneously, the versions superimposed to see which prevails, which blots out and invalidates the other. But beyond reasonable doubt? As if all the pages of a book, all the twists and turns of a marriage, could be savoured together simultaneously, in instant, unimaginable immediacy. By the reasonable man, no less. Had they loved each other or not? Had they behaved properly towards their children? If every action has a cause and if each cause another ad infinitum, how can I reasonably be held responsible, since inevitably the chain of events began long before I was born? These are old conundrums. Ladies and gentlemen of the jury – the prosecution counsel likes to finger his gown, pout his lips as his eye moves over one piece of paper or another – ladies and gentlemen let me remind you that the moment on which we must concentrate our attention is that moment of March 22nd, the time was 10.52 p.m. to be precise, when a stone weighing nine pounds and seven ounces, I repeat nine pounds and seven ounces, was thrown from the bridge where Malding Lane crosses Simpson's Way, otherwise known at that point as the ring road.

Ladies and gentlemen, Daniel told the jury as the trial began. Many of you will perhaps already have heard and read something about the case you are to try. It is natural in such circumstances that one forms an opinion, tends to one interpretation rather than another. The twelve good men and true were a rather younger group than was normal. Eight women and four men. I must now ask you to forget whatever you have heard and dismiss any views you may have had about the case. It is your duty to base the decisions you will eventually make only on the evidence you will hear in this court.

But if one is to superimpose all the conflicting versions and apparently discrepant facts relating to such a terrible crime, in what order must they be laid down? An ancient mechanics establishes the sequence of the speakers. The prosecution will begin. The defence will answer. But prosecution counsel is the least likely to begin at the beginning. He begins at the end with the ugliness of the crime. He impresses on the jury the seriousness of what has happened. The victim, ladies and gentleman of the jury, has now spent five months in coma. He seeks to encourage the idea that somebody must be found guilty. CPS had given the brief to Trevor Sedley QC, the most experienced lawyer locally available. A week ago, she gave birth, by Caesarean section. Her doctors, he said quietly, looking up from his papers, are unable to predict whether she will ever emerge from that condition.

Almost a whole day had been spent pre-trial arguing about admissibility and procedures. I see no reason why this trial should be severed, Judge Savage told two of the defence lawyers. There will be ample opportunity for each defendant to justify him or her self. At the same time Daniel couldn't understand why he wasn't being asked to justify *himself*. At least to the press. It was already more than a week since his statement to Mattheson. He had seen Kathleen Connolly only yesterday in a court users meeting and she had been brightly jolly, almost excessively friendly. Does she know, Daniel wondered? Would the policeman have discussed the situation with the CPS? He had no idea. But if she did know, why had Judge Savage been allowed to start this high profile trial? Defence are a very mixed bunch, he thought, watching the wigged heads lean over to whisper to each other. In a joint enterprise trial of this size, Daniel knew, there would inevitably be an element of intimidation. Or at least the fear of it. The order in which the defendants were to be heard was crucial.

When the doctors removed his eye-patch, the eye saw nothing. Not even darkness, he said. More like milk, bright milk. He was less frightened than he had expected. Do you sense any change in light intensity? His good eye was covered. Now? Now? He didn't. The doctor said only time would tell. He began to give instructions. I've already applied for a disabled licence, Daniel told him. Then on impulse he drove directly to see Mattheson. I'm seeing fine, he thought. My vision is fine.

The inspector will be back shortly, an assistant said. He took a seat by a coffee machine. It is ridiculous, the judge told himself, for a crown court judge to wait for a police inspector. This is ridiculous, he had said a thousand times in imaginary conversations with Hilary. Now that she was gone, he spoke to her all the time. The first day of her absence he had left Tom with the Crosbys. When he returned, the boy was gone. Hilary picked him up a couple of hours back, Mrs Crosby explained cheerfully. She has taken Tom's things, Daniel noticed back at the house. His clothes were gone, his bike, his Discman. This is ridiculous, he told her. Ridiculous.

The waiting room was neon lit. Picking up a magazine Judge Savage read about a man sexually obsessed with anorexic girls who had tried to starve his chubby wife. Attractively chubby, Judge Savage thought, studying the photograph. Said he'd be back any time, the assistant insisted of the bulky Mattheson. The man didn't know what to make of a judge coming down to the police station. The obsessed man, of Latin origin, had previously been cautioned for stalking. I'm afraid I can't wait more than a moment or two, Judge Savage told the assistant. As if it were Mattheson had asked him to come. Can't you chase him on a mobile or something? But he stayed to read the feature article to the end. I have no trouble reading with one eye, he thought. The man denied charges of paedophilia but admitted imprisoning his wife in their bedroom to prevent her eating. He locked her up a whole week allowing her only oxtail soup. I never imprisoned Hilary, Daniel thought; if anything I was her willing prisoner. Enjoying my occasional escapades. Now his gaoler had flown. But did it matter what the relationship had been? Where was she? Where was Tom? What on earth is going on? Judge Savage demanded when Mattheson finally appeared.

Inspector Mattheson called for coffee. He was robust and avuncular. He took the judge into his office, sat him down. A man entirely in tune with his environment, Daniel sensed. What is happening? he demanded. Why haven't you made any arrests? Or have you? The policeman sighed. The whole thing has got rather complicated. Daniel waited. He himself had never quite been in tune with his surroundings. In all sorts of ways, Mattheson added. I imagined you would arrest them at once, Daniel said. If only to avoid any danger for the girl. He didn't even try to hide his nerves. I thought the story would break and I'd be forced to accept paid leave or something. Instead I find myself starting a big trial. I don't know how to behave.

The inspector held a pen between two fingers and tapped it on the desk. Behave exactly as you always have. Well, bar an indiscretion or two. He coughed. Sorry, no, to tell the truth, there are complications. What complications? Mattheson's repeated sighing was theatrical. In confidence, he said, it emerges that your people, the Koreans, are being investigated over another matter. Your people? Daniel barely took in the room they were sitting in. There was a fire extinguisher, a framed certificate, golf clubs. What other matter? he asked.

The inspector sat back. I haven't been told myself. He watched the other man. He's lying, Daniel thought. Mattheson was overweight, complacent. He says in confidence, Daniel thought, to flaunt the fact that there can be none. Is it immigration offences, he asked? It could be, the policeman said. Judge Savage didn't tell Mattheson what he knew. Or drugs, he asked? It could be drugs. The policeman tapped his pen. This pen tapping, Daniel sensed, is a way of making another person aware of time and tension. It could be all sorts of things, the policeman sighed. When I was playing my own institutional role, Judge Savage was aware, I felt superior to the policeman. I rightly refused him PII for that informer. As a result, however, a possible drug dealer had gone free without even facing trial. Have you interviewed the girl at least, he asked, the Korean girl? What other girls are there? Mattheson laughed. Hold your horses, he smiled, no offence meant. Then he said: Actually, we haven't.

But why not? As I see it, she needs protection. I would never have got into this position if I wasn't concerned for her safety. I appreciate that, the inspector said. But he offered no response to Daniel's question.

Mattheson asked if Daniel minded him smoking. The cigarette was already in his mouth. Actually yes, Judge Savage said. The policeman was squinting down to the flame of his lighter. I'm afraid smoke of any kind stings my one good eye. It wasn't true. Mattheson laid cigarette and lighter by his papers. They really did put you through the mill, he sighed. Perhaps you should have taken a little longer convalescing. It takes a while for all the shock to come out after an incident like that. I'm sure, he went on quickly, that if you told them you weren't up to it yet, that you needed another month or something, everyone would understand.

Daniel struggled to impose a professional voice, a legal syntax: On the last occasion we spoke, Inspector, I was under the impression, that you were eager to proceed rapidly to the arrest of the perpetrators of what was after all a most serious crime, and one that captured public attention in a spectacular way. You said yourself, if I rightly recall, that to make some convincing arrests would raise public confidence in the police. You also assured me that if she were in danger, the young Korean woman would be protected. As a result you told me in no uncertain terms to brace myself for public disapproval. You praised me for taking a courageous line of action that would be disastrous for my career and private life. You should know that in view of those remarks I explained the situation in some detail to my wife and family, provoking exactly the consequences that you can well imagine. And then despite my evidence nothing happens. We also agreed, if you recall, at that meeting, that on the following day I would deliver a full, signed statement. Yet early the next morning, one of your assistants phones to tell me that for the moment that won't be required. Now, just as I have undertaken an important and high profile trial that will go on for at least two weeks, you suddenly suggest that I might go off sick. What is happening?

The policeman sucked his lips. When the phone rang he leaned across his desk and pressed a button to silence it. You have two possible courses of action, he announced. His voice was brusque. For the first time Daniel had the impression that he was being candid. You can continue as you always have and await developments. In that case I promise I will do my best to give you due warning if and when something is about to happen. He stopped. Yes? The policeman looked at him. Alternatively, you could go and speak directly to the press. That would make things happen extremely quickly, I imagine. If that is what concerns you.

Mattheson paused, perhaps to study the judge's response. Daniel was sitting perfectly still. Actually such a course of action would be most inadvisable, the policeman added. In all sorts of ways. He paused again. He was tapping his lighter on the table now. For my own part, I can assure you, I would be delighted to arrest these people, regardless of your private situation. With due respect.

What *was* all this about? In court Judge Savage would have insisted that a witness respond more straightforwardly to the questions put to him. He was under oath to tell the *whole* truth. He must disclose what he knew. But Mattheson was not under oath. So I just go on? he asked. Mattheson said nothing. The interview seemed to be at an end. Daniel was seized by the anxiety that there was something important he had forgotten to say. He did not want to go back to the emptiness and uncertainty of his private world with something important unsaid. He sat still. What was it?

I gather, Mattheson finally offered, that your wife's taken the kids on holiday to think things over. Apparently he was being kind. He sat back, lifted his eyebrows. Yes, Judge Savage agreed. Yes she has. He stood up. Mattheson said vaguely: Of course we do still have our other suspect. Judge Savage sat down again. What? The Inspector rubbed the butt of his pen up and down the side of his cheek. The truth is that you can't actually be sure it was the Kwans committed the crime. Can you? We have no evidence but the circumstantial business of your all being together in the café a few minutes before. Daniel said nothing. You didn't see your attackers, Mattheson insisted. No, Daniel said, that's true. I didn't actually see them. I was hit from behind. Mattheson lifted the phone. Dennis, could you bring in the Savage file? A moment later he was asking: Do you recognise this man?

The photo was a grainy still from a security video. The time and date were printed in the top left corner. The original image must have been blown up to give the head and shoulders of a man yelling, fist raised; a white man, with tousled hair, beefy face, eyes lost in deep hollows. Daniel shook his head. Never seen him. That was recorded outside court after the Mishra verdict, Mattheson said. And this, he handed Daniel another photo, was picked up by the Barclays security video beside the pedestrian entrance to the car park. Seen from above in half profile the figure might or might not have been the same man. The time is right. We've identified the man in question and he does have a record for violence. Quickly, Judge Savage handed back the photo and in the same movement got to his feet. Let me know when there are any developments, he said.

NINETEEN

Following the order on the indictment, the prosecution began with the case against David Sayle. However, I must establish this initial premise, Trevor Sedley cautioned. He was a man who generated conviction by eliminating any hint of charisma. This is very much a case of joint enterprise. The Crown will be inviting the jury to bear in mind that the nine defendants, together with two others who were not with them on the evening of the twenty-second, but whom we will be hearing as witnesses, were very much a group. Whenever possible they spent their time together. The Crown will be bringing evidence from both inside and outside the group to demonstrate that this was the case. They regularly drank together, either at a pub called the Tally Ho, on the corner of Craeburn Street, where they had been on the evening of the crime, or at another pub called the Belgrave on Canada Avenue. They listened to music together, usually at the home of the Crawley sisters, two of the defendants, or at the home of James Grier, another of the defendants. On occasion they played games together at a church youth club. St Barnabus. David Sayle, in fact, is a regular member of the St Barnabus congregation. He frequently reads the lesson in church. So is Mr Davidson. Sedley looked up from his notes. He spoke tediously slowly. A solid group, then, as my learned friends for the defence will not be contesting. It will be noted, for example – he coughed – that two of the defendants admitted in an initial interview with the police that they had been present on the bridge at the time of the crime and seen stones thrown from the bridge by a member of their group. Released pending further enquiries, however, and thus exposed to the peer presure of their friends, they then both denied this.

Three defence lawyers sprang simultaneously to their feet. I am sure, Judge Savage said calmly, that Mr Sedley will be explaining to the jury the relevance of the interviews to the case against each defendant. As for the differences between the early and later interviews, the defendants themselves will have the opportunity to explain how these came about. However, Mr Sedley, while the fact that this is a close knit group has been well-established, your remarks about peer pressure have not and the objection of my learned colleagues is quite understandable. Your honour, I myself was about to say, Sedley conceded, that the Crown's interpretation of these interviews will be hotly contested by my learned friends the counsels for the defence. Thank you Mr Sedley. The defence lawyers sat down. At the same time it struck Daniel that he himself, far from being part of a group, was now entirely alone. Exactly, he thought, as society most applauds me – there was the invitation to wait upon her Majesty on September 30th, the very day of their twentieth wedding anniversary – I find myself most alone. Nobody is putting peer pressure on me at all.

Very slowly, and as if a man just couldn't be more even-handed, Sedley started to explain that the Crown would be maintaining that David Sayle was the group's leader and that as such he must bear the greatest responsibility for what happened on the evening of March 22nd. This is why Mr Sayle's is the first name you will see on the indictment. Mr Sayle, ladies and gentlemen, is the man sitting on the extreme left of the dock and his defence counsel is my learned colleague Mrs Wilson directly in front of him. The jury found themselves looking at a pleasant chubby young man with a blond pony tail, who nervously returned their gaze.

Martin was skeletal and serene. He didn't turn the television off when his guest arrived and the shifting colours of the screen's melodrama played uncontested across the pallor of his face. The curtains were drawn. The once black hair had turned suddenly grey. His beard was gone. The once powerful voice was a whisper. That's Shirley, she's seeing her ex-husband on the sly. We're supposed to feel sorry for Damian who doesn't know the boy isn't his. Judge Savage noticed that the room had a slightly sweet smell to it.

Daniel had driven straight from court to clinic. For ten days now he had been left entirely alone. He had seen no one. Exactly as had happened at The Cambridge a year before, the moment there was a split with Hilary, it seemed impossible for him even to talk to anyone else. My wife is a catalyst who makes other intimacies possible, he thought. Without her, without the children, I am inert and alone. He couldn't even respond to the most ordinary messages on the answer phone. He listened to Christine's voice and didn't answer it. He couldn't offer sympathy or ask for it. It's quite inexplicable, Judge Savage told himself. He ate pre-packed sandwiches in the kitchen and went to his work mechanically. I have no individual existence, he realised. I go to court to be jerked into action, like a marionette who only comes alive on stage. I lock into the ugly world of a group of undistinguished youths telling lies about the evening of March 22nd. He thought about his own children, and it was some way into the trial before it occurred to him that March 22nd might have been the very day that he and Hilary had decided to buy the house.

And is this, Sedley asked, the stone that you refer to? From under his bench the lawyer produced a white box and from the box a large rough whitish stone of the variety one might use in a rockery. The usher took the stone and carried it across to the witness box. It is, said the constable. And where was it exactly? On the floor of the car, where a front passenger would put his feet. It was covered in blood. I would like, Sedley said, in his quiet voice, for each member of the jury to take this stone into his or her hands and feel its weight.

The usher took the stone across to the jury. Sedley watched. If one speaks quietly, Daniel thought, all around you must strain to listen. Take your time please, ladies and gentlemen, the lawyer was saying. It's a style that imposes silence. One or two jurors clearly did not want even to touch the thing. When someone dropped it on the bench the clatter was startling. It was as if Sedley had wished this to happen. Then the prosecutor continued with his case. A forensic expert was called. Your honour, someone stood up. The young man's voice boomed. I object. The courtroom hadn't really been designed for nine defence counsels, each with his or her solicitor. Your honour, my learned friend is leading his witness. This was true, though fairly innocuous. The defence lawyers are diminished in stature, Daniel thought, by their number. It was an important aspect of joint enterprise trials. They seem shrill, even when their objections are reasonable. The wisest say as little as possible. Mr

Sedley, could you rephrase your question please? The jury was unimpressed. And when the expert had finished and the jurors were taken to the secure car park behind the court to look into the boot of Grier's father's Mondeo, the whitish grey fragments were so evident on the coarse black under-carpet over the spare wheel and so clearly of the same stone material that they had examined earlier in the day that this aspect at least of the prosecution's case became biblical truth. It was the same grey white, Daniel now saw, as Martin's face, expressionless as a fallen stone on the hospital bed.

Mr Shields is no longer with us the nurse told him at St Steven's General. Judge Savage had set out to visit his friend with a sudden determination to break the spell of isolation that had fallen on him. Hilary had not been in touch. The children had not phoned. Minnie Kwan had not phoned. Martin will be happy we have broken up, he told himself.

The nurse gave him the name of a private clinic. This was the third day of the trial. Daniel had been in court since nine. To his surprise Kathleen Connolly had appeared at the afternoon session and seemed to be focusing her attention entirely on him. Has my whole private life, he was wonder-ing, been discussed among the various powers that be? Is the advantage of making those arrests being weighed against the disadvantages of disgracing the first black judge on the circuit, and a national hero to boot? How had Mattheson reached the conclusion that Hilary was off on holiday with Tom? I live a charmed life, perhaps, he thought. After a few minutes watching television in a tiny private room, Daniel said: You know, Martin, that stuff you once gave me about having no secrets in marriage: well, I told Hilary everything.

The private clinic was out of town, to the west, not far from the Shields' home. So, having spoken to nobody for so long, Daniel found himself returning to Martin. He and

Martin had lived in the glow of each other's mutual esteem for twenty years. It was a friendship that had seemed as much part of his life as the colour of his skin. Martin was the person who most enabled me to overcome any racial disadvantage, Daniel had often told himself. He had been there when the Savage family broke up. He had provided a security beyond that family. Then, mysteriously, the friendship died. Was the death blow my getting back together with Hilary? Or my becoming a judge, being promoted beyond him? You understand all this, Daniel thought, no more than you understand your relationship with your daughter. Or the reason why a group of young people heave a rock onto a fast road. They could see no way of shedding their innocence. What an odd remark that was! Had there been something innocent about the friendship with Martin? As if an aspect of adolescence had been protracted long into adulthood. We were close for years, Daniel kept saying to himself in the car, then something came between us.

Sitting beside the man's bed, the judge was suddenly determined to tackle this. Do they still not know what you've got? he asked. Oh some obscure viral complication, Martin muttered. Unlike most sick people, he did not seem eager to discuss his ailment. You-had-the-flu-twenty-years-ago-and-now-you're-paralysed-for-life kind of thing. He shrugged. He seemed resigned and unconvinced. His nose, Daniel noticed, had become prominent between sunken cheeks. It had become an imperious nose. And despite watching TV inanities all day, he still retained an imperious manner. Soap opera, Dan, he pontificated while the ads came on, is the triumph of the age. It's made up quite casually from day to day by a group of authors who all have their different takes on the various characters; but you invest emotion in it anyway: completely random and completely engrossing.

Judge Savage laughed: Ever since you first talked about them, I keep seeing moths, he said. He was trying to please. Before tackling the issue. There was one enormous one in the bathroom last night. About an inch long maybe. Very gothic. But you don't want to crush them because their bodies are so soft, their death would be such a mess. Easier to chase them out of the window. Martin grunted. It was the sort of grunt Tom came out with when his father belatedly showed interest in some computer game the boy had already half forgotten. Will I be forever without Tom? I told Hilary everything, Judge Savage said. And I told the police who beat me up.

It was extraordinary how quick Martin's mind still was, how immediately this corpse of a man grasped the situation. His attention was galvanised. The television was forgotten. He was pleased, excited, condescending. You've always had a desire for self-abasement, he explained to his old friend in a cracked, husky voice. You want to be known and *still* be loved. He shook his head. So when you become a judge and circumstances have apparently put you beyond all abasement, you go and look for a way of destroying yourself. You can't bear being above criticism.

Daniel was respectful, but didn't agree. He hadn't looked for trouble at all. The girl had come to him. He had been obliged to check that she was okay. Martin smiled wanly. Look at it any way you like, he said.

What *is* wrong with you? Daniel demanded. There was silence in the small and no doubt expensive room. Or rather, there was the chatter of the television. Despite the uncertain weather the place was air-conditioned. You do know, don't you? Martin lay still. The interest that had flared in his intelligent eyes was swiftly extinguished. Daniel started at the sound of a phone ringing from the TV screen, as if someone were calling them into that world of interminable melodrama. I'm sure you do know, Daniel said, and that if you told people, something would change. Martin's face was quite expressionless. What does it matter to you? he asked eventually. We were close friends, Daniel said.

So?

This one croaked word seemed to contain oceans of stubbornness. So, I want to help, not to let something that was part of my life just dissolve. You look pretty ill, you know, Daniel insisted. Martin said nothing. Does Christine know? Daniel tried. Again he waited. I think she does, doesn't she? Christine being another of your close friends, Martin said weakly. He held the remote tightly in two clawed hands. You two were going to split up, weren't you? Daniel insisted. Anyone could see, Mart. Only since you're now ill you don't have to. Martin shook his head. I can't understand how my problems could possibly matter to you. Lying on his back, eyes turned to the ceiling now, he clasped and unclasped the remote. We live in different worlds, Dan. Rubbish, Judge Savage said. Martin seemed to hesitate. Okay, Dan, okay, for the sake of old friendship, let me tell you something about Christine. At once Judge Savage felt tense, felt he'd made a mistake. On the television, the chatter of the soap turned to a tinkle of music. It was Christine told Sarah about you and Jane. And all the other women you had. Christine. Your friend. At last they exchanged a long look. Martin's eyes were surprisingly alive. Why? Daniel asked. His old friend shook his head: Caprice?

TWENTY

Mr Whitaker was a nondescript, overweight man in his late thirties. He worked in a building society and had come to court, as he would go to the office, formally but not carefully dressed. Mr Whitaker, could you tell the jury what happened on the evening of the twenty-second of March? He is on tranquillisers, Judge Savage saw at once. Any time you need to take a break, Mr Whitaker, all you have to do is ask. The young and rather brash woman on the front row of the jury kept twisting round to make remarks to the man behind her. Elizabeth, that is my wife, and I were driving along the ring road, the witness said, on our way back from a visit to my mother. He spoke in a low voice. We had been driving about ten minutes. Could you speak up, please, Mr Whitaker? We do appreciate how difficult this is. His hands were limp on the rail. His voice was a monotone. That was the day Elizabeth had her scan. Then the windscreen sort of exploded. I think I lost control of the car for a moment, then I braked on the hard shoulder.

Sedley invited the man to say exactly where this had happened. And could you describe to the court the scene after you brought the car to rest? Yes. After I stopped the car, I saw that Elizabeth . . . Mr Whitaker took a breath. He cannot look at the defendants, Daniel noticed. The man's eyes were fixed on some distant point above the jury's head. He knows it will make no difference to him whether they are found guilty or not. Well, she was covered in blood, Mr Whitaker continued. Her face was gone.

Only one defence lawyer ventured a cross-examination. Mr Whitaker, did you actually see the stone fall from the bridge? No. The man's voice was a whisper. Perhaps you could repeat that so that we can be sure everyone has heard. No, I did not see the stone coming. And could you tell the court, Mr Whitaker, how far away you were from the bridge when you stopped? Mr Whitaker said perhaps a hundred yards. And how long was it after the accident before you looked at the bridge and saw, as you said in your statement, 'quite a few young people', running away. The man hesitated. I was trying to pull Elizabeth out of the car. I've really no idea. She had the mobile in her handbag, you see. I wanted to get it out to call for help but she'd fallen over it. It . . . There was so much blood. How long do you think it was, Mr Whitaker? Perhaps a minute, the witness said vaguely. Not more than two or three. So it might have been as many as three minutes, the lawyer repeated with great deliberation, between the moment you stopped the car and the moment you saw these young people. Yes. Thank you, Mr Whitaker, he said.

That evening, Daniel called Hilary's parents. These people always disliked me, he knew. He had never understood if it was a racial thing, or whether they would have disliked any partner of Hilary's. If he had never worried about it, it was because it seemed that the dislike of her parents was a necessary condition for being loved by Hilary. Certainly they had hated Robert before him. Our marriage is strong, she said once, because neither of us feels at home with our boring families. How ominous this seemed in retrospect. They were held together by opposition to the world without.

Are you fully recovered now? his father-in-law enquired. Hilary is not sure of her plans just at the moment. The man had the sharp, cautious voice of one always ready for argument. He was waiting for this phone-call, Daniel realised. Of course we will tell her that you phoned. And that I asked her to phone me, Daniel insisted. He had been hoping that she would not have been in touch with her parents at all. If he hadn't spoken to anyone these last two weeks it was partly because, not talking about it, it seemed the split hadn't quite happened, or might still be harm-lessly reversed. For Hilary to go to her parents, Daniel knew, to speak to her parents against him, this was a huge step. She was gone.

Then, in the space of an hour he called everybody: Jane, Frank, his daughter, Christine, Max. In the empty house he needed to feel people around him. He sat with the newly installed phone in the kitchen, the communicating doors both shut. Max said he had been on holiday and only just returned. What is it, Mr Savage? For a moment Daniel imag-ined the boy was lying. Could he really not know? Have a good time? he asked. Max began to talk about Chicago. There were relatives he had never seen before. Judge Savage decided he couldn't tell him: Hilary said to tell you to feel free to use the piano while she's away. If you stop by one evening, I'm to lend you the keys. Oh that's so kind. She's on holiday with the kids, Daniel explained. They've gone to the coast. I can't talk, Jane whispered. I'm with Gordon. Just tell me how's it going, have you managed to hush it up. Fine, Daniel said. It's going fine. *A bientôt*, she said. Frank was merry. Found the dear Asian damsel safe and sound, did we, squire? Desert flower, jungle orchid. I've been keeping an eye on News at Ten to see if you'd been brained again. Daniel felt an intense impulse to confide, at once blocked by an equally powerful impulse for self preservation. Instead, he talked about Martin. Repressed queer, Frank said. Alas. He laughed. The worst. By the way, if you're really hard up for cash, we might even be able to pay you something back, we're doing a roaring trade. People just can't get enough of antiques, even the most obvious fakes. Even the immigrants are buying antiques, he laughed. The Pakis, you wouldn't believe it. Everybody wants to live in a stately home. Pillars of Georgian society. Frank talked on and on. He seemed to have taken a liking to his brother. It's unbelievable, he cried. People are gaga with the idea they're getting something unique, something with a history. He bellowed with laughter. The duller the world they live in, the more they want antiques, get me? Come and visit the stall and you'll see. They're just begging to be taken in. Most of the stuff's mass produced of course. When I see you in the dock, Daniel said, I'll say it's a case of homonymy. They'll never guess. Frank has been drinking he thought. His brother couldn't stop laughing. The old pigmentation was always on your side in the end, he joked. You were born at the right time, squire. But I forgive you. The Savages really were a bit too pale for their name, n'est-ce-pas?

On putting the phone down, Judge Savage felt oppressed and dissatisfied. The sound of these familiar voices, each so miraculously distinct, instantly gave him back a part of himself. Then it died the moment he put the phone down. He was no one. For a moment, going through to the sitting room, he found himself in the black glass of the TV screen. It had become rather frightening sitting here alone. The television is frightening, he thought. How could Martin lie there for hours allowing his mind to be absorbed in the television? Daniel Savage wanted to tear a scab off. But where was the wound? Do I really feel that bad? I do feel bad, he thought, but it doesn't matter. Mr Whitaker's face was present to him. What a nondescript face that was! This man who had suffered so much. The world is so irretrievably routine for today's youth – this was something he had read in a newspaper article – that only the most extreme gestures can pierce its suffocating sameness. I'm in danger, he sensed. He had felt less sorry for Mr Whitaker after his appearance in the witness box than when he first heard about the calamity. When you read about suffering, in a newspaper article or in case papers, you imagine it is your own. How intense it would be! You imagine you are capable of the most intense suffering. You imagine the pathos of Hilary hit by a rock, her face is shattered, torn away by stone and shattered glass. You are sitting on the roadside weeping. Mr Whitaker is not up to the tragedy that has befallen him, Daniel decided. He was a mediocre man who had been heavily and effectively tranquillised. Not even a reliable witness. Those three minutes could save the defendants.

Christine? he demanded. Christine. He felt belligerent. Yes. Christine, listen, I saw Martin last week and he told me it was you who told Sarah about me and Jane. How clumsy it sounded. Why on earth did you do that? Why? I know it must sound mad calling out of the blue, but I need to know. Why did you do that? You changed my life. There was a long pause. The woman seemed to be in difficulty. Why? he demanded. I just don't understand it, he shouted. Is it true? Dan. She was upset. Dan, I . . . Abruptly a different voice came on the line. Who is this? Who am I talking to? Daniel Savage. Oh Dan, it was Martin's father. The voice dropped. Dan, I'm afraid Martin died this afternoon. Christine's in a state.

He called his daughter, but no one replied. She even took the dog, he told himself for the twentieth time. I can't even stroke the bloody dog. The ringing tone sounded for the tenth or twelfth time. Sarah wasn't answering. If I'd had to feed the dog I might have fed myself too. He wasn't eating at all except lunchtimes in the judges' dining room. The fridge was empty. In the one private conversation he had had during the day Crawford had complained that the Government's new human rights legislation would double their work load. There would be endless complaints. Whole new categories of victims have been created! The potential for litigation is vast. Where will it end? Daniel thought: Perhaps the powers that be don't want to lose a judge when they're expecting a flood of new cases. The phone rang on. Minnie is there, he suspected, but not answering. It occurred to him that he didn't know whether or not the girl was in time to have an abortion. These are not my problems, he told himself.

He went out and climbed into the car. Nobody replied at Carlton Street. He drove to the country, to the Shields' house. The place had undergone a transformation. Everything had been cleaned and tidied away. Seriously cleaned, Judge Savage sensed. The once cluttered hallway was spick and span. There were no bottles to recycle. In the sitting room, the air of shabby inertia had been replaced by an equally unsettling show-house look. Coming here so soon after the phone conversation with Frank, Daniel noticed for the first time that all the furniture was antique. All the surfaces were freshly dusted. On a low table, copies of *Tatler* and *Cosmopolitan* had been arranged in a fan. He wasn't a man who usually noticed furniture. Hilary hated DIY and Ikea and she hated antiques too. Though she always dusted. The glossy covers stood out against the dark varnish. People should make beautiful things now, she said. Hilary seemed to hate everything that might be considered the norm of English middle-class life. No wonder she married a man who wasn't white. Everything classy is black, she used to laugh. Cars. Dinner jackets. Pianos. On the Victorian sideboard stood a huge framed photo of Martin in full black barrister's regalia. That was new. It was a rather young Martin, but with a Dickensian look to him, his eagerness still intact. You were his closest friend, old Mrs Shields murmured, and she pressed Daniel's hand between hers.

They sat in the austerely clean room. Christine kept getting up from her seat and sitting down again. Even the sofa covers had been dry cleaned. Christine drew the curtains, sat down. She went to get glasses, sat down. The floral curtains have been cleaned, he noticed. He remembered making the phone-call to Ben, from that seat. Mr Shields was talking. Christine's dress had a neat floral pattern. All her dresses, he was aware, had frills at the bosom. She placed various bottles on a low table beside the *Tatler*s and *Cosmopolitan*s. She sat down. She has nice knees. Then she stood up to pour.

With all the advances in medical science, Martin's father was rambling, it seems you can still die of some obscure disease without them even being able to tell you what it is. He had exactly Martin's long, lean face, his curling, self-confident lip. They can't tell you. They've never even *heard* of it. The posh old voice was a rehearsal of outrage. He doesn't really feel outraged, Judge Savage sensed. He feels he should be. Pouring sherry and whisky, Christine's floral sleeve trembled. The frills on her breasts trembled. But it seemed with repressed energy, not grief. Probably they were fed up with Martin and his disease. The woman is having to hold herself back, Daniel thought. Martin had bored everybody sick. She wants to get going. It seemed it might be Creutzfeldt-Jakob at first, Mrs Shields confided. The mother had exactly Martin's soft eyes. The early symptoms, she said, were very similar. He'd had the father's sardonic lip, the mother's soft eyes. Oh Mother! Christine protested. The older woman had burst into tears. You were his only friend, Dan, she was mumbling. The only one who came to visit him in hospital. Then they said it must be something to do with all those moths he kept playing with, Mr Shields picked up the story. Perhaps more to drown out his wife than anything else. He was pacing the carpet beside the coffee table, glass in hand. These were hours to be got through, Daniel thought. When he tried to exchange a glance with Christine, she looked away. Some oriental thing, Mr Shields was saying, half-heartedly. She went to fetch an ashtray. Could she really have told Sarah, Daniel wondered? It had never occurred to him that Martin might die and they would never speak again. I'm sure I wasn't the only visitor, he said. Martin had so many friends. Mrs Shields lost control. Our world is over now! It's gone, Dan. She was sobbing. She sat crumpled on a low stool. Then she put her arms over her face, her hands pressed on her grey hair. There's nothing left. There are no children. We might as well be dead ourselves. Sometimes I think we *are* dead! Shut up, woman! Mr Shields lashed back. With hatred, Daniel thought. He put down a cigar. I'll never have grandchildren, she was weeping, shaking her head beneath her arms. Martin cut off what friends he had, Daniel realised. Christine sat rigidly in her seat, one hand reached out to touch her mother-in-law's arm. She is waiting for us to be gone. The moment we are gone, she will jump to her feet and live! She can't wait. Old

Mr Shields looked disgusted. Daniel stood up himself. Christine will change her life overnight, no sooner than we are all gone, he thought. She has been waiting for this moment. She knew it was coming. Mrs Shields, he bent down to the woman; she was small and shrunken and shaking: Martin was a wonderful man, he said. You know that, Mrs Shields. The words seemed both true and preposterous. Turning to go, he found himself face to face with the photograph of the younger Martin in his black gown. How persuasive his friend had been! I can find my own way, Judge Savage said. But Christine had sprung up, a haunted smile on her face. In the passageway she squeezed his hand. We must talk, she said. He didn't know how to respond. Did she mean about Sarah? Dan, I want you to speak at the funeral. It will be Friday probably. Will you? Only you could do him justice, she was saying. Please, Dan, just a little speech. Justice. She was pleading and intimate. She reached out to him and did something motherly to a button on his jacket. You do know Hilary has left me, he said. Hilary has left me, he told her. Yes, I know, I know, we must talk. Outside Daniel sat in his car rubbing a finger fiercely at the corner of his lips. His old friend was dead. When he stopped at Carlton Street the windows were still dark and no one answered.

By the time the prosecution was approaching the end of his case the styles of the various defence counsels had become clear. There were those who objected constantly and chose to cross examine all the Crown's witnesses, and those who kept silent, sat still. It was also clear that there was a certain friction between one or two of the lawyers. Perhaps, Daniel thought, Sedley had tried to split the defence pre-trial by hinting at his accepting a lesser charge – perhaps section 20, GBH through reckless behaviour, rather than section 18,

GBH with intent – for the less important of the group's members. In return for a plea of guilty of course. Both initial interviews given by the Crawley sisters indicated Sayle and Grier as the culprits. That none of the defendants had accepted the offer was an indication of how tight-knit the group was, how much they feared Sayle perhaps. Unless of course they were indeed all innocent. At the same time the lawyers defending those offered the lesser charge, if such an offer had been made, would have understood that they could perhaps best serve their clients by leaving the spotlight on the two defendants whom the prosecution had now unequivocally indicated as the main targets. Or if he was truly devious, this might have been Sedley's plan, not to have the less important defendants accept his offer, but to encourage them to believe that it was worth attacking each other from the witness box. But that phase of the trial was yet to come. Meanwhile, another remarkable indication of solidarity among the defendants was that all but one had told the police that they were actually at the bridge. Perhaps they had decided even before they were arrested that it would be too dangerous to deny this, since there might be evidence to prove their presence there. As it was the prosecution had only one witness, the elderly cyclist, who had positively identified only two members of the group, Sasha Singleton and Ryan Riley, as present on the bridge at the time of the crime, more or less. Their accounts, in interview, of those with them on the bridge would not become evidence against their co-accused until they actually gave their versions in court, after the prosecution had presented the case. If all the others had flatly denied being on the bridge, Sedley might well have found himself threatened with having his case dropped at half-time for lack of evidence even before the defendants were called to the witness box. Yet only one had denied it, and as a result of that he was clearly being ostracised in the dock. The others were not speaking to him. No sooner had Sedley closed for the prosecution than Stuart Bateson's counsel was on her feet. Your honour. She wished to consult with the judge upon a matter of law. The jury were invited to leave the court. Your honour, may I submit that there is no case to answer in respect of Stuart Bateson. No witness, this sensible middle-aged woman pointed out, had identified Bateson as present at the scene of the crime, he himself, unlike the others, has always denied it. Counsel for the prosecution had had nothing to say about him. There was an immediate and angry stir among the defendants. You bastard! In the dock, a police constable moved quickly to get between Bateson and Grier. Daniel withdrew to consider the matter.

From the case papers Judge Savage knew that the other eight defendants had all named Bateson as one of their number on the bridge at the scene of the crime. But again this could not be considered evidence against Bateson until stated in the witness box. At this point, the prosecution's case against Bateson rested on his having been engaged in the orgy of mobile phone conversations in the early morning after the event and having been seen to leave the pub with the rest of the group when they set off for the bridge. The law requires that Judge Savage separates in his mind what he knows will be stated in court by the other defendants and what the court has already heard. And what he has heard is really not enough evidence to try the man. Other youngsters were known to be members of the group and were not on trial. They too had made many phone calls on the morning after the crime. One girl in particular, Virginia Keane, had also left the pub with the group, but then not gone to the bridge. Her alibi was solid and none of the rest of the group claimed she had been present. Judge

Savage put his head in his hands. Then before returning to court, he quickly wrote the following note on headed paper: Dear Hilary, not having an address for you, what can I do but hope that your parents will forward this, or hand it to you. Despite having written the thing at least a thousand times in his sleepless head, he found himself stuck when committing it to paper. I myself don't understand the psychology of it, he wrote, or the real nature of the damage that has been done. I just want to say that whatever I did and said, I am still essentially the person you always thought I was. The things we talked about were over ages ago. I want to live with you and Tom and Sarah. Meantime, have you heard that Martin has died? When I found out, I realised how much I longed to have you beside me to talk about it.

Give my love to Tom. You have all of mine.

Dan.

When the jury eventually returned and took their seats again it was to hear Judge Savage explain in careful detail why he must now invite them to return a verdict of Not Guilty on the defendant Stuart Bateson.

TWENTY-ONE

It had long been impressed on Daniel Savage that you could recognise people by the way they played the piano. But could you then go on to recognise whom they were playing for? Drinking whisky over newspapers while Max practised in the sitting room, Judge Savage found himself puzzled. His wife had a particular kind of virtuosity. It was the virtuosity of precision, of controlled excitement. That *is* Hilary, Daniel often thought, that energy and its contrasting restraint. Don't be boring, she always said. Don't be boring, Sarah mimicked. And she might equally well say it to invite you to express strong emotions, or to ironise when you had launched into them. She wanted those emotions, then ironised them. She found them cloying. The two of them had made love together in the empty house, with great tenderness, but then it had been most unwise to speak of what was most on his mind. When they went for walks, he remembered, she hurried on ahead, straight-backed; she turned round and beckoned you on, Come on! Then she stopped for hours to pick blackberries by the side of the road, stuffing them, if she had nothing else, into a paper bag

that immediately fell to pieces. Or she would talk to someone at a bus stop, ignoring you. She was cheerful, patient,
charming, then intolerant to a degree. I became addicted,
Daniel thought, as he sat listening to Max's piano playing,
to the difficulty of being with Hilary. Though perhaps she
is no more difficult than any other woman, or man for that
matter. Now I am suffering withdrawal pains. And Max is
playing differently too, he thought. You could tell he wasn't
playing for her today.

Listening, Daniel tried to concentrate on his newspaper.
A man dressed as a woman had killed his psychiatrist and
the psychiatrist's wife in a major London shopping street. I
am drinking too much again, Daniel thought, pouring
himself another drink. Max was playing quite differently. The
murderer had no history of cross-dressing. After killing the
husband he had chased the wife, whom he had never previously met, into a department store, shot her, then locked
himself in the ladies toilet and, after two hours of negotiation with the police, shot himself. It was as if a flood tide
of music were slopping over lush banks. Daniel lifted his
head. The boy was playing as if no one were listening.

Murderer's Wife in the Dark. That was one subheading.
This woman had told the police that she didn't realise her
husband had a gun. The murderer was a successful architect,
but retired. The wife was a third wife. More remarkably, she
wasn't aware that her husband had been seeing a psychiatrist.
Daniel went out to stand in the back garden. The new grass
was thin and long now. A horse was grazing in the field
beyond the hedge. I won't mow it, he decided, until they
come back. Actually, he didn't know whether Hilary had
bought a mower. I expected scandal and tumult, he thought,
and drama, but not this emptiness. All day at the court, then
an empty house. You thought work filled your life, then found

time hanging heavily. How Tom would thump things out on the piano! Get back Joe! Hilary didn't control or criticise him the way she did with her students. How excited she got watching him play football. Pass, Tom! Pass! You're too wooden, she used to tell Sarah. You're too cautious. Suddenly, Judge Savage was storming back into the drawing room.

Max! The young man stopped. Daniel saw his face return from a sort of vacant transport, to polite alertness. His hands left the keyboard and fell to his side. Max? Yes? What is it, Mr Savage? Max, when exactly did you meet Sarah? A breeze from outside rustled the music score. On the table the flowers of two weeks ago had still to be removed. I'm not quite sure. Max hesitated. Last winter. Yes, before Christmas. And she was handing out tracts? Yes. In His Image? Daniel asked, for Your Salvation? That's right, Max half smiled: She stopped me in the street. And she was very intense I suppose?

The young man turned the stool to face Judge Savage properly. He seemed glad of the conversation. Yes, she was. When we started to talk, she said actually she was far more confused than I was, about God. She said she was only handing out tracts to see if she really did believe. Which I thought was funny. Daniel was struck by this picture of his daughter. Finding he was still holding his newspaper, he folded it. Quite, he said. Then she took you to one of her mother's concerts? Yes, I'd told her I was a piano player. She said if I came to a church service with her there was a concert afterwards. I think there was a piece by Satie, I don't know who played, and then Mrs Savage played Ravel. So it was Sarah introduced you to her? Yes. And what relationship do you think they had, Sarah and her mother?

Daniel had been speaking very quickly, almost brusquely. It would be evident that he'd already drunk too much. How do you mean? Max's face contrived to give an impression of complete candour. How *do* I mean, Daniel wondered? Every evening he came home from work and immediately was filling a tumbler. I'm not sure how I mean, he said. Then another. Just give me your impression, of how they were when you met. What did you think of them? Well, Max said, Mrs Savage was very excited. That's normal after performing. He hesitated. I think after a few moments Sarah sort of disappeared. I can't remember, she must have wandered off, then we started talking about arranging lessons. I'd stopped playing for a while and I wanted to start seriously again.

Have you seen Sarah over the last few days? Again Daniel was brusque. I did phone, Max said. When no one replied here, I tried Carlton Street. Daniel tried to understand what this pleasant young man was thinking. Surely he must find it strange that Daniel was alone with breadcrumbs all over the table, dirty glasses, wilting pinks. Mrs Savage, you see, hadn't told me she was going away. We were supposed to have our regular lessons. So you called Sarah? That's right, but then of course I only got her flatmate. Why of course? Max seemed confused: Of course? Well, I mean, because as you said they're on holiday. He thinks I'm drunk, Daniel saw. In fact, she told me that Sarah had gone off with her mother. She told you that, the Korean girl? Yes. Max was increasingly uneasy. Where have they gone by the way? How old are you? Daniel asked. The boy's extraordinary civility actually invited you to be rude. Twenty-five, he said. Twenty-five? Can I ask you a brutal question, Max? The young man shrugged: If you like.

Judge Savage was sitting on the sofa now. He had spread his legs out. He held his tumbler in both hands, elbows on his knees. Sarah had left the flat and gone off with Hilary. How improbable that outcome would have seemed only a short while ago. He tried to assume a posture of ease, as when he used to tell court stories at dinner parties. Max, I'm presently trying a case where a group of people your age or there-abouts are accused of throwing a rock from a bridge over the ring road. That's right, we've already talked about it. Have we? That evening I drove you to the hospital, remember? Oh yes, well, I wanted to ask you, Max, can you imagine why they would have done that? Max was puzzled. The boy couldn't see how this could be considered a brutal question. The judge explained: It seems, you see, that statistics show that the culprits of such crimes are almost always in their early twenties. And in fact that's the case with the defendants we have. Max shook his head. There are three couples, Daniel said, in the nine accused. Max looked up: Oh are there girls too?

Outside it was dark now. Daniel stood, turned on a lamp, went to draw the curtains. Does that surprise you, that there are girls? A sudden movement startled him, but it was only a moth outside against the pane. I'm so nervous, he thought. I suppose I thought it would only be boys, with vandalism, Max said. But this isn't vandalism, Daniel sat down. These people have no history of vandalism, Max. That's why I wanted to ask you. They all live at home with their parents. Like you do. They are all employed. They have quite decent jobs actually. Certainly they all have mobile phones. They call each other incessantly. The morning after the crime there were something like eighty phone calls between them. Anyway, I just wanted to throw this idea at you.

He paused. It was actually extremely indiscreet of him to discuss a case under trial. But what difference could it make? Yes? Max was dutiful. There's a psychologist, you see, who has served a statement on the relationships within the group, and he remarked on the fact that none of the couples involved, none of them, had normal, well, sexual relations. Oh, the Jewish boy said. They form tentative couples, but their real solidarity seems to be toward this adolescent group, though they are hardly adolescents any more if you see what I mean. Yes and no, Max said. Well, what I'm driving at is that the psychologist suggests that this, oddity if you like, this prevalence of the group over the couple, has something to do with the crime. What do you think about that?

I . . . Max began. Daniel waited. Well, I don't see how, Max said. He tried to laugh: Psychoanalysts always think everything's to do with sex. That's true, Daniel agreed. On the other hand in this particular case, not fifty yards from the bridge from where the stone was thrown, I think we drove under it ourselves didn't we, there's a place where prostitutes stand. You know. Probably you have seen them yourself. Yes, Max said. Actually I've heard the police are thinking of asking the papers to publish the names of the men who stop for them. Are they? Judge Savage asked. Really? He hadn't heard about that. Anyway, those prostitutes must have been in view when whoever it was threw the stone. What I want to know is, do you think, someone your age, Max, might, out of sheer sexual frustration, out of not being able to get started in life, as it were, do something quite mad like that, to show off to the prostitutes, to send a message to his girlfriend? Do you see? Or to another member of the group. Apparently there was some kind of dispute going on between two of the male members of the group.

Max was perplexed. Very directly, he demanded, But what does it matter, Mr Savage? Daniel sensed resistance. The boy's amenability was gone. Who cares *why* they did it? As long as there's enough evidence to show that it was them. They looked at each other. Fair question, Daniel said. This had once been Minnie's objection of course. If we know he raped her, who cares what he was thinking?

Or perhaps it does matter, Max asked more cautiously, does it? He didn't want to seem stupid. Exactly as he spoke,

Daniel became humiliatingly aware of not knowing quite why he had started this strange discussion. I'm drunk, he told himself. In a trial – he tried to think – in a trial, in order to get a conviction, Max, the prosecution has to put together a body of evidence, make a convincing story if you like, and of course it has to make sense. I can see that, the boy agreed. They call it the burden of proof, but it's rarely really proof, of course. There's almost nothing you can really prove, in the way that you can do an experiment to demonstrate some scientific formula. Legal proof is a convincing story, a series of persuasive links between the things which appear to be indisputable evidence: in this case the stone, the bridge, a car driven by one of the group with traces of stone in its boot, the nine young people with their mobile phones, two more or less corroborating confessions in an early interview with police, later withdrawn. Right, Max agreed. Right, I see that.

And stories, Daniel went on, these days are above all psychological, you see. They have to be psychological. When people tell a story they're thinking psychology. They're thinking, what is the mind that this collection of facts implies? Actually, Daniel wasn't even sure whether he believed this. Yes, Max agreed. Rightly or wrongly, of course. So if the jury feel the psychology of the prosecution's story is crazy, that means they can't imagine that mind, and the lawyer defending of course will do everything to make it look crazy, or at least suspect. At that point, however convincing the evidence, in terms of who saw whom where and when, the jury may still decide not to convict. Or at least hesitate. They feel it doesn't add up. This bloke couldn't have done this. I hadn't thought of that, Max said.

But the trouble is, Daniel concluded, that so many things that happen, even ordinary everyday things, don't seem to add up at all. I suppose not, Max was dubious. And anyway they're so complicated. Which is why people perhaps exaggerate some things and play down others when they start talking about their lives. Or even when they're giving evidence to the police. To give it a shape and a story. Yes. Max had his youthful body bent forward, clutching his hands together. Yes, I can follow you there, I know people who do that. It's an aesthetic thing. But looking at the handsome young man, it occurred to Daniel now that he was merely offering a repertoire of postures that might please. He shuffles a pack of pleasing attitudes. This conversation is pointless, Judge Savage thought. Why on earth am I blathering on like this?

So the thing about the psychologists, he tried to wind up, when all the exaggeration and so on is stripped away, is that they are very good at bridging the gap between what happened, the various facts, and the mystery of the mind that made them happen. In fact, although obviously that's not officially their job, you could say that it was their secret task, if you see what I mean. Their function. Depending of course on whether they're serving a statement for the prosecution or the defence. A psychologist can put the jury's mind at rest that another mind could indeed have operated in this way. So in this case someone comes up with this story of throwing stones in response to sexual inhibition. And I just wanted to know what you personally thought of that.

Max shook his head. It's fascinating, he said carefully. He bit a lip. I mean, Daniel went on blindly, I mean you could say that Sarah, for example, had thrown a lot of stones at her father, couldn't you? Max was silent. Do you see what I mean? Max sat still. Daniel made one last drunken attempt to puncture the boy's defences. Just think, he said sharply, for example, of the way you met her, Sarah. There you are, walking down a street in town in late spring early summer. You come across a young woman, fresh, attractive I think, sexy even, am I right? Someone you might have looked on as a possible girlfriend, I would have said. How often is it that a man is actually approached in the street by a beautiful girl? Oh God, I've drunk far too much, he realised. We all dream of such things, don't we? But instead of merrily a-courting her, as it were, you spend most of your time with the girl's mother who's a good twenty-five years older.

Judge Savage's voice had become quite harsh. He wanted to force some sense into the man. But Max replied at once: Well, that's because she's a piano teacher. Daniel sighed. Quite, he said. The anger went out of him. He stood up. Yes of course, you're right I'm sure. Then he announced: Oh they went to Cornwall, by the way. It was a bit of a last minute decision. Hilary said to tell you she was sorry, but it seemed the only way of enticing Sarah out of the flat. You remember we'd had problems. Oh, I see, Max said. His eye had wandered back to his score. Daniel was struck by the fact that even he himself was not really suffering. He picked up the newspaper, spread it on the table and very quickly pulled the rotting flowers from the vase. He rolled them up in the newsprint and found himself to his surprise face to face with the psychiatrist murdered by his architect patient. He burst out laughing. Actually, Max . . . The boy had been poised to start playing again, but waited. Actually you know, Daniel wrapped up the flowers tight, her flatmate's quite nice too, if you feel like flinging your cap. Max looked perplexed. Sarah's flatmate, the one you spoke to. Korean, petite. Mid twenties. Probably quite a sack artist, I would have said. I'm sorry? Sack artist, Max, good in bed. One hears these expressions in court from time to time. Oh I see, the boy said.

TWENTY-TWO

On impulse, Daniel was driving to Carlton Street. I will wrench this into shape were the words that repeated in his head. He drove very fast through a fizz of city light. Already I am in the lift. I will wrench this into shape. The word wrench is very powerful. But he couldn't get his key in the door. What is wrong with these keys? He checked again. Now the landing light was out. She has changed the locks, he realised. This flat is no longer ours. Christine has changed the locks. I hate Christine. He knew this. He pushed on the bell. He pushed the button down and held it. He held it down. It is late at night to visit, people will be asleep, but he must wrench this into shape. There were footsteps. He heard a chain guard released. We never used a chain. Someone is scared. There was a rattle. Somebody is frightened of opening the door. The door didn't open. He waited. Open up! The footsteps were retreating. Judge Savage shoved the door which swung effortlessly open onto a cavernous sitting room. Sarah! Her figure was retreating in a dark nightdress. Sarah! He stumbled toward her. Why are my legs so leaden? I'm ageing, Judge Savage thought. I'm no longer young. The figure turned in a doorway. Minnie Kwan was streaming blood. Her face had dissolved in blood. But it was also alight. It was on fire. It was consumed in red flame. You let me die, she said, and Daniel awoke.

He lay in bed, savouring his dream. A nightmare can be a pleasure when it's over. The shiver of horror almost immediately became a pleasure. Let her die was what I didn't do, he thought. Why had he dreamed the opposite? Why did one wake from such a terrible dream to feel so complacent? I don't have nightmares of being beaten up, he noticed. I don't regret what I did.

Experiencing a strong sense of being himself and sure of it, Judge Savage got up in the night and found a piece of paper. Hilary, he wrote, if you are quite decided, let's sort out terms so that then I can see Tom and Sarah. He felt dispassionate. I will no longer fight for my marriage, he thought. It was more a fact than a decision. There is no kindling in me, he announced, rather oddly. He wrote. Obviously you will have the house. I won't make trouble about money. I shall move out. Actually, I love you, he concluded. Dan.

He addressed the letter to her parents and in the same strange mood of assurance and even serenity that the nightmare had brought on, lay down in bed again to doze. At last he could see the future. How strange to feel so calm! I find a small place in town somewhere. I give myself entirely to the court. Judge Savage put his hands behind his head and closed his eyes. I become the finest of judges, the very finest. I give all my energy to it, to the business of running a court efficiently and honestly. I write important articles proposing far-reaching reforms. Somebody must improve the quality of prosecution in this country. Somebody must find a way of saving time and money without undermining anyone's rights. It would be gratifying to have reached the pinnacle of the judicial system. The children are too old to be taken from me, he decided. Tom and Sarah will always be my children. They are too old to think of anyone else as their father. Then he thought: If the scandal does break, I could go into legal consultancy. Race issues. I will always be in demand.

He felt blissfully calm now, completely and utterly decided and serene, as if drifting on his back in some comfortable canoe down a gentle mental stream through the soft late summer morning beyond the town, a distant barking of dogs just penetrating the muslin mist that hung over slopes of wet stubble. It's all done, he thought. That's over. Living alone, I need no longer torment myself with the mysteries of those around me, what they might want, what my rela- tionship with them might be. He felt strangely posthumous to himself, as though saying goodbye to the life of one who was dead. I won't even ask Christine about her talking to Sarah, he thought. The woman's unhinged, Judge Savage decided. He remembered Father Shilling. Even if I sleep with her, he smiled, I won't ask her. He chuckled. You don't rule a woman out of your bed just because she's unhinged. Who shall I sleep with now I'm no longer married? If I sleep with Kathleen Connolly, he thought, I'll just sleep with her. I won't ask her any professional questions or be in any way indiscreet about trials in progress. She's an attractive woman. I will avoid conversation about her sick child. Work, and have the occasional fling, he decided. And I will never need to lie to anyone. Never need to say where I am, when I'm coming home. There will be no separate compartments in my life, no false bottoms. That had been exhausting. I will support the children, he decided rather solemnly, with- out insisting on knowing too much about their lives, without tormenting myself whether they are successful or not. They can do what they want. They can become evangelists and marry pygmies. I will not interfere. I will sit out.

What a blissful image this was! Daniel Savage seemed to have detached himself from the hard earth. I will be entirely understanding, he thought, and tolerant. A judge's responsibilities are enough for one man, he decided. I didn't let her disappear or die, the thought came back. I didn't. At least that part of my identity I was true to. That's the bottom line. I didn't find her face streaming blood. Again he saw the corridor, the bloody, burning, faceless figure and was not horrified. On the contrary, his soft dozing was cushioned on the pleasing falseness of that nightmare. It was curious that the dream unfolded in the place that used to be his home. Now I don't have a home, he thought. Double lives happen in homes. Now I don't need to wrench anything into shape. Not even the stone-throwing trial. I'm just the referee, he told himself. I'll become a sort of legal priest, Daniel Savage decided, presiding over the sacrament of justice. I can see Frank, perhaps, some Saturday mornings. I can drop by Frank's stall. This was a charming thought. He and his forgotten brother would chat together at the man's market stall, all past rancours forgotten. All relationships will be drained of rancour, Judge Savage said out loud. He said it again. Even Hilary. Separated, their relationship would be drained of rancour. Yes, yes, that will happen very soon. He could imagine them all having a drink together. Down by the river, perhaps. Myself and Frank and Hilary. Perhaps Christine too. I'll take a rowing boat with Tom. His relationship with Sarah would also be drained of pain. I will never slap her again. There would be no more embarrassing conversations of the variety he had embarked on last night with Max. I won't do that any more because

I won't be trying to comprehend the incomprehensible. It was curious how such a nightmare, a banal nightmare really, the simplest rearrangement of various anxieties, could provoke such a profound change of attitude, such a deep sense of well-being. This story has a happy ending, Judge Savage thought. Suddenly he saw the trajectory of it very clearly. He was convinced. It was stupid to be seduced by the difficulty of these long-term relationships, with wife and children. You set yourself goals, then are overwhelmed by them. You've worn yourself out, he decided, that's the truth, being two and more people at the same time, Hilary's man, your own man, the courts' man. A double, indeed a triple life. It was stupid to seek approval, stupid to abase yourself. Duplicity is exhausting, he decided. All the same, there was no need to go down Martin's path of nihilism. On the contrary. This is blissful, he thought. There would be new interests. Frank seemed perfectly happy with his new friend and his antiques. I'll allow myself an amorous adventure from time to time, Judge Savage told himself, floating blissfully on the early morning mist. Something a bit more classy and discreet than a Brazilian streetwalker. A conscientious judge is a valuable member of society after all. He deserves his little adventures. He can afford them. Or I might do the rounds of old girlfriends. That was a possible variation. Even Minnie. He hadn't just abandoned the girl, as he might have. A friendly night together was not out of the question. Now you are free to help anyone you want and likewise to make a pass at anyone you want. So long as they are not sitting on a jury. Those seemed to be the two fixed points of his character, helping and leching. A moral man, with appetite! Judge Savage laughed out loud. He felt good. I must make the stone-throwing summing up an exemplary performance, he thought, I must say quite clearly what's at stake. You cannot reduce a woman to a faceless mass of gore.

We was in the Tally Ho till about ten. I've said that.

Well, I'm asking you to say it again, Mr Sayle. Could you please remind the jury whom exactly you mean by we?

Well, there was Sasha and John and. . .

Could you give us their surnames, please, Mr Sayle.

I've already told this part.

Mr Sayle, I'm asking you to tell it again. You have been questioned by your defence counsel who invited you to present your version of the story. Now I, as prosecution, am questioning you about that version which I suggest is actually a pack of lies.

Sedley shocks, Daniel observed, by being suddenly offensive without any change of pace or delivery. But it seemed poor advocacy to him. There was the danger that the jury wouldn't come on board.

Okay, there was Miss Singleton, that is Sasha, Jamie Grier, Ryan Riley, Stuart Bateson and Ginnie Keane. Five plus me.

Sedley ticked off the names painfully slowly.

Stuart Bateson has denied he was there. Did he tell you why he denied it.

You'd have to ask him.

Mr Sayle, I didn't ask you why he denied it, I asked you if he talked to you about it.

I won't talk to a liar, Sayle said firmly. As far as I'm concerned he doesn't exist. He was there.

Do you mean that you are angry with him because he departed from a prearranged story?

There's no prearranged story. He didn't tell the truth, because he was scared that then people might think he did it. Which he didn't.

294

But that is speculation.

What? Sorry.

You are speculating as to why he said what he said. You don't know.

I do know, Sayle said. It's clear as daylight.

Mr Sayle, all of the names you mention as leaving the pub with you were originally among the defendants, with the exception of Ginnie Keane. Did she come with you to the bridge or not?

Ginnie went off somewhere else.

Good. We will come back to Ginnie later. So, there were six of you when you leave the pub; one of the six goes off on her own, but in the meantime you phone various others.

As I said.

You had a mobile?

Yes.

In fact I gather every member of the group has a mobile.

I've said so, yes.

Mr Sayle, could you explain to the court the way in which the telephone numbers of the group were recorded on the memories of each mobile.

David Sayle had no problem with this request: Each of us, had, like, a number, in the group, and that was also the number you had in the memory on everybody's mobile.

Mr Sayle, Judge Savage interrupted, are you chewing gum?

'Fraid so, your honour.

Could you please remove it, Mr Sayle? At once.

David Sayle put his fingers into his mouth, then stopped. The court usher offered him a tissue.

Thank you, Mr Sayle.

So if I can get this business of the numbers straight, Sedley began.

Yes, for example, Sasha, Miss Singleton, is two which means if you press number two and hold it down on any of our phones that automatically calls Sasha.

Ah, I understand. And whose idea was this?

Mine.

And what was the reason for it, Mr Sayle?

I liked to feel we were a close group, like, that we was all good friends.

I see. Presumably this sort of tight-knit community was something you also appreciated about the church.

Yes. I liked the youth club.

But that was for under-twenties.

That's right, though some of the people that goes are a bit over. I mean, it's not a hard rule.

Thank you. Now, who was number one on those mobile memories, Mr Sayle?

Beg pardon?

Each member of the group had a number and that was also their number on the memories of the mobile phones. Who was number one?

I was.

And why was that?

Sayle shrugged his shoulders. Because it was my idea, I suppose.

And not because you were the leader of this, er, close group of friends.

Not really.

Not really, meaning you were a little bit, or meaning some people thought you were, but in fact you were not.

Sayle looked puzzled.

Judge Savage said: I think counsel is suggesting that 'not really' is not as clear an answer as yes or no. Were you or were you not the leader of this group?

Sayle hesitated. He had an honest, open beefy face. No, he said.

And your girlfriend Sasha Singleton was number two on the mobile memory?

I just said that.

And was she the leader of the group?

No, definitely not.

Ah, definitely not. And what number was Mr Riley.

Ryan is five.

Not quite the order in which you appear on the indictment, Sedley mused aloud. It was improper comment, but the defence counsels wisely refrained from objecting. Just one member of the jury chuckled. David Sayle again looked puzzled.

And was Mr Riley the leader of the group?

Now the defendant smiled broadly. Not at all.

Could you explain your merriment, Mr Sayle?

Sayle took a breath, then fell silent.

Could you explain why you thought my question about Mr Riley amusing?

If you knew him, Ryan's not the kind to be a leader, Sayle said. Of anything.

So who was the leader?

Sayle shrugged his shoulders.

Mr Sayle, you know perfectly well that you were the leader of this group, indeed the only reason it was formed was so that you could be leader of it and the truth is that you decided and dictated everything that the group did, where they spent their evenings and how they were to arrange the memories on their mobile phones. You lived in a delirium of power and self-importance, did you not?

That's not true, the defendant said immediately. He hesitated. I just proposed things from time to time. Sort of. I have more ideas. Often it's hard to know what to do in this town. There are no facilities like, are there? For young people. After a pause he added: Just because there's a group there's no need for there to be a leader. He hurried on. Or it's like, they was relying on me knowing what to do, not me bossing anyone around. If there's a group it's because people like to rely on one another. Same at the church, he said, they often ask me to arrange tournaments and outings and things. Because I have ideas.

Mr Sayle, I shall have to ask you to keep your answers brief and to the point. Let us get back to the evening in question: what was it that at 10 o'clock on the night of March 22nd outside the Tally Ho pub, where you had consumed, let me see, how many, yes three pints of beer you say, of Caffreys to be precise – what was it that you proposed to the members of this group of which you were not, you claim, the leader, but let's say, the ideas man?

Sayle sighed. I said, Let's call the others and meet somewhere and chill out. That was normal.

The others being?

Sayle rattled off the names.

Or perhaps you'd like to give us their numbers?

4, 7, 8 and 11.

You seem to know the numbers very well Mr Sayle.

It was a joke we had.

It sounds ominously paramilitary to me, Sedley remarked.

Your honour! Sayle's defence counsel stood up. I object. This is personal comment of the worst kind.

Objection upheld, Daniel said. He had often noticed how it was the QCs far more than the humbler lawyers who tried to exploit this kind of weapon. As I am sure you are aware, Mr Sedley, he said drily, you must put your thoughts to the defendant as direct questions, not disparaging remarks.

Quite so, my apologies, your honour. Sedley paused, as if gathering important thoughts: Was there, Mr Sayle, something deliberately paramilitary about your thinking of each other as numbers rather than names? Paramilitary, he repeated.

I don't understand the difference, Sayle said, between military and paramilitary.

How ably this defused the question! The jury were amused. Unexpectedly, Sayle was coming across as a very ordinary and quite candid boy, Sedley as a man pompously exhibiting his superior education.

Let me put it another way, then. Was this business of using numbers part of a general habit of seeing yourselves as engaged in war games?

Not at all, Sayle said sensibly.

And yet, Mr Sayle, what you proposed to members – he consulted his notes – 4, 7, 8, and 11 of your group was that they meet you on the bridge where Malding Lane crosses the ring road.

That's right.

Why?

Beg your pardon?

Mr Sayle, please. My voice may not be of the loudest but I am quite sure you heard my question. I asked, Why, why go there?

Sayle didn't respond.

Why would 4, 7, 8 and 11, want to go and meet, 1, 2, 3 or whatever on a busy road bridge? Was there entertainment of some kind to be had there? Was there a supply of food and beverages? Was there music?

The young man stared across the court

Why on earth would anyone agree to meet together in such a place. It is hardly a convenient location for a chat, is it Mr Sayle? Or for contemplation of the night sky?

The defendant said nothing.

Mr Sayle, in your statement to the police you claim that when you and the others arrived at the bridge, in two separate cars and a motorbike, one car from one direction and one from another, it was to find yourself looking at the scene of an accident that had already happened. Is that right?

Yes, that's what I keep saying. We were getting to the bridge, you know there's a bend, then the road climbs a bit and just as we get to the top we see these kids running away down the embankment.

Please, Mr Sayle, we'll come to that in a moment. What I would like to ask you now, though, is why you went to the bridge in the first place? In your statement to the police you say the group, and I quote, 'frequently met there'. What I want you to tell the court now is why. Why did you choose to meet on the bridge?

Dressed in dark suit and tie, shoulder length blond hair in a ponytail behind, Sayle seemed for the first time completely nonplussed. Could he really have come to the witness box, Daniel wondered, without expecting he would be asked this question?

Was it to throw stones at the cars?

No! I've said it a thousand times.

Why then?

The defendant's fingers fidgeted with each other and his weight shifted back and forth from leg to leg. Why hadn't he pleaded guilty, Judge Savage wondered, looking at the young man? A show of remorse, an admission of one drink too many, some statement to the effect: I can't believe I did it, I want to pay the price. In that case the sentence would probably not have exceeded six years, of which he would serve only four and might even be paroled after three. And instead here he was facing the impossible question. Why did you frequent the bridge? The jury, who had seemed rather sympathetic, were watching intently. The three benches of the public gallery, mainly relatives and friends of the defendant, were clearly excited.

Sayle said nothing.

Mr Sayle, Daniel interrupted, once you decide to give evidence you are bound to answer all the questions you are asked. You have sworn to tell not just the truth, but the whole truth.

The young man was looking blankly across the court to the public gallery. He opened his mouth then shut it again. A full minute went by.

Mr Sayle. Daniel used his gravest judge's voice. The question as to why you chose to go to the bridge over the ring road on the night and at about the time of the alleged crime is a proper question and you must answer it.

Mr Sayle, Sedley nodded to the judge and began again. He spoke as one obliged to undertake a task as wearisome as it was essential. Let me repeat my question in the clearest possible fashion: can you explain to the court why you and your group liked to go to meet on the bridge where Malding Lane crosses the ring road?

Again there was a long pause. Then Sayle flexed his hands, gripped the box, and said: We went to talk to the prostitutes.

Sedley was taken by surprise. There had been no mention of this in any interview given by any member of the group. Nor had Sayle spoken of it during examination in chief with his own counsel. The barrister put his hands together as though in prayer, fingers to lips, swaying back and forth. To talk to prostitutes, he repeated. Now he will be obliged to improvise, Judge Savage thought. To talk to prostitutes, Mr Sayle! Sedley went for a rising note of incredulity, but he was stalling. The young defendant came ingenuously to his aid: There are always a couple of girls doing business, you know, down on the circular in the lay-by near the bridge. We used to go and talk to them.

I see. And why did you go and talk to them?

I think it's quite normal actually, Sayle said. Lots of people chat to prostitutes.

Do they indeed?

Course they do. You should look around you, Sayle said. He was embarrassed, but defiant.

You are saying, let me check that I have this right, Mr Sayle: you are telling the court that you think it is quite normal to spend an evening in the pub and then gather together a group of carefully numbered friends to drive off to a busy road and talk to some prostitutes. Did they have numbers too?

I said you should look around you.

I am looking around me, Sedley replied. And what I see is a group of young people on trial for a most serious crime. Perhaps you would like to tell us what you used to talk to these ladies of easy virtue about.

Life, Sayle said. This and that. Sometimes we'd bring along some cans of beer or a take-away. We'd talk about where they were from, why they were on the game. They're mainly immigrants, you know.

How fascinating, Mr Sayle. And your girlfriend, Sasha isn't it. . .

Miss Singleton, Sayle said with some irony.

Miss Singleton didn't mind this entirely normal interest of yours in these ladies of the night.

Sasha likes to talk to them, Sayle said. They know a lot about life. Everybody's so wrapped up in their own little bit of the world. But they see everybody.

Quite so, quite so, Mr Sayle. I can see that three pints of

Caffreys does nothing to blur the spirit of philosophy. But let's get this straight – you are telling the court that you regularly visited to the bridge to bring a couple of friendly prostitutes beer and burgers?

That is correct.

And stones?

What, sorry?

And stones? You take these friendly women, cement of society and source of worldly wisdom, beer, burgers and stones. The back of the car you were travelling in was full of stones, Mr Sayle.

The defendant sighed. I've explained that the mess in Jamie's car was to do with the building work his uncle has been doing.

Ah, yes, of course. I'd forgotten about Mr Grier's DIY uncle, how silly of me. We shall come back to him. But for the moment, could you perhaps explain to the court why you have, to date, never mentioned these engaging soirées with our local courtesans, not in any of the statements made to the police.

Sayle hesitated. He sucked his lips: His manner was a strange alternation of belligerence and compliance, each quality manifested in such standard and immediately recognisable social postures that it was difficult to get any sense of what he might really be like. If not just the normal modern youth.

Mr Sayle, I am asking you why you never mentioned that you and your girlfriend, not to mention the other members of the group, visited prostitutes of a Saturday evening? What are we supposed to imagine? You were inviting them to abandon a life of shame and to come to church with you the following morning?

Course not.

Mr Sayle, you spared the police no detail of your church-going, but you omitted to mention these visits to prostitutes. Can you explain why?

Sayle didn't respond.

There's nothing wrong, Mr Sayle, in trying to recuperate a woman who has fallen into sin. Even the most noble of our nineteenth-century Prime Ministers, William Gladstone, was actively and personally involved in a mission to help the ladies of the street. I wonder, therefore, that you didn't tell the police at once. I wonder you didn't offer glowing accounts of the souls you've saved. Or is the truth of the matter, Mr Sayle, that actually you just thought up this clever answer two minutes ago, on the spur of the moment, when you found yourself in a rather tight corner?

Sedley has lost it, Daniel thought. All this aggressive colouring and irony was getting him nowhere. The defence counsels were wise not to object, however objectionable it was.

I wasn't trying to convert nobody, Sayle said.

Ah. You were not trying to convert them. We will not then be able to hear testimony from some charming young lady as to how you snatched her from the jaws of hell.

Sayle said: I don't know why we went to talk to them really. We had some laughs. It was our way of chilling out.

Mr Sayle, let's leave aside the pleasures you may or may not have had in talking to women of easy virtue, and let me insist on my previous question: why did you not mention to the police this motive for going to the bridge? Or indeed to your solicitor, since this fact did not emerge from the evidence we have just heard?

After another long silence, David Sayle said glumly: To tell the truth, I didn't want my mum to know.

Not only did the remark provoke titters all round the court, but it was delivered in such a way as to seem entirely authentic. An unhappily fat woman in the front row of the public gallery had covered her face with her hands. The whole story has suddenly shifted, Judge Savage sensed. Admit to something embarrassing and people believe you, even if perhaps it's not true. Ten minutes later, as he was closing the door of his room in chambers he found himself face to face with the young clerk Laura. In her hands she held a copy of the evening paper. Mystery, ran the headline, over Savage Attack.

TWENTY-THREE

Dan, hello there. A disturbing and improbable intimacy was creeping into the policeman's voice. You got my message then? He should not speak to a judge like this. Yes. Daniel was breathless. Good man. And you've seen the evening paper, I presume? Yes. You don't know how they came to have this story? No. Who do you think could have told them this? I'm shaking, Daniel noticed. I'm not ready for a scandal at all. He said: My wife. I think not, Mattheson said at once. In fact, I was just on the phone to her. I'm sure it was not your wife. Oh. Mattheson had Hilary's number. My daughter perhaps. Mattheson said nothing. Judge Savage could hear a sound of voices. The policeman was on his mobile. My brother Frank knew something, he said. For some reason, he couldn't bring himself to speak of Christine. He had told Martin the whole thing. Would Martin have had time or energy on his deathbed to have told his wife? Miss Kwan herself wouldn't have done it, he suggested. Would she? Dan, the policeman's voice was condescending, I believe Miss Kwan has gone back to her family. I doubt if she would have any interest in shooting her mouth off to the press now she's living with her family again. I beg your pardon? The girl's gone back to her family, Dan. As of three days ago, I believe.

Daniel felt lost. His life had foundered on a young girl's ambivalence toward her origins. She had cut herself free. Now she had gone back. It had been for nothing. Trembling, he said: But the story is quite accurate. I mean, they didn't pluck it out of the air, did they? It must be someone who knows something. It doesn't mention the jury business, Mattheson remarked. Which would have been the most damning thing of all, the thing that would sink you. No, no it doesn't. Judge Savage had hardly had time to think of this. Was there a warning note in the man's voice? Who would blow the case to the papers, the policeman asked, without mentioning that, assuming they knew it?

Daniel found he was looking up from the phone to see if anyone could be listening, a ridiculous gesture when he was in his own room with the door closed. It does say she was Korean though, he pointed out. Actually, Asian, Dan. Asian. Sorry, I'm not concentrating. It's natural, the police-man said. Then after a pause and with a mighty sigh he went on, Okay, okay, so somehow someone's picked up this story, probably in rumour form, and fed it to the evening paper and for all sorts of reasons the editor felt confident enough to risk running it. They know that even if it's not true the last thing a judge wants is to launch a highly publicised libel case. Right? Look at it this way: you've been set up as a hero, now you're ripe for a scandal. That's life. MBE for extramarital sex, etc. On the other hand, he paused, on the other hand, Dan, there's nothing in this but hearsay, is there, nor any suggestion that you yourself did anything illegal. Right? There's no allegation that could lead to charges being made. It's an entirely personal attack and I think we should bear that in mind. Then we should also bear in mind, with regard to the assault, that you yourself never saw your assailants. You may be quite wrong in supposing that these people attacked you. Actually, and with respect, though I appreciate your motives for telling us what you did, I've never been entirely convinced by this version of events. There was a brief silence on the line. Why not, Judge Savage wondered? Why wasn't he convinced? It seemed clear as daylight. In fact, Dan, I was initially trying to get in touch with you to say that we've now pulled in Craig Michaels for questioning. We'll be talking to him over the next forty-eight hours and he has previous convictions for assault and for stirring up racial hatred. So that should reinforce the official position.

Judge Savage didn't know how to react. Good, Mattheson concluded. Now Dan, you're no doubt going to find a lot of journalists on your back over the next day or two asking all sorts of questions. Presumably you'll be in court tomorrow morning? Daniel explained that all the courts had been adjourned for two hours tomorrow morning to allow lawyers and staff to attend Martin Shields' funeral. I'll be speaking, he said. Will you? Poor Mr Shields. There was a pause while Mattheson took this in. Yes, come to think of it, I see I'm supposed to be going myself. Yes, anyway Dan, I can't imagine a man of your experience will have any trouble with a few questions from pesky reporters. All the same, it might be wise to sit down a minute or two and think over what you're going to say. Just to make sure you give them no corroboration at all. Meantime, we'll have a car sent up to your house so they don't keep leaning on the bell. Yes, Daniel agreed. On the desk, beneath a large photo of himself with prominently patched eye, a sub-heading asked: Was Black Romeo Bashed by Ex's Boyfriend? Scores of Affairs? ran another title. In one corner a vignette of a head in judge's wig reclining between open thighs. Daniel asked: And the Kwans? Inspector Mattheson snorted. He seemed entirely relaxed: When the powers that be are onto something, they don't give us mere mortals progress reports. It's drugs, I suppose. Could be, the policeman said. And Dan? Yes. One other thing. Yes? Mattheson seemed amused. Every cloud has a silver lining, he chuckled, you know? So they say, Daniel said. He felt guarded. A situation has developed, he was suddenly aware, where a crown court judge is deeply indebted to a man at least nominally responsible for many of the cases brought to his court. Expect a pleasant surprise when you get home, mate, Mattheson said. I won't say any more.

Having put the phone down, Daniel stared at the article on his desk. Informed sources. He found it difficult to read the words that described himself. Repeated allegations. He felt physically sick. Though it was all accurate. Now the phone was ringing again. Judge? Judge, it's Kathleen, Kathleen Connolly. He didn't know what to say. Your honour, I know it's perhaps improper for me to phone you like this but I just wanted to tell you how ridiculous we all think it is. Thanks, Judge Savage said. She liaises with Mattheson every day, he thought. Thank you. At least she wasn't calling him Dan.

A policeman was standing beside the gate at the bottom of the garden. Cars were parked all along the usually empty road. A knot of men and women were chatting together. As he arrived other car doors opened. The policeman made a clearing-the-way gesture. He stretched out his arms. Cameras flashed. I am in this now, Judge Savage knew. The story had changed again. It is beyond my control. But he was good at talking to people. Talk to them, his instinct told him. He could have driven straight into the garage, but instead he stopped the car, waved the policeman away. At the same moment Hilary's face appeared at the front door. He had guessed as much. I believe, he told a reporter, that the police are questioning a man in connection with the attack on myself. That is all I know. I didn't actually see my attackers, and so cannot identify the man and cannot comment on rumours as to who these people might have been.

A dozen reporters were now crowded round him. There were two or three TV cameras. Is it true that you were having an affair with a twenty-two-year-old Asian girl? The shout appeared to come from behind him. Judge Savage was struck by the bad taste of it. Sounds like an exciting story, he grinned. Raising his voice, he said: If the gentleman who asked that question is eager to discuss his own private life, I'd be more than happy to listen and advise. A woman shrilled: Don't you have anything to say on the matter? He stood still and appeared to think. One of the things that really surprised me, he said, when I was a child reading the Bible, was that when Jesus said: he that is without sin among you, let him cast the first stone, everybody went away. In today's more upright society, he smiled, I'm sure there would be a hail of stones.

Judge Savage was surprised that he had said this. And frightened too. He hadn't thought about Biblical parallels for years. It must have been the stone-throwing case brought it to mind. Does that amount to my admitting it all, he wondered? He said, Now if you could, please, let me go home, I suspect my dinner is waiting.

As he spoke, the dog appeared, barking at his feet. Woolfie! Hilary was walking down the path to embrace him. Sarah appeared behind her mother, a faint smile on her lips. She wore a short top that showed her belly. There was a tattoo.

Her hair was growing. Tom was pulling off his headset. Daniel felt completely false. It was not unlike the moment when he had crossed the floor of the Capricorn to meet the Koreans, or when he had walked along the balcony to the flat on Sperringway. Everything was at a remove. He had often sensed how witnesses and defendants became exhilarated by the public role they were playing in court. Their mannerisms became exaggerated, their language more pompous. These events turn us into marionettes. My life is a subject for cameras, he thought. He felt strangely exhilarated. One of them flashed to capture a scene of perfect solidarity as Daniel met his wife's warm embrace. She was pretty and petite in jacket and skirt. He pressed her to him and her body was hard. Inside, the moment the door closed, she told him: This is just for the duration, Dan. They stood facing each other. Don't nurse any illusions. Sarah was watching them. To stop you going under, she said. She turned away. Tom hurried to the drinks cabinet and poured his father a whisky. His young eyes were full of consternation. Meantime, I'll be sleeping on the couch, Hilary said.

It was eight-thirty when finally he announced: So here we all are together at last, in our new house round our marble fireplace with our grand piano. First time. For more than an hour he had sat quite silently while the others moved about him. Hold your breath, he told himself. For some time he had closed his eyes. The curtains were drawn. The phone was turned off. He had heard Hilary speaking low on her mobile on the landing. Tom was at his computer games. It would be nice to join him. In the end, Judge Savage enjoyed computer games. But he couldn't move from the place he had taken by the empty fireplace. His wife busied herself with the Hoover. She insisted on hoovering. She didn't sit down and talk the matter over with him. She was making the house hers again, he thought. Hoovering. Avoiding conversation. Can I talk to you alone, he asked. What about? she said. Let me clean this mess up. There's nothing to talk about, Dan. We just have to lie for a few weeks. We just say it's rubbish. I talked to the inspector about it. He's sure it will work out.

Sarah seemed eager to help her mother. Truth to tell, the house was a mess. She has put on weight, Daniel noticed from his place on the sofa. Once again his daughter had changed. She was cleaning the bathroom. Nobody came to talk to him. Tom scuttled upstairs to his room. His face had been red. He loved his father. He's ashamed of me, Daniel thought. He could hear the computer beeping. Grimly Hilary hoovered. She hurried back at once, Daniel thought. She didn't wait and think it over. She came rushing back the moment the story broke. The story was an excuse, he thought, to hurry back without losing face, to have her house again, and now she is making it hers. Fair enough, he decided. Is there any point in my trying to think clearly, he wondered? He waited an hour at least, sitting quietly on the sofa. He realised he wasn't suffering in any simple way. He felt angry. At last he announced: So here we are everybody, together at last in our new home.

It was eight-thirty. Hilary had switched off the Hoover. Daniel's voice was loud. His wife didn't interpret it as a cry for help. Sarah was sorting out clothes to be washed. There were suitcases on the floor. We could have a concert, light a fire, Daniel said. Come on. Tom, he called. To-om, do you want to come downstairs and play Get Back for us. The boy appeared on the stairs. The open plan room with the stairs coming down between fireplace and front door was attractive. You were right to want a fireplace, the judge told his wife. Let's light it. Let's sit round it. Without looking at him,

Sarah said: Leave off Dad. Hilary stopped at the door to the kitchen. She shook her head. Are we a family or aren't we, he demanded. Sarah, he turned to the girl, this is your first time here really, isn't it. Your first night in the place. He wasn't sure himself whether he was sarcastic or pleading. Play something Tom, he encouraged. Come on, if we're going to be together, let's be together. Let's light the fire.

Hilary put a hand on the boy's shoulder. Dan, she said. She gave a small false smile. Dan, leave off. If you want, we can discuss what exactly we're all going to say to people over the next week or two. She paused, took a breath: That I've been on holiday for a couple of weeks with the kids and came back because of this ridiculous story, which is rubbish. That's it. Nothing more to say.

Fiercely, Tom shook off his mother's hand, went to the piano and banged out a couple of chords. He stopped, looked up at them. His boyish face was disheartened. He was unable to settle. He looked up at them, down at the keys. Come on Tom, kid, Daniel coaxed. You're just a bit rusty. Or shall we light the fire. Dan, you're sick! Hilary told him sharply. She was shaking her head. Stop it! Am I? he demanded. It upset him to see the boy like that. Why? Why am I sick? His wife didn't reply. Okay, he said, let's be sick to the end. Let's discuss *everything* at once with everyone here, let's have it all out, everything, so that everyone knows everything absolutely and completely once and for all and then we can have done. Dad! Sarah said. Yes? Her eyes were raised in silent pleading, like any adolescent signalling that a parent is beyond the pale. Please, Dad. She shot a glance at her mother.

Listen, your father is in disgrace, Judge Savage began. Since a judge's position depends on his being seen as a figure of absolute integrity, I could well be invited to resign. You understand that? Tom nodded solemnly. This is all wrong, Daniel thought. Not to worry, he said quickly. Or not about the financial side: if necessary, the house can easily be sold and exchanged for something less expensive. I can easily find other work. I haven't, after all, done anything illegal. No shut up, Tom, wait a moment. I'm not going to be put in gaol. Now, your mother has returned after two weeks away and tells me she will support me officially in this crisis, but she doesn't want to live with me as a wife. We all know why and I'm not going to argue with that. She wants to live in the same house, but separately. Now let's find out what everyone else wants.

Dan, Hilary said. She was staring at him. Dan you can't do things like this. Why not? You're just trying to railroad everyone. No I'm not. How am I railroading everyone by asking them what they want? I get letters from my daughter accusing me of hypocrisy, so I'll be open. I spend all day listening to people lying under oath, so let's hear the truth. I'm fed up with it. What do you want Tom? He turned to his son with grim cheerfulness. What would you like to see happen?

The boy sat on his hands at the piano stool, rocking back and forth. I want it to be like it was before, he said. He spoke straightforwardly with no catch in his voice. Why can't we do that? Good, that's one position, Daniel said. I second it. Sarah? he asked. Hilary was shaking her head as if the whole scene were something that would be regretted for ages to come. You're impossible, she muttered. Sarah seemed perversely at ease. She smiled at her mother: I only agreed, to come to this dream castle of yours on the basis that you two would never get back together. That it was just to help you because of this scandal thing. That's my position. It's right to help you, because it would be silly if you lost your job and nobody had any money. But something's got to change. Daniel looked at Hilary. She met his gaze. It had been weeks since they looked in each others' eyes. You've agreed this between you, then? She said nothing. Answer yes or no, he demanded, have you two agreed that we two are finished. Dan, Hilary protested, you're not in court for Christ's sake!

Daniel Savage stood up and shouted, Yes I am! I'm always in court. I'm always on trial! Dad! Tom pleaded. Have you agreed this between you or haven't you? I think we should call a doctor, Hilary said. Ostentatiously, Sarah had lowered her head and started to iron. Sarah had always refused to do housework. Now she was folding clothes. Stabbing the iron, she said: We've been all right the last couple of weeks, Dad. Everybody feels better. I agreed to leave Carlton Street on that basis, okay? That I would stay with Mum. Looking up at her father, she said: I've started doing piano again, Dad. Hilary said: She's going to re-take her exams in November, Dan. Tom looked from daughter to mother. He was crying. So we all live together here, Daniel said, pretending to be a family while the press do their best to destroy me. Two months say, three. Then at the end, we break up. Hilary muttered: You've destroyed me in so many ways, Dan. As she spoke, her voice broke up. He had known this would happen. She was overwhelmed by emotion: You said, in your letter: All that was over ages ago . . . She was unable to go on. Tom seemed to be in despair. His hands clenched and unclenched. Offhand, Sarah explained: We've been staying with Christine.

So this was the scene Daniel had always feared. My whole life, he was intensely aware, has been based on avoiding this scene. Yet now it was happening he was merely astonished by the details, the *how* of it all. *Christine's*. You've been *there*?

I thought you were with . . . He couldn't take it in. But, listen, I went to Christine's when Martin died. We were upstairs when you came by, his daughter said. She was smiling, like a child who has managed to hide when Daddy sent her to bed. Her dark eyes were warm. Your daughter is perverse, he decided. My own flesh and blood. She was cruel.

Hilary said carefully: Christine told me about you two. It was the last straw. I get a letter from you saying all that was ages ago, I am on the brink of saying, okay, let's try again, and then I hear that no, it was only a couple of days ago. And after that . . . After that I couldn't. . .

Now Sarah also went over to stand by his wife. So Hilary had the two children one on each side, Sarah a half-inch taller than her now, willowy, beautiful, quite self-confident, Tom chubby and bewildered, unable to look up. Daniel asked: And what exactly did she tell you? That you always kiss and fondle her when you stop by. She's mad, Daniel said. It was mad that they were saying this. He stared at his family. His daughter had his hands round her mother's neck. Crying, Tom was saying, Don't cry, don't cry, don't cry. The only discretion you can hope for, Judge Savage decided, is from a whore.

And I suppose she told you, he suddenly found himself saying, that she has asked me to give the main speech at her husband's funeral tomorrow? Did she tell you that? That I'm good for a speech as well as a fondle. Yes, Hilary said. Yes, and I think you should do it, Dan. You and Martin were good friends.

The thought of Martin Shields' death allowed her to dry her tears, to look up and sound reasonable. But where's the sense in it, he asked. Where's the sense in her telling you that, then asking me to make a funeral speech? She likes and admires you, Hilary said. She likes me and slags me off to my wife, where's the sense in that? Where's the sense, Hilary retorted, in your making love to me then kissing her every time you went round? She said you'd made it clear you were planning to have an affair with her the moment she left Martin to move into Carlton Street. She said she thought you were in a hurry to get Sarah out of the flat so you could start something.

Daniel closed his eyes. His voice was tense. I kissed her twice, he said. No, sorry, I kissed her three times. Let's be perfectly accurate. I kissed her once ten years ago. When I was drunk and we were fighting. I kissed her twice in the last couple of months when she absolutely begged me. She was so depressed with what was happening with Martin. Oh she absolutely begged you, Hilary mocked. She used the same voice her husband did when he mocked. Sometimes it seemed he was arguing with himself. Poor, poor Daniel, she mocked, so used to kissing anything that comes his way, he doesn't know how to resist. Sarah's eyes were gleaming. Anyway, how can it matter how many times, Dan? It matters a great deal, Daniel shouted. Can't you see that I've been keeping away from her precisely because she's being so bloody predatory and I'm so useless at resisting. Stop it, Tom screamed. Stop arguing! He had his hands over his ears. No, sorry Tom, we must sort this out, Daniel went on. But another voice told him he was exhausted. His one eye had blurred a little. La-l-la! Tom started singing loudly, hands over his ears. La-l-la-l-la-l-la! Shut up, Sarah said. La-l-la-l-la-l-la! Tom shrieked. Let them have it out, the girl yelled.

There was a pause. No, Tom's right, it's all beyond me, Daniel Savage announced. All at once he was decided. Shush, Tom. I'm not going to argue any more. I love you all, Daniel Savage found himself saying — he sensed as he spoke that it was final — I've missed you these last weeks, really, I was constantly wondering where you were and what you were up to, but this is hopeless. You've lost faith in me. So let's kill it. Let's kill it. Then he repeated the words again. Let's kill it, kids. Tom ran to him. The boy buried his face in his lap. Daniel moved him aside. I'm off, he said. I have to go.

Ten minutes later, breathless, trapped in the drama of it, he came down with a few things in a case. His family were waiting listlessly. Where are you going to go? Hilary asked. The locks have been changed, at Carlton Street, she said. Daniel stopped at the door. He shook his head: I gather Minnie went back to her family, he said. I did everything to stop her, Sarah announced. Daniel looked at Tom. He shook his head at the boy and left.

TWENTY-FOUR

Why did Judge Savage go to deliver the funeral address for his old friend Martin Shields as asked? Was it defiance, or inertia? Well, there's no point in hiding, Frank told him. Then they'll know you're running scared. On the other hand, what had been the most intense male friendship of his life could no longer be thought of positively. Martin had been cold and contemptuous at the end. They were strangers. The man's wife, herself an old friend, had sought to seduce him, then betrayed his trust. We are all becoming strangers, Daniel thought. The more we reveal ourselves. Even the decision to buy their flat on Carlton Street now seemed ominous. As if they had deliberately wanted to worm their way into our lives, Judge Savage told his brother. He had driven straight over after abandoning the struggle at home. Frank had agreed to put him up on the sofa. He found a ragged undersheet. Some people just can't keep their gobs shut, squire. The lady was jealous of your nice kids, your new job. Jealous of you shagging around. She didn't have any and she wasn't getting any. And to top it all you're not even white.

Daniel was sure this explanation was inadequate. Frank unfolded a pillow-slip with a can of lager in one hand and a cigarette waggling in the corner of his mouth between squinting eyes. He was unshaven. You don't want to get into conspiracy theories, bruv, he warned. Sitting at the table, oiling the workings of an ancient clock, Arthur chuckled. Frank's a master of the conspiracy theory, he said in his polite American voice. No one is more conspired against than Frank. He's sure the council are trying to get us out of our pitch.

Frank laughed: We all feel more important with a few enemies. Still, Dan, really, you brought this lot on yourself, didn't you, squire? You shag the chinky ticket, then you want to be moral about her welfare, you're playing husband and family man and major public figure and getting your leg over left and right as well. You're even confessing it all as you go along to Mr Moral Repression himself, Martin-never-used-a-Shield, rubbing it in that he's not getting any and suggesting if he doesn't wake up you might just tidy his wife as well. Fantastic! Dad would have been impressed. Frank laughed. You remember how furious he always was about not having another war to fight, preferably on at least six fronts? So there you are battling along, all guns blazing, until one day the supposedly watertight bulkhead gives and HMS Savage begins to list. Hardly the wreck of the Mary bloody Deare, is it? Across the room, Arthur burst out laughing. Not exactly – Frank was enjoying himself – that we have to revise our position on sea serpents and ghost ships, do we?

Looking at his watch Daniel saw it was only ten-thirty. Life had reached a point where the most momentous shifts seemed to take place in the space of a couple of television programmes, causing no more than merriment on the part of his newly reconciled brother. Drinking from a can, he himself felt removed from it, beyond anxiety.

Still, Frank went on, there should be plenty of time to take to the lifeboats and no harm done, you know. You can go into politics if they chuck you out, the voters love a candidate who shags. Don't they, Art? Gets you in the papers. Better still a transvestite. Daniel found that he was smiling. He liked being with Frank. He liked being called squire and bruv. The funny thing is I can only shag around when I've got Hilary there to stop me. The other two men shared a long smile. Shaking heads at each other they said in perfect unison: He-te-ro-fackin-sex-u-als, p-lease! Arthur clapped. He seemed a charming man. Daniel went to sleep wondering if anything that had happened to him was remotely serious. Tom, he thought. Tom.

I will say nothing to Christine, Judge Savage decided. She was standing in impeccable lacy black outside the porch of a neo-Gothic façade. She was even wearing a hat with a lacy black veil. Performing the widow, Daniel thought. He had chosen not to look at the papers. I will not read what they are saying about me. Was it fear or courage? I'm so sorry, Christine was saying, she reached her arms up to him, about all your troubles, Dan. It's so good of you to come. She embraced him as if nothing had happened. His cheek brushed the lace of her veil. I will not look at the papers, he had thought, and I won't ask her anything. This was her husband's funeral after all. She must perform the widow. Probably she does like me, he decided. He needed to save his energy. But the woman was shaking with sobs. She held him tightly. He killed himself, Dan, she was crying softly. If you knew. If only you knew. Her body trembled against his. He killed himself. He made himself die. He made me watch him doing it. She held Daniel tightly and he softly detached her.

He sat in the front row. The coffin was brought and the packed church sang, Abide with me. How could they, Daniel wondered? How can you sing, Fast falls the eventide? Martin himself had become contemptuous, Daniel told himself, of what he used to believe in. Help of the helpless, they sang. It was irritating. Helpless is helpless. Get on with it, he muttered. Martin himself had come to believe that all these social functions were the merest theatre. Daniel was sure of this. Tom will get over it, he thought. We'll meet often. He'll begin to understand me, to see how it could have happened. All married men know how it can happen. O thou who changest not, all these people were singing, abide with me. Nobody changest not, Daniel smiled. Perhaps Martin believed in Christianity, Daniel thought, the same way as he believed in the rituals of the crown court: a tradition that allowed you to get on with things. The witnesses' oath allows you to get on with things. The ritual gestures set the wheels in motion. Ills have no weight, the congregation sang, and tears no bitterness. This hymn is purest kitsch, Daniel thought. Once somebody has sworn an oath you can get on as if they were obliged to tell the truth. When really they're not. You know they're not. We wrap ourselves in purest kitsch, he thought, when there's nothing we can do. Presumably everyone saw that.

He sat in the front pew where he had often sat at concerts, where he liked to let his mind wander with the music high up in the fake Gothic vault. My mind always wanders in church. Churches were designed for that, perhaps: a space for the mind to wander. He had read somewhere that fake Gothic had only become so popular for churches because the nineteenth-century ecclesiastical authorities had discovered that the style cost less than neo-classical designs. Hold thou thy cross before my closing eyes, people were singing.

There was a swooning self-indulgence to the voices. How completely detached I feel. How ready for the worst! He almost burst out laughing. This is the worst possible farce, he thought. The public lynching will be a trifle. Yet when the coffin was awkwardly lowered onto its trestles, it did seem important that his one-time friend was in there, inside that polished box. The difficulty the men had setting it down suggested a certain weight. It was serious. It is terribly serious, he thought, that Mrs Whitaker is still in coma, even if her husband is a non-entity and David Sayle a charming performer. Mattheson would never, Judge Savage suddenly realised, try to bring Craig Michaels to court, because he knows, he *must* know, that under oath *I* would tell the truth. I would. And he *knows* that. That in court, under oath, *I* would tell the truth. He felt immensely relieved by this reflection.

There were other hymns, but Daniel didn't join in the singing. The words were stupid and at the same time there was the problem that his voice would break with emotion if he once began to sing. If I joined in the singing, I would be overcome with emotion, Daniel Savage realised, even though I know that the words are stupid. Behind him he heard voices overcome with emotion. To his left were Martin's parents. The mother was singing through tears. She is happy to be overcome, he thought. Perhaps she knows the words are stupid. Then after the vicar had asked, Oh Death where is thy sting, Daniel himself was invited to go up to the chancel steps: to say a few words, the clergyman said, about our deceased brother in Christ. Judge Savage stood up, and as he turned, at the very place where they put the organ console at the concerts his wife worked so hard to arrange, it was to find himself one of only half a dozen non-whites in a substantial congregation. The legal profession is still predominantly white. There was a faint shiver. The police force likewise. They will listen the more carefully because of what the papers are saying, he knew. He had prepared nothing.

I have prepared nothing, he began. Which I know is unusual for a lawyer. There were faint smiles. So I'll be brief. He saw Hilary at the back. I am not a believer, he said, nor at the end, I don't think, was Martin. Sarah was on her left, Tom on her right. They weren't wearing black. Yet, oddly – he looked around their faces – church does still seem the only suitable place to speak of a friend who has just died. I came for Hilary of course, he understood.

The congregation, many from the courts, people he knew, solicitors and ushers and court clerks, sat more intently than usually they might. Daniel was a good speaker and their colleague Martin Shields had died young. You speak effortlessly, people said. You are so convincing. There were people from the rowing team they had once got together. There were people from the tennis club. You have a natural authority, they would tell him. They marvel all the more because I'm not white, Daniel often thought. They were wearing black. Jane was there and, yes, one or two other women he had slept with. All showing respect, wearing black. He never had any problem convincing women. Everybody will have read the papers, he thought. They love that mix of power and vulnerability. I love you. How many people had told him that? The powerful man caught with his leg over. He said: Our friend and colleague, Martin Shields, has died young. Then he was disturbed to see his daughter was crying. You must perform, he decided. You're in public.

Martin Shields was my friend from boyhood until a year ago. My closest friend. I needn't speak to those present of his brilliance as a lawyer. For myself, I know of no one who took his vocation so seriously. Despite many offers to go into more lucrative fields, Martin remained in criminal law because he believed in it absolutely. He absolutely believed that every defendant deserved the fairest of trials and that there was nothing more serious than taking a man's liberty from him.

This remark was greeted by a rather fruity Hear-hear! Daniel paused. I must not use this speech to make any remark that could be construed as having to do with my own predicament, he thought. At last he was alert. And he sensed that not making any such a remark would be precisely what might most improve that predicament. The press were here. Mattheson was here, he saw, and Kathleen Connolly, and the very senior Judge Carter, head of the disciplinary committee. Forever ill.

In court Martin preferred to defend, Daniel went on, as I think we all do, but he was also happy to prosecute. He believed in prosecution, as few still do. He believed that the sense of lost security that overcomes the victim of any crime is the next most important thing to the loss of liberty. He understood that there can be no liberty if we don't feel secure, if we don't feel we can go about our own business at ease. Again somebody called, Hear, hear! Counsel for the defence, Daniel said, defends one man, counsel for the prosecution defends us all. He casts the first stone, even if he himself is a sinner. That is his unpleasant duty. Martin was brilliant at both.

Again Judge Savage paused, he breathed. He put a hand behind his neck. Then as well as a fine lawyer, the Martin I knew was also a husband, and I must say for my own part a friend of great loyalty. He was always ready to listen. He gave me more advice than anyone else I have known. And some of it was good. This raised a faint laugh. There are few of us who don't need good advice. Again there was a faint titter. Whether I used it well or not is another question. Again people smiled. People eat out of your hand, Hilary once said. Even when you don't stretch it out.

About a year ago, I lost touch with Martin, Judge Savage went on. Perhaps many of you did. We all know that he was not well this last year, since his car accident. He stopped his work in court. He fell into a depression, a negative state of mind that coincided, perhaps, with the beginning of this nameless illness which eventually killed him. We do not know what it was. It seems pointless to speculate. In any event, we stopped seeing each other. I confess I didn't realise he was dangerously ill. I thought him merely changed and miserable. I criticised him. When we did see each other the things he said were disturbing and out of character. He repeatedly told me that life was a farce. He said he preferred watching soap opera to coming to court. In the space of our last two or three conversations he wrote off as the crudest parody everything that seems precious to me and that had once been precious to him. I felt angry with him. I felt our friendship was over.

The public were surprised, and hence attentive. Christine, Daniel saw, had turned white.

I know such reflections are not usually the stuff of funeral orations. I would like to remember Martin as he was before he lost faith in what he did. Yet it seems important to be honest at a moment like this. So I must tell you that I found it difficult to fault his reasoning even when he spoke from his illness. Daniel paused. Perhaps his illness was even more eloquent than his health. In any event, I have no choice but to remember that Martin too as well as the friend I played chess with, and snooker, and loved to watch in court. I can't tell you how many times I would slip into a courtroom for a few minutes on the off-chance of watching Martin perform. He was brother and mentor to me. Remembering this, Daniel felt moved. It was true. It was a big part of his life. But once a phase is over, what does it matter? He paused, As I said, at the end Martin had ceased to believe in any form of religion. Yet church and in particular this church where both he and I were married, many years ago – he looked about him – well, it still seems the only appropriate place where one can say a few public words about a friend who has died. He hesitated. Or to put it another way: whatever Martin himself said, life and death do still seem sufficiently serious for us to come along to the funeral of a man we loved. That's really the only way I can think to put it. Let's not forget him.

Daniel returned to his seat. As if nothing out of the way had been said, the Reverend Cornwell immediately began the collect: O Merciful God, the Father of our Lord Jesus Christ, who is the resurrection and the life . . . Later outside, waiting for the coffin to be slid into the hearse, Daniel found himself standing beside the ancient Judge Carter. But his eye was searching for his family. Do you really not know, the old man rasped, why Shields gave up practice? No, Daniel said. I have lost my family, he thought. Judge Carter swayed very slightly back and forward and said nothing.

TWENTY-FIVE

Judge Savage wrote a letter to the Palace, announcing, with regret, that he would be unable to accept the MBE. In court Sedley seemed to be making no headway with the eight defendants still charged with Grievous Bodily Harm in the incident that had destroyed Elizabeth Whitaker's life. The evidence against the group of young people remained where it was and largely circumstantial, while the chorus of denials grew louder and louder. Called as a character witness, the Reverend Mrs Gosse described David Sayle as the most promising of St Barnabus's young folks and a born youth leader. The jury were perplexed. If he went to talk to prostitutes, the Reverend Mrs Gosse said, and she seemed an intelligent woman, that was no doubt part of a laudable curiosity, his willingness not to be governed by prejudice. He didn't have sex with them after all, she pointed out. And certainly in this regard, as in others, David Sayle was unlike Judge Savage who, having heard that evidence, now returned to the ring road and after visiting three or four lay-bys on two separate evenings eventually tracked down his Brazilian girl, if she was Brazilian. She took him to the same house, but a different room. Euphoric with the wild risk he was taking on a day when he had received more than one offensive letter, Daniel tried to make the encounter more conscious and more generous than the high-speed accident that their first meeting had been. The girl responded up to a point. She took out her chewing gum. For a moment she giggled when he pulled a face. Give me your mobile number, he said. Judge Savage has a mobile himself now. Mobile is an excellent word, he had thought, in the extremely unstable state of mind in which he was buying the thing. Identity fizzed away like aspirin in soda water. The judge was elated, but prone to moments of panic.

Most of her clients were white, the girl answered him. Then she said: But you seem real English more than the rest. She had registered the contrast of his colour and his class. He was pleased. They are jealous of the dark secrets of your body, he told her. He was joking. Or maybe not. He had felt before how you could get an echo of romance by aping it, by being honest about aping it. They fear they may be innocent, he said to her in a soft deep voice, so they come running to your dark mystery. She didn't understand. For a few moments I'm enjoying myself, he decided, though the letters he had begun to receive over the last few days made his mouth dry with fear. Filthy black bastard stealing our women. He dropped them the moment his eye took in an insult. Pompous black ponce, go fuck yourself. My mother was Brazilian, he told the prostitute. I'm British bred, but the genius is in the genes. He raised his eyebrows in fun. Again the girl didn't appear to have understood, but conceded her mobile number and allowed him to stroke her. How beautifully young she was! The time slot was fifteen minutes. A name for the mobile memory? he asked. Sue, she said. He knew he would never be able to think of her as Sue.

While taking her back to the road, Judge Savage enquired, Do people ever come just to talk to you? Sure, she laughed. She said: But Gabriel come and he chase them away. With great amusement, she mimicked: You don't fuck, you fuck off, little white prickies. She was a coltish girl with long legs and an endearing way of clutching her handbag as she trod off across the lamp-lit gravel. Clutching your prick more like, Frank laughed. He shook his head in admiration. You're mad, Dan. Daniel felt the pride of the little brother who has at last managed to upstage the older.

Meantime, to his own considerable surprise, despite all the allegations in the press, Judge Savage has not been suspended or invited to resign, or even reprimanded. Not yet. He has a charmed life it seems. You always had a charmed life, Frank told him. Palace, colleagues and newspapers all urge him to change his position on the MBE. You should accept it, Dan, a voice from London tells him, on behalf of other non-white barristers if nothing else. With exquisite pomposity *The Times* reflects that the country must choose between doing an injustice to one individual on the basis of hearsay, and ensuring that the public retain its respect for the administrators of justice. The editor thinks the dilemma is a real one. But the climate is on Savage's side. His authority in court doesn't seem diminished, despite a stare or two. If anything, the sense of his charisma has increased. After a lifetime fearing conspiracy, or just some instinctive closing of white ranks, he now finds the *Guardian* attacking the tabloids for seeking to revive moribund myths of black bestiality. It should be remembered, the *Guardian* tells its readers rather sternly, that Judge Savage takes his surname from his adoptive white parents and *not* from his natural ancestors.

Did you see it, Sarah phones him to ask. He's sitting in

his office going through papers, but at the same time wondering, If you go to a prostitute, why return to the same one, why seek affection? You toss up a dust storm, Judge Savage tells himself, and grope for roots. Mum and I are cutting out all the articles, his daughter says. Immediately, he is nostalgic for home, for a living room with a table and scissors and paste. Did you see *Cosmopolitan* praised you for not rehearsing the farce of family solidarity? I didn't, Daniel confessed. He held the phone carefully as if it might be fragile. How are you? he asked. All right. I'm back at school for re-takes. That's wonderful, he said. I knew you'd say that, she laughed. But his daughter too, Daniel sensed, was asking for approval. Having kicked me out of the house, she longs for me to approve. How's Tom? he asked. The usual pain, she said. And Mum? There was a pause. Busy with her lessons? Sarah hesitated. Mum's not teaching, she's a bit depressed. But Max comes over no doubt? No, Sarah said. Why not? Mum says she can't see him any more. But why? She liked teaching him. His daughter's voice became vague and distant. She says she's already taught him all she can. So what is she doing? Playing herself, I suppose. No, she's not playing at all. Daniel didn't know how to continue. It was their first contact since he had left. But you're happy, he asked. Yes, she said. Good. Still going to the Community? he asked. She said no. She said, That was all a bit stupid.

Again there was a long silence. Then she asked: Dad? Her voice had altered. Yes? Minnie got in touch. Oh? You've made friends? Kind of. I went to see her, in their flat. On Sperringway? Right. That's nice, he said. She asked if I could promise one thing: that none of us would mention her name, in these stories that are coming out. She said she'd told her parents a lot of lies. Daniel said: Whether her name comes out or not will depend on who's giving these rumours to the press and how much they know. I suppose so, Sarah said. She asked, Who could it be, Dad? He reflected. It was positive, he thought, that she was calling him Dad. He felt pleased that Hilary had banished Max. I've sometimes thought it might be Christine, he said. Sarah said nothing. What do you think? he asked, any ideas?

Dad, she whispered. What is it? Oh nothing. Then with a charmingly girlish change of tone, she announced: I'm seeing someone Dad. Seeing someone? A man, silly. Immediately he responded to her cheerfulness. And may I ask whom? This was why she'd called, he realised. You may, she giggled, but you won't get an answer. You're happy though? *–er*, the girl said, happi*er*. I seem to have a daughter again, Daniel decided when he put the phone down. It made him want to speak to Hilary. Our twentieth anniversary is two weeks away. Then he saw: Whoever gave this information to the press, seeks to destroy my life as a man, a family man. But only that. Four affairs had been dug out from the woodwork, but there had been no mention of girls on juries or professional misconduct. By denying nothing, *The Times* said and suing no one, Judge Savage has shown that he is not scared of these stories being aired in public and thus not susceptible to blackmail. From this point of view, however regrettable it might be for those concerned, his separation from his wife is salutary. He is not in the vulnerable position of the man defending a sandcastle. He has declared his independence. The judicial system can ill afford to lose men of this calibre, men capable of surviving first a brutal physical attack, then a ruthless exposure of their private life. Who, Judge Savage wondered, having set out to harm him and seeing this paradoxical result, would not deliver the death blow, the story of Minnie?

Who, Sedley asked, was the leader of the group?

Having surrendered herself at last to the police, Janet Crawley was now in the witness box.

No one, she said.

It was growing wearisome. There were eight defendants to be examined then cross-examined, first by their own defence counsels, then by each of the other defence counsels if they should see fit and finally by the prosecution counsel. A total of seventy-three examinations if each barrister availed him or herself of each opportunity, and this without even taking into account the other witnesses called. Inevitably Sedley was doing most of the work. Let me approach the question differently, he said for perhaps the hundredth time. Which of the men in the group seemed most eager to show-off, to establish his manhood, if you like?

David, she said at once.

Mr Sayle, Sedley said.

Fortunately not all the lawyers were eager to stand up whenever they could. Counsels for Davidson and Simmons in particular were following the time-honoured strategy of saying as little as possible, calculating that at the end of the trial almost nothing specific would have been said about their clients and consequently that the jury would feel unable to convict them for so serious a crime. Daniel himself had often been at pains to reassure clients that he was doing better for them by keeping his mouth shut than by questioning witnesses, since in the end one can never quite know what this or that witness might say. It had been established, or at least all the defendants agreed, that Simmons had arrived at the scene on a motorbike carrying Janet Crawley on the pillion, while Davidson had driven the car that brought Stuart Bateson and Gill Crawley. Both vehicles, their drivers and passengers claimed, had arrived at the scene to find Sayle, Singleton, Grier and Riley already on the bridge.

And would it be fair to say, Sedley tried, that there was a certain amount of animosity between the male members of the group?

I don't know what you are getting at.

Miss Crawley, due to your absence, you have inevitably missed a great deal of what has been said in this trial. However, it is not important for you to understand what I am getting at, but to answer my questions. Let me be precise: Is it true that Mr Sayle and Mr Grier were in competition to impress the girls?

I don't see, Janet Crawley said petulantly, why I have to answer questions about our private life. The girl's counsel stood up. Your honour . . . Mr Sedley, Daniel asked, can you explain to us how these questions are relevant to the trial? Your honour, Mr Sedley began, as I have said from the beginning, this is very much a joint enterprise trial and one where the dynamic of the group of people involved is both complex and important. I am seeking to establish that the motivation for the crime lay in that group dynamic, in the relationships of the different members of the group to each other. Judge Savage considered: I will give you just a few minutes, Mr Sedley, to see if this line of questioning will lead to anything.

Sedley paused to concentrate. Miss Crawley, the qualities of sensitivity and loyalty to friends are most admirable, but may sometimes prove misguided. Let me approach the problem in a way that will perhaps make it easier for you to answer.

The girl stared at him. She was a small, tense, abrasive creature, the face crudely pretty with bright lipstick and sharp eyes.

You are part of what Mr Sayle has described as a 'tight-knit' group. At what age would you expect such a group to form?

Don't know. Mid-teens.

And at what age would it normally break up?

Early-twenties, I suppose.

You are in your early-twenties.

Right.

Your group hasn't broken up.

No.

What kind of thing do you think could make a group like yours break up?

Your honour, the girl's counsel was on his feet again. Not only is the defendant being asked a series of irrelevant questions about her private life, but now she is being invited to launch into the purest speculation. She is not, so far as I know an expert on social mores.

I shall rephrase the question, Sedley conceded. Miss Crawley, did you and your friends ever talk about the kind of things that broke up groups like your own?

Yes.

And did you reach any conclusions?

Well, people get married, don't they, Janet Crawley said. Couples get wrapped up in themselves and pull out.

Is that why Ginnie Keane was not present on the bridge on the night of March 22nd?

Again I have to object your honour. The defendant is being invited to speculate.

Mr Sedley. . .

Did Ginnie tell you why she wasn't coming to the bridge?

She was with her boyfriend, yes, if that's what you mean.

And the boyfriend is not part of the group?

No.

Did Ginnie tell you what she and her boyfriend were doing while you were on the bridge?

The girl laughed: What do you think they were doing?

I've no idea.

Bet you have.

Did she tell you they were making love?

You've said it, the girl said. She seemed at once pleased and grim.

When people form strong couples, that destroys groups, doesn't it? Sedley suggested very quickly. Is that the conclusion you reached when you talked together about such things?

I suppose you could say that.

Who was most opposed to this?

You what?

Who was determined to keep the group together at all costs?

She didn't reply.

Sedley sensed he was getting somewhere. Daniel was anxious that he was allowing the man to get away with too much. But all at once the questioning had geared in to his own intuitions.

David Sayle didn't have sex with his girlfriend, did he, Miss Crawley, despite their having been together for some years?

She hesitated.

Miss Crawley, in an interview with the police, you. . .

Okay, no, he didn't, they didn't.

And you all knew.

No, *I* knew because Sasha told me. We was like sisters.

Ah, so no doubt she also told you why he didn't, or they didn't.

Your honour, I object. It was Sayle's counsel this time.

But Janet Crawley was already answering: It's true he had this thing about us staying together as a group. He wanted us to go to youth club as well.

Sayle's counsel hesitated, then sat down.

Mr Sayle had a thing about sex too, didn't he?

Your honour! Now she was on her feet again.

Yes, Mrs Wilson.

Your honour it seems admirable rather than unnatural for a young man not to have sex with a girl he is not married to and entirely consistent with his evident religious vocation. I really do not see how my learned friend can deduce some kind of perversity from this abstention. In general, can I submit that this whole line of questioning seems quite irrelevant to the facts of the case.

Mrs Wilson, the prosecution counsel has not said anything about perversity. For the moment I shall allow him to continue.

Miss Crawley, did Mr Sayle have a very particular position on, or shall we say *against* sex?

The girl took a breath. You could say that, she said.

Some of you must have thought, surely, that Mr Sayle was a bit, er, nutty, talking to prostitutes, then not having sex with his girlfriend.

She shrugged her shoulders. Course we did.

And who, in this group of eleven, I believe the numbers on the mobiles go up to eleven, do they not, who most keenly opposed Mr Sayle?

I don't know what you mean.

Miss Crawley, has it ever occurred to you that you yourself might be the victim of Mr Sayle's obsession with keeping a group together?

Sometimes I've thought he was a bit queer.

Did any member of the group think David Sayle was a complete nutcase and a tyrant?

She didn't reply.

Somebody who was only frequenting the group to be near one of the girls perhaps?

Judge Savage was impressed by the mileage Sedley was getting out of this from the purely psychological, general interest point of view. But as ever there was the danger that a great deal of court time would pass and nothing substantial would be proven or demonstrated. It was his task to make sure that that did not happen. Listings officers rightly disliked judges whose trials went on forever. In another few minutes he would have to force Sedley to arrive at the point.

Was there somebody else – I shall be as clear as I can – who fancied Sasha Singleton?

The girl had her lips pressed tight. She folded her arms.

Miss Crawley, can I put it to you that one of the other men in the group regularly mocked Mr Sayle in order to impress Miss Singleton.

Janet Crawley's stare had now become belligerent. The lipstick had gone from her lower lip.

In your first police interview, Miss Crawley, which you later claimed was made under pressure.. . .

Your honour. . .

Mr Sedley, you must allow the witness the time to reply, you cannot go on building up this web of implication without us having a clear response from the witness.

Of course, your honour. I apologise.

Did Mr Grier show an interest in Miss Singleton?

Yes, the girl said at once.

Were you all aware of this?

You could have seen a mile off.

Did. . .

If you want to know, the witness announced, Jamie was the really nutty one not Dave.

338

Immediately the girl volunteered this piece of information, Daniel noted the movement among the defendants. From glazed boredom they went to a flutter of concern. Glances were exchanged. Janet Crawley had skipped bail, then surrendered herself to the police only shortly before it was time for her own evidence. Was this planned? The jury were staring. In the end they would have to decide what had happened that night on the bridge.

By Jamie, you mean Mr Grier.

That's right.

In what way was he, nutty?

He'd do anything, Jamie would.

Was he seeing Miss Singleton away from the group?

The girl looked at Sedley and a sudden shrewdness passed over her features. Yes, she said. Then Judge Savage guessed that spite had overcome fear at last. Or perhaps she had always planned to play it this way? People can be so cunning. In any event the next morning's paper would summarise the girl's evidence thus: Grier had long been seeing Sasha Singleton away from the group but was unable to detach her from it, or from her relationship with David Sayle who had become a respectable fixture in the girl's more than respectable family and to whom she had long been engaged. Indeed, the Sayles and the Singletons had clubbed together and promised to buy a flat for the couple when they married. On at least three previous occasions, while the Crawley girls necked with Davidson and Simmons in the cars in a quiet parking space among trees beyond the bridge, and Sayle and Singleton went down in the lay-by to talk to prostitutes, Grier with Ryan Riley and Stuart Bateson had thrown stones from the bridge, Miss Crawley claimed, onto the carriage-way near where the others were talking to the black girls. This had caused David Sayle to rush up on the bridge to stop them. On the night of March 22nd, Janet Crawley claimed she had distinctly heard Grier say: I'm going to keep throwing stones till Sasha owns up how much she likes sucking my dick. Miss Crawley had further claimed that she and Simmons had been walking back across the bridge to say that they were leaving. I looked up, the girl was reported as saying, and saw Dave (Sayle) had a big stone in his hands, like, a really big one, and was going to smash it down on Jamie, who's much smaller. Sasha is screaming, Don't, and Dave turns in a fury and chucks the stone way over the bridge. Then we heard a bang and brakes screeching. Miss Crawley's evidence, said the paper, led to such an uproar in the courtroom among the defendants and their relatives in the public gallery that Judge Savage was obliged to interrupt the hearing and adjourn. The paper was not in a position to remark that immediately afterwards, as if high on the emotional charge generated by this court drama, the judge drove out into the country to confront the newly widowed Mrs Shields.

TWENTY-SIX

It was always a relief to leave the rigid grid of the centre for the softer, more seductive topography of the countryside. A grid promises simplicity, Judge Savage had often reflected, and yet simplicity was exactly what was denied you in the city, whether as a driver or a lover. I will get the truth out of Christine, he told himself, however tortuous.

Don't think you can cross-examine me, she said to him. He found the house standing beautifully picturesque in an autumn twilight. The Shields family residence is purest England, Hilary used to laugh, the best and the worst. How often I see things through Hilary's eyes, he thought. A generous red brick pile rose a little lopsided in pools of green lawn beside the slow deep turbulence of the river. No one responded when Judge Savage rang the bell. Don't think of Hilary, he thought. He rang again. It was about that time when you might expect a light to be turned on, a curtain to be drawn. Judge Savage knew the house was sometimes left open at the back. He walked round and pushed the handle of a long unvarnished door. Locked. He put his face against the window pane and focused his one useful eye.

Then he understood that the house was empty. This place wasn't lived in any more.

But the determination to have it out, now, to get the truth out of her didn't leave him. Even though he knew he had promised himself he wouldn't do this. He had promised himself he wouldn't look for truths, except in court. Yet it was precisely in court that the young girl's evidence had put him in a sort of fever for revelation and resolution. If the right questions were asked, a secret spring might be released. It had always excited Judge Savage how there came a moment in a trial, or in some trials, when everything could be understood in a quite different way, and somehow this new understanding always seemed superior to the old. If nothing else, Daniel thought, Janet Crawley had told an excellent story. The jury might be convinced. But Christine was defensive. You can't *force* me to tell you anything, she protested, can you? She smiled. Despite the freshness of her bereavement, her voice had recovered all its old verve and teasing silkiness. I'm not under oath you know, Dan. Apparently, Daniel thought, this is something every barrister's wife or daughter says.

Even driving rapidly, by the time he had crossed the ring road, then followed the town grid to Carlton Street, it was eight-thirty. Yes, I've moved, she laughed, wasn't I quick! She greeted him in her dressing gown. Her hair was freshly washed and hennaed. How often she must wash, he thought. I'm never going back to St Gwen's, she told him. Thank God we bought this place. She had been in a bathrobe the evening he drove round with Max. Perhaps she was obsessive about cleanliness. Have you eaten? she asked. He said, Christine, I want to know why you told Sarah what you did.

He invited her out to dinner. She hesitated, then went to

342

change. Already their old flat had been re-furnished, albeit provisionally. There were a few old pieces of furniture from the country house. I couldn't stay out there, she said lightly. She picked up her handbag and he caught a wave of perfume. I'm a city person really, she told him. It was a mistake to live out there. The perfume was a strong, sweet polite-society thing. Well, this is jolly, she remarked, climbing into the car. How lovely to go out to dinner, she said. Oh how nice of you, Dan! I do want to know, Christine, he repeated. She had pulled down the sunshade above her head to study herself in the mirror. I'm worried my mole may be getting bigger, she said loudly. Christine . . . You can't browbeat me, Daniel, she said sweetly. I'm not under oath, am I? After a little silence, she asked: By the way, where are you living?

He started to tell her about Frank. Rediscovering his brother, he told her, had been the only good thing that had come out of all this. It seems I had to be disgraced before we could get on. I know what you mean! Christine almost giggled. So now you're sleeping on the sofa in a terraced slum? I don't mind, he said evenly. Anyway, it's not a slum. I could easily go to a hotel if I wanted. Then when he told her Frank was dealing in antiques she was immediately interested. Really? Do you think he could clear out St Gwen's for me? Some of the furniture will be worth quite a lot. He'd be delighted, Daniel said. If you could trust him. Well, could I? Is he trustworthy, you mean? Daniel hesitated. She said: Martin never liked Frank, you know. He thought he was one of those people who always live off others and never take life seriously. Immediately, this seemed unfair. Daniel said, As much as you can trust anyone. Martin always had harsh opinions of everyone, she said. Daniel couldn't tell if she was remembering with emotion or merely reflecting. You should have heard the things he said about you.

343

Oh yes? He thought you were weak and vacillating, she said. He thought you lacked self-esteem. She spoke lightly offhand, leaning her head to one side and shaking out her hair. Why, Judge Savage asked, very calmly, did you tell Hilary I'd been kissing you? Oh, did she mention that? Christine smiled. That wasn't important. She frowned a little and pouted. I also told her she should go back to you, she said. Did she mention that? Actually, I hardly thought another fact or two would make much difference at the point you were at. I wanted her to see it was just something you did, I mean a sort of natural physical thing, and that these affairs weren't important to you. I told her if she left you she would be full of regret, you know? I mean, I know *I* did the right thing not leaving Martin. At least I've nothing to regret. Almost in a daze, she added: I stayed to the end.

They ate in a Chinese place that Christine had known of old. Let's see if it's still there, she proposed. She seemed pleased. He barely noticed what he was eating with all the plans that kept forming and dissolving in his mind. Frank called on the mobile. Okay, squire? he asked. Dinner only went cold an hour ago. I thought you might have got yourself knocked about again. Oh, but how sweet of him! Christine exclaimed. How brotherly! She clapped her hands. I *will* get him to clear the house. You must give me his number. She fussed with her notebook and shaking her head, she added, I never thought Martin was a good judge of character. Calling you weak was just silly. She had chosen her food with care. Her husband might have been dead for years, Daniel thought. Dabbing her lips, she asked brightly: Do you really want to go back to Hilary? At the same moment Judge Savage said, Tell me about your plans.

Christine said as soon as she had recovered she wanted to find work with some charitable organisation that would put her in contact with reality and people. She must be with people, she felt like a hot-house flower. Then once she'd sold St Gwen's there would be really no need for her to have a salary. She thought she could go back to Save the Children. She had done fund-raising for them in the past. For a moment she looked solemn. I need to be near poor Mumsie. She hasn't been well you know. The good thing about volunteer work is that I can always be free to help Mumsie or take a holiday or whatever. She added: I need to enjoy myself.

They fussed over their food. Daniel felt feverish. He found himself saying: The funeral the other day started me thinking about church and Christianity. Hmm, oh yes? She covered a yawn. I'm exhausted, Dan, sorry. I mean, when it's over and the emotion suddenly leaves you, you feel totally, totally exhausted. But he was close to deciding he would stop at nothing. You and Martin, he said, used to be very Christian, didn't you? Having bent to concentrate on her chopsticks, she raised her eyes, face sideways to the table. The smile seemed to be mocking. And of course Sarah went through that very Christian period, you remember, right after Hilary and I got back together.

Ye-es, she said.

And now in this trial I'm involved in, it turns out the main defendant, a very odd character, is the most stalwart of churchgoers. Hmm, and so? she enquired. Again she batted her large eyelashes. Daniel tried to get a grip on whatever it was he meant to say. In each case, he hazarded, there seems to have been something ominous about it. It preceded a catastrophe, if you get me. As though the engagement with religion was an alternative that failed, you know, an attempt to escape something else that they had foreseen and feared. They tried to be Christian in the hope they could avoid something else, but in the end they couldn't. Martin falls into that depression, Sarah writes obscenities over her exam papers. Quite probably this defendant did in fact hurl a rock on the road. Though I shouldn't talk to you about this of course.

Well, Christine sighed, it doesn't make much sense to me. She popped a small spring roll in her mouth, closed her eyes and swallowed, then spoke patting the corner of her mouth. She seemed to have so many facial expressions, at once sophisticated and brittle. Don't you think you're reading a bit too much into it? The restaurant was quiet and the waitress bent over them ceremoniously, bringing more dishes. After all, I never felt Christianity let *me* down, she smiled. I still like my polished pew and the Ancient & Modern. I think it's good to go to church, though I don't suppose anybody really believes they're going to heaven any more, do they? For the third or fourth time she came out with a shrill little giggle.

Talking about religion, he insisted, you are Sarah's godmother, aren't you? Of course, Christine agreed, but that's all just a lovely formality, isn't it? Hilary always made it clear she didn't even want her baptised anyway, that she was only doing it because of your slavery to convention. So I could hardly feel I had a serious duty to undertake. Hilary's always been very anti-Christian, hasn't she?

Daniel had forgotten this. Hilary had indeed been annoyed, he remembered now, that he had wanted to go through with a ceremony neither of them actually believed in. Tom wasn't baptised at all, Christine asked, was he? Daniel said no. He had forgotten this part of their lives. At our age there's so much that isn't present to the mind. Hilary had been right, he thought. If you don't go to church, she would say, except when there's an organ recital, what's the point in baptising your kids. Be consistent, Dan, his wife insisted. Confused now, Judge Savage said: Anyway, the thing is, after the service, the funeral, old Judge Carter asked me if I really didn't know why Martin had stopped practising. Did he indeed? Christine didn't look up. And I said no. But I thought he was suggesting something, that there was something I might have known, but didn't. Now her face did lift and she was smiling brightly. I do like Chinese food, she told him. These spicy aromas. I think they're truly marvellous, Dan, and it's so awful, isn't it, that this lovely place is almost empty while all the stalwart Brits are at the Angus Steak House or some kitsch bistro. Don't you think?

Would you like me to stay the night, he asked. He had parked the car on Carlton Street. His voice was low and steady. While he waited for her reply, he said, by the way, you can always rely on this spot being free at night, because there's a frozen food van here till about eleven or quarter past, then it drives off for some reason and you can park right by your front door. You extraordinary man! she squealed. You're terrible! She might have been a little girl being propositioned for the first time by a brutish stranger. You extraordinary Savage! You can't ask to stay the night. It's disgraceful! Yet ten minutes before, Daniel remembered, as the waitress was pouring the *sake* into thimble glasses, Christine had let her hair brush his ear to whisper, Watch how the bottom of your glass changes when she fills it up. The prim Chinese girl, all formal smiles, tipped the bottle; the glass was filled to the brim, and at once, in some trick of refraction, the transparent alcohol turned what had been just thick colourless glass down at the base into a tiny image of, what? Putting his good eye right down by the glass he saw through the liquid that it was a woman stretching her hand between her thighs. Jolly, isn't it, Christine chuckled a very male chuckle. Her voice could move very suddenly from a shriek to a rumble. What's yours, he asked. She giggled and put a hand on her breast. Oh, a rather large bottom, by the looks! The orientals love this stuff, she laughed. Isn't it charming. Sex at the bottom of a glass. But then you would know all about that, I suppose! She giggled again. Bottoms up and the bottom's gone, she said, she downed her drink. Daniel looked. The glass was no more than glass again, the image hidden in the thickness of the base. Isn't it fun? Christine cried. Now, twenty minutes later, sitting together in the parked car, she protested: The man complains I've ruined his marriage, I've made it impossible for him to go back to his wife, and now he wants to go to bed with me, when my husband's hardly dead a week! Do you want me to stay or not? he asked. She reflected: Couldn't we just have a kiss and cuddle? She turned to him. He kissed her very determinedly. He was quite quite determined and when she gasped, Oh Dan, in a way that, again, was patently false, he asked, What's to stop us? Trembling, she began to fuss with her hair. You can come up for a bit of a chat, she told him.

On the sofa they kissed again. He couldn't tell whether he was excited because he had his hands on her breasts or because he was sure he would get the truth out of her any moment now. But she broke off. Drink? She stood up. There was the ancient gesture of smoothing down the skirt. Whisky, please. No, tea, she said. But . . . Tea! she cried. He came to stand behind her while she put the kettle on. He brushed his lips on the nape of her neck. She turned to detach herself, then found a pack of cigarettes. Have you made arrangements for seeing the children? No. Why not? He shrugged. Inhaling the smoke, she asked: You want *me* to tell you why? I suspect I'm going to hear, Judge Savage said. You haven't made those arrangements because you still haven't accepted that it's over. Could be, he said. And you only want to know things from me, dear Daniel, because deep down you hope that they will reopen things with Hilary, you'll find something else, someone else you can lay all the blame on, and you can start again. She cocked her face to one side, puffed out smoke and returning to her most high pitched little-girl voice demanded, Am I right? Could be, he repeated. She put her cigarette down, took his hands and stood to face him. The kettle was boiling. Hmm, she said. Then, breaking off, she stood back and slapped his cheek very hard. It was unexpected and completely clinical. She was laughing. Oh you should see your face! She turned to snap the kettle off, then turned again and began to kiss him feverishly. She was biting his neck. She wants to leave signs, he told himself. How many times had Daniel Savage convinced himself that he had seduced a woman only to realise then that it was he who was the prey. But he had never minded this. She pulled him to the bedroom and rapidly undressed. She sat on the bed to kick off her shoes, but then kept on her underwear. This is my old friend Christine, he told himself, Martin's wife. He lay down beside her. In the midst of kisses, she broke off again. Again she found a packet of cigarettes, she pulled herself seated, back against the bare wall in a room yellow with streetlight. There's nothing to tell you, she said abruptly, blowing out smoke. You're a silly schoolboy. He reached out to touch her. Leave me alone! She wore lacy cami-knickers, a shiny bra, robustly ribbed. She giggled, you must think you're fucking your wife here, in this room again. Anyway, there's nothing to tell. Nothing, no secrets, no reason why Martin stopped work. She began to shout: He just went like that! I don't know what it was. He got ill.

Naked, Judge Savage now felt ridiculous. You're lying, he told her. He looked around for his pants. I'm not going to insist, but you're lying. You know you are, you said as much at the funeral. Why did you tell Sarah? he asked. She sat forward and put her hand on his shoulder. Can't we just forget all this ugliness and have a lovely kiss. Again, he obliged. They began to kiss. She kissed with great softness now, but very wilfully. She is making her mouth melt, he thought. Breaking off a moment, she said, what lovely, lovely skin you have Daniel Savage, you are so dark and so sexy! She shivered, theatrically, and now was kissing him again. Often, he knew, you had to go through all kinds of trials before you could actually have a woman. But when his hand found its way between her thighs, she tightened. To his great surprise it seemed she was completely shaven. She pushed him away and jumped up off the bed. Tea! she announced. Oh I must look awful. I'm all mussed, aren't I. Milk? Sugar? I need a shower. Coming back with a tray, she said: Dan, the truth is I don't have sex with strangers. And least of all with little boys. She smiled, Not to worry, there are always the twenty-year-old Asian chicks. I thought it was in pretty bad taste by the way introducing the child to Sarah. He was dressing rapidly now and started to pull his socks on. Oh don't go, Dan, she said, let's have some tea and chat a bit. Then his mind clouded. He stood up and smashed the tea tray from her hands. Bitch! he shouted. She screamed. She was scalded. She kept screaming, crouching over her knees. Daniel was scared he had hurt her. Get in the shower, get in the shower. He pulled her up and hurried to the bathroom, turned the water on. Get in. Now she was in the shower with her underwear on, shivering, directing the cold jet at the top of her leg. Is that better. Yes, she said. She sighed. He stood there in his old bathroom. Nothing had changed here. You must forgive me Dan, she laughed nervously – no, it's not that bad, I'm just not used to these things.

You know. I've never done them. Poor Martin, she began to cry under the cold water. I'm sorry, he said. Are you okay? With another change of tone she asked, Why don't you get in the shower. She turned on the hot tap. What? Come in, the water's lovely. She stretched her arms out. Again he complied. He took his clothes off. She kept her underwear on. In his ear she whispered: It was you asked to stay the night! She took his sex in her hand. Tell me about all the women you've ever had, she said. Tell me. Tell me. While she was towelling herself dry, she said: about Sarah, I don't know why I told the girl, I just did. I'm sorry, but I'm like that. You can't trust me. On leaving in the early morning he knew he had never felt so humiliated.

TWENTY-SEVEN

M iss Crawley, yesterday you described how Mr Sayle threw a stone onto the ring road from the bridge, a stone that hit a car travelling toward the bridge and caused the crash that led to this trial, is that right? The girl said yes. The public gallery was packed with angry faces: Sayle's relatives, and Grier's. The defendants too looked intent, possibly belligerent. The jury were all on the alert after yesterday's excitement. Two or three listened with pencils in their hands.

You claimed – Sedley consulted a piece of paper covered with tiny writing, he adjusted his spectacles – that the stone was thrown as a result of an argument between Mr Sayle and Mr Grier over their relationships with Miss Singleton. Is that correct?

Yes.

You said that Mr Sayle appeared to be about to use the stone to attack Mr Grier, but then tossed it instead out onto the road when Miss Singleton begged him to stop. Have I got that right?

Yes.

Sedley lowered his papers and stared at the girl. Had he

too, Daniel wondered, been up all night. The barrister had bags under weak eyes. Again he adjusted his spectacles.

Where did Mr Sayle find the stone, Miss Crawley?

The girl appeared to think.

Dunno.

Can you tell me where each member of the group was at the moment the stone was thrown?

David and Jamie was right there, right by the parapet like.

That is Mr Sayle and Mr Grier.

Right. Sasha, Singleton, was right near them, behind Dave. Sayle. Me and Mr Simmons was walking back onto the bridge to say we was off.

You were approaching from the town side of Malding Lane.

Don't get you.

As if you were coming from town.

Yeah.

So how far were you from the incident.

Dunno. Maybe here to that wall.

Miss Crawley, Judge Savage interrupted, since your evidence is being recorded, could you please give approximate distances, rather than referring to the size of this room, which will mean nothing to those listening to the tape away from here. To help you, I should say that the length of this room would be about ten yards.

The girl frowned. Okay then, ten yards.

Ten yards, Sedley repeated. And you say that immediately before the fatal accident you heard Mr Grier say, and I quote your words of yesterday: I won't stop throwing stones till Sasha admits how much she likes sucking my dick.

The words sounded wonderfully incongruous in Sedley's dry lips. No one smiled.

Right. I don't know if those was the very exact words, but more or less.

Miss Crawley, the ring road is a busy road, is it not?

Yes, sir.

It was the first time she had called him sir. Sedley let it ride.

And a busy road makes a lot of noise.

Right, it's noisy. There's a sort of roar.

A sort of roar, Sedley repeated. And yet, over ten yards distance, and above that roar, you were able to hear what Mr Grier said to Mr Sayle.

The girl took a deep breath, but didn't reply.

Miss Crawley you might imagine that as counsel for the prosecution I would be grateful to hear from a defendant that another defendant had committed the crime, but I must now put it to you that your testimony is riddled with inconsistencies, many of which I suspect are the result of your lying. Is that the case?

The court waited.

Is what sorry?

Sedley asked: Miss Crawley, you have said that the first interview you gave to the police, in which you described Mr Sayle as throwing the stone under very different circumstances, was full of untruths.

Yes, she said. Like I said, I was put under pressure.

Sedley took a breath: Do you feel you are under pressure now?

Yes, I suppose so. In court and everything.

Am I to assume, then, that you are telling untruths again?

You can think what you like, she said quickly, you weren't there.

Miss Crawley, are you going to insist that you could hear what Mr Grier said to Mr Sayle from ten yards away on a bridge over a busy road?

Maybe I was nearer, she said. I can't remember.

Judge Savage began to lose patience. Miss Crawley, this question of distance is important. You are under oath to tell the whole truth.

I need a rest, the girl said flatly. I got a headache. I can't concentrate. Or I'll faint or something.

Judge Savage adjourned. How are you? he asked. He had dialled the number on impulse. Okay, Hilary said. Sarah said you were depressed. I'm not jumping for joy. Sarah sounded in good spirits, he tried. She's been a great help. So, you're getting on together? Daniel asked. We always got on, his wife replied. Well, I'm glad. She even said she'd got a boyfriend. This caused a short pause. First I've heard of it, Hilary told him. Oh, well that's what she told me. Did she indeed, and you believed her? Why shouldn't I, he asked. Who is it then? Hilary said. She wouldn't say who it was. I bet she didn't. Daniel stopped. And how's Tom? Tom is upset, she said. At once he sensed that her voice was franker. What's up? he asked. She lost her temper: What do you mean, what's up, don't be so stupid, what's up is his Dad's not here. He doesn't talk. He's in front of the TV all day. Can I see him? Who's stopping you? I'll call this evening, he said. Call when you want. Hilary, he tried, I didn't want this, even now I . . . Well, you've got it, she said. The conversation was completely different from those he had had from the phones of the Cambridge Hotel. He waited a moment. Look, I miss you all. He knew he was being honest. Hilary I love you. Is there no way . . . What does it mean, I love you? she demanded. What does it mean? Come on, tell me what it means to say that. He thought, I mustn't give a stupid sentimental answer. It means, he said, he hesitated, it means that I only made sense to myself as a person when I was with you. I don't know if . . . When you were with me you were betraying me, that's a lot of sense. But Hilary, I said all

355

that was over, it was a sort of weird phase, sometimes I think it had to do with Dad's dying and . . . You were with Christine last night! his wife shrieked. Who told you? Christine, she's here now. Then Daniel said: Christine is the person who's been talking to the press, Hilary. She's poison. And every word she told them, his wife said, is true!

Hilary had slammed the phone down. Daniel called straight back. When my mind engages with my family, he thought, I can't leave well alone. No it isn't true, he said, as soon as she picked up. Dan, for God's sake! What she told them isn't true, Hilary. Daniel, I don't care . . . You know why I went to see her last night? His wife answered promptly, To go to bed with her. Did she tell you that? She did indeed. How ridiculous, he said. You do seem to have a track record. He knew she was acting this sarcasm from things she had seen in films. He said: It's ridiculous because anyone can see that Christine is incapable of going to bed with anyone. Her femininity ends with her perfume and frilly dresses. Can't you see that. I wouldn't be surprised if she never had sex with Martin at all. She's not a flesh and blood woman like you are, she's a nutcase! He knew his wife wanted to hear this. Your difficulty was juggling career and babies. She didn't have either. She's a complete nothing, and a lunatic too. That's probably why Martin got so depressed, he hazarded. She wouldn't fuck.

Hilary lowered her voice. He sensed she was walking somewhere with the cordless phone. From what she's been telling me, she said softly, the real lunatic was Martin. You should have heard the stuff that came out.

Judge Savage sensed the possibility of complicity. Their marriage had always been strongest when criticising those they knew. He said: Okay, so let me tell you why I went to see her last night. There was silence at the other end of the line, but not refusal. I told her something that wasn't true, deliberately, to see if it would get in the papers. I told her I'd had a fling with . . . He named a famous television presenter. A news anchor woman, no less.

Suddenly his wife was laughing hysterically. It was disquieting, but Judge Savage went on talking. I said we'd met in London when she was reporting on some conference and I'd invited her up to my room. You always said you fancied her, Hilary said. Suddenly she seemed light-hearted. Daniel couldn't remember saying anything of the kind. Anyway, I gave her the story so that if it goes in the papers, we'll know where it came from, and there'll be such fierce denials all round, won't there? You can't imagine someone with that public profile accepting such a rumour, and then maybe people will begin to see that all this news is bullshit. His wife said: To date, all the stories in the paper have been true, Dan. With sudden weariness she said: I'll tell Tom you'll call him this evening.

He had adjourned for fifteen minutes. Now he called Mattheson and waited till the man got off another line. I know who's been talking to the press, he said. Oh yes? The policeman listened but seemed sceptical. Well, we'll see if the story comes up, but I doubt if the paper would have the courage to publish a name like that, the libel tab would be enormous. Daniel felt foolish for not having thought of this. He was a judge and he hadn't thought of the legal consequences. He asked what had happened to the suspect, Craig whatever-his-name-was. We've released him for the moment, Mattheson said. Clearly he didn't want to talk. Daniel couldn't understand whether he was dealing with an institutional procedure or a man with an agenda all his own. The only thing I'd say, Dan, Mattheson was now signing off, is keep away from the Korean ticket. Why do you say that?

357

Just a word of warning, the policeman said. He chuckled. Come to think about it, the less we talk, and the less you talk about it, the better. Especially as, for the moment you seem to be getting away with it all famously. You don't see my mailbag, Daniel said.

Then he was Judge Savage again. He put on his wig. The usher knocked three times on the heavy door. The court rose, he took his seat, the court sat. Miss Crawley stood and came to the box. Okay I was right near, she said at once. She was trembling. Judge Savage now had no difficulty concentrating. The truth is, about the stones, that David, Mr Sayle, had this thing they would only hit someone if God meant them to hit. There was an uproar. Judge Savage ordered that two members of the public be removed. The defendants were silent. They weren't exchanging glances. Four prison officers now sat with them in the dock. Yes, Janet Crawley admitted, we all knew stones would get thrown one way or another when we were at the bridge. Even if it was only one on an evening. It was a sort of thing between Mr Sayle and Mr Grier. It sort of wound the evening up. I don't know. It was a thing they had.

Sedley stood watching. Are you returning to the version you gave in your initial interview with the police, Miss Crawley? The lawyer was taking great care, Daniel thought, to be neutral. He just wants to keep this flow going. With her hard pretty face, brash eyes, tight lips, the girl seemed the least likely candidate to break. Had the group stayed compact, Judge Savage was sure, a conviction was unlikely. There had been room for reasonable doubt. Sedley started to take her through it again. On how many previous occasions had stones been thrown and who threw them, who brought them to the bridge? Why does the truth out? Daniel wondered. And why does it out *when* it does? Loads of times, the girl said. Please try to be more specific, Sedley asked. You should have heard the stuff that came out, Hilary had said. Grier was just wild, Janet Crawley was saying, her voice had taken on a low, trance-like tone. David said the stones would only hurt people if they weren't pure because in the end everybody only got what they deserved in this world. No sooner was the girl out of the box than her counsel asked for an adjournment, no doubt to reconsider her position. But when the court was reassembled he did not ask for the indictment to be read out again. Her plea of not guilty remained.

TWENTY-EIGHT

Chloe Cummings, the TV presenter, was not mentioned in the papers, except with regard to the ongoing story of her sick child by a previous marriage. The boy was dying of leukaemia. On Saturday morning Daniel took his own son to play football in an outlying suburb south of the town, then drove him to Doherty Street market. The match was exciting. The boys were fourteen now and many full grown. The autumn air was full of memories *We go up in a line or not at all*, a big black defender kept shouting. *In a fucking line!* Tom lurked between bigger feet. Very occasionally he broke free on his own, shoving with his elbows. *Bastard*, he cried and right after half-time shot home a loosely cleared ball. He raised his arms, he was mobbed by his team-mates. The yellow-and-black shirts mingled, the black boys and the white and one Asian. Daniel watched in the cool September air.

Just beyond the pitch old men leaned on the parapets of the walkways round their flats. Sperringway again. And later, driving Tom back to town, without expecting it or choosing his route on purpose, Judge Savage caught a glimpse of the improbable Sue in her lay-by. She was leaning against the side of a van, talking to a driver. I belong here, Daniel thought, smiling. I am a citizen of this town, inside and out.

But now Tom was demanding a trip to McDonald's. If I got a shake for every goal I scored, he boasted, you'd be broke. Daniel parked the car. Mum said you were depressed, he told his son over the tabletop. The boy raised his eyes, chewing. He was lighter skinned than Daniel or Sarah, but with the same black eyes. Now they seemed clear of any pain. They shone with youth. No time to be depressed with all the homework they're giving us, he grumbled. We're training three times a week now. Great, Daniel said. The games master was saying there'll be scouts round looking at us this year, from the big youth teams. Great, Daniel repeated. Sarah? he asked. God what a *pain*! Tom shouted, his mouth full. For days, nothing but chat chat chat with Mum, you know – he made a quacking gesture with one hand – like it would never end. Chat chat chat. Only now she's out most of the time, thank God. Never at home.

Perhaps she's got a boyfriend, Daniel said lightly. It was nice to be with his son; with Tom his father's role seemed so obvious, something that was not the case with Sarah. Boyfriend! That'll be the day, the boy laughed. A *boyfriend*, Sarah! Then even more emphatically, That will be the *day*, alrightie-oh! He punched one fist in the air, gripping the remainder of his burger in the other. His voice was gratingly loud.

But why shouldn't she get a boyfriend? She's pretty. Oh yuck, Tom said. Tom, don't be so childish, she's lovely. No she isn't, he insisted. Tom, she is, take it from me! Tom sneered: It's just that you're old Dad, you'd make do with anything. Daniel stared at the boy, but he was munching away quite candidly, as though there were nothing offensive in what he'd said. The judge made a gesture with his head. There were three girls sitting at the table to his left. Do you think *she's* pretty, he asked. Tom chewed. Comically, he shifted his eyes without turning his face, frowned. Then rocking back and forth he sang: All right in a kind of a limited way for an off-night!

He giggled. The beautiful girl raised her head. I see beauty everywhere, Daniel thought. Don't show-off, Tom, he said. Chewing the last mouthful, wiping his hands under his armpits, the boy defended himself: Anyway, *Mum's* always saying she never will. What? That Sarah will never get a boyfriend. Mum says that? Yes. No she doesn't. But she does, Dad! But why? Daniel asked. Tom wiped his mouth, laughed. Dunno!

Stirring his shake, the boy went on: Oh, one piece of good news though. Mum said I could stop piano. Oh really, and what's good about that, I thought you liked it. Dad, come on! Where have you been! Again Judge Savage had the feeling he was trying to penetrate an enchanted thicket. They can't cut you out though, it suddenly crossed his mind, because you are part of the tangle. What on earth do I want to go to the market for, Tom was complaining. I'll get you a sheath knife, Daniel tried. There's always someone selling second hand stuff like that. Dad, I only gave up with sheath knives about three-and-a-half centuries ago. As it turned out there was more than one stall selling used computer games.

The afternoon was warm and bright, the market less busy than it would have been in the morning. Around the fruit stalls the ground was littered with boxes and rotten grapes. Halfway along the street, outside the Westward Ho, a group of youngsters were sitting round two black men tapping on drums. Arab women shifted and dawdled in their veils. The beat was soft and urgent. Tom wasn't interested. They picked their way through. His chest bared, an old white worker sat on a low wall, a pint held between hairy nipples as he peered into the crowd. There were tunnels of shade between the stalls and a hard glitter of sunshine on awnings and wind-screens.

You know, when I first came here, right after university, Judge Savage told his son, I was pretty well the only non-white around. I even remember people looking at me. Tom was unimpressed. Grudgingly he asked, So, is it better or worse now? It's different Daniel said.

Across the crowd the rhythm of the drums came and went. Then they were passing by a store selling oriental drapes. Daniel was alert. Why had Mattheson said that about not trying to contact Minnie? Did I ever say I had any desire to see her again? He bought Tom an ice-cream, then went back and got one for himself.

My nephew! Well, would you believe it! Frank broke off a conversation with a man holding a heavy-framed mirror. Tommie boy! Tom stood sheepishly behind his ice-cream, embarrassed by this effusive uncle with a cigarette in one hand and a rag in the other. Hilary despised smokers. Tommie boy! Jesus, you *are* tall! The kid's embarrassed, he said to the customer. Last two times we met was at funerals. Wasn't it, Tom? Funny you can't say, last twice. Now, thirty quid, take it or leave it, Reg. He raised his voice as if talking to a large crowd. Take it or leave it. I never go lower than list price or old customers would feel cheated. You among them. Three guesses where Art is, he threw in an aside to Daniel. The customer, stooped with thick glasses and thicker eyebrows, said he'd give twenty, but no more. Oh please, Reg, don't be an arsehole! Gone to check out what's at Mart's place. Daniel looked up. Yep, had Madame Bovary-Shields on the blower early this morning, quite a voice, all flirts and squeals, thanked me *most* warmly for coming to the funeral. I thought: better send Art or I'll have to spend all day reminiscing. Thirty, Frank repeated to his client. Not a penny less. No, not one hay-pen-ee! Reg remembers ha-pennies. Don't you old mate? Still with an embarrassed smile, shaking his head as though in pity, Tom had started to leaf through a box of old letters on a trestle table. Oh, by the way, Reg, you're probably wondering – Reg is an old customer, he confided – this is my brother, yes brother, Daniel. Dan, Reg, a regular customer and a hard bargainer at a stall that never bargains. Ha ha! Reg, Dan. I stick by the list price, old mate. The queen's not for turning! He aped a female voice. Reg was grinning at Daniel in affable disbelief. Your brother? Doesn't fackin' well believe us, does he Dan? Frank clapped Judge Savage on the shoulders, winked, lit another cigarette. The prices are on the list over yonder, he shouted to a woman who was searching the surface of a small chest. He blew out smoke. My adopted brother – that's better – recently separated from his legally wedded whatever and presently causing bloody havoc sleeping on the sofa of the otherwise immaculate Savage residence; but has promised to move out soon, haven't we, Dan? Yes, in the darkest interior Madam, the gloomy sanctum, hanging from the rail. There, you've got it. Only staring her in the bloody boat-race, he muttered.

But now, shambling and bespectacled, shading his pale eyes from the sharp sun, Reg had begun to look perplexed. Aren't you . . . he squinted, Sorry, haven't I seen you somewhere.

My God! Squire, he's recognised you! Yes, it's Regency, love. You're famous, Dan. Reg recognises you! The recognition scene. Yes, genuine, Madam. Can promise. Bring someone along to check it out, if you're worried, if it's still here when you get back that is. Three hundred is not a gift,

Madam, but we have to get rich somehow. He laughed, Yes, my old black bruv, Judge Savage. Again he clapped him on the shoulder, alias Don Giovanni. Let's get out of here, Dad, Tom whispered. Pleased to meet you, sir. Reg set the mirror down to shake hands, truly honoured to meet you, sir, I've seen you on the telly. And as he did so, exactly as he set the mirror down beside Frank Savage's stall, Daniel caught a glimpse, in its old and uncertain silvering, of his daughter. Yes, as the mirror was set down he definitely caught a wobbly glimpse of Sarah's head and shoulders, as if photographed, clumsily, from a low angle. Was it her? Already extending his hand to Reg, he swivelled, distracted, knowing he would offend, and there she was, not four yards away, picking up tiny pieces of pottery that a community of ex-addicts had moulded into caricatures of public figures. There she was! But most of all there was a big be-ringed hand gently resting on the tight butt of her jeans, a man with his firm hairy forearm clasped around her in a gesture of candid sexual possession. It was only a second, a glance, but Daniel took in, for future reflection, a solid paunch and a small blond ponytail of dirty hair.

I'm sorry, he turned back, but it's so embarrassing, being recognised. Pleased to meet you, Reg. And don't trust this man an inch. If you knew how we were brought up! Again he turned a second and glimpsed a scoured face. How old? But now his eye switched to check that Tom wasn't looking. Right, I saw you on the news, Reg was saying, undeterred by the other's distraction. He couldn't recall why. He chattered on. Tom was still bent over the old letters. I promised the kid a computer game, his father finally said.

An hour later Judge Savage parked the car up on the hill at the bottom of the drive beneath the new house. Tom rushed off. The dog was tied to a bench that had appeared beneath the sitting room window. It yapped and strained at the leash. Hilary was crouched by a great pot of white flowers. She had scissors in her hands. All right? she enquired, without looking up. Daniel felt he might be returning as any husband after a brief outing. Did you win Tom? she called. He was gone. Three nil, Daniel grinned, he lowered his voice. He seems fine to me. Now she looked up. She frowned. Well, maybe that's the way he wants to appear to you. Daniel shrugged his shoulders. How can I know? She was laconic: Since you don't see him here, Dan, you can't, can you?

The afternoon was mild and seemed beneficent. Perhaps we could have a cup of tea, he suggested. No whisky? she asked. Actually no. I'm not drinking that much. It was the truth. She had crouched down again to cut off another couple of dead flowers. Perhaps you're happy, she said primly. Now she looked up with a more pleasant smile, pushing back hair with the back of a wrist. She went through to the kitchen and turned the tap on. I'm dying to hear the scoop on Martin, Daniel said. Behind her the window was open on their patch of lawn, the brick wall, the fields rising beyond where a distant horse lifted its head and snorted. It seemed so much more airy and attractive than it had when he had been here on his own. Tom's terrible during the week, she said, if you want to know. He's even given up piano. He refuses to play at all. Daniel chose not to answer.

She made the tea in silence. Then she laughed and said that the dog was driving her mad bringing in rats all the time. You wouldn't believe it, there must be rats in the ditches beyond the close. Big brutes. You wouldn't believe it. Every time he escapes, he comes back with one. Please, don't ask me how I am, she said quickly when she caught some look or other in his face. She bent down to pour.

Give me the dirt on Martin then, he said brightly. He felt determined to be bright. She half smiled into her cup. Oh, better not. But why? Christine swore me to secrecy. Daniel was taken aback. Hilary, you never . . . But this is new, isn't it, she told him. She looked up hard. We're hardly united against the world now, are we, Dan? United against the world had been an old expression. He stared at her. She was wearing neatly creased trousers and a small white blouse that showed how solid, but not fat, her body was. Had she lost weight? Oh come on, he said. No. She was sardonic. But God, Hil . . . Anyway, she conceded, turning away for sugar, they certainly weren't any worse than we were, now I've had time to think it over. He shook his head. Oh and your famous story wasn't in the papers, she said. Chloe what's-her-name. She grimaced, Was it? No, he agreed. But I'm still waiting. It's only twenty-four hours. Tell you what, she said jollily, the day that story's in the papers, I'll give you the dirt on Martin.

Tom, I'm off! he called. The boy was at his screen, his games. I'm off, Tom! You should have seen the second goal he scored. I've seen so many, she said. Bye Dad, the boy shouted from upstairs. Don't come down, Daniel shouted.

They were passing through the sitting room now. How attractively she had furnished it for him when he was ill, when she sat by his bedside. How arid these paintings and embroideries had seemed when he was here alone. He lingered by the piano. She is getting nervous, he thought. He noticed her old habit of shifting her weight from foot to foot. She is waiting for me to go. But he was determined this encounter would end well. I can't believe we can be so easy together, he said. So offhand, you mean, she corrected. No, it's not offhand . . . It is for me, Dan. The more she resisted him, the more he knew he would insist. Only a couple of months ago, he said, not even, Hil, we were so passionate, and now . . . Oh Dan, stop it, we weren't passionate. Passion died with us years ago. We're too old for passion. No we're not, he said. He thought of the man with Sarah. How old? Why am I not going to tell her? he wondered. We're too old for passion *with each other*, Hilary corrected. Now you've been listening to Sarah, he protested. You always said she was trying to split us up. There was a brief pause. He had annoyed her. Tom tells me she's got you to dump Max too, he said.

I beg your pardon?

You've dumped Max, haven't you. It could only be because of Sarah. You adored the boy. No, I did . . . but Hilary Savage burst out laughing. She was shaking her head and sat down. No, you can't get me like that, Dan. I'm not going to fall for that. I didn't dump him. I simply stopped all my lessons, because I needed to take stock. It hasn't been an easy time. Sarah was delighted, he insisted. I've no idea, Hilary said.

So nobody's playing the piano, he tried. No, she said, not at the moment. It seems such a shame with . . . Cut it, Dan. They were staring at each other. I feel I could seduce anyone but you, he suddenly confessed. Go ahead then, she said. Who's stopping you? He hesitated: Do you mind if I keep trying with you? Yes, she told him. It'll make me cry when you've left. Going out, he asked: Have you lit the fire yet? Hilary didn't answer.

Sometime later, climbing the stairs to the fourth floor, he was still reflecting on this meeting, on the completeness of his wife's refusal of any sort of intimacy, when Frank appeared above. He was excited. Is that you, squire. Dan? Come and take a butcher's at these. Get your black bastard arse up the stairs.

Arthur had found them taped underneath the second

drawer of the Georgian dresser in Martin's bedroom. In two separate folders, he said. On the sticky wooden top of Frank's kitchen table, among glasses of Verduzzo and hunks of Battenberg, were a dozen photos of young children, girls and boys, in obscene poses. Most were oriental, Indian, or black. The faces had been scratched away.

TWENTY-NINE

You have heard various conflicting versions of what happened on the evening of March 22nd. The time has now come for you to weigh up all that evidence and decide whether each of the defendants is, beyond reasonable doubt, guilty as charged. It is my duty to assist you in that task.

Thus, in routine fashion, would Judge Savage begin his summing up in R. v. Sayle and others. But that moment was still four days away, four days and four nights during which, it seemed, the judge slept not a wink. Nor had he eaten. Colleagues noticed that he looked haggard. It's a delayed reaction, Kathleen Connolly told herself, for there had been nothing adverse in the press about Judge Savage for some days now. That phase was over. He had survived. Nevertheless, patch over his eye, shoulders slumped, clothes crumpled, he did not look in the best possible state for delivering the authoritative summing up that a complex trial like this required. Aside from which, there was now the added intricacy that on the night of Saturday, September 15th, Mrs Whitaker died. Sensibly, the prosecution asked for no alteration in the indictment. Grievous bodily harm with intent was crime enough. But would the defendants later be able to argue that the death had hardened the attitude of the jury? Juries were known to be more willing to convict when there had been a death. All the same, at this late stage there seemed no reasonable alternative but to proceed. In the early hours of Sunday morning, it seemed, the woman had simply ceased to breathe. This was the same night that Judge Savage had sat up, towards three o'clock, sharp and frightened, on the sofa in Frank's flat, as if jerked rigid from a sleep of years, and cried out loud, I feel utterly betrayed.

Utterly betrayed, he announced. He shivered, sitting bolt upright, though it wasn't cold. His heart beat fast. It was as if the words had been given to him and now he must make sense of them. What sense did it make to feel betrayed when it was you who had done all the betraying? Now he remembered the photos. Surely that wasn't the dirt Hilary had kept from him. Those photos were so much more than what his wife would have called dirt. He stood up and began to walk about the sitting room. Hilary has cut me off, he announced. I am utterly betrayed, he said. I would never have done that to her.

To avoid confusion, Judge Savage would tell the jury four days hence, before you consider those conflicting stories, it will be worth going over the facts that are not a matter of dispute between any of the parties, facts with which any satisfactory version of events must be consistent.

Reading slowly, he began: On March 22nd of this year at 10.52 p.m. a motor vehicle was struck by a stone as it passed under the bridge where Malding Lane crosses over the ring road. He looked up. This is not disputed.

The impact of the stone meeting the car at a speed estimated to be about forty-five miles per hour and thus within the fifty-mile-an-hour limit in force on the ring road, led to the coma and eventually, as we have recently heard, the death of Mrs Elizabeth Whitaker. This is not disputed.

The eight defendants all admit to having been present on the bridge the night of the incident and to having seen the damaged car on the hard shoulder before the arrival of ambulance and police vehicles. They neither aided the victims of the incident, nor informed either hospital or police. This is not disputed.

Data from the telephone company Orange shows that 85 telephone calls were made between the eight mobile phones of the defendants in the hours between 6.30 and 9 a.m. on the morning of March 23rd. No similar intensity of phone traffic has ever been recorded between these phones. This is not disputed.

Judge Savage seemed exhausted. Why was he repeating that phrase so insistently. It was an unusual way to proceed with a summing up. Looking up from his notes his seeing eye was bloodshot.

So much then, he told the jury, for the undisputed evidence. It is all, as you will have observed, *circumstantial* evidence, by which I mean that it is not the same as the testimony of an independent eye-witness identifying the perpetrator of a crime at the moment he or she commits that crime. We have no such evidence in this case. A witness did see a group of youths on the bridge around the time of the crime and has positively identified two of the defendants. But he did not see any stones thrown. No one saw the crime committed. However, it is permissible for you, as the jury, to infer from circumstances proven and accepted by all parties any other facts necessary to complete the elements of guilt or, for that matter, to establish the defendants' innocence. What I am saying is: to call evidence circumstantial is by no means to deny its importance as evidence. The dirty bastard, Frank had breathed over the photos. He was shaking his head. Someone else could have put them there, Arthur said reasonably. Maybe he didn't even know they were there. It doesn't prove anything. Oh but it fits! Frank cried. Doesn't it, squire. He turned to Daniel, splashing out wine all round. It fits! Art, if you'd known Martin you'd understand! It explains everything. The bloke was sick. It's him, Dan! It must be. What you must bear in mind, however, Judge Savage would go on to tell the jury, is that even the strongest circumstantial evidence can often allow for various interpretations, however unlikely they may at first seem. It is with this caveat, then, that you must consider the various divergent versions of events which you have heard, versions which can be understood as different attempts to explain those circumstances that are, I repeat, not a matter for dispute: the throwing of a stone, the impact with the car, the presence of these nine young people on the bridge. It is also important that you understand, he warned, how your acceptance, or otherwise, of any given version will affect the position of each single defendant.

Jerked from sleep in the early hours of that Sunday morning, after his afternoon with Tom, the conversation with his wife, the shock of the photos, sitting shivering and stiff on the sofa, Judge Savage was aware that something new had happened in his life, something important had changed. I feel utterly betrayed. He said the words out loud. But was that reasonable? He stood barefoot, rather frightened, on the gritty carpet. He didn't understand how he could have been so violently tossed out of sleep. When he woke, he was already sitting up.

He waited. In the dark his vision was blurred. He had no perspective on things. He felt vulnerable. Perhaps it's a dream I'm about to remember. He felt that kind of pressure. But no dream came. Rather, the simplest and most lucid of observations suddenly spoke itself with great conviction: Hilary sees a different version of our lives. He stared into the dark. His wife wasn't being hysterical, as once at the Cambridge Hotel. She wasn't even being aggressive or actually in any way unpleasant. Quite calmly, he told himself, even *sensibly*, Hilary considers our life together as over. My marriage is finished. At the very point where she had been about to crown him as her dream hero, the wounded Savage, the heroic Savage, the strong moral figure who had at last replaced her first love Robert, at that very moment, circumstances had prompted her to change position: they weren't even partners. We are no longer partners, he announced. Though *I* haven't changed at all. She isn't saying there was *never* a story, he thought, I *never* loved you, as she had said before, beating on his chest in the foyer of the Cambridge Hotel. That line had been easy to refute. She was saying, this is how that old story ends: we don't grow old together. It still doesn't seem possible, Daniel thought. I am dead to Hilary, he announced out loud and rather strangely in the street-lit shadows of his brother's flat. She has put herself away from me.

In boxer shorts he paced the filthy carpet. He saw his wife crouching by the vase of white flowers. Tom had gone up to his room. She snipped off the dead flowers. It came home to him that he had no home now. Christine had been right that he hadn't taken it in. You are sleeping here on the sofa like an adolescent runaway, like a teenager staying a week with his brother. Christine *told* you this. Christine isn't all bad, he thought. She herself hasn't taken in Martin's death. How could she? How can you take in, in the space of a few hours, that somebody you have lived your life with has been cremated. I am dead to my wife, Daniel thought. The

374

dead softness of Christine's body had been most disturbing. His wife's flesh was solid, robust, healthy. It no longer has anything to do with me.

And Frank wanted him out too. You have rediscovered Frank, you have reconciled yourself with a large part of your past. This had been a great relief. All the same and quite naturally your older brother doesn't want you sleeping on the sofa for ever. Frank is changing, Daniel thought, from the merest adolescent rebel, a man who never grew up, into a successful if rather irritating adult with a thriving business. Frank accepts you because you fell from grace, he thought, but all the same he needs to concentrate on his business. This is Arthur's doing, Daniel thought. And the consequence of his father's death, his mother's decrepitude. Our parents are gone.

Then Judge Savage rushed into the kitchen and found the photographs again. The tape that had held two thin folders to the wood was brown with age. Can you tell how old Scotch tape is? I know nothing of Martin's life, he thought. He couldn't remember a case that hinged on the age of Scotch tape. The man had been a regular churchgoer until his car accident. He stared at a little girl urinating. The body was chocolate brown. He shook his head. The face was scratched out. There was a shine to the child's skin, the enamel shine of young brown skin. The photos were large, larger than those photos of moths. He turned on the kitchen light. He stared. He brought them to within an inch or two of his eye. How could you identify a child, without the child's face? Do I know a single distinguishing mark of my daughter's body, he wondered? Martin had scratched out their faces. They were gone. The evidence is entirely circumstantial, he reflected, but it does seem reasonable to infer that Martin did the scratching. The child was peeing onto an erect and decidedly adult male member. Surely Christine wouldn't have done that, he thought. She wouldn't have scratched out the faces and hidden the photos. And even if she had, she wouldn't have told Hilary. No, the single indisputable fact of these photographs, Daniel told himself – they were A4 in size – alters everything I know about Martin. He remembered the odd girlishness of Christine's behaviour in bed, his unease at her squeaky voice, the shaven skin between her thighs. What was that about? Sarah had wept at the funeral. It had surprised him. Suddenly his mind was fizzing. Don't you know why he stopped work? the old judge croaked. And the car crash. Going no one knew where. I have to hide so much, Christine said at the funeral. She wept. There had been a sardonic look in Judge Carter's eye. Why had the Shields decided to buy the Carlton Street flat? The possible connections between these events are multiplied ad infinitum by the appearance of a dozen A4 photos of naked children in obscene poses. Just matter, Martin had insisted. How earnestly he had leaned across the table, the beer-mats. His one earnest moment in all the evening. I was defending a man who had killed a child on a bicycle. Was it the ring road? It was a revelation, he had claimed, not something you arrived at by reasoning, Dan. You're not ready for it, Dan, he said. He had laughed. Had he been trying to confess? These photographs are a revelation, Daniel thought. If not exactly a confession. Why hadn't Martin destroyed them?

We mustn't be caught with these photos, he had told Frank at once. A moth fluttered under the naked bulb of the kitchen. The world is full of moths. As harmless as they are irritating. There was a fly too that had settled on the table's stickiness. Photos like this would take a lot of explaining. And now it seemed he didn't know Hilary either. She would never again be the person she had been for him by the fire that Saturday afternoon. And with her refusal the past began to shift too. The fire died and went out. It went out in the past. There is no need to deny the past, Judge Savage told himself, to pretend it never was. It will shift on its own. A decision like that, today, he thought, alters a person's identity to the core. And retrospectively. History was changed. Should he show her the photos? Should he show Hilary? He was quite sure this wasn't the so-called dirt Christine had given her. That would be paltry stuff. Should he run to his wife apparently flabbergasted with these incriminating photos? I understood nothing of the core of Martin's identity. He could show Hilary the photos. They would confront Christine together. Look at these photos! Christine, we demand to know the truth. Would that force something out of her? Who are these children? they would ask. They could go to the police.

Extremely agitated, Judge Savage rushed to the oven and started to burn the photographs. He turned on a gas ring, lit it, held the photos one by one over the flame. He watched young bodies curl and burn. Burn them, he thought. Get all this stuff behind. Tom and Sarah will be fine without you, he thought. I'll see them regularly. The room – but how ludicrous to think it might be Tom! – stank with smoke and he hurried to open a window, burning the photographs one by one. He gathered the ashes. He was breathing hard. Think of all the damage you're avoiding, he told himself, making an end of this. His mouth was dry. Don't pursue it. Hilary is right to make an end, he decided. Start again.

But then, once more on the sofa, still unable to sleep, Daniel's mind raked back and forth across the ashes of their lives, the arguments, the reconciliations, the being with

Hilary and the betraying Hilary, the being with her *by* betraying her – another strange thought – two ongoing states that curled on and on together like smoke and flame, or two twigs curling together as they burned and now burned quite out. We are burned out now, he announced. And the sequence of all that burning from beginning to end, the excited kindling, the tall blaze, the little spurts, the sparks and coloured gases, the winking embers and lively unexpected flickering over and over – how it flared and sparked and blazed again out of the dark! – was beyond him, beyond all comprehension, but somehow had gone on and on for twenty years fed and fanned from here or there – winds that came from you knew not where, breezes that blew and blew themselves out – how could you know or understand why your wife suddenly wanted to make love, was she thinking of Max, did Max remind her of Robert, surely not, she blazed with excitement, there in the empty house, until now the coals were suddenly hard and charred and the old embers raked apart.

Raked apart, Daniel Savage announced. The words felt cool. They cooled him. Still he couldn't sleep. It wasn't just they two, he told himself now, but a whole world that had been burning, burning in ways he couldn't imagine, in ways no one was controlling. To control a fire you set it in a Swedish-made cast-iron fireplace with a surround of Regency stone. But it had already been over when they did that. The flames were already dying. He sensed he wasn't going to sleep now. The world was never even remotely as you thought it. Frank and Martin and Hilary and Christine. They were fuelled by fires you never dreamed of. You too, he thought, perhaps have fuelled fires you know very little of: in Jane's life, in Minnie's, perhaps even in Martin's. Didn't I speak to Martin of unseen chains? No, I *boasted* of them. He had been deliberately provocative. When you make love to a woman, he had told Martin, you bind yourself to people you know nothing of. That was the excitement. The loss of control, the secret links. But it was more like a fire than a chain. Everything you do could set a flame alight, elsewhere, perhaps years from now. How deeply his relationship with Jane would burn into stupid Crawford's heart. There had been other women too. The more their marriage goes on, Daniel thought, the more her relationship with me will smoulder on. It was a burning net of fire. Could it have been Crawford feeding these stories to the press? Yes! Why didn't I think of that? Daniel had other women, Jane might tell her stupid husband one night. I was only one of many, Gordon. When you're old you'll make do with anything, Tom had sniggered. Daniel sat up again. Of course the children are involved! A poor woman on a distant continent makes casual love to an older man, making do perhaps. Two dry sticks are rubbed together. Or perhaps it's an adolescent, drawn to the blaze of first experience. The prostitute takes him in her arms. He must lose his innocence, he is Tom's grandfather! A flame is lit. The boy's eyes sparked with dark and casual life. When you're old you'll make do with anything, he sneered.

Oh why can't I sleep! Daniel cried aloud. Why? Burning the photographs, their secrets possessed me, he decided. Martin's malignant secrets. I'm possessed. He jumped off the sofa. This most English of friends! The carpet was full of grit. I hate portentous thoughts! Taking pictures of moths had been a sort of penance, for Martin perhaps. I will not have portentous thoughts! Martin used to think in those terms. Had he confessed to his mother, to the frail old woman who had wept in their sitting room? Christ! Daniel sat up again and stared around the dark room. It was curious he didn't pour himself a drink. You could pour a drink over your burning mind, he reflected. A whisky. Frank has some whisky somewhere. He was afraid it would flare up on him. How the sleepless mind sizzles in the quiet dark of the early hours. Was that when Martin went out in his garden to photo the moths? In the early hours. The world of matter falls silent and the mind sizzles and burns.

Yet in the end it's good that one gets burned, Judge Savage muttered. What is life if not people setting each other alight? How frightening not to be burned and consumed. To sit still and watch soaps, to have the burning mind extinguished by wet soaps. It was right, he thought, that a marriage should wear out, wear *you* out. Me. How terrifying to be forever soft and fresh with soaped and perfumed skin and the pudenda of a child. Could that be Christine's case? She was unconsumed. What if she were still a virgin? Daniel asked himself. Are such things possible?

Daniel Savage stood undecided, pacing about his brother's sitting room. There was a soft deadness to Christine, a perfumed mummification. Unconsumed and seeing her husband burnt out with contradictions, Christine craves to have something happen. Determined to start a fire, she talks to your daughter about her father's philanderings. There's a spark. Christine is a pyromaniac, he told himself. That's obvious. Unconsumed herself, she would burn up those she knew. From the smoking ashes she runs back to her Sunday school. I'll work for Save the Children, she said. Part time. But Daniel was furious with himself for thinking of such things. Speculation is an *illness*, an inextinguishable fever! I must always interrupt when counsel engages in speculation. Always the paranoid, Frank laughed. He was right. But Frank *had* cut those strange lines in his back when they were at school together. How can you not be paranoid when people do that to you? How could you fail to imagine you were somehow important, if people insisted on doing that to you? We will be blood brothers, Frank said, as if etching those wounds he could kindle some love between them. Decades later three men he didn't know had beaten him within an inch of his life.

Judge Savage went to the corridor, picked up his dispatch case, returned to the kitchen, switched on the light and banged out files and notebooks on the table. He slapped them on the unwiped surface and at once began to draft notes for the summing up. R. v. Sayle and others. He strained his eye. The light wasn't good. There were still at least two days of the trial to go and still one more defendant to be examined. But the case is clear enough now, he thought. The evidence is pretty well there, he decided. You can set up the outline at least. Sum up then. Work is solid, Daniel Savage told himself. I have this good fortune. I have some-thing solid. My work. Crawford, he thought, was one person who might know of his philandering in general, but not about the girl on the jury in particular. It could have been Crawford. His eye strained in the yellow light. It was five a.m. Work is a slow controlled burn, he told himself, over a sensible stove. He wrote:

The first, the most determining, and possibly the easiest decision you must take, members of the jury, is whether the stone that caused the death of Mrs Whitaker was, or was not, thrown by one of the eight defendants. Mr Sayle, Mr Grier, Miss Singleton, Mr Davidson, Mr Simmons and Mr Riley have all claimed that as they arrived on the bridge from the city side of Malding Lane in Mr Grier's car they saw three children, whom they have placed between twelve and sixteen years of age, running in the opposite direction and into the wooded area beyond the bridge. They presume these children perpetrated the crime. No independent witness has been found to corroborate this evidence.

This was not the proper tone for a summing up at all, Daniel Savage told himself. Why was he writing like this? But never mind. The thing was to concentrate, to think. Not to think of other things. The form could be altered later.

Three of the defendants, Mr Riley, Mr Grier and Mr Simmons, have spoken of having been more than once accosted on the bridge by a foreigner, a journalist they believed, who offered money to anyone hitting a car with a stone. They believe this man may have encouraged the young children they saw. Two witnesses have corroborated this account. Both of these witnesses, we must remember, were erstwhile members of this group, and albeit not present on the bridge on March 22nd they may be considered to be in a special relationship with the defendants and their evidence must thus be considered with due caution. There is also a certain discrepancy to be considered here, in that although, in the witness box, the three defendants and the two witnesses all agreed that the man was white and middle-aged with an East European accent, one of the two witnesses, in her first statement to the police referred to the man as young and of Indian or Pakistani origin.

Apart from these accounts, there are also two initial interviews that two defendants gave to the police in which, independently of each other, they stated that the stone had indeed been thrown by one of the defendants. These interviews, however, contained notable discrepancies with regard to the numbers of stones thrown and the attitude of the other members of the group who did not throw stones to those members who did. The remarks were later withdrawn and it was claimed that they were made under extreme police pressure. However, one of the defendants has given here in court what we might think of as a more articulated and complicated version of her original account in interview. Again, however, this account contains a number of serious discrepancies, and should in any event be treated only with the utmost caution as it includes elements which might be considered self-serving at the expense of other members of the group.

Judge Savage paused. He had been scribbling very fast in the early hours of the Sunday morning, quite unaware, of course, that a few miles away the victim of the crime under consideration had only minutes ago stopped breathing. He was beginning to feel better and again set pencil to paper:

Throughout the trial, and this is one of the most problematic issues for you to decide ladies and gentlemen of the jury, no evidence given by the defendants or by any other witness has explained the presence on the bridge of such a large stone, a stone, we remember, of a kind not to be found in the woodland around the bridge, or indeed for a distance of some miles. Examining the ring road that same night, the police found two other such stones within fifty yards of the bridge. Counsel for the prosecution has pointed to the circumstantial evidence of the presence of fragments of similar stone in the back of the car used by Sayle and Grier to arrive at the bridge, arguing that the stones were loaded into the car with the express purpose of throwing them from the bridge. It is largely on the basis of this circumstantial evidence that the prosecution has rejected all the defendants' versions of the evening's events, including that of Miss Janet Crawley, insisting that *all* members of the group were equally involved in the reckless behaviour that eventually caused grievous bodily harm. Mr Grier, we will remember, however, has accounted for the stone fragments in the back of his car, by offering evidence of the rockery he set up with his uncle in the garden of the latter's home using similar stones. It has been established that this rockery, which does indeed use such stones, was set up in May of 1998, almost a year before the crime we are here to consider. However, it is not impossible that fragments of stone should remain for many months in the boot of a car.

Sitting in Frank's kitchen, Judge Savage could already see how he would raise his eyes, his eye, from his notes at this point and gaze for a moment at his nondescript jury with the irritating, unattractive, brash young woman in the front row. Then having highlighted what he was about to say with this anticipatory pause, he would continue:

The first question you must ask yourselves, then, will be: Is the circumstantial evidence together with the fact that two defendants albeit amid discrepancies and withdrawals have offered incriminating eyewitness accounts, sufficient to convince you *beyond reasonable doubt* that the stone was thrown by one of the defendants? If you are *not* so convinced, you need proceed no further and the defendants must be acquitted. If, however, you are absolutely convinced, so that you are quite sure in your minds, that the stone was indeed thrown by one of the defendants, then you must proceed to the more difficult task of establishing who did what, who abetted whose actions and, in general, who is responsible for what. At this point we should consider the evidence we have for each of the defendants. . .

Judge Savage put his biro down. He had been writing swiftly and confidently and this aggressive purposeful motion of the mind in the silent room, had left it rapt and calm, as if cooled and assuaged by its own fierce speed. He was intensely aware, powerful and quietly waiting, like some well-tuned engine ticking over in the early hours of a silent street. The near panic of an hour before had been transformed to near pleasure. This is a hellishly complex case, he thought, and yet he was confident that what was at stake could be sorted out into a series of decisions, and that each decision could reasonably be taken on the merits of the evidence presented to the court. He could direct the jury how to do this, he could explain to them how they could arrive at a series of verdicts congruent with the laws of England.

But what if the same expertise were applied to his own life? What if a skilled judge were to direct the jury in that case? Immediately Daniel Savage felt uneasy, his mind clouded. How many witnesses would have to be called, how many decisions about the admissibility of evidence? He pulled himself up abruptly. Your life is not a crime, he said. There is no charge against you. So it is nonsense to think of a judge summing up. Why do I keep thinking of my life as a crime? The expertise of the judge summing up, he thought, has been developed over centuries in the closest symbiosis with the criminal code and the technicalities of the laws of England and Wales. It is an expertise that allows the judge to instruct the jury on how to take decisions with regard to acts that this country considers illegal. It is not a general wisdom, he reminded himself. You cannot apply this technique to a marriage or a friendship.

But far from cooling him down, this reflection now had Judge Savage on his feet again, pacing the room. If it was a crime we were considering, what crime would it be? Was there one crime that could define a life? Daniel felt something looming now. More and more over recent years he had begun to experience mental activity as a physical thing, something as sensible as wind when you turned a street corner, or the first rumble of distant thunder that raises the head from the desk, that turns the jury's faces to the window. What crime?

It was ten to five. It is just before dawn, he thought. He pulled on trousers and sweater and let himself out of the flat. Nothing to do with fucking a girl on the jury, that's for sure. He hurried down the stairs and stood in the street. It was quite silent in this exhausted inner suburb. He breathed deeply and felt calmer. The crime of letting a fire go out? he wondered. He was calmer now. I let the fire of my marriage go out. Weren't there ancient religions where it was a crime to let a fire go out? Not to mention *The Lord of the Flies*. The last book he had read to Tom. I am just chattering to myself, Judge Savage told himself calmly, even cheerfully, striding along this yellow-lit pavement through the uneven volumes of these makeshift streets, the decayed housing and low, prefab discount stores.

He breathed deeply. Yes, he was almost enjoying himself. I'm chattering. I did the right thing to come out. The insomniac makes the night present. He had read that. But then he stopped. There was the crime against Sarah. What crime? He shook his head. Ladies and gentleman of the jury, the Crown will be seeking to show that Miss Savage's unhappy behaviour patterns over recent months are the result of crimes yet to be defined and identified but indisputably perpetrated by her legal guardians and parents. He smiled. There had always been something odd with Hilary and Sarah, oh from way back, an odd attraction and attrition. But that's not a crime. It's *family*. If there's nothing odd, it's not a family, Daniel thought, it's not a *life*. Martin did *not* take pictures of your daughter pissing over him. The fact that she wept at his funeral means nothing. Everybody weeps at funerals. I myself have wept at the funerals of people I hardly knew. That is not the crime. Then at last he saw he was guilty of not having understood. You have understood nothing, Judge Savage told himself. Nothing. The jury's verdict would be unanimous.

He walked the streets. The town sprawls and changes and you cannot keep track of it. But the houses that come down, he reflected, are not the oldest. Some fixed points do remain. Most of the world, then, is in flux around a few fixed points, the undisputed evidence that remains. But not in this part of town. There was rubble to his left now and three bill-boards carrying artists' impressions of utopian shopping centres. In this part of town everything is up for grabs. There was corrugated iron and the domestic solemnity of curtained windows. This is an Indian area, Daniel thought. The iron gates closing a building site were plastered with posters in Indian languages. How could you understand them? The corridors of the courthouse likewise had posters in Indian languages. Judge Savage could only presume that they meant the same as the posters in English beside them. The evidence was circumstantial, but convincing. It does fit, Frank said. So Martin was a paedophile. Or had that tendency, Daniel thought. As his closest friend, I never knew this. For years, decades, I was his closest friend, yet I never understood that Martin had dangerous tendencies. Martin had often defended paedophiles. But then as often as not he prosecuted them too. We all did. And equally effectively. My children were often visitors at his house, Daniel thought. That means noth-ing. Childless, his wife Christine was a willing babysitter in the days when Hilary and I went out of an evening. The last times Hilary and I went out together, he thought, we always had Tom with us, but never Sarah. We went to concerts with Tom. Oddly for an Indian area there was a Madonna with baby Jesus in a niche beside a front door. They're thick as thieves, Tom said of mother and Sarah. And a dwarf on a bicycle in the garden. She's punishing you for betraying her mother, Martin told him. They're very close, Martin insisted. If he had known something of Martin's difficulties, would Daniel have been able to help him? Six months ago we bought and furnished a large house, Judge Savage told himself, to be happy in. You had decided to be happy, Daniel remembered. You wrote something about it in your diary. It was a clear day. A day when you imagined you were seeing things with immense clarity. But in fact you had understood nothing. The jury would return their decision in a matter of minutes. You must find a place to live now, he decided in the cold streets as the air turned grey among a tangle of traffic lights and hoardings. Shops were opening this side of the park and someone was walking a fat dog. Judge Savage picked up a newspaper, sat in a café and learned from the headlines that once again the police had arrested upward of a hundred illegal immigrants. There will never be any shortage of work for a judge, he thought.

THIRTY

Your effing mobile, squire. Frank was furious. At six-thirty. Six bloody thirty! Daniel apologised. Arthur, as always, smiled quietly, leaned on a doorframe. Don't say sorry! Just take the fucking thing with you when you go a-shagging. That's what mobiles are for, aren't they! You can leave it in the chariot if you're afraid they'll nick it. Frank, I'm sorry. Twice, he insisted. Twice! At six-thirty. Then I got up and turned it off. When I'd managed to find it. It was inside your bloody bag! Idiot! Frank repeated. He was in his bath-towel, portly and pink, cigarette in one hand, ashtray in the other. Judge Savage didn't bother to say he hadn't been shagging. Was Frank jealous? Arthur raised his blond eyebrows. There is something immensely reassuring about Arthur, Daniel thought. The man seemed to wait in the background for all negative energy to exhaust itself. He has rescued Frank. I'm moving out today, he announced. Good, Frank said. Found a place? Arthur asked. No, Daniel said.

The mobile told him the caller's number had been withheld. Where are my papers? he asked then. I made some notes. The table's for eating on, Frank snapped. He blew out smoke with a mocking smile. Arthur intervened. I recovered them, he said. He produced five sheets of paper that had evidently been crumpled, then smoothed. There were traces of something brown and sticky. Yeah, sorry about that squire, Frank said. He was fiercely sarcastic. Some of the words were illegible. All the same, far more than this mishap with the kitchen bin it was the evidence, the following Monday morning, of the last defendant, Janet Crawley's sister Gillian, that would oblige Judge Savage to rewrite even these few notes for his summing up. The tone had been quite wrong in any event. Meantime, there was Sunday to be got through.

While the others ate their breakfast, Daniel found a phone directory and called the Cambridge Hotel. At least a week, he said. Dressed, Frank seemed more amenable. Want to give us a hand, Dan, moving a couple of sideboards? After Arthur's visit yesterday, Christine had agreed to let them have some items for their stall in return for moving the big old sideboard into Carlton Street. You never know, kid, we might find a few shrunken heads, pickled toddlers' testicles, what have you. Pint at the boozer afterwards. There's an excellent set of Victorian fire-irons, Arthur enthused. Poke her with a poker said the poker-faced poker partner, Frank laughed. And don't imagine, he turned to Daniel, that I'm feeling guilty about your bloody notes, because I'm not. I hate being woken up. And I hate the smell of burnt photographs. You are one nutcase. God knows how the wife put up with you so long.

Daniel phoned Hilary. Somebody called my mobile, at 6.30. Well, not me, she said. Oy! Tom, Sarah, did either of you call Dad? He could hear their voices sing out no. Then he experienced, most intensely, as if he were physically present, the routine intimacy of family breakfast, the smell of the milk and coffee and children in the early morning. So why didn't you answer the phone yourself, Hilary was asking. Where were you? I'd left it in the car, he lied. Does one of the kids want me to take them out? This time she must have put her hand over the receiver. There was the remains of mirth in her voice when she said: No, they've both got full days. They're not five-year-olds, she added. He was struck by something in her voice and suddenly found himself saying: Hilary, I keep thinking you're seeing somebody else. Oh God! But she seemed indulgent. That's because you keep imagining everybody's like you! She didn't seem angry. I thought maybe you were seeing Max, that you'd stopped doing lessons so you could see him away from home. Now the shrillness of her laughter forced him to move the receiver from his ear. Poor Max, she confessed. She added, Oh when the dust's settled, Dan, we must do some sums. She seems perfectly in control, Daniel realised. As he put the phone down, he heard a dog barking.

The idea was, Gillian Crawley said, that we could always, like whenever we wanted, call each other, you know, so we wouldn't ever feel alone.

Perhaps people had expected the trial to wind down fairly rapidly after Janet Crawley's evidence, but no sooner, on Monday morning, had her sister Gillian settled in the box for her examination in chief, than Daniel knew that something was up. Her counsel had an apologetic look on his face. Never sum up before the end, Daniel told himself. Never work in the middle of the night. Waste of time. At this point it was two nights since he had slept. The dust never settles, he thought, or never all of it. In the end, Frank laughed, after he had returned to the kitchen Sunday morning, when a woman's got the house and she's got the kids, she doesn't need a bloke any more, does she? He was chewing toast. They're very materialist, don't you think, Art? Art has an interesting line on women, Dan. I mean either they're fucking everyone so they can take just a little cash from each, like your Brazilian babe on the ring road, or they're pleading monogamy so they can take all the cash from one. Isn't that right? I always loathed Hilary, Frank added. It was quite mutual, Daniel assured him.

.The idea was, Gillian Crawley claimed – her defence counsel had asked her why they went to the bridge – that when we went to the bridge, but only then like, and only if enough of us went, well then we could all kiss and cuddle whoever we wanted like, among ourselves, in the cars there where there's a parking spot in the wood by the bridge. What I mean is, it was a sort of agreed thing that you had to kiss anyone who wanted to kiss you, but only when we were at the bridge. And no more than kissing and cuddling. You know? I don't know when it started exactly, it was a thing that had built up in the group. A tradition really. There had been people before us that left and sometimes there was someone new who came along for the first time and then they had to kiss everybody and that was Janet, my sister just a few months ago. Do you get me? The bridge was a kissing place. So that's why we went there really, and that's why the others stopped going, like when they wanted to be steady, or somebody didn't want you to kiss everybody else, and that's why we all agreed we wouldn't tell. It was something you were sworn to.

Miss Crawley, her counsel said gravely, the man had barely said a word throughout the trial, could you explain to the court what happened on the evening of March 22nd.

Jamie, Mr Grier, had some stones in his car, she said quickly. She was taller than her sister, and plainer. The hair she brushed from her face was mousy.

Why?

I don't know.

But you must have had an idea.

No, really.

Had he thrown stones from the bridge before?

Small stones, she said.

Why?

She drew a breath. About, I don't know, a bit before, a couple of months maybe, I mean before the night everything happened, about a month before, three other girls in the group, well they had stopped coming to the bridge. We called it playing bridge.

I'm sorry, but are you saying that that constituted a reason for Mr Grier's throwing stones?

Her counsel was a stout, elderly, moustached man, at once avuncular but solemn. Unlike her belligerent younger sister, Gillian looked scared and fragile. A nervous shrewdness twisted her mouth and tensed her voice. Watching her bitten fingers as they flexed then clutched the rail of the witness box, Judge Savage wondered if she was making them so visible on purpose.

Well what I was trying to say was, there were more boys, like, now than girls.

And so?

So Jamie got bored when he wasn't, like, with someone. So sometimes he picked up stones, they were pebble size things really, even smaller, and threw them on the road. Because he was pissed off. I mean, he made sure everybody saw him do it. Especially Dave, Mr Sayle. He wanted to sort of show he wasn't having a good time.

Ah, to show he wasn't having a good time.

Yes. She hesitated. And to frighten Dave.

Miss Crawley, I'm sure some members of the jury will

find this difficult to understand. In what way would Mr Grier's throwing stones have frightened Mr Sayle?

David, Mr Sayle, he always felt sort of responsible, you know, for all of us. He liked this sort of secret society thing. He wanted us to be happy. He was always asking if everybody was having a good time. It was, like, his community. You know. Anyway, he shouted at Jamie. He was afraid of what would happen if he hit a car. He was upset. He didn't want people to know we went to the bridge to kiss.

Miss Crawley, please tell us what happened on the night of March 22nd.

The girl sighed. They had arrived at the bridge. They had all parked in the clearing beside the road and the woods. They got out of the cars and chatted. They had the car radios on. Both on the same station loud. They leaned on the parapet and watched cars stopping for the prostitutes in the lay-by. There were two black girls, she explained. It's about fifty yards away. There's a path down the bank through the wood. We sort of stood around chatting and smoking and listening to music. That was the usual thing. Anybody who wanted just had to sort of pull the sleeve of someone else and kiss them. But if the other person didn't want that much you sort of understood and stopped after a bit.

Counsel kept his voice perfectly neutral: Could you explain to the court who was with whom and where that evening.

Well. Gillian Crawley swallowed. Again she brushed hair from her mouth. Her face was pale and plain, but not unpleasant. Okay, so, nobody ever kissed Ryan Riley. Except maybe sort of at the end. Dave said it was only fair. Dave and Ryan were sort of special friends. You know? They did a lot of things together. Ryan followed Dave around. He's his little dog.

Miss Crawley, please, just describe the sequence of events as carefully as possible.

Her sister Janet had gone with Simmons, she said. As per usual. She told me a couple of days before she wanted to stop going to the bridge and be his regular girlfriend but he didn't want. He kissed everybody as much as he could.

Miss Crawley . . .

Right, so Janet with Simmie, me with Stu, Mr Bateson. At least at first me and Stu used to go out, like, when we were little, anyway, and we only recently started talking again. But anyway when we were in the car, that was Mr Grier's car, the bigger one, because the seats come down, at the front, there was a big argument on the road with Sasha and Dave and Jamie.

That is the defendants Miss Singleton, Mr Sayle, Mr Grier.

Right.

And what was the cause of that argument?

Well, we had the radio on loud in the car and there was the noise from the ring road, which is very noisy, so even if all the windows were open, because it was mild like and it was better not to let the car steam over we didn't hear. Anyway we weren't listening.

So you saw rather than heard the argument?

That's right. You could see them shouting at each other, I could like see from the corner of my eye over Mr Bateson's shoulder. Jamie had had a lot to drink.

And what happened next?

Mr Sayle went down the path by the road to where the prostitutes were. I saw him go.

Ah. Is this something he did regularly?

Yes.

Please continue.

Well anyway, Sasha wanted to be in the car with Mr Grier. I could see her pulling his sleeve.

And presumably this was something Mr Sayle objected to.

Dave? Oh no! Gillian Crawley was shaking her head. For the first time she smiled. No, anybody could go with anybody at the bridge and Dave was like the first one to encourage all that. I mean, it was his idea.

Please continue.

Well, Sasha, Miss Singleton and Jamie Grier started arguing, without Mr Sayle now. Then he started shouting.

He who, sorry? Who started shouting?

Jamie, he started shouting at Sasha, and we could hear him a bit now because he came over to the car. I mean, it was his car, and he told us to get out and put the seats up and either Sasha went away with him now, or never. He said it was all . . . beg your pardon. She stopped and looked around.

Yes? What did Mr Grier say?

He said it was all, er, wank what we were doing and kiddies in the playground playing silly wankers.

So, Mr Grier came to the car and insisted Miss Singleton left with him.

That's right. Then I think somebody telephoned Sasha, on her mobile, like, because she stood there talking on the phone forever, I remember she had a hand over her ear because of the traffic while me and Stu got out of Jamie's car. She must have talked at least five minutes because Jamie was getting really angry like and making faces at her and like scissor movements with his fingers, meaning cut the conversation and we were winding up the seats. Like I said he was pretty far gone. Like with drinking.

Miss Crawley, we are all doing our best to follow your account, but could you please just remind us exactly where everybody is at this point.

Gillian Crawley looked alarmed, as if terrified that she wouldn't be believed. I'm scared of them, she announced. She jerked her head towards the dock at the back.

The court was dead silent.

Judge Savage interrupted: Miss Crawley, you have sworn to tell the truth, the whole truth and nothing but the truth.

Could you tell us where everybody was at this moment, counsel repeated.

I said: Janet was with Simmons in Simmons's car. At the other end of the bridge. Away from town. Riley and Davidson was standing at the parapet looking at the road. Stuart Bateson was with me and we were winding up the seats of Grier's car because we thought like he wanted to go. Dave wasn't there, he always went down to talk to the prostitutes. He loved doing that, only sometimes there was a pimp with them who got pissed off. Sorry. Angry like. Sasha was on the phone. I remember she was laughing. You see, Ginnie Keane used to phone us when we were on the bridge and ask who we were snogging while we were there because Mr Sayle had used to try to get her to kiss every-one and she stopped coming. Jamie was like really furious and banging his fist on the car. It's his dad's car.

Gillian Singleton had started to speak very quickly and breathlessly. Her counsel exchanged glances with Judge Savage who remained impassive.

Sasha stops talking on the phone and says if he was going to be so bloody possessive he could forget it. Something like that. She went to get hold of Riley. Riley, I mean, he's sort of the group loser. But Dave liked him. Jamie shouted, if you do that, something is going to happen. He had opened the back of the car and got out a big stone and he carried it to the road. He's always very jokey, like you don't know if Jamie's being serious. He shouted, and we could hear because he was really really shouting and we were right there: Whoever hits a car can take his woman off and enough of this shit. I don't know if he brought the stones on purpose.

397

Anyway he threw one off right away without even turning to look at the cars. Sasha like was terrified and runs down for Dave. He came running up and Jamie threw another. We were standing in the road, I remember, on the bridge, like, because a car went by fast, I mean over the bridge, and we had to get out of the way. David said: You're drunk Jamie. That was about when my sister got out of the car, the Golf, with Simmie, it was John's car, John Davidson. And that was when Jamie said I'm going to keep throwing stones till she tells you how much she likes sucking my cock in your bed. We heard it because we were less than five feet away. When you're in church, he shouted. At Dave this is. Jamie kept shouting and calling Dave wanker. And then I missed some because my mobile rang and I went and got back in Jamie's car so I'd be able to talk.

Who phoned you? counsel asked.

It was Ginnie Keane, said Gillian Crawley. Like she'd called Sasha, now she's calling me.

And why did she call you?

She – Gillian Crawley hesitated – she was in bed with her boyfriend. She was phoning all of us and asking when we were going to stop playing silly buggers and have real sex in a bed, Ginnie's sixteen. She's younger than the rest. Then I heard the accident, there was a kind of bang, and everybody was saying run. Run. I didn't know what had happened really.

Do you know the time of that phone-call?

The girl shook her head. I remember what was on the radio. It was The Offspring. My friend's got a girlfriend and he hates that bitch. I was annoyed like because Ginnie was talking and I wanted to listen. It was like my favourite song.

Counsel turned to the judge: Your honour, the defendant informed her solicitor of this phone-call only yesterday. I was immediately in touch with the phone company involved and various radio stations, after which I discussed the matter with my learned friend Mr Sedley who agreed that he would make no objection to admission of this evidence. In fact – counsel consulted his notes – the phone-call is recorded as commencing at 10.48 on the evening of March 22nd and as terminating at 10.52. Meanwhile the Yeah Channel, a local radio station, has confirmed that the song Miss Crawley has mentioned was the penultimate song before their 11 o'clock programme change on that evening. Mr Whitaker, you remember, made his emergency call from the side of the road at 10.55.

All this, then, seemed to fit. But who had telephoned Daniel Savage on his mobile early on the Sunday morning? And why did his life now seem to be a tightening net of telephone conversations or discussions about telephone conversations or verifications of telephone conversations, all of them on mobiles, when only a few months ago, he had sworn he would never get a mobile, so superfluous did they seem. Only a few months ago, Hilary had said: We should never have put the phone in the bedroom. And she had said to Max that same evening, In the new house we will be ex-directory, won't we Dan? All this started with a phone-call, Daniel thought. Out of the blue. Even if the marriage was burnt-out then, it was happy. Actually, it was happier burnt-out than not. He had been exquisitely happy, he thought, that evening, watching Hilary bend down to pull that cake from the oven, while the phone rang in the background. After calling his wife to ask if she had phoned him, he called Max. It was rather early for a Sunday morning.

I'll get him for you, said an abrupt male voice.

Hello, Mr Savage, the young man said.

I hope I didn't wake you up?

No, not at all. What is it?

Since he hadn't even given Max his mobile number Daniel had nothing plausible to say. Closing the door of Frank's flat behind him, he took refuge on the stairwell.

Yes? Max asked.

I'm worried about Hilary, Daniel said. I suppose you heard that I am not living with her at the moment.

I'm very sorry about that, Mr Savage.

And now I hear you are no longer taking lessons with her.

That's right, Max said.

It's rather sad, because I thought this was just the kind of thing that would keep her sane.

Well, it's nice of you to say that, Max said warmly.

Anyway, I just spoke to her and she seemed so frantic, I thought perhaps it might be an idea, if you were to get in touch, I mean, if you could spare the time.

There was a pause. Max said: I can't do that Mr Savage. I'm so sorry.

Daniel didn't know what to say. He had walked down two floors and now started walking back up again, his footsteps echoing in the stairwell. There was such a solemn and decisive ring to Max's voice that it seemed evident there was something behind it. And at the same time a determined hostility to any enquiry.

I'm sorry I can't be more helpful, Max now said at his most formal. How's the music getting on, Daniel asked. Max explained that he had had to ease off a little because of pressure at work. We're installing a new computer system. He had to relearn all his software. Give my regards to your parents, Daniel said. If the boy suspected irony he didn't show it.

I've only given the number to two or three people, he then found himself saying quite incongruously to the young clerk Laura. So I thought it might be you. Oh, Mr Savage! The young woman didn't disguise the fact that she'd been woken. I'm so sorry, I was sleeping late. Daniel had an obtrusively clear image of how Jane used to answer the phone in bed. He begged forgiveness. He remembered how, in some hotel bed together, she would take phone-calls from Crawford, winking at Daniel as she spoke. I'm so sorry, I just wondered who it could have been, he said. Not to worry, judge, she told him. Arthur popped his head out of the door above. We're off, he called. We only have the van till lunchtime.

THIRTY-ONE

Daniel hadn't slept. Moving even the smallest pieces of furniture exhausted him. I really mustn't be alone, he thought. A sharp pain shot up the side of his face with the damaged eye. The sideboard was massive. Then towards twelve Christine arrived. They had almost finished. What shall I do with the ashes, she confided. She was heavily made up. Daniel didn't understand at first. Martin's of course! They would be ready Thursday she had been told. Her dress was downy peach. What can there be to be ready? she shrilled as if scandalised. Grinder, Frank told her calmly. They grind up the bones, love. She stared at him, eyebrows wrinkled in shock. Usually people stick'em in the garden, Frank went on. Oh, but I'm selling the house, Christine cried, I won't have a garden! The men were carrying out the last small things. There's only a window box in the flat, she protested. You know Dan's old flat I suppose? I can't put his ashes in a window box!

This nervous frivolity is obscene, Daniel thought. He carried out the famous fire-irons. She's definitely on drugs, he decided. What shall I do with them, she said again. He couldn't think what to say. It'd be like the pot of basil, she insisted, in Byron. Keats, Arthur said. Christine burst into tears when the van was loaded. She hung on to Daniel. Come and stay with me tonight, she muttered. Please. He was exhausted from sleeplessness. He oscillated between dazed disorientation and a shiny, talkative lucidity. She muttered the words, but not so low that the others couldn't hear. It was more as if she herself didn't want to know what she was saying. Don't go to a hotel, Dan, stay with me tonight.

To-ni-i-ght! Frank sung as soon as they had pulled away. To-ni-i-ght's the ni-ight! Oh, with one custom-made, record-breaking, ocean-going Panama barge pole, thank you very much, he laughed. The swamps you get into Daniel Savage, the jungles. Daniel in the lioness's den, Arthur laughed. She could chuck the ashes in the zoo, Frank laughed. That small Georgian tallboy is a gem, Arthur said. A killing, he announced. He rubbed his hands. Daniel had never seen him so excited. Then going round the ring road they saw that the bridge where Malding Lane crossed the road was at that very moment being festooned with flowers, with wreathes, with a banner announcing Goodbye Elizabeth. She must be dead, he realised. Public have gone soft, Frank opined unimpressed. Soft in the head. Every death is their own death these days. Lady Di syndrome. Left here for the pub, Art, he shouted. Where are you going, man. We'll deliver the battleship later. Hang a left! Arthur braked hard. The furniture shifted. The van drifted into a quiet side street, a traditional beer garden. And it was here, sitting at a wooden table outside the Belgrave that the phone rang again, Judge Savage's mobile. Oh, don't mind us, noble Squire Juan! Frank cried. I'm desperate, Minnie whispered. Dan, help me!

Call the police, he told the girl. He wouldn't listen. I'm

with people, Minnie. He was harsh. He hadn't slept. He had spent the morning helping to sort out the gloomy furniture in his dead friend's gloomy house. Martin was dead. It was Martin wanted this stuff not me, Christine kept saying. Isn't it gloomy? They had found nothing on pulling out the sideboard drawers. Above all, though, Daniel had spent the morning seeing himself through Frank's eyes. I am ridiculous in Frank's eyes, he thought more than once as they shifted the furniture. Oh, but you were always a pushover, his brother had been saying. He mussed Daniel's woolly hair affectionately, sitting at the grey wooden table, outside the Belgrave. To-ni-ight! Almost anybody could get Dan to fag for them, he told Arthur as the American arrived with the pints. That word fag kills me, Arthur smiled in his soft way. He shook his head. To-ni-i-ght! Always a pushover, Frank repeated. He was mussing his brother's hair when the mobile rang. I'm desperate, the girl said.

It's a sort of formula she has, Daniel thought. Or women in general. From memory he was able to give the Broughton Drive police station's number. I can't, she said. Call them. He gave her Mattheson's name. When the desk sergeant answers, you tell him you have to speak to Inspector Mattheson, okay? You can even say I told you to call. Judge Savage. M-a-t-t-h-e-son, he spelt it out. Walking up and down the pavement with the phone at his ear, he saw the two gays with their beers were giggling their heads off. Please Dan, the girl was saying in a low voice. Please, let me explain. He was exhausted. It went far beyond the sleepless night. I'm with someone, he said. Such a pushover, Frank was laughing. I was telling Art about when you let me cut those druidic signs on your back. Yes, with a knife, Frank shook his head. I had this sharp little sheath knife. It was Martin stopped it. I was going through a wild patch. I told him it would make him more English having druidic signs on his back. Daniel didn't remember that part. Anyone else would have told me to get stuffed, Frank laughed. It was just a quirky memory now. Call the police, Daniel had closed the conversation, if you're really in trouble, Minnie, call the police. I personally cannot help.

In a warehouse behind Doherty Street, they went meticulously through two chests and three cabinets and found nothing. Yesterday's photos had been burned. Martin is gone, Daniel thought. What I choose for myself, he used to say, I choose for the whole human race. He had chosen to die. I burned all the photos of moths, Christine said when they delivered the sideboard at Carlton Street. There were thousands, she protested. Her voice again became theatrically shrill. Thousands! I told the gardener to burn them. I hope the buyer will keep him on. Would you like some tea? He's such a nice old stick, she said. I want nothing to do with the place, she confided in Arthur. I'm not going to put the ashes in the garden. He was trying to find a piece of cardboard to balance up one wooden leg. The sideboard wobbled. Nothing! She had taken a liking to the American. Hot damn, he said. Now a drawer wouldn't fit. He was crouching down. As she had previously taken a liking to Max, Daniel remembered. They had left together that day he came home, hadn't they? Was that why Hilary had stopped the lessons? Let me try, he told Arthur. The younger man was mopping his sweat with a red handkerchief. Trying to force the drawer into its slot, Judge Savage dropped it on his foot. He hopped about his old living room in pain, causing considerable amusement. Then they sat down in his old Carlton Street kitchen to drink Christine's strong black tea. Done, Frank said. That's it. Back at his brother's flat toward five, Judge Savage packed his case and his dispatch bag and descended the stairs. Sorry about this morning, Frank laughed. Got out of the wrong side of bed. He stood, penitent and portly, at the decaying door to the street, while Daniel climbed into his car. See ya.

Judge Savage drove to the Cambridge. I should have chosen another hotel, he told himself, climbing up from the underground car park. But he and Martin had studied at Cambridge. He and Hilary had had a blazing row in the foyer of this hotel. He stood for a moment with his bags just inside the swing doors. He felt he had loved her then, when she shrieked at him in the foyer of this hotel, when she beat her fists on his chest. You're worn out, he told himself. His head was spinning. Always a pleasure to see you Mr Savage, the man on reception said. The word gent came to mind. The old receptionist is a gent. He took coats and carried bags. Soon to be Sir Daniel, I believe, the gent said. Daniel didn't disabuse him.

In his room, he watched a programme about the migration of birds. Nature programmes fascinated Hilary. Almost the only good thing about England is its nature programmes she once said. She had that habit of speaking of England as if she wasn't English, though they almost never went abroad. Daniel felt uncomfortable abroad. In England he was English, but in France he was just black. Sleep will overtake me, he said out loud, taking a beer from the fridge. This isn't even a crisis, he laughed. Just a Sunday evening to be got through.

But I'm desperate. Minnie told him. She phoned again while he was in the shower. Desperate. He rushed out, slipping on the tiles and stood naked and dripping on the pale pink carpet before the mirror. Who had he hoped it would be? It's hopeless, Minnie said. I've called three times, this Mattheson, and he said he would call me back. He didn't.

The shower hadn't cleared Daniel's head. It was an effort

to understand. They're holding me here, I can't leave, she was saying. A pushover, Frank had laughed. Did you hear, Minnie said, that there was a raid yesterday. It's complicated. They arrested loads. . .

The call was cut off. Just matter, Judge Savage thought, staring in the mirror. You're not ageing well, Savage, he told himself, seeing his naked body, beer bottle in one hand, mobile in the other. He had dreamed of a gentle civilised ageing beside a fireplace with a wife and children and a dog. One might well just be matter, but one dreamed these things anyway.

Her name was Sue, he was saying a few hours later. She gave me her mobile number, but it's not answering. Sue. Dark skin, he described. Yeah, pretty much like mine. More or less. She's Brazilian, I think. Sue, the girls laughed. Sue! Oh come on! The bridge was fifty yards away with the flowers flaming up white and red in the rhythm of headlights, a great bank of burning flowers along the ring road. But I'm called Sue, a little Indian girl giggled. What's wrong with me. Me too, another voice said. I'm called Sue. What's wrong with me? He couldn't see anything wrong with any of them. We're all called Sue, they giggled. But then he could barely see them in the dazzle of headlights and the gloom of the lay-by. Goodbye Elizabeth, the banner on the bridge said. The girls stood together in their short skirts giggling. It was two in the morning. Police! someone shouted. Judge Savage spun round. Just joking. Spinning round he had almost fallen over. Oh Sue, behave! a voice shrilled. Be-have! They should-n't let me drive at all, Daniel thought, driving carefully to the house where she had taken him. It's a scandal that I'm driving, he thought. What's wrong with the other girls, sir? the Hispanic man asked. With all respect, sir, he said. He was most polite. When pressed, he shrugged his shoulders: Some of the girls, the police wanted to see if they entered the country illegally. They've been rounding them up.

Judge Savage circumnavigated the ring road. The police had been checking the residency status of the prostitutes. They were arresting illegal immigrants. He turned off at the first lights and stopped the car. He fiddled with the mobile, then remembered that Minnie's number had been withheld. It didn't come up on the display. He couldn't call her back. For a while he sat still, staring at the houses. It was familiar. Where was he? He remembered. This was where the Community was, where he had come all those months before to pick Sarah up the day she savaged her hair. She had looked very pretty in the market yesterday. The Community would welcome, he thought, a middle-aged professional man experiencing a religious crisis. They would be glad he wasn't white. He saw himself sitting, singing hymns to the twang of the guitar. David Sayle had been obsessed by some odd notion of community, religious community. The two words went together apparently. It's such a tight community, Minnie always said. The Koreans. They kept their odd religion, their little altars to dead relatives. Twenty minutes later he found Christine's car parked in the space the frozen food delivery van always left in Carlton Street. In life I took her husband's job, and now she has taken our flat. If you ring that bell, I'll kill you, Daniel told himself.

Back in the Cambridge at 4 a.m. he still couldn't sleep. Why hadn't he gone to a pharmacy? It's pills I need. He turned off the mobile in case he did sleep, drank a few shorts at random from the fridge, watched a film he couldn't make head nor tail of. One-eyed and fiercely wakeful, he reflected. The usual themes of love and money seemed recklessly muddled. His head ached. The phone is ringing on the screen, he told himself. Not in the room. But the film was set in the Middle Ages. So he picked up the receiver. It was one of those solid, old grey dial phones they have only in places like the Cambridge Hotel. You told me you were at this number, Minnie said. She had been trying for hours. I've got something to tell you. They think I'm responsible, she said. For what? For all the people they're arresting. They think I'm the grass. I'm scared. I called the police but nothing happened. Now Judge Savage was wide awake again. Immediately, he called the Broughton Street station. I really can't wake the inspector at this hour, the desk sergeant said. I'm sorry. There is an inspector on duty, if you'd like to talk to him. It's about the Korean girl, is it? Everybody knows, he thought. Well, sir, Inspector Mattheson did take all the details and told me to assure you he has it all in hand.

Then it was morning. It's Monday. Have I slept? He hadn't turned the television off. The talk was of Montenegro. It was eight o'clock. In the shower he shook his head violently from side to side. Wake up, Savage! A pushover for Serb troops, the earnest reporter was saying.

Are you all right? Mrs Connolly asked. He bumped into her quite by accident in the car park behind the court. Unless she had contrived to bump into him. I'm fine, he told her, fine. In his room in chambers he immediately phoned Mattheson. The man was on the line almost before he knew he had the connection. Hello? Didn't recognise you, the policeman said, you sound odd. Sure, we've got the score, it's okay, and we're monitoring the situation. Not to worry. Daniel was struck by something American in Mattheson's delivery. There was a tone of facile reassurance. Don't worry, Mattheson repeated, but if you don't want trouble yourself I would keep as far away as possible.

Fortunately, no sooner was he in his place in court than there was Gillian Crawley to keep him awake. In no time at all his mind was wonderfully concentrated on the trial in hand. It is within my power to have you sent downstairs so that the defendant can give evidence in your absence he told James Grier. The young man had begun to shout. I am not and never was a pushover in court, Daniel told himself.

The elder of the two Crawley girls completed her examination in chief and went on through the late morning to survive two aggressive cross-examinations from Sayle's counsel and from Grier's. Fragile as she had seemed at first, she grew in strength. She would not be drawn on the question of who had actually thrown the stone. She had been talking on the mobile to Ginnie Keane and at the same time trying to listen to the words of The Offspring above the noise of the road. She liked that song. The name of the song is: I won't pay, she said. So she hadn't seen the fatal moment. She'd heard a sudden bang. The other lawyers felt their clients' interests were best served by letting the story stand.

Both cross-examinations sought to ridicule the account of the kissing game. Sayle's counsel in particular, the buxom and embattled Mrs Wilson, asked the defendant how long she had had to rack her brains in order to come up with such a preposterous fabrication. The girl wasn't shaken. Have you ever kissed, she asked, when there's loud music and a real thunder of traffic, I mean so it's deafening sometimes? And the radio like on full, and you can put it on full *because* of all the traffic. Everything booming.

I am not here to answer your questions, Mrs Wilson told her. She was sixty if she was a day. The idea of her kissing in a car with crashing music had set one or two members of the jury smiling. Well, it's easier, the girl said.

Easier? You must excuse me, Miss Crawley, if I can't always follow.

I mean, the girl was patient, when they're people that are

not, like, your boyfriend, the noise and the rush, it's exciting, and sort of, I don't know, it's less embarrassing. With the road. We called it playing bridge. She hesitated: I mean, like that night, I was only kissing Stu, to warm up before John.

John Davidson?

Yes. He's my real boyfriend.

But. . .

With the noise, it's less embarrassing, she said. Being with someone who's not your boyfriend, she said. That was playing bridge. It's like you could be with anyone. Like being at a concert. Because of the sound of the traffic. Like standing under a waterfall. It's easier.

Mrs Wilson gave up.

Grier's lawyer was a bright-faced black woman, a thoroughly negro African woman with an even posher accent than Daniel's. She was a brilliant barrister, a born actress, swaying about and swirling her gown back and forth. Derisively, she asked Miss Crawley whether this wasn't all schoolgirl fantasy, a heated fantastical adolescent story designed to hurt the lives of people she resented for reasons that it would be as well to confess. Intelligently, Gillian Crawley waited for a real question. Daniel was often surprised by the astuteness of the least educated witnesses. When I leave court, I'll collapse, he thought. I'll break down. Only the enigma of this impossible trial is keeping me awake.

If we are to believe your version of events, counsel was saying, we shall have to suppose, shall we not, that Miss Singleton and Messrs Riley, Davidson, and Simmons have all lied to this court, repeatedly and under oath, *not* – the black woman's face gleamed with intelligence as she raised her eyes and her voice – to save their own skins, *on the contrary*, but merely to protect Mr Sayle and Mr Grier!

Not Jamie, David, the girl said quickly.

I beg your pardon?

To protect Mr Sayle, the girl explained. There was a pause. Nobody would have done it for Jamie, would they?

The answer was entirely convincing, for its obliqueness, its splendid missing the point. The girl was a liquid they couldn't cage. Judge Savage raised his eyebrows to the handsome black counsel. Smart as she was, she had allowed herself to be drawn into a dynamic where her next question could be no more than an instinctive reaction to the defendant's remarkable claim: Why then, Miss Crawley, have you broken ranks? What makes *you* different from your friends? Aside, that is, from a decidedly feverish imagination.

The girl stared.

Counsel tried to give the impression of being in control. Miss Crawley, I have put it to you that the overwhelming flaw in your ridiculous story is that it obliges us to assume that five people are risking prison sentences out of a misplaced sense of loyalty to two of your number. You have insisted that that loyalty exists, at least to Mr Sayle, but at the same time you yourself are not being loyal. Now why is that? Why are you different from them? Why are you telling us this 'truth' as you claim, when they are not?

At last a question had been posed that the girl did not expect, or did not want to answer.

Isn't it rather, counsel insisted, that you have invented this complicated and steamy story because it lets you off the hook?

The court hummed. The jury looked fatigued. A press reporter's eyes were glazed.

Miss Crawley. . .

A voice from the dock called out: Tell her, Gill.

It was Janet Crawley. Half a dozen lawyers were on their

feet protesting. There were the usual remonstrances and warnings and as a result nobody heard for a moment what the defendant had said. She had spoken softly. I'm sorry Miss Crawley, Judge Savage was obliged to interrupt, we didn't hear your answer.

I'm pregnant, the girl whispered. I'm going to marry Mr Davidson, and my kid's not going to get born in prison for anybody, not even for Dave Sayle.

Mrs Whitaker had also been pregnant, Daniel was thinking, some six hours later. But perhaps Sedley had been wise not to stress the point. The policeman helped him into a cab. In the late afternoon, prosecution had made his closing speech. Then counsels for Sayle, Grier, and Singleton had made their final speeches. I think you'd better take a cab, sir, the constable said. They had been remarkably brief, as if seeking to deny the complications of the case, to insist on the obviousness, one way or another, of their positions: these people were on the bridge and threw stones; these people arrived at the bridge after stones were thrown. I was afraid you'd hurt yourself there, sir, he said, dusting off Judge Savage's jacket. Let me get you a cab. And Minnie too is pregnant, Daniel told himself, giving the driver the name of the hotel. I did the best I could by the girl, he thought.

In any event, the day had now passed and he could sleep. The whole thing started, he thought, in the back of the cab, clutching his dispatch bag, because a young woman got pregnant and began to dream of a different life for herself in a different community. He watched the streets sliding by, the brick and shiny glass and the dull press of windblown shoppers against the brittle light of Salisbury Street. He hadn't known then that she was pregnant. That was where he had stood and waited for her when she hadn't come. The corner with Drummond. He had bought a bottle of champagne, drunk it with Christine and Martin. They had sold the house but Martin was dead. Martin never had a child. I have to do my duty by the child, Gillian Crawley said in the witness box in explanation of her extraordinary evidence. I don't care what we swore to each other, or what we said we'd say. The defendants stared. Daniel put his face in his hands in the cab and laughed.

I thought for duty's sake I should give you a call, Kathleen Connolly said, when I heard you'd fallen like that. Is there anything seriously the matter? He had fallen down the steps at the back of the court, the judges' separate entrance. How had she learned about it? He had banged his head. How did she know he was staying at the Cambridge Hotel? They agreed to dine together. When really he should have gone to bed. My babysitter's away, she was telling him, but if you don't mind Stevie, why not come here? I'll sleep better this way, he thought. He would go out and eat properly, come back at elevenish, then fall asleep. As easy as falling down a flight of steps. Coming out of the back door, facing the small flight of steps, he had blacked out. No damage done, he told the policeman. He had banged his head, hurt his knee. Probably my whole life, he thought, this old girlfriend will occasionally call me and tell me she's desperate, she's been imprisoned, beaten up, whatever. She knows I have to respond because of the way our relationship started. You keep out of it, Mattheson said, and all will be well. Tomorrow, at the rate we're going, Judge Savage told himself, you'll be summing up. You sum up, then you ask for a holiday. Pressing private reasons.

But Kathleen's aperitifs gave him an unexpected rush of energy. He began to speak volubly. Call me Dan, he told her. He spoke about the Crawley girl, her extraordinary evidence. Could she have made up such a complicated story?

This was indiscreet. He spoke about barristers' fees. He spoke about the folly of the proposed new legislation on the recognition of sperm donors. What does it matter who one's natural father was? He spoke about Ireland and Montenegro and Martin Shields and the Mishra case. Why hadn't they been found guilty of unlawful abduction? He spoke excitedly, perhaps wittily. Stevie, it turned out, couldn't speak at all, but made moaning and grunting sounds. Walking jerkily, arms held high like a puppet, the boy wanted to touch Daniel's face. He's fascinated by your colour, Kathleen Connolly laughed. I don't think we've ever had a guest who wasn't white. He likes to touch people he hasn't seen before. The boy seemed to be trying hard to say something. Uh, he said. He bellowed, *uh*! Not an entirely unheard of phenomenon, Daniel laughed. I'm in fine form he thought. Not tired at all. The boy was unsettling. *Uh*, he insisted. He turned to his mother and came out with a shrill, high-pitched scream. He likes you, she said.

It was a small terraced house in an area that couldn't decide whether to gentrify or not. Kathleen Connolly was only a modest cook. When he began to eat, she replied to him earnestly on a number of social issues. She couldn't agree with him on the question of spanking children. Oh I really think you're wrong there, she said with reference to his remarks on the minimum wage. I can't understand, she said, your distinction between ABH and exploitation in the workplace; they're both forms of violence, aren't they? In the end one's beaten up once, she insisted, and it's over with, but the low wage is a form of violence that is practised day in day out your whole life. She wore track-suit bottoms and a polo-neck, as if determined to offer a reverse image of the crisp dress and heels she wore at work. It's never over when they beat you up, he told her. In your head, it's never over.

Dan, she said. Forgive me, I hadn't thought. He sensed at once how pleased she was to stand down like this. Do you think about it a lot? Then she told him she was convinced society was drowning in its own selfishness. Drowning. She opened a bottle of wine that he knew was cheap. She would not be well paid herself, he thought, knowing the CPS. The whole problem with prosecutions was the miserable funding for the CPS. People simply had no reason for not being selfish, she insisted. Almost everybody, she became extremely intense, who ends up in court, don't you think, has been blinded, blinded by selfishness. Why shouldn't people be self-ish? she demanded. The only reason is the law, and even if they're caught, most of them get off. The percentage of acquittals is mad, she said. I wouldn't even be surprised if these stone-throwers didn't get off. Would you? Why *shouldn't* they be selfish?

Daniel was taken aback. People aren't selfish in regard to their children, he told her. Then he remembered her husband had bailed out as soon as he saw their child was handi-capped. Suddenly he felt overwhelmed by it all. The energy left him. He had no intention of seducing her. I never seduced anyone, he thought. Moaning softly, Steven had been sitting in front of the television. When Daniel rose to go – I'm so tired, he said – the boy pawed him, he wanted to embrace him. Fourteen or fifteen years old, he must be wear-ing a large and cumbersome nappy.

I can drive you back to the hotel, Kathleen insisted. If it's only for half an hour or so, I can leave Stevie with the TV and tell the lady upstairs to keep an eye out. Only now did Judge Savage appreciate that the house was divided into flats. Why hadn't he realised? She only had the downstairs. Why did I imagine she would be more fun, he wondered, as Kathleen left the room and climbed the stairs. He felt vaguely angry. Her eyes seemed brighter at work. He heard her talking in a soft voice from the landing above. There was a photo on the sideboard of a group of friends in a rubber dinghy. She hurried back down. Just half an hour, Stevie, she told the boy in a suddenly loud, Women's Institute voice. Just half an hour. Protesting, Stevie pawed at her. She invites people here on purpose to have them witness these scenes, Judge Savage thought. Who would feel ready to make a pass at her after witnessing such a scene?

Oh he's done so well, she was saying as they climbed into the car. Unexpectedly, it was a white Peugeot 205 convertible. Impossible to get a taxi to come out here at this hour, she repeated. You may as well phone for a spaceship. She buckled up rapidly, pushed the key in the lock and turned to him. Forgive me for insisting, she smiled, but you do look ill, Judge. I've been quite worried for you.

She sat looking at him in the dark of the car. The smile lingered. Having done her best, he thought, with the spectacle of her son, the talk of social issues, the indifferent food and indecent wine, she suddenly turns on the intimacy. Anyway, it's been great to get to know you away from court. She turned to the road. Know me? he asked lightly. I thought everybody knew everything about me. Sometimes I think they know even more about me than I do. Well, it's not *all* bad, she laughed, is it? I don't know, isn't it? No, I think the girls rather like a man who's wicked from time to time. Selfish you mean, he said. She referred to herself as a girl, he noticed.

Oh, it's not quite the same, she told him complacently. I don't think people think you're selfish. Shooting out into the road she drove far faster than he could have imagined, far faster than the speed limit. The white needles leapt in the glow of the dial. Sometimes, she laughed, you can be wicked just by giving where you shouldn't, if you see what I mean, or really just by living too much. Now Daniel was on the alert. Having done penance all evening with her son, she had the right to be more audacious.

Define the difference, he said. He was laughing. Inevitably he was becoming more pleasant himself. Though he might well pass out at any moment. Define the difference between wicked and selfish. Go on. She hit the brake hard for a traffic light. The car was in the wrong lane. Turning to him, her eyes were embarrassingly wide. Hmm. She put on a theatrical thinking face. Hmm, let me see. The woman has cast off ten years in two minutes, he thought. Her face glowed in the light of the dials of her peppy car and her wrinkled forehead, as she puzzled for an answer to his question, was pleasantly girlish. With complete candour she told him: Well, selfishness is ugly, isn't it, Dan. It's ugly. Daniel Savage caught his breath. But wickedness – she stretched out her gear hand, palm downward and waggled it – wickedness isn't, or not always. It might even be fun. Abruptly he said: Oh by the way, Kathleen, I had been meaning to ask: Why, when I told Mattheson who it was that had attacked me, why didn't he make any arrests? Why didn't he pull the guys in? There can't be anything uglier than assault, can there? She wasn't at all perturbed. Oh I wouldn't know the answer to that, she said at once. I mean, the CPS isn't privy to all the police do? I know they had various suspects. They didn't want to make a move and find you were wrong. From what I gather, yours was only a suspicion.

Daniel turned to look out of the window. She's lying, he thought. He waited. Don't you find it hard, she asked, moving into a hotel all of a sudden. Living out of a suitcase. I mean . . . It was the first direct comment on his marital position. Brutally, almost using Frank's voice, he said: Well, the beds are nice, and they've got a nice bar. He didn't even turn to her. Want to come in and grab a night-cap?

She slid the car very neatly into one of the spaces to the left of the entrance and pulled up sharp with the hand-brake. Okay, she told him. Then she was just saying the words, teensy-weensy, I'll have to hurry back you know, I can't leave Stevie long – this as they passed through the rotating doors – when he felt a hand on his sleeve. Sarah! Sitting on a deep armchair in the unfocused desolation of the hotel foyer was Minnie Kwan, pale as death.

THIRTY-TWO

We have spoken, Judge Savage said, of . . .

He stopped. It was here that the notes he had made ran out. He rubbed a hand over his face. He looked up at a court humming with expectancy. He had planned to make further notes before trial continued this morning. Everybody was eager for the end now. But he had not. The defendants, their relatives, the jury, the press, the lawyers, they all wanted it to be over, quickly. He could have made notes during the final speeches of the last three defence counsels. We have all had enough, Judge Savage thought, of this burdensome story. But again he had not. Not that he was fascinated or even really interested in what they had said. Judiciously, they had said very little. Their clients were not the main players. It was not even that he was too tired, though it was hard to believe he could ever have been more so. But he found himself marooned. He was paralysed. He knew that when he emerged from this trial, when at last the jury withdrew and the defendants and relatives held their breath while the twelve jurors sifted through mountains of evidence to arrive at eight separate verdicts – when, in short, his day's duty here was done, then a greater and final trial would await him. I should never have come, he told himself. My real duty was not to come. Not to do my duty here, but to do another duty. This pompous form of self-address seemed to offer some respite. I had another duty to do, he thought. But he had been a pushover for Mattheson. Dan, the inspector had said. His voice was triumphant. The phone had pierced a troubled state that was neither consciousness nor sleep, but more an intense mesh of blurred images and cries and fierce colours. God! He sat up. Dan, forgive me for waking you. I thought you'd want to know at once. We've got them all. All? Daniel asked. The Kwans, plus all their connections, Dan. And you'll never have to see them. We've got them on other stuff. It's serious immigration and prostitution charges. They'll be away for years and you'll never be mentioned.

All of them? Daniel repeated. We got everybody, the inspector said, everybody. He was a happy man. Except the girl, he added, your young lady, he chuckled, and her husband fellow. Ben Park. It's a false name by the way. Park. Yeah, we wanted to detain her for her safety and so on, but they must have slipped through the net. We had to pick up more than forty people simultaneously. It's been quite a night in all sorts of ways. But we're still looking. Bound to find them soon. The hotel's digital clock said four-fifteen. I've got the girl, Daniel said. He slumped back on the pillow, the phone at his ear. Is that so? Really? The policeman was delighted. Weight off my mind. Where is she? She's with me, Daniel said. But she wasn't.

She wasn't with me, Judge Savage muttered to himself in court. He had said Minnie was with him and she wasn't. So that while counsels for Davidson, J. Crawley and G. Crawley had been speaking, he had written no more on his notepad than: Sacrificed to protect an informer. The informer rules the world, he thought. Deliberately sacrificed, he wrote. And now, at this crucial point of the summing up, it came to him: What if the stories leaked over recent weeks had been deliberately put about by the police to draw someone's attention to Minnie and away from whoever was giving them what they needed. Somebody coughed. For a moment Judge Savage was paralysed by the impossibility of proceeding. I am numbed, he thought. Minnie too had been numbed. What's the matter, Kathleen Connolly had asked? She had bent over the sofa in the hotel foyer, then squatted down beside the girl. What's the matter? Minnie wouldn't reply. She shook her head. There is nowhere to go, she moaned when Daniel suggested a taxi. The rules offer no way for me to proceed, he thought. A judge should be a master of procedures.

We have spoken, he finally looked up at the court, of those defendants who claim that the stone was not thrown by a member of their group despite their presence on the bridge. Recalling the story helped him to gather his wits. If you accept that claim you must acquit all defendants on all charges. We have spoken of the prosecution's position, backed up, as we have seen, by considerable circumstantial evidence. The prosecution maintains that *all* members of the group were involved in a joint enterprise to throw stones onto the ring road. If you accept this version, a verdict of guilty must be returned for *all* the defendants, though it will be left up to you to decide, for each separate defendant, whether he or she was merely reckless as to whether serious harm was caused, or whether serious harm was caused with intent. If a defendant is considered only reckless then he is or she is guilty of what we call section twenty, grievous bodily harm through reckless behaviour. If a defendant is considered to have acted in joint enterprise with the others and with intent then he or she is guilty of the more serious section eighteen, grievous bodily harm with intent.

Daniel paused. In the end one hardly needed notes. But now we must consider, he went on, the two more complex explanations of the events of March 22nd which have been offered to us by the Crawley sisters. It is not my intention – actually, I would hardly be able, he thought – to examine these once again in detail. On the one hand they offer a fullness of motivation lacking in the versions both of the prosecution and the first six defendants. And a motive, as we have said, may be an important element of proof. Put very simply, these versions *explain* more. On the other hand I must warn you to be cautious of this evidence, precisely because of that fullness, that explanation. A complex account of motivation may be more the work of able fabrication than a proof of the truth. Whenever someone we know does something strange, we ask: why did they do that? This was hardly the tone of a proper summing up, Judge Savage told himself. Yet not inappropriate perhaps. And if we think of a reason, however complex, we feel satisfied. Indeed, the more tortuous and complex and unflattering the reason, the more satisfied we may feel, because we now convince ourselves that we know this person, that we are clever at deducing their motivations. But of course unless we have strong evidence that supports our idea, it may well be that we are quite wrong. What I am saying is that you must not be impressed by the *story value* of these two rather different accounts. You must simply consider whether one or the other is true. Nor must you be swayed by the declared motivation of the defendant Gillian Crawley. She claims that she decided to confess the story because she is pregnant and does not wish her child to be born in prison. You must recognise that such a desire, a desperation perhaps, might well lead someone to invent a story of great complexity. And since the other story has been offered by Gillian Crawley's sister, you may be concerned that her, I mean Janet Crawley's, initial decision to break ranks was also motivated by concern for her sister's pregnancy.

This really is lamentably confused and unprofessional, Judge Savage thought. A number of the defence counsels were staring very hard. All the same, he sighed, and given that you treat the evidence with due caution, you may nevertheless reach the conclusion that one or other of these stories, that of Janet Crawley, or that of her sister Gillian, is indeed the truth of the matter. In that case, you must ask yourselves, Who now becomes responsible for what? Who must be found guilty and who acquitted of which charges?

Again he made a huge effort to gather his wits. In the version offered by Janet Crawley, you will remember, Mr Grier threw two stones which did not hit cars – two such stones were indeed found by the police close to the bridge – while the stone that *did* hit a car was thrown wildly and in intense frustration by Mr Sayle after choosing not to use it to attack Mr Grier. Should you find that you are convinced of the truth of this story, satisfied, that is, so that you are quite sure in your minds that it is correct, then Mr Grier cannot be found guilty because there is no joint enterprise and the two stones he threw did not hit cars or cause harm and indeed we cannot know if perhaps they were deliberately aimed to avoid cars, the primary intention being to annoy Mr Sayle. All other members of the group must then also be found not guilty, with the exception of Mr Sayle, who, always assuming that you are convinced by Janet Crawley's version of events, becomes guilty of grievous bodily harm through reckless behaviour. This was extremely shaky, Daniel thought. But the whole thing was beyond him. Alternatively, if we accept the version of the elder sister Gillian Crawley, we are in even greater difficulty, since Miss Crawley tells us that she did not *see* the stone actually thrown but *understood* that its being thrown must have been the result of the clash she had witnessed between Mr Sayle and Mr Grier. This story exculpates its teller, without explicitly blaming anyone else. Some people might feel this was merely ingenious. But if you should come to the conclusion that it is true, you must then decide whether it is at all possible to arrive at a position where you are absolutely certain so that you are sure in your minds that one or the other or both of these men is guilty of grievous bodily harm. Did that make sense? But how could he be expected to be lucid having spent the night as he had? Where is she going to spend the night? he had asked his daughter in a low voice. With you, Sarah smiled. Who else? And all the time, Judge Savage concluded, you must constantly bear in mind the essential, the one absolutely undisputed and indisputable fact: a woman was severely injured as a result of a stone being thrown from a bridge. And the essential question? Can we be sure, on the basis of the evidence presented to this court, who should take responsibility for throwing that stone and how far this was or was not a joint enterprise common to all the defendants? Inviting the jury to retire, Judge Savage wondered, Would he himself ever be satisfied so that he was sure as to who had been responsible for Minnie's death? Her father, her brothers, Mattheson, himself, his daughter, or even his wife?

Mother threw a complete fit, Sarah had said. She drew her father aside in the foyer of the hotel. She went completely hysterical. His daughter seemed quite pleased about this. She wore a short tight skirt. Her lipstick was bright. Her eyes clear. A fit! Hadn't it only been a few weeks ago, Daniel thought, that Hilary had been telling him of Sarah's hysterical fits. This is my daughter, he beckoned to Kathleen Connolly. Sarah, Kathleen Connolly. The older woman froze into formality and embarrassment. Pleased to meet you, Sarah offered a knowing smile. Kathleen stiffened the more. Daniel was at a loss. Your mobile's off, Dad, the girl was saying. That's why I brought her here. I tried to phone. Mum just refused to let her in the house. She went completely nuts!

The Asian girl sat on the sofa in the foyer, glazed eyes looking away from them at the wall. She looked sick. A small group of businessmen clattered through the door. Daniel remembered how the foyer of the Cambridge would echo. The businessmen had been drinking. I'd better be on my way then, Kathleen laughed nervously. I was just driving your Dad back to his hotel, she said unnecessarily. The men clattered into the lift. He had a bad fall, Kathleen Connolly insisted, coming out of court. Glad to have met you, Sarah smiled. Her smile said not to worry, she enjoyed meeting her father's women. Kathleen Connolly was hurrying to the door when Daniel caught up with her. That's *the* girl, he said. *The* girl, you know? Kathleen was frowning. She keeps phoning to say she's in some kind of trouble, that her parents are violent, and so on. I've told Mattheson on numerous occasions. I can't get involved. He tells me he has it under control. But she keeps phoning. Now she turns up at our house. Obviously my wife got upset.

Then he said, perhaps you could talk to her. Kathleen Connolly looked dubious. To your wife? To the girl! She's called Minnie. Find out what we can do for her. I don't know, Kathleen said. At the same time she seemed tempted. There was a soft gleam in her eyes. Her mouth softened. She ceased to be the embarrassed creature caught entering a hotel with a colleague. Okay, she said, I'll try. Oh no, Sarah shook her head, she won't talk, it's pointless. His daughter had appeared beside them, blocking their path. I've been with her a couple of hours now, Dad. She's in a terrible state. She won't say a word. Mum went quite mad. Sarah beamed at her father. She didn't want the older woman to solve the problem.

As they stood by the revolving doors with the Asian girl shivering twenty feet away, head in her hands on the sofa, paying them no attention, Judge Savage suddenly found himself more interested in his wife's rage than in the practical question of what to do with the girl. Mightn't such anger mean Hilary still had an investment in their marriage? Kathleen was pulling him aside. Holding his arm, she whispered: From what I gathered from Inspector Mattheson, they are arresting the people who attacked you tonight, the Korean family you know, together with various others. It's been in the planning for many months. What I'm saying is, you can't offer to take the child home.

Hands pressed to her sides, Minnie Kwan rocked back and forward. Kathleen went to her. Pulling up the creases of her slacks above the knee, she squatted down. Do you need to go to hospital, she asked kindly. Her voice had a faintly Irish accent. Rocking back and forward the girl shook her head. Kathleen looked up. We should call the police. No, Minnie gasped. No! The CPS woman was perplexed. Would you like to come back to my house then? It's only ten minutes in the car. I have a spare bed. Nobody will know where you are. Again the girl shook her head. I'm terrified, she muttered. Where is she going to spend the night? Daniel asked his daughter. With you, Sarah smiled. She told me she wouldn't go with anyone else. She's sure she'll be safe with you.

Nor would Minnie take a separate room. Are you sure you don't need to go to hospital? She shook her head. But what's wrong? Just feeling bad, she finally said. Because of the baby, she whispered. Kathleen was now offering to drive Sarah home, but at that moment, Daniel became aware of a man coming through swing doors, a tall figure pushing against the glass, hesitating, now walking over to them. Why is he familiar? There was the pony tail, the slight paunch, a wide grin. Forty if he's a day, Daniel thought. This is Trevor, Sarah said brightly. The man wore trainers, jeans, tweed jacket on white tee-shirt. Trevor, Dad. The two were shaking hands. Gather we're having a bit of a drama, Trevor said charmingly. Pleased to meet you, Mr Savage, heard a lot about you of course. His voice was warm and fruity. Sarah was radiant. Trevor works with Max, she whispered to her father, as if that made the man safer. We were just talking about who was going to drive who home, Daniel said. Right, I believe I'm here to do the honours. Trevor rubbed his hands: Or at least that's what the lady said on the blower. It's so sweet of you, Sarah cried. Off we go then, Trevor said. Anybody else? No? Sure? Well, goodnight all. In the space of no more than a minute, the two disappeared, the man spinning his car keys round a finger, the girl remembering to slip an arm round his waist as they entered the revolving doors. This caused something of a tussle, for the doors were small for two. The sound of laughter echoed across the foyer of the Cambridge Hotel.

Daniel stared after them. What are you going to do, Kathleen whispered. More solemnly she said, Dan, I think she should go to hospital. I'll call an ambulance, Daniel announced. No! Minnie shrieked. It was loud and embarrassing. The foyer was cavernous. I'm fine, the girl insisted. Just scared, a bit shocked. There was a pause. Again a group of men wandered in and across to the lifts. Could he force her to go? Daniel wondered. He tried to assess the situation. I'm fine, she insisted, just a bit shocked. I had a bad experience. I got scared. Would you like a cup of tea? Kathleen asked. Again Minnie shook her head. She kept her hands pressed to her sides. I just need a bed, she said. Please. She was speaking through gritted teeth. Daniel sighed: With the reputation I've got these days, I don't suppose it'll make any difference.

He said goodbye to Kathleen and waited till the foyer was empty. The old receptionist studiously ignored whatever was going on. A hotel receptionist, Daniel thought, does not object when a judge and national celebrity takes a young girl to his room. In the lift, Minnie leaned heavily against him. I need a bed, she whispered. They just knocked me about. It was nothing. The bed wasn't even a proper double. More a solution for honeymooners, weekends away. The young woman lay down in her coat. Why? he asked. He waited. He was experiencing little rushes of adrenalin, of hyperattention, followed by moments when he might easily have fainted.

She had closed her eyes. The police stopped a lorry loaded with immigrants. They must have known. It's the second time. My brothers think it's me told them. They knew about me and you. All this rumour in the papers. They think I'm telling things. So I'm locked in the flat all yesterday. I had the mobile at first. They didn't know. Then it ran out. In the evening two men came and hit me. They kicked me. I didn't know them. Ben's mother wasn't there. I told them, I hadn't said anything. Minnie was shaking her head, crying. This afternoon I wake up and they've all gone. I had to smash the door.

He covered her up, pulled a chair to sit beside her,

smoothed her hair. She looked grey and bloated. At least it's over, he said. What do you mean? she asked. He hesitated: If they went, if everybody disappeared, it will be because they were afraid of being arrested. Anyway, you can't go back now. We'll find somewhere else.

The girl shivered, staring at him. She seemed suspicious. He went to the cupboards and found a spare blanket. I can make a tea, he offered. I can get you a drink from the mini-bar. He wasn't sure what to say to her. She said, a tea. Very carefully, he tore open the little Twining's bags and pulled out the sachets of tea. He plugged in the kettle. I should call the police, he kept thinking. But his aversion to Mattheson was insuperable. He felt embarrassed that the girl should come to him. Mattheson had explicitly said to keep away. I'm too tired to make sensible decisions he thought. In the morn-ing, then. If only he could consult Hilary. Methodically, he wound the strings around the handles of two pink teacups. In the morning he would be able to think. Minnie cupped the tea in her hands. She seemed more comfortable now, her head propped up on the pillow. She asked: You have left your home? Yes. He sat in an uncomfortable armchair at the other side of the bed. There was no room for his feet. Are you happy? No. He twisted sideways, jamming his knees against the bed. She sipped her tea, looked at him. You always said you were just about to stop. Stop what? he asked. She even managed a thin smile. What was the word you used? I don't know. For what? Fil – Philandering? Yes. You said: This can't go on! I must stop philandering. Did I? She nodded. He remembered saying the words to Jane.

They sipped their tea. It was past midnight. The room was optimistically decorated in a rose wallpaper with pink curtains and carpet and bedspread. Now with the weak light of just one pink lamp beside the bed, a sort of wounded calm had been established, as of softly dying embers. They sat and sipped. She said: Was it my fault? What? That your wife found out. Are you angry with me? He shook his head. Go to sleep now, he told her. You need to sleep. And so do I. I've got a big day tomorrow. You always went home early, she said. I always felt you were in a hurry to get home. His uneasiness increased. Call the police! Then, as she slid down into the bed, she cried out in pain. He hurried round to her side. Are you all right? I was punched, here, it still hurts a bit. Look he said, with the baby and everything, you really must go to hospital and get yourself checked out. I'm going to call a taxi and take you now. No, she said. But . . . Tomorrow, she insisted. Really, I'm all right. I'd know if there was something serious, wouldn't I?

She lay in the dark now. He went to the bathroom. Undressing quietly, he thought the girl had gone to sleep. He would slip into the sheets and sleep himself. In the end, this wasn't all bad news. The Kwans would be arrested. The girl will be sorted out elsewhere. The drama is almost over. One way or another I can reconstruct my life, Judge Savage thought. He pulled back the sheets on his side. The girl's quiet voice asked, Dan, would you mind turning the television on? I can't sleep. I'll sleep if you put the television on, just softly.

Sighing, he found the remote. What do you want to watch? Oh, it doesn't matter. Then she said: Canned laughter puts me to sleep. Daniel zapped past the news, a gunfight. On the fourth or fifth channel there was a crackle of applause and an all black cast on three brightly coloured sofas were jumping up and down despite the takeaway food on their laps, joking and arguing intensely in the accents of the American south. That's fine she said. She didn't seem to want to watch.

But Daniel found it difficult not to pay attention. Somebody was complaining that a daughter was out late. I'd give the hussy a good whipping, an elderly woman's voice announced complacently. Listening, the judge contrived not to touch the girl at his side. Then a precocious little boy was launching into a lecture on the evils of corporal punishment. Came a roar of laughter. We'll see tomorrow, honey, someone said. We'll talk to that hussy tomorrow. Tomorrow it will be over he thought. He would deliver his summing up. He could call in sick for a week. He *was* sick. He would find a flat. Well now I'll be doggoned! Was it possible people still spoke like that?

Then quite suddenly he was speaking to Mattheson. He was heaved out of sleep by the trilling of the phone. It drew him up like a line tossed into a violent sea, and Mattheson was saying: We got them all, all but the girl and her husband. *I've* got the girl, Daniel said. The television now emitted only an intense blue glow. She's here with me. Is that so? That's excellent, Mattheson cried. Excellent news, Dan. The man was calling him Dan again. He shouldn't do that. Now I think we really can get this story behind us, the policeman was saying. Was it his problem? Judge Savage said: She claims you didn't come after she had repeatedly told you they were treating her badly. There was a pause. Mattheson spoke in common-sense tones. Dan, we needed just twelve hours. Twelve hours. It would be too complicated to explain. There's been more than two years' work gone into this. It was a huge operation. If we'd moved any earlier, we wouldn't have got the evidence we needed. It's pointless getting the people without good evidence that will stand up in court. But no harm done, hey, if you've got her there now.

Judge Savage turned off the television and lay back in the dark. Occasional headlights crossed the curtains. They must have had an informer to protect, he thought. They were happy to have the Kwans imagine it was Minnie. He sat up in the bed. From the road outside headlights sent pink rectangles stretching and creeping around the wallpaper over prints of English country gardens. It was monumental vanity, Judge Savage thought, on my part, to imagine I was important because I was in the paper for a few days. There was a print of Chatterton House: the view to the lake. One light passed and then another. It had been a terrible error, Daniel told himself, to imagine that Hilary couldn't leave you, because you were too important a part of her life. Then it occurred to him that Minnie hadn't woken when Mattheson phoned. She must be in a deep sleep. She had been exhausted. But he too had been exhausted. Alert, he listened for the girl's breathing. There was the rumble of a truck accelerating. You notice it more at night. The headlights passed over a neat pattern of hedges and flowers. Hatfield House. Sedley was right that Janet Crawley could never have heard somebody say anything above a busy road from ten yards away. He reached out and touched the girl.

THIRTY-THREE

Judge Savage had arrived at court at nine-thirty. He began his summing up towards four and invited the jury to retire before six. Sedley was shaking his head. Impossible to call, one of the defence counsels muttered to his second. More than eight hours, Judge Savage was thinking to himself, carrying his papers along the corridor, eight incriminating hours in which he had said nothing, done nothing. You look ill, Kathleen Connolly told him that morning. She had been waiting for him by the judges' entrance. All this is horribly improper. A judge should be quite separate from other authorities. How did it go? she made her voice low. All right, he told her. Is she still there? Yes. He said, I'm afraid I should really be making some notes for the summing up. I'm behind. Right. But she hung on a moment at the bottom of the steps. He turned. She was dressed in a sharp black skirt. Her hair was washed. They arrested them all, she told him. It was a big success. So I gather, he said. He didn't know what to say. All this time I've been a pushover for Mattheson, he thought. Perhaps after you've finished today, she was saying, we could talk for a moment about what we can do for the girl. I mean, she can't go home.

Daniel hesitated. This was the moment when he should have spoken. He didn't. He felt a growing aversion, almost a physical inhibition, to telling anybody anything. No need to clean my room he had told the hotel housekeeping on the phone. It's in too much of a clutter. I've got papers all over the place and they mustn't be muddled. Do Not Disturb, he hung the notice on the door. And now, nine incriminating hours later, he was sitting in chambers again, at his large desk, with this large and impossible hurdle before him. It is of no interest to me, he thought, what verdict the jury return in the trial of R. v. Sayle and others. He sat down, and it was only after five or ten minutes, sitting motionless behind his desk that he noticed a small white envelope with Hilary's writing: Dan, we can't not see each other today. Come over. Judge Savage closed his one good eye.

It's only our twentieth anniversary! The phone had rung at eight sharp. She knew he was always up before eight. I wanted to apologise, she said. I rather lost it yesterday when the, er, your Korean person turned up. I'm sorry. I could have handled it better. Sarah said you were in difficulty.

Daniel hadn't known what to say. Looking through the curtains onto a blowy September morning, he had no idea how to proceed. It's only our twentieth anniversary, Hilary said. She laughed nervously. I know the circumstances could have been more propitious, but I thought I should call anyway. Dan? she asked. Dan, are you there? She's dead, he said.

Reaching out across the bed after Matteson's phone-call his fingers had found her skin cold. There was no tension at all. No hum. He understood at once. I feel numb she had said the previous night in the foyer. I can't get warm, she had complained in bed. He heaped a second blanket on her. Daniel touched her cold wrist, recoiled and even before he found the light-switch he knew that she was dead. He pulled the lamp off the bedside table, then found the switch to the main light on the wall. The girl's mouth was open. Her face was grey and empty. The glassy eyes stared at the ceiling where the light hung in a shade of pink glass.

He rushed out of bed, then froze with indecision beside the corpse. He knew at once it was a corpse. Minnie, he said softly. Minnie, he called. Minnie. He put his mouth to her ear and shouted, Minnie! She was quite still. He rushed into the bathroom, filled the tooth-glass, threw it over her face. Someone banged on the wall from behind the bed. For a moment he didn't understand. The girl hadn't moved. Then they thumped again. Oh Christ. He pulled an arm out and felt her pulse. He knew there was no pulse. The body was already stiffening. This is like so many dreams, he thought. He knew he wasn't dreaming. Impulsively he tilted the small head back and put his mouth to hers. He breathed into her. The lips were stiff and rubbery. He breathed hard. There was a smell. You won't forget the cold touch of those lips, that smell. He took away his mouth and pressed both hands on her chest. There was a faint gurgling. He put his mouth on her mouth and breathed again. But now immediately withdrew. You know she's dead. The face was yellow grey, the brown eyes glazed. She's been dead for hours. Again he thought he heard a sound of trickling liquid. He threw back the sheets. She was still in jeans, loose maternity jeans. Between the legs the cloth was sopping. The sheet was black. Frightened, he pulled up her sweater and shirt at the waist. The skin was livid, blotchy. She has been bleeding for hours, he realised. Bleeding inside. She is dead and her child is dead. Elizabeth Whitaker's child had survived. This baby is dead, he thought. You should have taken her to the hospital. He ran to the phone. He didn't have the number for the hospital. Call 999. But now he put the phone down. He dialled the three numbers, then quickly put the phone down.

Why didn't I call 999, or Mattheson, he asked himself, sitting at his desk this evening, turning over his wife's strange note in his hands. How could his wife invite him after what he had told her in the morning? You *what*? she demanded. She's dead. Minnie. She must have had a haemorrhage. When I woke up she was dead. But, is she in your room? Yes, he said. Obviously Hilary hadn't realised this. Sarah hadn't told her. There was a pause. Dan, have you called a doctor? There's nothing a doctor can do, an idiot could see she's dead.

It was one of those rare occasions when his wife could think of nothing to say. You've got to call someone, she told him eventually. Mattheson, she told him. This is the end of me, he was saying. You do understand that. Hilary said nothing. But it's not that that frightens me, he insisted. He felt it wasn't. He felt that was an unworthy response. It's not that, he repeated. What then? she asked. I don't know. I can't deal with it. I mean, the talking about it. The going over and over it all. I feel so sad for her. You know my job is stupid, he began to say. I don't mind losing my job. It's stupid. It's the *process* of losing it. The cameras and the press and the *interest*. Was it this Martin hadn't been able to face? Daniel wondered, looking at the dead girl's face. She had been so pretty. He felt completely responsible, utterly ashamed. I could have done something. I can't face it, he told his wife. I'd rather die, he insisted. Had Minnie known she was dying? Probably not. She had simply misread the dull pain of internal bleeding. He remembered how her voice had sunk to a whisper. Had she actually said goodnight? She hadn't. She had passed out. He should have guessed. But he himself had been overwhelmed by tiredness. Not lucid. She died without a sound, transformed into matter.

Dan! Dan! He heard his wife's voice calling. Are you still there? Dan, say something! Yes, he said. I'm sorry. Listen, Dan, are you listening? Yes. Is she there now? Who? Minnie. Of course she's here, she . . . Dan, call Mattheson, now, at once! Things can only get worse if you wait. Call him now! Mattheson's been playing a double game, Judge Savage said. I don't trust him . . . Dan, call him. You've got to call someone. He might be able . . . It was Mattheson leaking those stories to the press. He was . . . Dan, don't be ridiculous! Hilary's voice was loud and harsh. Call him! He's on your side. You've got to call the police.

He put the phone down and turned back to the girl. Gently, he pulled the eyelids down. Her face was still wet from the water he had thrown. But more dignified with the eyes closed. Remembering what they had done to his dead father, he went to the curtains, detached a velvet pink sash and tied it round over the top of her head and under the chin to close the mouth. The jaw was stiff and he had to pull hard. The sash was garish round the grey face, but she looked more dignified with eyes closed, with mouth closed. Closed in on oneself, one is more dignified. He saw that.

He went to the bathroom to shower. But no sooner was he in there than he was overcome by anxiety, by a strange longing. He got out and dressed. It was twenty past eight. He hadn't called Mattheson. There were three or four hand towels. He filled the basin with warm water and went back into the other room. As expected, the mattress had a plastic cover under the sheets. How often did we make love? he wondered, stripping off her clothes. He had never taken her to a hotel. The arms wouldn't come. At least four times. Maybe more. He took the nail scissors from his washing kit

438

and sawed through the thin sweater. They went to the warehouse with its piles of rugs. The jeans were filthy. In the end that was more fun, less romantic. He wiped her hard with the top sheet, then eased out the under-sheet and wrapped the filthy clothes into them. She was on her side, on the plastic. It was Jane who always complained about the plastic sheets hotels used. With Jane he went to hotels. In the bathroom he dipped a towel in warm water. He wrung it out carefully, then hurried through to the bedroom and washed the sweat off her back and the mess from between her legs. He soaked another towel. He wiped her limbs, her small breasts, her belly. The stiffness of the belly was frightening. At least four times, he told himself, in her father's warehouse, probably a cover for God knows what. At least they won't be able to say I didn't wash the girl.

He didn't call Mattheson. Will the jury be out all day tomorrow? Laura asked, putting her head round the door. For an eternity, he told her. Daniel waited. His desk was stacked with papers accumulating information on people's crimes and misdemeanours, their alibis and confessions. Footsteps hurried along the corridor. The walls were full of files. And each of five judges' chambers were similarly crammed with such files and in the basement of the court complex room after room was stacked from ceiling to floor, shelf after shelf after shelf, with the immensely complicated details of crime after crime after crime and all the mad invention and tedious bureaucracy that surrounded every trial in the interminable antagonism of true and false. Surely ninety percent of what had been said in R.v. Sayle wasn't true. Before being reduced in the end to microfiche. While ninety percent of what was true hadn't been said, or even imagined perhaps. Minnie was reduced to matter while I slept beside her, Judge Savage thought. But she wouldn't dissolve. He had washed her, but he couldn't wash her away. I don't want to wash her away, he decided. Minnie was a nice girl.

What am I waiting for, he suddenly asked himself. He didn't know. For someone to advise me, perhaps. For a phone-call, from Kathleen Connolly, a knock on the door. Yes, once again I am waiting for someone who will advise me, as Hilary and Martin always advised me. I am waiting for someone I will be a pushover for, as I was always a pushover for Frank, and for Mattheson. And Christine. Suddenly resolute, he stood up, gathered his things and hurried out.

Feeling better this evening, sir? the policeman at the back entrance asked. Judge Savage half smiled. Thank you, he said. He found his car where he had left it the previous morning, drove to the centre of town in a thick drizzle, stopped briefly at a pharmacy, then drove down into the underground car park beneath the Cambridge. He had always appreciated the fact that with the card that opened one's room one could also enter the Cambridge from the elevator in the underground car park and thus go straight up to bed without being seen in reception. I have always liked not to be seen, he thought.

The elevator stopped on the third floor. He hurried down a crooked corridor past white doors in beige paint-work. The narrow carpet was beige too and there was a faint buzz of televisions from within the rooms. Behind him, as he approached the end of the corridor, he heard a door open and close, a mother fussing with her child. Then he saw that the Do Not Disturb notice had been removed from the handle. He stared. Alarmed, he put the card in the lock and pushed open the door. The room was dark and fresh. The curtains must be drawn, but he knew from the roar of the traffic that the window behind them had been opened; the town in the early evening was busy.

He swallowed and prepared himself. A small green light in polished brass showed him where the card-key must be inserted to turn on the lights. They all went on at once. And the TV too. There was a flicker and hum. The room was clean and empty. The bed was made and turned down. There was a chocolate on the pillow. Aghast, he looked around. Mr Savage, Welcome to the Cambridge Hotel. You have one message. The words glowed from the TV screen. The remote was on the bedside table. He pressed Messages. From Inspector Mattheson. Message taken, 12.38 p.m. Nothing to worry about, Dan. All sorted.

He sat down on the clean bed and began to shake. She had been taken away. Likewise the decision he must make. He knew at once it was a loss. She was gone. Only now did he appreciate how intensely he craved some consequence, however dire. I need to be punished, he told himself. He was shaking his head. The whole thing has been removed from me. He repeated the words over and over. Removed from me. I didn't act. Then his eyes found the screen again. Nothing to worry about. The words had a quiet blue glow.

Abruptly, Judge Savage stood up and snatched the TV cable from the wall. The plug dangled from his hand. How stupid. Removing his jacket, he became aware of the weight of the mobile in his pocket. It had been off all day. He turned it on. You have four recorded messages. He took off his tie, locked the door, pressed the appropriate buttons. How you doing, you old bastard? Frank's voice. Kathleen Connolly said she had had a lovely evening with him and she wished circumstances had been less traumatic. Dan, listen, Hilary said, if you feel up to it, do come round. You must be in a state. Then came a voice he didn't recognise. Mr

Dan, the phone crackled. I'm Sue. Mr Dan, my friend say you are looking for me. If you want, I work tonight. Goodbye Mr Dan.

Daniel Savage stared at the phone. How had she got his number? Had he called her mobile from his? Thinking hard, the judge undressed. My hands are shaking. They had taken Minnie away. He checked again that the door was locked. For a moment, he stood with his forehead against the polished wood. Everything has been removed from me. Turn off the phones. Turn everything off. Quick, quick. Tearing open the bag they had given him at the pharmacy, Judge Savage measured out a powerful dose and lay down on her side of the bed to sleep.